Some visions are
dead wrong...

SPIRITED

A TIDEWATER NOVEL

MARY
BEHRE

B

**BERKLEY
SENSATION**

$7.99 U.S.
$9.99 CAN

ISBN 978-0-425-26861-2

Praise for

SPIRITED

"Great! A real page-turner. Once you pick it up, you won't want to put it down until you're done!"

—Lynsay Sands, *New York Times* bestselling author of the Argeneau Vampire series

"Rich with mystery, hot romance, and sneaky humor, Mary Behre's *Spirited* absolutely delighted me! The solid dose of supernatural thrills it offered—along with one of the hottest, most divine heroes EVER—had me curled beneath a blanket, shivering with the thrill of being swept up in the drama, magic, and unexpected fun of heroine Jules Scott's paranormal encounters. Beneath the ghostly mysteries lurks a sexual chemistry between Jules and detective Seth English that sets fire to the pages. It's been a long time since I've come across as unique a premise as Ms. Behre offers her readers in *Spirited*. No magic crystal ball is needed to foresee this writer is bursting with talent! I can't wait for more from her!"

—Shelby Reed, author of *Games People Play*

"From the moment the heroine, dressed like a hooker, stumbles through the window of the cop hero's bedroom, you know you're in for an unusual story. Behre's sweet, sexy, funny debut has twists and turns (and an occasional ghost!) to keep suspense readers happy, and a poignant love story that will have you grabbing for a Kleenex."

—Lena Diaz, author of the Nursery Rhyme series

SPIRITED

Mary Behre

BERKLEY SENSATION, NEW YORK

THE BERKLEY PUBLISHING GROUP
Published by the Penguin Group
Penguin Group (USA) LLC
375 Hudson Street, New York, New York 10014

USA • Canada • UK • Ireland • Australia • New Zealand • India • South Africa • China

penguin.com

A Penguin Random House Company

SPIRITED

A Berkley Sensation Book / published by arrangement with the author

Berkley Sensation Books are published by The Berkley Publishing Group.
BERKLEY SENSATION® is a registered trademark of Penguin Group (USA) LLC.
The "B" design is a trademark of Penguin Group (USA) LLC.

For information, address: The Berkley Publishing Group,
a division of Penguin Group (USA) LLC,
375 Hudson Street, New York, New York 10014.

ISBN: 978-0-425-26861-2

PUBLISHING HISTORY
Berkley Sensation mass-market edition / March 2014

PRINTED IN THE UNITED STATES OF AMERICA

10 9 8 7 6 5 4 3 2 1

Cover illustration by Tony Mauro.
Cover design by Sarah Oberrender.

For Donna Graham,
who believed this was possible from the moment
she read the first story I wrote.
I miss you, every day.

And for Valerie Bowman,
who refused to let me give up on her book boyfriend.
This one's for you.

ACKNOWLEDGMENTS

So many people influenced me, guided me, or just plain buoyed my spirits as I endeavored to put words to paper, it's only fair to thank them here.

My editor, Leis Pederson, thank you for taking a chance on me. Nalini Akolekar, I'm so grateful for your guidance and that you're my agent.

Elle Cosimano, your idea for writing retreat weekends was brilliant. I've never pushed myself harder or written more in one sitting than in those cabins.

Kim Kenealy, you'll always be my best friend. Too late to run now. It's in print.

The Berry Best Betas: Valerie Bowman, Elizabeth Clark, Jamie Disterhaupt, Kim Kenealy, Yvonne Richard, Chris Behre Sr., and Gayle Shlafer, thank you for the excellent feedback. Thank you, LaLaLas for being such an amazing writers' group.

Also, thank you KG YMCA staff for letting me hide in your offices and write while my children played or took classes.

A quick shout of thanks to Lee Lofland for introducing me to Chief Scott Silverii at the Writers' Police Academy. Any mistakes made in this book were purely my own and sometimes intentional.

And thank you to Lynsay Sands, Shelby Reed, and Lena Diaz for the fabulous cover quotes. All three of you are brilliant authors and to have received your praise means so much to me.

And finally, to Indy, the Captain, and Chris. You are the most important people in my life. I love you three so much, it amazes me when I wake each morning and discover I love you all a little more than before.

PROLOGUE

"WHAT DO YOU mean, she took the diamonds?" He tightened his grip on the cell phone.

"She says she can't find them now."

I'll just bet she can't.

Little whore probably had this planned from the moment she found out what they were doing. She'd assured him he needn't worry about her. Convinced him to trust her.

And this is how she thanks me?

The voice on the crackling line rambled on. "We'll find the diamonds. You'll get them back. *I'll* fix this, I swear!"

More broken promises. More lies.

His fingernails dug crescents into his palm and he imagined repaying her for her betrayal.

It wouldn't take much. Just the right placement of his fingers on her throat and a little pressure. Then a little more. Her lovely swan neck would feel like silk beneath his fingers. He'd kill her slowly. Give her time to catch a wisp of breath before he strangled her again.

The idea of making her suffer and beg him to spare her worthless life brought a smile to his face.

"Okay?" The idiot stopped rambling.

"Sure." He didn't know what he'd agreed to but didn't care. He'd stopped listening. Tapping out a text, he chose his words carefully. The message was brief, but believable. She'd come out of hiding . . . and he'd make her pay.

CHAPTER 1

JULIANA SCOTT LOOPED the strap of her black Prada clutch over her wrist and imagined scaling her apartment building in five-inch stiletto boots.

Where was a radioactive spider when you needed one?

The fire escape ladder dangled about seven feet up. She'd just have to jump for it. Or she could continue to stand there like some kind of crazily dressed prostitute turned damsel-in-distress at three in the morning. Someone might come along and help her; then again, the way her night was going, she'd probably end up a statistic. Or arrested.

But her heels were freaking five inches high. And she hated climbing, boots or not.

"Come on, Jules," she sang to herself as she plowed her hand through the contents of the bag for the third time. How could she not have her keys? She might be directionally challenged but she never forgot them. Ever.

A nearby streetlight flickered off, then on again, casting a dull yellow glow.

She shuddered; goose bumps rushed up her arms but it

wasn't cold. That could only mean one thing: she wasn't alone. She listened for whoever—or more likely, *what*ever—it was to make its presence known.

Nothing. Not a sound except the ocean waves washing against the sandy shore a block away. The gentle lapping water soothed her and a small, relieved sigh slipped from her lips.

"Who, whooooooo!" A barred owl swooped low and she let out a small yelp of alarm.

Crazy bird. Jules laughed softly at her own paranoia and rubbed her weary eyes. She hadn't seen a ghost in six months. Why did she think she'd see one in Tidewater now?

She refocused on finding her keys. She shoved aside the bags of dried lavender and oregano she'd picked up from the herbalist. Skipped over the Waitress Red lipstick she'd bought for tonight's party. Dug beneath her first prize blue ribbon. And came up empty.

She shook the purse. It felt oddly heavy, but it contained nothing else.

Even her cell phone was gone.

Dang it! Another fabulous blunder to add to an already freakish night.

How was she supposed to find her missing sisters if she couldn't even find her flipping keys? Finding lost things . . . now *that* would be a gift! Instead she'd inherited the freakish ability to talk to the dead. Unless a dead person could tell her where she'd left her keys, or help her find her lost sisters, she considered it more of a *crift*—cursed gift. She shook her purse one last time.

Stupid ghosts.

She glared at the ladder's twenty rusted stairs leading to her bedroom window. Hitching the purse strap up to her elbow, she heaved a sigh and jumped twice before her fingers connected with metal. The ladder lowered with a screech. The sound echoed against the brick as she stepped one precariously high-heeled foot on the first rung.

Man, tonight totally bites.

First, Mason Hart, that overgrown jock, tried to cop a feel at their college reunion. Now, she was wriggling up a fire escape in a skirt and bustier so tight, they squeezed all the breath from her body.

I'm burning this outfit tomorrow.

Finally on the second level, she pulled up the ladder behind her and latched it in place. Every other step, her boots snagged in the grooves of the metal deck. She started past her neighbor's partially opened window when the goose bumps returned.

An incredible sense of anger and sadness swept over her. Someone else's pain. The feelings smothered her sense of self and stole her breath. Bracing herself against the brick, she fought to erect the mental shields that she used to block out a spirit's projected emotions.

She visualized gray castle walls rising around her, the same mental image she'd used since childhood. Castles were strong and safe . . . impenetrable. With her mental shields in place, her breathing eased and she rested against the wall.

Below, the street sat eerily quiet and dark. Even the owl stopped hooting. As far as she could see she was alone, but her senses screamed she had company.

Minutes ticked past and nothing moved. A warm ocean breeze carried the sound of the rushing shore. Otherwise, silence.

Home and her bed waited less than a foot away.

"Help me . . . please . . ."

The high-pitched voice grated against her senses.

"Not now," Jules whispered, wishing she could just ignore the girly-sounding disembodied voice.

And a fresh one at that. New specters hadn't yet mastered the ability to communicate without rubbing against the corporeal plane. The effect on her body was like fingernails on a chalkboard. Unlike the dead, living people didn't make her skin crawl just by speaking.

Jules tried to open her window. It didn't budge. She eyed the lock but it was open. Why wouldn't the darn thing open?

"I . . . need . . . you . . ."

Frustration tinged with a healthy dose of fear whipped through her. She shoved at the window again. It still didn't move. Rubbing at her goose bump–covered arms, she turned to her neighbor's window. It was open and dark inside. She dismissed the fleeting thought. She'd sooner scale down the building naked than . . .

Her mind muddled. She shook her head to clear it. The

scent of sandalwood filled her. Warmth suffused her bones and she couldn't resist the pull to the open window.

The aroma intensified. Never before had anything smelled so wonderful. A warm, gooey, just-ate-the-best-caramel-brownies-ever feeling filled her. She had to get closer. The urge to get inside was overpowering.

The scent wafted through the open window and her body tingled, needing to get closer. The leather skirt hugged her thighs too tight as she tried to step through. Instead, she shifted and pushed through headfirst. Each movement dreamlike. Jules's belly on the sill and her booted feet still outside, the scent drew her in until she tumbled to the floor. Breaking the trance, the specter whispered one word.

"Finally."

WAS HE DREAMING? Detective Seth English of the Tidewater Police Department rubbed his eyes. Nope, no question about it. Someone *was* breaking into his apartment.

Criminals are just stupid.

Of all the nights to leave his window open, Seth had to pick tonight. He damned his recent bout of insomnia. Stress always did that to him. The sound of the ocean usually soothed him. Not tonight. His much-needed peace was shattered by a felony in progress.

He sat up. The blanket fell to his waist. Sliding noiselessly out of bed, he grabbed his gun and handcuffs from the nightstand. He slipped into the shadowed corner and waited.

Damn. The last thing he needed was a trip downtown and a night full of paperwork. Lately, it seemed to be one thing after another: his daughter's engagement, his new partner, their unsolvable case . . . and now this.

Could his life get any more complicated without his head actually imploding?

The window frame groaned then gave another inch.

The streetlamp outside cast her in silhouette. And she was definitely a she. Delicate feminine fingers slipped into the opening and wrapped around the frame, pushing the window slowly upward.

Seth watched, barely breathing, as she wriggled through

the window. When she'd made it mostly through, her hands
flew wide in front of her as if searching for leverage. Then she
tumbled to the floor with a grunt.

"Stay down!" Lunging forward, he planted a knee in her
back. He pressed the gun into the base of her skull. His other
hand twisted each of her wrists behind her and cuffed them
together.

"Ouch! Stop!" she screamed. "Help! Police!"

"I *am* the police." He ran his finger along her wrists to
ensure he hadn't snapped the cuffs too tight. "You're fine."

In the dim light, Seth reached down to help her up. He
couldn't very well leave her on the floor, regardless of the
temptation. Fumbling in the dark, his hand brushed the warm
satin skin of her bared midriff.

"Get your hands off me! Somebody! Help me!" She
shrieked a banshee's wail next to his ear.

"What the hell are you yelling for?" He tugged her over to
the bed and shoved her down.

She thrashed and screamed incomprehensibly.

"Enough! Or I'll charge you with disturbing the peace too."
When she kept shrieking, he added, "*You* broke into my place,
ruining the first night's sleep I've had in a week. I don't need
you bursting my eardrum too. Now be quiet. I'm getting the
light."

Her cries instantly died in the shock of blinding light.

When Seth's eyes focused, he pinched the bridge of his
nose.

The hooker—she had to be a hooker—wore knee-high
black patent leather stiletto boots, a black miniskirt that could
have doubled as a headband, and a leather bustier. Her legs
were long and lean and covered in fishnet stockings. And the
swell of her breasts was, in a word . . . succulent. Her short,
straight midnight-colored hair was too dark to be real. The
woman personified sex, as was her obvious intention. But her
green eyes made his pulse thrum.

They were astonishing, as if emeralds were cut and layered
around the pupils. The most beautiful eyes he'd ever seen, in
spite of the appallingly thick black eyeliner surrounding them.

And strawberries? God, she smelled like *strawberries*. His
mouth actually watered.

Attracted to a hooker. I've sunk so low.

Chalking it up to his sexual drought, he focused on dealing with the handcuffed home invader thrashing around on his bed. He tried to shove his sidearm into his shoulder holster before remembering he was shirtless. Stomping over to the bedside table, he yanked open the drawer and dropped the gun in.

He hoped she'd think the heat creeping up his cheeks was from anger instead of embarrassment. Folding his arms across his chest, he asked, "Do you have any idea where you are?"

JULES SAT DUMBFOUNDED in the bedroom of a Greek god. He had espresso brown eyes, curly black hair, a long nose that had probably been broken a time or two, and a sexy, dimpled chin. His tan, muscular body was covered by a chest full of springy hair that begged to be touched. Dang! He even smelled good, like soap and the salty Tidewater air.

Ohmigawd, he's a walking condom commercial.

He scowled at her, waiting for an answer. Although to save her life she couldn't think of anything. Where *was* she? More important, what was she doing here? Then a mental switch flipped and it all became clear.

That freaking ghost! Jules couldn't very well tell a cop she stumbled into his apartment because a ghost made her do it. He'd haul her off to the loony bin.

"Well." Jules fidgeted against the cuffs and tried to adjust to a more dignified position on the bed. So not happening. "No, not really. I was trying to go home but, uh . . . locked myself out."

He arched an eyebrow at her but didn't say anything.

"I know this looks bad but just ask Big Jim. He'll vouch for me."

"And Big Jim? Who's that, your pimp?"

"What? No!" She laughed and shook her head at the absurd thought. "He's my dad."

"Is that what they're calling them these days?" He scoffed but didn't give her time to respond. "There's no one named Big Jim in this building. Try again, the truth this time."

"Ernie Ward! *Ernie* is my dad."

"I thought his name was Jim." He shook his head. He made a sound like a buzzer. "Wrong again. I've known Ernie for years but I've never seen you before. Want to try another name, honey?"

His biceps flexed, arms still folded across his chest, as if he wanted to move but barely restrained himself. The sight was distracting. He wasn't exactly muscle-bound, just finely honed. He stood fierce and masculine like an ancient warrior. Intimidating but ruthlessly sexy. It made her want to . . . She shook herself inwardly.

Why couldn't she think straight? This so wasn't like her. She didn't go gooey over any guy, regardless of how ruggedly handsome. But her heart pounded at an erratic pace and she'd once again lost the thread of the conversation. What had he just asked?

Think, Jules! Ignore the instant pull of pointless physical attraction. It had never done her any favors in the past anyway. *Something about him must be repellent. Find it!*

She looked at him again, this time skating her gaze past his naked chest and sexy arms and moving down.

Oh, it couldn't be.

She blinked, astonished.

He wore bright yellow pajama pants, covered in *lambs*.

Resisting the urge to laugh, she latched onto righteous indignation and straightened her shoulders. This condescending jerk treated her like a criminal, handcuffed her, and called her a liar. Oh, he was going down.

"My name's Jules. Not *honey*," she snapped. "And Big Jim—Ernie—*is* my father. He lives in this building and I live with him."

"I highly doubt it. Hookers don't live here," he said, tugging a red T-shirt over his head.

"Excuse me?" she yelled. "I'm not a hooker, and you owe me an apology!"

"Really?" he said, giving her an obvious once-over, his gaze settling on her bustier.

Her cheeks burned.

"Wait. I can explain."

"Enlighten me." He narrowed his eyes, doubt etched on his face.

"See, there was this costume party and . . ." Her words trailed off. How to explain the theme of her college reunion without sounding like an imbecile for dressing in the ridiculous outfit just to win a blue ribbon? Now that she thought about it, *stupid* might aptly describe her decision-making skills tonight. "Well, there was a Pimp and Ho party earlier tonight. I was on my way home from it—"

"And you just happened to climb into my window?"

Jules opened her mouth to respond, but doubted he'd believe her anyway. So she settled on a half-truth. "It was a mistake. I meant to climb into Big Jim's window, but it was jammed and yours was . . . open."

"Ah ha!" His mouth twisted into a satisfied grin. "You admit to breaking and entering."

"Not breaking. Just entering. And who in his right mind sleeps in this city without a screen in his window anyway?" Oops! She hadn't meant to say that last part, but she pushed on. "If you'll just let me go find Big Jim—"

"Don't think so." With a grim expression on his face, he tugged her to her feet. "Time to go."

"Where are we going?" Jules dragged her heels, her stilettos scraping the wooden floorboards.

Still in his pajama bottoms, he jammed his feet into a pair of loafers.

Jules gaped. The gladiator image of him fizzled with each passing second. "Are you *really* planning to go out in public dressed like an overgrown four-year-old?"

"Shut. Up," he growled, jerking on a knee-length, brown leather coat. "Say another word and I'll charge you with resisting arrest."

"Wait, uh, I think there's been some mistake."

"You bet your sweet ass, there has."

"Where . . . where . . ." Jules swallowed in an effort to keep her voice from shaking. "Where are we going?"

"You're gonna spend the night in lockup."

"Please, not jail!" Her words ended on a squeak, but she couldn't help it.

Earth-bound ghosts, bent on driving the living crazy, seemed to love hanging out in graveyards and jails. When they realized she could actually hear them, she'd be defenseless.

The needy ones would annoy her, but the evil ghosts—who'd managed to elude the hell beasts that usually put them where they belonged—they could attack en masse.

Their vicious thoughts would seep into her consciousness like a staticky radio she couldn't turn off. They could strip her of her sanity. A single night in jail nearly drove her mad once before. She doubted she'd survive it a second time.

She pleaded, "If you'll just let me talk to Big Jim, he'll straighten this out, I promise."

He glared at her, wrenching open the front door. "You have the right to remain silent."

Guess again.

She rushed into the hallway, screaming at the top of her lungs. "Big Jim! Big Jim! Help me! Big Jim!"

"Quiet!" the cop shouted. He grabbed her from behind and clapped a hand over her mouth as the door slammed shut.

He pulled her against him. With her cuffed hands behind her back, she pushed against him, trying to twist away. Leveraging her weight, she clutched and got a fistful of coat leather in one hand and warm, cotton pajama bottoms in the other. She froze. Her hands were lined up with the apex of his thighs.

Could this get any worse?

Of course it could.

His body reacted to her unintended groping. Jules attempted to push away, but only succeeded in pressing harder against his tightening groin.

No, no, no.

Images of their naked bodies joined together slammed into her mind, stealing her breath. Never in her life had she experienced such vivid fantasies, only these weren't hers. Like the entrancing smell that drew her into his apartment, these images were coming from outside of her, manipulating her senses.

The sex scenes playing through her mind had to be courtesy of the cop holding her too close. Jules nearly swallowed her tongue at the onslaught of the explicit images he'd somehow sent winging into her mind. Before she had time to wonder how a living person managed to project his thoughts—and they *had* to be his—he'd spun her around to face him.

Her gaze dipped past his abdomen before zipping back to his implacable expression. She hadn't intended to look, but in his fantasies he was huge. According to the sword tenting his pajama bottoms, that part of his fantasy was real.

And the gladiator image sprang to life again.

He cleared his throat, drawing her attention to his lethal gaze.

"I, uh . . ." Her cheeks heated as she stammered a muffled apology. His hand loosened, but remained pressed over her lips. "P-please—"

"Look, Happy Hooker, do you really want to add soliciting a police officer to your list of offenses tonight?"

"No," she whispered and shifted farther from him, pressing against the wall behind her. He crowded closer. At first it seemed threatening; except he emanated desire, not hostility.

A stream of heated images flitted through her mind, images of his lips exploring her . . . everywhere. Her breath skittered, her cheeks burned hotter, and her mouth went dry at the flare of attraction in his eyes.

"Mmm . . ." She tried to speak, inadvertently moistening his salty palm with her tongue.

The cop sucked in his breath. His darkening gaze flicked from her eyes to his hand on her mouth and back again. Then he drew his fingers across her lips in a manner so sensual, she shuddered.

"Don't push this any further," he whispered against her ear. He lightly traced her bottom lip with the tip of his index finger. Time stopped as his face lowered to hers.

Lost in his nearly obsidian gaze, she waited for him to kiss her.

And he was going to kiss her.

Somewhere in the back of her mind, she knew this was a bad idea.

But, God help her, she couldn't think of a single reason why she should stop him. His gaze lowered to her mouth and Jules licked her lips.

He leaned closer.

Her heart raced.

A rusty-hinged door squeaked open. Big Jim—who wasn't really big at all—appeared out of nowhere.

"Seth? What's with all the noise?" Big Jim yawned, stepping out into the hallway and closing the door behind him. "You're gonna wake April."

The cop leapt away from Jules but kept a firm grip on her upper arm. "Hi, Ernie. Sorry for the disturbance. Police business. I thought you and April were in Florida this week."

"Nah. We leave Monday." As if seeing her for the first time, Big Jim turned to her. "Jules? Is that you?"

She glanced at the man, barely twelve years her senior, who'd adopted her shortly after her thirteenth birthday, then back at Seth the Cop. Thanks to Big Jim's appearance, her illogical and ill-timed desire quickly morphed into anger.

Glaring at the cop with triumph in her eyes, she shook free of his hold. With as much pride as she could muster, which wasn't much considering she *was* dressed like a prostitute in handcuffs, she strode over to her rescuer.

"Hey, Big Jim." She planted a kiss on his cheek.

"Oh Lord, Jules! You look like a hooker." Big Jim's lips twitched.

"I won first prize in the Pimp and Ho contest."

"Oh God, you really did it! April said you were going to . . . but I never dreamed you'd actually have the guts to wear *that* in public." Big Jim laughed out loud. "I hope she took a picture."

The cop, who must have followed her, now stood so close his warm breath feathered across her ear. It sent electric tingles down her spine. *Oh boy!* She liked it. A lot.

This needed to stop. Jules slid from between the men.

"Do you know this girl?" the cop asked, oozing disbelief. "She climbed into my bedroom window tonight. She claims to live with someone named *Big Jim.* Then she tried to tell me she lives with you."

"I'm not a girl, I'm a woman." Jules bit off the words. She lifted her chin and added, "I do live here. I moved in this morning."

"She's my daughter. She—she calls me Big Jim. Family joke," Big Jim managed to say before lapsing into a guffaw.

"See?" Jules narrowed her eyes. "I told you so."

The cop took a step back. His eyebrows disappeared beneath the curly locks that fell over his forehead.

Big Jim's whooping laughs filled the hallway. Not seeing the humor in her situation, Jules glared defiantly at the cop.

He gaped, clearly bewildered, but made no effort to let her go.

With waning patience, she tapped her stiletto-clad foot on the linoleum and cleared her throat.

"Use your key next time, *precious*," the cop growled in her ear, spinning her around. Then the cuffs were blessedly off. "You could have climbed into the window of a psycho. Good thing for you it was me. You got lucky."

Jules rubbed her sore wrists. "Gee, I never knew getting lucky could be so disappointing."

The cop opened his mouth, then snapped it closed. "Good night, *Big Jim*," he said, looking pointedly at Jules.

" 'Night, *Lambkins*!" she called out, wiggling her fingers in a mock wave as his door slammed shut.

Big Jim guffawed again. "Jules, for a woman determined to lead an ordinary life, you're off to an exciting start."

"Thanks a lot." Jules frowned at her salacious costume. Jeez, she needed to change into her own clothes.

With a sigh, she reached for the knob and twisted it. It didn't budge.

"Juliana . . ." Big Jim held open his front door.

Dang it! That cop had her so flustered she had tried to enter the wrong apartment again.

"You know," Big Jim said with a snicker when she finally crossed her own threshold, "you have a terrible sense of direction for a psychic."

STRETCHED OUT IN bed, she forced her mind to clear. Considering it was four in the morning, Jules should have been exhausted, but her mind raced. Across the room, her clothes and black wig lay in a pile on the dresser. The costume had been killer, but that wig itched all night. She scratched her head, capturing the coppery strands of hair between her fingers briefly and examining them with a grin.

Shock value. She won for that alone. After all, who would have suspected that she—a former preschool teacher, who never swore—would dare show up dressed as a member of the world's oldest profession?

Pride flooded through her. All through college she'd been the oddball. The one who was different. For a few hours tonight, she was normal. No one looked at her as if waiting for her to talk to a wall or an invisible person. Or a ghost.

Being crowned "First Ho" wasn't quite the same as being Homecoming Queen, but the general acceptance had been glorious.

Okay, so she had veered from her plan to be completely normal and boring, but it had been fun. After what she'd been through in the last two years with her divorce, she needed a little excitement. At least the party had nothing to do with ghosts or psychic abilities.

Tomorrow, she'd go back to being plain, ordinary Juliana.

For some reason, the neighbor-cop's face flashed through her mind at that moment. The man topped the charts on the sexy scale. He met her three *H* rule: hot, huge—the man had to be at least six foot two, not to mention where her hands had been earlier—and oh, so handsome. Yep, he could send a nun's hormones raging. And she wasn't a nun . . . she just felt like one.

Jules stared at the ceiling. She counted all the tiles three times before her eyes drooped closed. Just before succumbing to the exhaustion, Seth the Cop's face appeared again. This time his lips curled up in a roguish smile, making him more handsome than ever. She'd slipped into the state between dreaming and waking and drifted along with the fantasy.

His rich brown eyes grew black as he leaned in close, captured her mouth with his, and drank her in. He tasted like hazelnut coffee. Jules sighed with delight. He chuckled and buried his hands in her hair, pulling her closer. She breathed in the scent of sandalwood as he licked a path from her lips down to her collarbone before returning to her mouth. He swept his tongue inside and her senses exploded with the heady taste of him.

She opened her eyes but Seth had disappeared. Thick, gray fog blinded her.

Her world tilted and twirled, like a carnival ride, spinning faster and faster until it jarred to a halt. Lighting, sounds, colors—everything . . . changed. She was no longer herself but someone else. Jules had taken this particular type of trip too many times not to know when she'd fallen into someone else's gruesome reality.

"Pleeaaasssse," she cried in the darkness and shoved at

the walls crowding in around her. She scraped her fingernails down the metal walls, searching for a release latch that wasn't there. The stench of copper permeated the tight space. Blood oozed from her raw fingers. "Let me out!"

The car's trunk flew open. White light blinded her, then snuffed out. She lay still, unable to focus. She didn't need to see who had rescued her. Only he would have come. He'd promised he'd protect her. How could she have doubted him? Relief washed through her.

Hands wrapped around her wrists and tugged her from the Buick. Free from the vehicle, he released her wrists and caressed her shoulders. She slumped against him, then jumped at the sensation of the foreign planes of his chest.

This wasn't her lover. She tried to pull away but he manacled one of her wrists, refusing to allow her to escape.

She searched his face. Even masked by shadows, he exuded a lethal air. He might have cared for her once but not now. This man was a cold-blooded killer who meant to punish her for betraying him. His gloved fingers traced around her neck, while his thumbs stroked the hollow of her throat. She swallowed convulsively.

"Where are they?" The whispered words made her flinch.

"I don't know. Please, don't do this." She flinched and tears sprang to her eyes. "I did it for all of us."

"Where are they?" His grip tightened. "Give them back."

"I c-can't." She couldn't return them, even if she'd wanted to—he knew that.

His fingers dug deeper into her neck. She clawed at his leather-encased hands. Yellow spots blinked before her bulging eyes. Her ears buzzed. No! She'd only wanted to do the right thing. She couldn't die. Not yet. It wasn't fair! She had a future. Two lives depended on her.

She jerked her knee into his groin. He grunted but squeezed her throat harder. The buzzing in her head became a tidal wave of noise.

Her vision narrowed to a sliver of light then winked out to black.

CHAPTER 2

"BREAKFAST."

"Nooo!" Jules cried out. "Somebody help me."

Sunlight streamed between the purple curtains into the lilac-colored bedroom. She stroked her neck, as if massaging it could excise the memory of the life being choked out of her.

"Jules?" April, Big Jim's tiny, blonde-haired, blue-eyed pregnant wife, stared at her with wariness from the open bedroom door. Softly she added, "You're safe now."

The smell of fried eggs wafted in at the same moment the rest of Jules's physical senses returned in a violent rush. Bile burned her throat. Sweat beaded on her forehead. Her stomach lurched. Clapping her hand over her mouth, she bolted to the door.

Racing past April and nearly knocking over Big Jim, she hurtled to the bathroom. Her body trembling, Jules retched and silently cursed herself.

"Juliana?" April knocked on the bathroom door. "Are you okay in there?"

"Fine. Just had a nightmare," Jules called back, pushing to her feet.

"Just a nightmare? Not a vision?"

"Not a vision," she said too quickly. Guilt pinched at her already cramping stomach for the lie. After all, April never judged Jules when ghosts talked to her or sent visions winging into her head. This *had* been a vision of death . . . and more. This time, she'd witnessed a murder. But this time, no one would find out. "Just a nightmare," she added, wishing it were true.

"Okay, good." April's relief echoed in the pause that followed, then she called through the door again, "Not to rush you, but we have a lot to go over at the store today."

With her parents leaving Monday, she and April had a lot of work to do. Jules couldn't let down the only woman in her life who'd always come through for her because some ghost sent her a vision. "Give me twenty minutes?"

"No problem, hon."

Jules dragged the shower knob to the On position. She stripped and climbed beneath the spray. Ten minutes later, she felt almost human again. She dressed but with her stomach still clenching, she skipped breakfast, opting instead for a glass of juice.

"I don't know if there's enough time to show you everything before we leave," April said to her before turning to Big Jim in the kitchen. "Maybe we should delay our trip to give her more time to learn her new job?"

"April, it's not a new job," Big Jim replied.

Jules finished her drink and rinsed out her glass as her parents continued to speak about her as if she weren't standing three feet away.

"Yes, it is, Ernie."

"April, she's been running the books for the flower shop for over two years."

"I know, but that was *remotely*. She wasn't even living here." April worried her lower lip and rubbed her protruding belly. "Don't get me wrong, Juliana has done a fantastic job creating the website and managing the accounting system. But now she's going to be in charge of the daily grind like deliveries, talking to customers, and resolving a thousand and one small issues that come up every day."

Big Jim glanced Jules's way, clearly inviting her into the conversation. He sighed and gave a little shrug as if tired of this particular topic.

Jules hid her smile and came to his rescue. "Speaking of deliveries, didn't you say the delivery guy's coming early today?"

April flicked her right wrist and stared at her blue and pink ribbon-faced watch. "Oh dear. We need to hurry."

Sufficiently distracted, she grabbed her purse and waddled from the kitchen then across the small cream-colored living room littered with boxes. How she managed to move nimbly around the dozen cardboard containers packed with every possession she had, Jules wasn't sure.

"I need to get my purse," Jules called out to April, who pulled a small note pad out of her bag and scribbled. A staple of her wardrobe, April never went anywhere without the book. Well, until she climbed aboard the plane on Monday morning, then she'd entrust it to Jules. At least, that was the plan.

Jules headed toward her bedroom, the only room in the apartment devoid of cardboard. She bumped her knee into the corner of a box outside her door. "Shoot!"

"Foul-mouthed as always." Big Jim chuckled, stepping into her room. He glanced around with a wry grin. "April insisted on painting this room the same color as your room from our old house."

"At least I still love purple." Jules turned to look for her purse, first on her nightstand, then under her bed.

She stood up empty-handed.

"Thanks for redirecting the conversation out there." He hiked a thumb over his shoulder. "April is really worried about the business, the babies, the move, visiting her mother . . . oh, everything. Not to mention, she wants you to feel safe and welcome."

"I've noticed." Jules smiled, gesturing to the walls. "It's fine. I'm fine. The business will be fine. The babies will be fine."

"From your lips to God's ears," he breathed.

Jules gave Big Jim a hug. Despite his stature of five foot eight, only an inch taller than she was now, he seemed as big to her today as he had the day they met.

"Juliana!" April called from the hallway, her voice heavy with anxiety. "We can't miss the delivery guy."

Big Jim stepped back, his blue eyes twinkling. "You'd better go."

"I just need to find my purse." Jules turned her back to him and crossed to the faded pink velvet wingback chair in the corner by her window. It wasn't there either.

"Are you sure you didn't leave it somewhere? I don't remember seeing it last night when Seth *brought you home.*"

"Dang," she groaned. She'd been handcuffed—sans purse—when Big Jim had come to her aid the night before. "I left my purse in Officer Lambie-Jammies's apartment."

METAL SMASHED AGAINST pavement, startling Seth out of a sound sleep. He bolted upright in bed and glanced at the clock. Seven a.m.

From the street below, garbage collectors steadily emptied their cans. Damn, he needed more sleep or his morning caffeine infusion. Maybe both. He stumbled toward the open window and his bare foot connected with an object. The cool, smooth item slid across the hardwood floor, taking him with it.

Like something out of an old black-and-white slapstick movie, his feet flew above his head and his hands grappled at empty air. The back of his head smacked the floor as he landed on his back, the impact knocked the breath from him with an audible *whoosh.*

For a moment he lay there, checking his body for injury.

Nope. Nothing but a throbbing head and a slightly wounded ego.

He crawled to the window and tugged it closed, then he searched the ground for the offending object. A shiny black handbag lay in the middle of his bedroom.

The Happy Hooker left her purse. Wonderful!

Okay, so she wasn't really a hooker. God had cursed him with a quirky, sexy new neighbor. Memories of her pinned between him and the wall assailed him. His body tightened.

Her firm body had been deliciously soft in all the right places. He'd wanted to take her right there in the hallway, handcuffs and all. The desire to shove up her skirt and drive himself inside her until they were both weak with pleasure nearly overwhelmed his sense of propriety.

God! How had she done that? No one, not even his ex-wife, had ever turned him on so fast. And how could his new neighbor still do that to him now? Just thinking about her made his libido leap to attention.

For a completely unprofessional moment last night, he'd contemplated acting on his errant fantasy. Crazy! Then again, in all of his thirty-five years, he had never met anyone, suspect or otherwise, as sexy as Jules.

And, she'd smelled like strawberries. On her it had been an erotic aroma that teased his starved senses. He lifted the purse and inhaled but it held no trace of her scent.

What the hell am I doing?

He didn't have time for this, his shift started soon. He flung the purse onto the foot of his bed. It bounced off and hit the hardwood floor, littering it with its contents. Bending over, he swiped up a first prize ribbon with the name "First Ho" stamped in the center. He chuckled despite himself. A black tube of lipstick stuck out from beneath the bed. Grabbing for it, his fingers grazed something thin and plastic. He pulled it out. A baggie of dried *herbs* dangled between his thumb and finger.

You've gotta be kidding me.

Now what was he supposed to do? Disbelief had him sinking onto the bed. Unable to stand the sight of the drugs, he crushed the baggie in his fist. The Happy Hooker had left marijuana in *his* apartment.

Familiar bitterness burned in his gut. Memories of another junkie nearly ruining his life had him moving toward the bathroom before he could think better of it. He shouldn't protect her, but his career couldn't afford another hit. Drugs found in his home twice would definitely destroy any hopes he had of advancing on the force.

He emptied the filth into the toilet, flushing it in record time.

His stomach rumbled as the last of the dime bag disappeared down the commode. He had a sudden inexplicable craving for his mother's lasagna. His Greek mother's only non-Greek concession to his father's half-British, half-Italian heritage.

Why am I craving lasagna?

Seth shoved aside the random thought and tossed the empty baggie, lipstick, and ribbon back into the purse. Laying it on the kitchen counter, he decided to return it after work. Maybe he'd have a little chat with his new neighbor about the consequences of drug use in his building. In the meantime, he needed a shower.

He headed toward the bathroom.

Three short raps sounded on his front door.

"This better be important." He circled back, regretting that he hadn't programmed his coffeemaker last night.

Flipping off the lock, he opened the door.

A pretty redhead stood there, her hand poised to knock again. She seemed oddly familiar, but he couldn't place her. She wore jeans and a blue polo with "April's Flowers" embroidered on the front. Damn, she wasn't just pretty; she was sexy in an understated sort of way. And since when was he attracted to *every* woman he met? He usually had standards.

Focus. "Wrong apartment, honey." He smiled. When she didn't do more than gape at him, he added, "April lives across the hall."

"What?" She glanced behind herself then back at him. "Wait, you don't know who I am?"

"One of April's helpers?" He gestured to her top.

"Nooo . . ." She drew out the word. "We met last night. I think you have my purse."

"Your . . . *purse*?" Seth turned to face the woman, carefully examining every feature until his gaze stopped on a pair of familiar emerald eyes. Lust and frustration rode him. "You're the Happy Hooker."

"I told you, *lambkins.*" She stared pointedly at his pajama pants and enunciated each word. "I. Am. Not. A. Hooker."

Seth pushed the door open wider and gestured for her to come in. In her current outfit she didn't reek of sex, but the image of her as she'd been the night before superimposed itself over her body as she moved.

Closing the door with a click, he flipped the lock and prayed for patience. Without a word, he crossed to the bar and snatched the bag from the counter. He met her irritated gaze and his temper snapped.

"What the hell do you think you're doing bringing drugs into this building?"

So much for patience.

"Are you on some kind of medication?" The words flew out of Jules's mouth before she had the sense to recall them.

"No, but it seems you like to self-medicate." The cop's frown deepened. "We need to talk before I have to do something that is going to royally piss off two people I consider friends."

"Talk about what?" She crossed her arms over her chest. This guy was too much.

"About the drugs you left in my place."

"You're nuts. I don't do drugs," Jules retorted, reaching for her handbag.

The cop held it in the air over her head. She jumped for it but he stood a full head taller. "Give that back. What, are you in the fourth grade?"

"I'm a police officer and you made a stupid mistake sneaking into my apartment."

"I explained that." She hadn't exactly admitted that a ghost lured her into his home, but her half-truth should have been explanation enough. "I told you. I got locked out."

"I'll just bet you did. I doubt you would have intentionally crawled through my window if you'd known I was a cop." He advanced on her slowly, reminding her again of an ancient warrior. A lethal air stirred about him as he moved.

A smart woman would have retreated, gone for help. Jeez, any woman with an ounce of intelligence wouldn't have walked through his front door in the first place. But something about this man made her want to stand up and fight.

"What are you talking about? Are you going to give back my purse or what?"

"Or what." He kept the purse out of her reach. "We need to talk first."

"Very mature. I swear you cops are all alike."

"Had dealings with police before?" The smile on his lips

belied the condemnation in his eyes. "Why am I not surprised?"

"Jeez! Not the way you think." She threw up her hands in
surrender. Sanity finally reared its head and she backed toward
the door. The cop kept coming.

Jules grappled for the knob behind her back, but the cop
slapped a hand to the door over her head before she could tug
it open.

She met his gaze and froze at what she saw.

A vermilion aura swirled around the cop like a red haze
originating from the center of his chest. Jules gasped. How
was this possible? She'd seen auras around ghosts, the flashes
of color reflecting the spirit's soul and mood, but this was the
first time she'd seen it around a living person.

For a nanosecond she couldn't think or even breathe for the
fear choking her. She needed to escape. Get as far away from
him as possible, but she couldn't do that until he let her go.
Masking her fear with an irritated tone, she snapped, "I
thought you wanted to talk to me. How is trying to scare me
talking?"

"Do I frighten you?"

"No," she lied.

The swirling aura around him faded to a muddy brown,
and he seemed almost sad. He held up his free hand, palm out.

"I'm really not trying to scare you. But you're headed down
a bad road." His deep voice had lost that gruff tone and came
out oddly soothing. His aura shifted again, this time to green,
and she sensed protectiveness and concern.

She swallowed past the sudden lump in her throat. "You
want to talk, fine, we'll talk. Just back up a little, please."

He nodded, lowered his arm, and stepped back three paces.
Disappointment darkened his features. He stared at the handbag, and the frightening aura receded until she could no longer
see or sense it.

"Ernie and April are good people. You could ruin their
lives by bringing drugs into their home. Not to mention you
could destroy *your* future." He sounded like a dad giving a
speech to an errant child.

She could argue with him or she could try to reason with

him. They were both adults; time to reason. "Okay, why exactly are you under the misguided assumption I'd do drugs?"

"I found the bag."

"What does my purse have to do with anything?"

He frowned. "Not your purse. I found the bag of drugs *inside* your purse."

"You went through my purse?" Jules crossed her arms, fury and a familiar pain knifing through her chest. He was just like her ex-husband. "You had no right!"

"It was in my apartment," he replied through clenched teeth. "It's *my* property!"

"That you left in my apartment after you broke into it last night. I could have arrested you for that alone."

True enough. Despite the anger pumping through her system at his invasion of her privacy, she at least owed him the courtesy of listening. Ghostly-induced mistake or not, he could have thrown her in jail. Her anger cooling, she found herself more confused than before.

She didn't have drugs in her purse. Did she? Panic flickered through her at the thought. Last night she and another guest at the party had bumped into each other in the bathroom. They knocked their purses on the ground and scattered contents everywhere.

Although the other woman snatched up her belongings in a rush, she had eyed the baggie of oregano on the floor. Sweeping through the exit, she'd muttered under her breath, "Just say no."

Her confidence strengthened, Jules lifted her chin and smiled her most placating smile. "What you found in my purse was not drugs."

"Right. And prisons are packed with innocent people who were falsely convicted."

"Listen to me!" A short burst of laughter escaped from her. Big Jim would have probably found this scene amusing if he were here. "Not drugs. Lavender and—"

"I know lavender when I see it. There wasn't any." He cut her off. "And since you think it's so funny doing pot, let me show you what would happen if another police officer had found it."

He backed her against the wall and clamped a hand around her wrist before she could think enough to react. Fear stole her breath, killing the nervous laughter in her throat. Still, some part of her mind rationalized that while he moved quickly and pinned her in place, his touch hadn't been rough or painful. Just authoritative.

Tossing the handbag over his shoulder, he patted her down with his now free hand. "Here's when he would Mirandize you. Should I continue this demonstration and take you downtown? I'll be glad to call Ernie to come pick you up at the station, where you can explain to him why you had—"

"*Oregano* in my purse," she shouted the first word.

His hand froze on her backside. "What did you say?"

"Or-eg-an-oh." She carefully enunciated each syllable to be certain he heard her this time. "The *herb* you found was oregano. And what kind of rookie cop are you that you can't tell the difference between pot and a bag of oregano?"

Jules wished she could laugh again but she was hyperaware of his hand on her behind.

Surprise and realization lit his expression. He rolled his eyes. "Ah, crap. My mother's lasagna."

"What?"

"Nothing." He met her gaze. A stain darkened his cheeks. "Oregano. Brilliant detective work."

The last comment seemed to be more to himself than to her. She might have sympathized with him if she weren't still pinned to the wall.

Jules rotated her hips and his hand slipped farther down her backside. Go figure! The only time anyone had touched her this intimately in three years had been Seth the Cop demonstrating his search-and-seizure technique. "Hey, are we finished with the pat-down?"

He jerked his hand away as if touching her burned him.

Backing away, he propped his hands on his hips. A decidedly distracting position given that the man was shirtless with wide shoulders, a narrow waist, and he'd just been touching her butt. Okay, so he had been searching her for drugs, but her traitorous body was turned on anyway.

"I guess this is where I'm supposed to apologize." He

rubbed the back of his neck as if it pained him, but didn't say anything else.

"And?"

"And what were you thinking? Normal people don't carry oregano in their purse."

"Sure they do."

He shook his head.

"Oh come on, see the world past the monochrome. The colors are really beautiful."

He leveled a glare at her but she was sure the corners of his lips twitched as if she amused him.

She shrugged. "Normal people carry around spices if they've just been to the health food store. April only eats organic. I stopped by the store and picked up some oregano and lavender for her. End of story."

The cop cocked his head to one side as if studying her. His stoic expression revealed nothing. Not doubt, not disbelief, not even suspicion. She would have described it as bored, except for his bird-of-prey gaze that locked with hers.

"I told you, I know lavender when I see it. I didn't find any lavender." He delivered the statements tonelessly. Still maintaining that hawklike eye contact, he added, "I thought you went to a party."

"I did go to a party. Jeez, you are so suspicious." Jules waved away his mistrust, then his previous statement registered. "Wait, you didn't find the lavender?"

"No." He glanced toward his open bedroom door as if to reassure himself. "The only baggie was the one in there." He pointed to the purse he'd flung onto his faded faux-leather couch.

"I can't believe I've lost something else! What is wrong with me, lately?" Jules raked her teeth across her lower lip. When was the last time she'd seen the herb? "I had it outside your apartment. I'm sure of it. I remember pushing it out of my way as I searched for my keys last night. I know I didn't take it out of the purse. Are you certain you didn't see it?"

"Maybe it slipped under the bed," he answered, scratching his stubbled cheek. "I can look—"

Jules didn't wait for him to complete his sentence; she hurried to the bedroom. Dropping to her hands and knees, she crawled partway under the cherrywood sleigh bed, skimming her fingers across the floor. She shouldn't be so upset over missing a three-dollar bag of herbs, but she was getting tired of losing things. It would be nice if she could find something . . . for once.

"April really needs this to help her relax," she called out to him as she shimmied beneath the wooden frame.

The cop made a sound that was cross between a grunt and a snort. "You don't seriously believe in that New Age hocus pocus?"

"It's not hocus pocus," she replied, then shoved herself farther under the bed.

She opened her mouth then closed it again at what she found beneath his bed. The man had the cleanest floor she'd ever seen. There was nothing under there, not even a stray dust bunny in want of a new home.

Wow, Seth the Cop's a neat freak.

She started to scoot back out when she spotted the shiny edge of the baggie poking out of a narrow space between the bed leg and the wall. Relief swept through her, and she grabbed it and scooted out.

"All ready to cure whatever ails with your magic lavender?" he asked, a chuckle in his voice.

"Don't believe me," she said, rising to her knees before him. She held up the bag of fragrant tiny purple dried flowers triumphantly. "But aromatherapy works, even on stodgy old guys like you."

"I'm not that much older than you," he answered, the corners of his mouth curling slightly.

"So says you," she teased, still smiling.

He nodded. His eyes lowered and an indefinable look crossed his face. Jules felt her own smile fade at his inscrutable expression, then she followed his visual path.

The top button of her polo had popped free, revealing the lacy edge of her pale pink bra.

No, he's definitely not a dirty old man. Dirty young man, maybe.

She tugged her shirt back in place and quickly re-buttoned it, certain her cheeks glowed in matching color to her underwear.

He stared down at her with his hands on his hips, his

chocolate-colored eyes nearly black, and his hungry expression sent her pulse racing. Then images zinged into her mind.

Like an erotic movie, she saw herself tugging down his pajama bottoms and taking him into her mouth. She practically felt his hands on her head, his fingers curling into her hair as he guided her back and forth over his shaft a few times until she delivered the long, wet strokes he craved. Her heart hammered as she listened to him groan and encourage her. It was so real, the silken steel of his erection, the heady scent of sandalwood and male musk, the way his hands caressed her hair and face as he murmured encouragement.

The only thing missing was taste. This had to be his fantasy, because if it had been hers, she would have imagined tasting him. Plus, in her short marriage to Billy, she'd been too self-conscious to try to please him orally. And Fantasy Seth was definitely pleased.

As quickly as thoughts winged into her mind, they were zapped out as if someone slammed a door closed on them. Or as if Seth crushed his desire by sheer will.

Too stunned to move, she wondered at what had just happened. She'd read the thoughts of another person. Oh dear God! This couldn't be happening. First seeing his aura, now reading his fantasies? She'd thought last night had been an aberration. What if it hadn't?

The last thing she wanted to do was start experiencing the thoughts of the living. Seeing ghosts was bad enough. But if she started hearing living people's thoughts, she'd never have a moment's peace.

He extended a hand toward her and she gasped.

She didn't want him to touch her. Not until she figured out how to block his fantasies from invading her thoughts. Not that she hadn't enjoyed his little one-sided sex show.

She had.

A little too much.

Falling backward onto her butt to evade his touch, she banged her shoulder against the bedframe behind her.

"Are you all right?" Seth pulled his hand back with a frown, then asked in an exasperated tone, "Can I have my bedroom back now?"

"Of course." For the second time in twelve hours, she'd

forced her way into his bedroom. And she'd thought last time had been embarrassing. Jules pushed to her feet, avoiding eye contact.

She hurried through his apartment. Clutching the knob of the front door, she tugged but it didn't give. A tanned, muscular arm reached around her and flipped the lock. Before she could escape, he tapped her on the shoulder.

Jules rotated on her heel, relieved none of his stray thoughts had filtered into her consciousness. Still, he stood so close the scent of sandalwood filled her senses and sparked memories of the vision she'd just had.

He frowned at her and held out her purse. She tried to accept it, but he didn't release it. The purse acted as a conduit and again she connected to him. Unlike last time, there were no images, just an electric current of awareness evident in his darkening eyes.

It was sinful, frightening, and strangely intoxicating.

He lowered his head.

Instinctively, she lifted her chin, keeping her gaze locked with his. Her breath caught in her chest. His lips kicked up in a small grin.

His cell phone rang.

The shrill tone severed the link they shared. Sanity returned as the cop retrieved the phone from his pocket and scowled at the caller ID. He opened the front door.

With one hand on her back, he pushed her through it.

"Wait, my pur—"

He tossed her the clutch, which she caught against her chest with both hands, then he gave her his back as he answered his phone. "Detective English."

The door closed unceremoniously in Jules's face. For some reason she couldn't name, disappointment settled in a lump in the middle of her chest, immediately followed by an overwhelming sense of relief. She'd almost kissed a near stranger—a cop at that—for the second time since three this morning. And to top it off, she was either losing her mind or she'd just discovered some new facets to the Scott family curse. She could read thoughts. Maybe not everyone's, but definitely his.

I'd rather be insane.

"You've got your purse. Good. Lock up please." Jules

glanced up to see April, arms full, waddle into the hallway. "I can't believe you own a Prada."

"Yes, well, I needed to get something out of the divorce," Jules said, taking a stack of forms out of April's arms. "Go on downstairs, I'll lock up."

That's when Jules remembered which two items were missing from her handbag, her cell phone and her keys.

Perfect! Hopefully they're together, at least.

Tucking the purse under her free arm, she hurried down the steps and caught up with April just as she stepped out into the morning sunshine.

"April, can I borrow your cell on the way to work? I need to call myself."

CHAPTER 3

"**W**HAT'S SO URGENT you couldn't wait for me to come into the station?" Seth said into the cell phone after closing the door on his neighbor. He crossed his tiny carpeted living room and headed toward his bedroom.

"They knocked over another jewelry store last night," Devon Jones replied in a dry tone.

Seth propped his cell between his ear and his shoulder and grabbed his note pad and a pen. "Okay, you got my attention. Go."

His partner gave him a quick rundown. "Owners just arrived and discovered the store had been broken into. Beat cops are questioning them now. I'm en route to the scene."

"Give me the address, kid. I'll meet you there."

Jones remained silent.

That might have been Seth's fault. He still hadn't adjusted to the idea of another partner, his third in the past five years. He was sick of teaching guys the ropes only to have them promoted before him. At least this one didn't lap at his heels the way the previous two had. Well, until they were promoted, moved to the homicide division, and believed they were too good to associate with him.

Breaking in a new detective was not something he wanted to do. Lately, it seemed the rookies were getting younger, or maybe just cockier. Usually, he didn't care if he annoyed Jones by calling him a kid. Today was different; he needed his *partner's* cooperation.

"Detective Jones." Seth made an effort to sound civil. "May I please have the address?"

"McGivern's on the corner of Sixty-eighth and Pacific, in a strip mall with some florist shop."

"The jewelry store across from April's Flowers?"

"That's the one."

"I'll be there in twenty minutes."

Seth didn't wait for Jones to respond, he simply ended the call. He needed a quick shower. No, what he needed was to get his head on straight. Jules had been right. Mistaking oregano for pot had been a rookie mistake.

Heading into the bathroom, he turned on the shower and stripped. Steam quickly filled his tiny bathroom, fogging up his mirror.

He climbed beneath the water and tried to convince himself his error in judgment had been an anomaly. On the force he'd only ever made one other mistake.

That one error nearly cost him everything. Since then, he'd spent the past five years determined to never miss a single detail on a case, often working twenty-hour shifts. He'd missed blind dates, his own surprise party, and last spring, he almost missed his daughter Theresa's high school graduation.

But he owed it to her and to himself to earn back the reputation her mother and her mother's lover had nearly ruined. So he worked.

Under the spray, Seth tried to focus on the Diamond Gang case.

Why did the damn press have to come up with such an idiotic name in the first place?

Diamond Gang . . . sounds like they should be covered in sparkling jewels.

Jules.

Her sexy body flashed in his mind, her wide green eyes and

her slender body supple in all the right places. The vibrant red hair she wore down around her shoulders suited her far better than the black wig. And this morning she still smelled like strawberries. It had taken everything in his power not to press his nose against her hair when she'd stood beside his bed. Okay, so he wanted to do a lot more than smell her hair. When she'd been on her knees a myriad of other things he'd like to do with her sparked in his mind.

Why did she have to be his neighbor?

There's no way he could start a casual fling with someone in his own building. Only one way that would end: badly. His daughter had been right when she'd pointed out, after his last relationship crashed and burned, he sucked at commitment. Every single woman he'd liked and had dated, hated him now.

That decided it. He couldn't like Jules. He refused to be attracted to her. If he was, he'd do something stupid, like break his own rules and pursue her until she was naked and writhing in his bed. Then it would happen.

After a week or two of steamy, sweaty, heart-pounding, soul-numbing sex, he'd grow bored and she'd grow attached. Just like every other woman he'd met in the past four years. And then he'd need to avoid not just her, but Ernie and April as well. And he liked them.

Then again, they were going on vacation, and when they returned, they wouldn't live in his building anymore.

No. He couldn't do it.

Jules was no one to him, absolutely no one. Too bad his body seemed to disagree.

He flipped the knob to cold and shivered, washing beneath the frigid water. By the time he'd shaved, all thoughts of his troublesome neighbor had been replaced by his case.

Dressing quickly, he focused on what he knew about the Diamond Gang. No one else on the force wanted to touch the cases that had been passed from one detective to another over the past two years. The burglaries were considered trivial and unsolvable to everyone but Seth and the four jewelers who had been put out of business.

The little mom-and-pop shops had struggled to survive against the influx of national chains before the robberies. After them, they couldn't stay afloat. The shop owners needed to know who had destroyed their livelihoods. They needed closure and Seth needed to give it to them.

"Solve these," Captain Peterson had said last week, as he handed Seth the stack. "And I'll see to it you're given the opportunity to take the sergeant's exam."

Yeah, he'd solve them all right. Seth's career had taken enough hits over the years. Nothing was going to stand in the way of his promotion now. He had no intention of remaining a beat cop forever.

Except, he wasn't a beat cop. Technically, he was Detective English. Ha, detective in name only, thanks to his second partner and Seth's dead ex-wife. He pushed away the familiar fury and focused his attention on current events.

It had taken two years, but the Diamond Gang had finally slipped up.

With the remaining businesses doing their best to tighten security, the owners at Holcomb's Jewelers had grown creative. It worked. Two weeks ago, while robbing Holcomb's, the thieves missed one of the recently installed cameras hidden inside the body of a cheap lamp shaped like a stained glass lighthouse.

While the camera hadn't been capable of recording sound, the video came out crystal. Thanks to it, Seth had his first solid set of clues. The thieves were coordinated, ski-mask-clad, and fast. They seemed to know exactly which cases to hit. But the biggest discovery from Holcomb's video came as a surprise. One of the gang members was a woman.

Just before leaving the store, she'd bent over a display case in the center of the room. She'd seemed enamored with a piece of custom jewelry. A rare red diamond. While lusting after the ring, her shirt rode up. The camera captured an image of the tattoo on her lower back: a light green snake coiled around three red roses.

When Mr. Holcomb itemized the list of stolen items, the red diamond ring was included. The ring was on loan from a local philanthropist who'd planned to use it as the centerpiece in a fund-raiser for the Tidewater Children's Network next month.

And yesterday, Seth had received a voice mail from a woman named Aimee-Lynn who claimed to have knowledge

of the case. While she didn't admit to being a member of the
gang, she did request to meet with him today to discuss what
she knew. She'd even claimed to have proof she wanted to
share in exchange for "help for a friend."

His gut quivered at the memory of returning her call. She'd
whispered on the phone as if she feared being discovered.
After setting an appointment to meet with him at four this
afternoon, she'd hung up. Unless his instincts failed him,
Aimee-Lynn was the female recorded on the Holcomb's tape.

That burglary, like all the others, focused primarily on
loose gems. This time, they weren't just any gems in the store.
While before the stolen gems had been a mix of semiprecious
stones and diamonds, at Holcomb's robbery they were all diamonds. At a carat each, they were high quality and easy to
fence, with the exception of the red diamond. The value of that
gem alone boosted the Holcomb heist to nearly a half-million
dollars.

· And now McGivern's had been robbed. Seth only hoped
this time the gang left fingerprints or something more sub-
stantial to go on than broken glass. He'd love to walk in there
with a little leverage when he met with Aimee-Lynn this
afternoon.

AFTER CALLING HERSELF and receiving only voice mail, Jules
winced. She had no choice. She'd have to come clean.

"Um, April. I, uh, have some bad news."

"What's wrong?" April asked as she pulled into the parking spot at the back of April's Flowers and cut the engine.

"Well, it seems I've lost my keys to the apartment and, the
uh . . ." Jules bit her lip. "Shop."

"Juliana, are you sure?" April's eyes widened. "Wait, the
shop key's missing too?"

"I'm so sorry." Jules hurriedly exited from the car and
raced to the driver's side to help April climb out. "I'll pay to
have the locks replaced if I can't find the key."

April gave her a wan smile. "That's not necessary. I'll figure something out. I'll call Ernie. He'll know what to do about
changing the locks."

A horn beeped. Jules glanced toward the loading dock to

see the delivery van waiting for them. She turned back to April. "Why don't you head inside and I'll get the delivery sorted out."

"Good idea." April nodded. "Once you've finished with him, there are nine dozen white carnations in the back room that need to be dyed before the store opens. Can you take care of them?"

"Sure." Jules nodded, then headed toward the large white van.

She dealt with the deliveryman quickly, leaving him to put the fresh flowers in the case and the boxes of floral supplies in the back room. She'd need to shelve them but April had wanted the flowers dyed first. Jules closed the loading dock door behind the driver as he left the building, then strode toward the back room.

Gathering her supplies—a bucket of flowers, floral paint, and her apron—she carried them to the table. She dropped the bucket to the floor and set the cans of paint next to the nine large green plastic vases on the worktable before tying the apron around her body.

Jules grabbed up a flower, an uncapped can and started spraying. Finishing the first flower, she set it in a vase then plucked another carnation from the bucket and dyed it. The problem with the mundane task was that her mind tended to wander. The last thing she wanted to do as she stood alone working was think about her vision.

Each time her thoughts drifted to the hum and bump of the wheels of the car from last night's vision, she moved around the table, as if shifting her position could push away the unwanted memory. Before the last flower was colored, she'd circled the worktable four times and whipped her mind through topics such as how she'd find her sisters, ideas for boosting sales during the holiday season, and even April's fears of losing the twins as she had the previous two pregnancies.

Between dropping one dyed flower in the bucket and beginning the next, the hum of the tires sounded in her ears again. At some point she drifted, carried away by the monotonous tonal memory until her nose burned with the stench of sweat, copper, and fear. She found herself sifting through the entire vision.

With her visions limited to the victim's perspective, there wasn't much to go on. Last night's vision consisted mostly of shadows, blood, and pain, nothing about the victim, the car itself, or the killer. Information wise, the vision bordered on useless but it did bring on a fresh wave of nausea.

Visions always did that to her. She lived or died each moment exactly as the victim had. Her body acted as a vessel into which a ghost poured her pain, physical and mental. And when the vision ended, the rush of reality crashed into Jules with enough force to leave her feeling ill. Sometimes for days.

It was all the legacy of the Scott family crift of psychic abilities. A curse and a gift. While no two members had the same gift, each was rumored to be cursed with some form of it. Lucky Jules got to see ghosts. *Ha, lucky!*

Her crift had cost her everything: her father, her sisters, even her marriage. Only Big Jim and April had ever stayed beside her, unafraid of her *talents*.

Her thoughts drifted to the hum of tires again. She realized that unless the murderer put his hands around her throat—something she seriously didn't want—Jules doubted she would ever be able to identify him.

What am I doing? Three years ago, when she had tried to help another ghost, she'd ended up arrested as an accessory to kidnapping. She needed to remember that.

Jules shook her head to clear it and stepped to her right, sidling around the table once more. No more ghosts. She'd never help another specter.

Resolute, she reached for another flower and blinked in surprise. With the can in her right hand, she searched the table for a fresh carnation but none were left. She'd dyed them all.

How long had she been lost in her thoughts?

"Juliana, I spoke to Ernie," April called out from around the corner.

"April, I'm sorry about the keys," Jules called back, sweeping stray leaves and broken stems off the worktable and into a trash receptacle.

"It's fine. I told you Ernie would take care of it." Her voice grew louder and the floor squeaked as she waddled down the hall. "He's called a locksmith to come to the shop but he needs to wait for the super to . . . Oh my!" Her blue eyes nearly as round as her belly, she seemed frozen in the doorway between the storefront and the back room. "Hmmm . . . well, at least the flowers are dyed too."

Too?

Jules glanced down. Bright orange paint was splattered all over her apron, jeans, and shirtsleeve. Not to mention the swipe on the workbench where her hand had smeared the paint when she cleaned off the table. Heat warmed her cheeks but she tried to joke away her embarrassment. "Well, pat my head and call me coordinated."

"I wouldn't recommend it." April pressed her hand to her mouth but laughed anyway. Leaning out the doorway she said, "Diana, you've got to see this."

April's teenaged Goth assistant appeared at her side moments later and snorted.

"Want the black paint now?" she asked in a thick southern Tidewater drawl. "We can paint a jack-o-lantern's face on your apron and put you in the front window."

Black lipstick, jet-black hair, ivory foundation, and black eyeliner combined with Diana's thick southern twang often made the girl's jokes seem funnier than they probably were.

"Thanks. I'll pass." Jules laughed and set the can on the table. "I know I was put on this earth to entertain the masses with my clumsy antics but I'd rather not risk April's storefront."

Jules lifted a hand to brush a stray hair from her face.

Diana and April yelled in unison, "Stop!"

Pumpkin-colored spray coated her right hand. Had she touched her face, she'd have walked around for the rest of the day painted orange. Even her bangs couldn't have spared her the complete mortification of being the color of a fall vegetable.

"You . . . you . . ." Diana giggled, appearing to enjoy Jules's mishap a little too much. "You've got a spot on your cheek. Whadja do, stand downwind?"

"What wind? We're inside." Her question sent April and Diana into fresh gales of laughter. With nothing else to do, she gave in and chuckled at herself, adding, "I'll be back."

She darted past April's office door and down the short hallway to the single restroom in the shop. After flipping the light switch, the overhead light buzzed to life. She strode to the sink.

It took several seconds for the energy-saving bulb to illuminate the bathroom enough for Jules to clearly see her reflection in the mirror. When she did, it taunted her.

"I look like a deranged Oompa Loompa with red hair," Jules whispered to herself.

She half-chuckled and half-groaned as she washed her hands. Floral paint wasn't permanent, but with her fair skin she might need to take a couple of showers to get it all off. And somehow she'd splattered paint onto her cheek.

She scrubbed the spot with soap, then closed her eyes to splash water onto her face. As the bubbles gurgled down the drain, she sensed she was no longer alone. Nothing changed in the room at first. No movement, no wind, just the impression of another soul crowding into the tiny bathroom.

Oh great, the new ghost-girl has returned.

"Thanks a lot for last night. You nearly had me arrested for breaking and entering."

She glanced up, but the mirror's reflection showed only her.

"What am I doing?"

Don't engage the specter. It would only work harder to stick around. *Ignore her.* No, not her . . . it. Jules couldn't humanize the ghost or she'd fall prey to past mistakes and want to do something really stupid. Like try to help.

Can't see it. Not there. Simple.

Nodding to her reflection in the mirror, she attempted to ignore her own niggling doubt. Jules patted her cheeks with a paper towel and tossed it into the garbage.

The temperature dropped fifteen degrees in the space of a few seconds. A frigid wind blew across her neck, giving rise to the tiny hairs there. The screeching voice echoed in her ears. *"Please."*

Jules rubbed her offended ears in a fruitless effort to deafen the noise. It seemed the ghost wasn't any closer to mastering the ability to speak to the living today than she had been the night before.

"Awww, dang it!" Jules said through clenched teeth and shut off the water. "I moved back to Tidewater to get away from things like you."

The ghost continued, not taking the hint. *"Help. Me. Please."*

Jules went for brutal honesty. "I'm out of the ghost-helping business. Go find a medium or check out the Psychic Life Foundation down on Eighty-first Street."

To Jules's surprise, the apparition departed as noiselessly as it had arrived. Only the absence of a chill against her flesh signified the change at first. Then the rapid elevation in room temperature sent sweat trickling between her breasts.

Air. She needed fresh air. Jules hurried out of the restroom and made a beeline for the back door. But April stopped her just as she reached it.

"Juliana, are you sure you're all right?" Jules turned around at the sound of April's voice, in time to see Diana disappearing into the back room muttering something about opening boxes.

April watched the door close behind Diana, then turned back to Jules and continued. "You've been really quiet this morning. I have a feeling it wasn't just because you lost the keys. You're not having second thoughts about running the business, are you?"

"No, not at all." Jules blinked in surprise. "I mean, yes, I'm annoyed with myself for losing my keys, but only because I love this place almost as much as you do. I would have been the manager years ago if I hadn't married Billy. Teaching pre-school was fun, but horticulture is my life. So, no, I'm not having any second thoughts."

"Good! I was a little worried after your vision last night."

"I told you it was a nightmare not a vision," Jules replied in a strained voice.

"Right. And I've known you a long time." April waddled closer then rubbed the small of her back with her right hand. "You screamed, stared at me with that wild I'm-not-really-aware-of–who-I-am stare, then you ran to the bathroom. It's what you did every time you had a vision when you were a kid. I didn't know you still had them after what happened back in Kemmerton."

Jules held up her free hand to silence April. She didn't want to discuss what had happened back there. What had started out as the beginning of life in a picturesque little town ended in blood and death. Even now, thinking of it made her stomach pitch. And really, it was pitching enough already.

If she wasn't going to discuss something that happened three years ago, she certainly wasn't going to talk about last night's vision. Not now, not with anyone. "I haven't had any visions since then. I just had a nightmare, that's all."

April arched an eyebrow. "Lie to yourself all you want, but don't go trying to lie to me. I know you too well."

Jules nearly winced at April's too-true words, but didn't respond.

"Okay, well." April stuck her hands in the front pockets of her apron then pulled out a piece of paper. "Oh! I almost forgot. Abigail Harris from Social Services left a message for you late yesterday. She said she can meet with you tomorrow morning at nine."

"She's working on a Sunday?" Jules couldn't quite hide her surprise.

"For me she is." April grinned. "I don't know if you remember, but I told you we were able to adopt you because a friend vouched for Ernie and me."

Jules nodded despite her confusion.

"Well, Abigail was that friend. She told me a long time ago that if you ever needed anything, to call. I think she expected you to want to find your sisters. Anyway, she's going to meet you at The Jewish Mother restaurant tomorrow morning at nine."

Jules threw her arms around April and pulled her in for a quick hug. "This is great. Thank you."

"You're welcome." April pulled back and pushed the note into Jules's hand.

She accepted it and tried to squelch the hope bubbling in her chest, having been let down too many times before. But it was hard. "Did she sound like she could help?"

"She didn't say, but you have to believe she can." She smiled then ruffled Jules's hair like Jules was eight years old. "Make sure you invite Hannah and Shelley to Thanksgiving dinner."

"April, that's six weeks away." Jules laughed out the words.

"Never too early to start planning for the holidays." April grinned.

Glancing at the note in her left hand, her mind raced. Would she really find them? Would they look like her? Were they raised in a loving home like the one she found with Big

Jim and April? Would they welcome her into their lives again or blame her for not finding them sooner? Her heart skipped and jumped, whether from excitement or the fear of facing another disappointment, she wasn't sure. She shoved the note into the back pocket of her khakis then blurted, "Do you think Hannah and Shelley will want me to find them?"

"Of course they will. They're your sisters." April waddled closer and lovingly wrapped an arm around her shoulders. "We never forget the family members lost to us. I bet they're looking for you as hard as you are for them."

"You're right. I'm being silly. It's just . . . Hannah was barely three years old when we were separated." Jules chewed her lip. She hadn't realized how much she needed to talk about them until this moment, but it felt wrong somehow to discuss her other family with the woman who adopted her. "I'm sorry. I shouldn't be talking to you about this."

"Why? It's on your mind. We'll always be family, Juliana." She patted her distended belly. "God willing, the babies will be here soon and you'll have a brother and sister. And I have a feeling before you know it, you'll find Hannah and Shelley. I'm so certain of it. I've already planned for two more settings at the Thanksgiving table."

"You got a crift you forgot to tell me about?" Jules teased.

"No, unlike you, I'm not *gifted*. I just have faith." April smiled wide. Then gave her another one-armed squeeze. "And when they come for dinner you can show them your room in the new house."

The new house. The place Big Jim and April would move to when they returned from the vacation they were scheduled to start on Monday. More than once April had hinted that Jules could move in with them.

That sounded about as tempting as getting involved with another ghost's problems.

"April, I thought we'd agreed I'd take over the lease on the apartment so you and Big Jim could move into your dream house. You know I love you both, but I'm too old to live with *my parents*." She gave an exaggerated shudder and smiled. "How appealing would I sound? A twenty-seven-year-old woman who works in her mother's store and lives with her parents?"

April laughed. "Juliana, you *run* my business. Without you, I wouldn't have been able to afford to move into the house so soon. Besides, I thought you weren't interested in *appealing* to anyone."

"I'm not!"

"If you're sure?" April's eyes sparkled with mischief. A look Jules knew too well. It reeked of matchmaking schemes.

Jules threw her hands up in the air. "Stop that! I swear you act more like the corrupting older sister. I can see you scheming now. Whoever you think you want to introduce me to, you can forget it. Between running the shop and searching for my sisters, the last thing I need is a complication like dating."

WITH THE STORE set to open in twenty minutes, Jules and Diana emptied boxes and stocked inventory in the back, while April worked in the front, watering plants and setting up the register.

"Do you want to finish stocking or recycle the boxes?" Jules asked.

Diana looked over from where she stood, arranging every can on the shelf so the labels all faced the same direction. "I'll finish this."

"No problem," Jules said. Leaving Diana to finish stocking, she carried empty, broken-down boxes out the back door to the loading dock.

A cool breeze ruffled her bangs. Above the sun shined in a brilliant sapphire sky. She licked her lips, relishing the salty taste carried on the wind. When it came to beauty, no place compared to autumn in Tidewater. Nestled in the southeastern corner of Virginia, next to the ocean, the smell of salt lingered all year round.

The oak and maple trees lining the road boasted of fall with leaves of red, gold, and brown. The late morning air had lost the crisp chill and was now pleasant. The making of another perfect day in the tourist town.

Well, it would have been perfect if not for the bevy of police cars, parked across the parking lot behind McGivern's Jewelers.

As she broke down the empty boxes, Jules watched a uniformed patrolman cordon off an area behind the jeweler's.

Yellow tape formed a giant rectangle bisecting the alley. A short distance from there, two police cruisers parked in a vee, blocking three Dumpsters, two for trash and one for recycling. The recycling, of course, sat farthest away. And it appeared the recycling bin wasn't part of whatever was going on.

With boxes stacked in her arms, she hurried across the parking lot.

A uniformed patrolman stepped in front of her with his hands up and an icy glare on his face.

"This is a crime scene."

Adjusting the boxes in her arms, she nodded to the recycling bin. "I don't see any tape up over there. I'm just going to recycling. Is that blocked off too?"

The last thing Jules wanted to do was contaminate a scene. With her luck, she'd get a vision from it and end up in jail for spouting some foolish comment.

"Huh?" The patrolman appeared confused as he glanced over his shoulder. Looking back at her, he shrugged. "Uh, no. It's not part of the crime scene. You can go there, Miss . . . ?"

"I'm Jules." She grinned.

"Chaz Gareth." He extended his hand as if to shake hers in greeting.

"Nice to meet you." She eyed him from around the boxes in her arms, then nodded at them to indicate her hands were full. "Sorry. Boxes."

"Oh, right." The young man's eyebrows arched so high, a wrinkle creased his forehead. Then he rushed forward to lift the tape so she could walk under it toward the recycling bin.

"I won't be long," she promised.

She ducked under the tape, and in less than a minute she'd disposed of everything.

Returning empty-handed, she strode past the second Dumpster and stumbled to a halt as a chill slid down her bare arms. Then she heard her cell phone ring.

At first she thought she might be having a vision, albeit an auditory one, until the young patrolman glanced her way as if he heard it too.

"A Hard Knock Life" from the musical *Annie* was the ring-tone on her phone. And unless she was losing her mind—possible, but she'd never been that lucky—it was playing.

The patrolman crossed to her. Without the boxes between them she could see he wasn't much more than two inches taller than her own five foot seven.

"Do you hear someone singing?" he asked.

"I think it's my phone. I lost it last night," she admitted. "But I don't understand how it could be in the garbage."

"Maybe you accidentally tossed it out?"

"Not likely." She crossed to the bin and flipped up the lid on the second Dumpster. The music abruptly ended with a triple beep.

Two-day-old chicken lo mein mingled with the scent of roses. Despite being brown and unsellable, the flowers were still aromatic. But as the combined scents wafted up, Jules nearly gagged.

She covered her nose with her hand to muffle the stench. The young officer did the same. His blue eyes watered and he took three steps back, waving his right arm.

"Lady, I wouldn't go in there if you paid me. I suggest you just call the cell company and report it lost. It's not worth fishing for it."

Maybe she should.

She'd never be able to rid it of the stink. She opened her mouth to agree, but it started singing again. At the same time, someone screamed from inside the Dumpster.

"Help me! Please!" The high-pitched wail sent chills down her back.

Jules hurried to the Dumpster and started to climb in. Officer Gareth seized her by the arm and yanked her backward. "What are you doing? This whole area is a crime scene."

"Help!" The scream coming from inside the Dumpster nearly drowned out the singing telephone.

"Can't you hear her voice?" Jules tugged her arm free.

"Of course I can. So what?"

Another scream went up, pitched higher than before and considerably weaker.

Still the police officer stood. Useless and unmoving.

"Well, if you're not going to do something, I will."

Rushing to the Dumpster before he could stop her again, Jules scrambled up the side and perched on top. Sunlight glinted off of black plastic trash bags, rotting food, and roses. But there wasn't a living soul inside.

Jules blinked in confusion, then it hit her.

The ghost had been screaming.

No wonder the cop hadn't done anything. Only she could hear the ghost. Great. Just great.

Glancing over her shoulder, she found Officer Gareth scowling at her. "Are you nuts, lady?"

Yeah, she just bet she looked like a lunatic. And worse, she needed to figure out a way to gracefully back down from her perch. "Uh, no. Sorry Officer. Um . . ."

"You want your phone that bad?"

"My phone?"

Oh, he thought she'd done all this to chase after her phone. She sagged in relief. Then her phone started singing again. She jerked in surprise. That little bit of a jump was enough to send her tumbling headfirst into the trash.

Scrambling to her feet, she slid this way and that. In a way, trying to stand on rotting garbage reminded her of the first time she'd tried surfing.

No traction, no balance, and she just knew she was going down. She slipped sideways and got a face full of what had probably been beef and vegetables.

"Oh, gross!" She swiped a flaccid carrot from her face.

Her phone started ringing again. Jules stared at the garbage currently surrounding her.

Whatever! I need a shower anyway.

She thrust her hand into the muck and dug for the ringing phone. Her fingers closed around it and she yanked it free. Brushing off as much of the muck as possible, she pressed the Send button. "Hello?"

"Help . . . me." The whispered words crackled weakly through the cell. The phone went dead.

It rang again. The caller ID read BLOCKED.

Jules answered it again, only to hear the ghostly voice whisper, "Help me! Please!"

Fear and irritation had her reacting before Jules could think better of it. "You've got to be kidding me. I'm getting phone calls from the dead now?"

"Help."

"Help yourself. You seem to be able to do a lot. Stop calling me!" Jules clicked the phone off.

She glanced up as a white light burned bright then faded to a hazy gray aura surrounding a pretty young woman with a jet-black bob. Sitting atop the Dumpster with her knees tucked beneath her, she leaned on her hands near the edge of the lid, just staring down. Dressed in jeans and a light blue T-shirt, the ghost looked vaguely familiar.

"Do I know you?"

A tormented look of rage twisted the girl's features and her gray aura swirled again, this time to thunderous dark crimson. She dropped her head back and opened her mouth in a voiceless scream. Instead, the razor-sharp sound of a hundred fingernails dragged down chalkboards ripped across the space, echoing against the metal walls of the Dumpster. Jules dropped her phone and clapped her hands to her ears, desperate to drown out the sound.

She barely registered that the ghost had finally tapped into the ability to manifest itself when the lid slammed closed.

CHAPTER 4

SETH PULLED HIS aging red Honda Civic into the parking lot outside McGivern's Jewelers. Not bothering to lock the car, he headed toward his partner. Jones, with his indeterminate heritage—a thoroughly American mix of cultures from his pale blue eyes to his light mocha complexion to his sand-colored hair—was directing a group of patrolmen.

"Why isn't the tape up yet?" Jones asked a freckle-faced pretty boy who looked like he'd be more at home at a frat party than working the beat this close to the Norfolk line. "We need to have this entire area cordoned off, Officer Harmon."

"We've already put it up in the alley." A surprisingly deep voice came out of Harmon's choir-boy-looking mouth. "And we're about to do the front now, Detective."

Harmon turned and barked out orders. Three other patrolmen appeared, two flanking the front door and one from around back. Perhaps Harmon wasn't as young as he looked. Or maybe Seth was too damned old.

"Sirs, this is weird." Harmon turned to include both Seth and Jones in the conversation. "It's still early yet, but the owners say so far, it doesn't appear anything's been stolen. It's like vandals came in and smashed up the place, but they got in the same way the Diamond Gang did at the other burglaries."

"Through a dismantled security system?" Seth shared a confused glance with Jones.

Harmon nodded then his eyes widened. He pointed at something behind Seth and Jones.

Seth followed the younger man's line of vision and turned around. He watched a woman climb into one of the Dumpsters and the officer beside her doing little to stop her.

"Stop!" Jones and Seth hollered in unison as they broke into a run.

From behind them, Harmon yelled into his radio, "Gareth! Stop her. This is a crime scene."

"Harmon, stay and keep this area secure," Jones called out over his shoulder.

The woman turned her head just enough to reveal her profile before she toppled headfirst into the garbage bin. Jules! Recognition hit Seth like a punch to his solar plexus.

He nearly tripped over Jones, who'd jerked to a stop in front of him. The pause had been momentary, as if he'd received a shock, then he started moving again, faster than before. Seth chased the other man's heels. As they ran, the Dumpster lid slammed shut.

Incoherent screams poured from inside the closed container. The high-pitched cries sounded as if Jules were being tortured. "Pleeeasse! Help! Ahhhh!"

The wails sliced through him. He added a burst of speed but still lagged behind Jones, who moved so fast he became little more than a blur.

Gareth leapt into action, trying to push the lid up. Jones reached the Dumpster and shouldered the useless patrolman out of the way.

"Fine, you try," Gareth muttered under his breath and spun around, bumping into Seth.

With a glare and a thought to have a chat with Gareth's supervisor later, Seth closed the last few feet to the Dumpster and started to tug at the lid.

It didn't budge. Almost as if it were locked in place.

Seth quickly traced his hand around the container's lid,

searching for a lock or at least a weak spot. Finding none, he caught his partner's eye. On opposite sides of the bin, they both reached to pry it open at the same time. Despite their efforts, it remained firmly in place.

Their hard work was rewarded with only mounting frustration and lines crisscrossing their palms from the lid's sharp corners.

"Help! Let me out!" Jules banged on the side of the container. The Dumpster walls shook and gonged with each blow.

"We'll get you out, Jules," he yelled reassuringly. "Just hang on. The top's stuck."

"I can't find what's keeping it closed," Jones called out from the opposite side.

Jules shrieked incoherently, taking large sobbing breaths between each cry for freedom.

"Just another minute, Jules. Hang on, precious." Seth leaned even closer to the corner of the container, until his nose rubbed against something wet. Wiping the muck from his face, he turned and shouted at Gareth, who stood idly off to the side with one hand covering his nose. "Call for backup, Gareth! Move your ass!"

"No!" Jules yelled the single word before she loosed a cry filled with anguish and terror. A sound so piercing, it dug into his psyche. It echoed from inside the bin, drawing out the horrified scream. Seth knew he'd hear that shriek again and again in his nightmares.

The cry cut off with alacrity. The silence that followed was more haunting than the scream itself. Almost as if there was someone in there with Jules. And that person had silenced her.

A cold lump formed in Seth's belly in the nanosecond that followed, then he and Jones renewed their attack on the lid. Digging his fingers between the shallow opening of the molded plastic corner and the cold steel of the Dumpster, Seth's flesh scraped away near his fingernails but he didn't relent.

At least when she screamed, he knew she was alive. Anything could have happened in there. In his mind, he riffled through a myriad of horrendous scenarios—heart attack, stroke, seizure, aneurysm, fainting. Although fainting would have been preferable compared to the others.

Then, as if by magic, the lid sprang free. One moment it seemed cemented in place and the next the lid flew up into the air like a rock flung from a slingshot. It slammed against the brick wall near the back door of McGivern's before crashing to a halt, half on the curb and half on the blacktop.

"Wow. Remind me not to piss you guys off," Gareth said, breaking the silence.

"Too late," Seth and Jones replied simultaneously.

Leaning over the Dumpster beside Jones, Seth peered inside.

Jules lay facedown on the heap of trash. Rotting food, torn black trash bags, and crumpled white foam containers with shoe prints in them were scattered around her.

Jones pole-vaulted over the side of the Dumpster and jumped in before Seth could move. The rookie slid his fingers against the side of her neck, checking her pulse, then rolled her over.

"What are you doing?" Seth demanded, his basic first aid training kicking in. "You aren't supposed to move an unconscious victim."

Jones didn't answer. He slid his arms under Jules's legs and shoulders, carefully lifting her. He appeared ready to try to climb out of the Dumpster with her in his arms. That seemed like a worse idea than moving her, so Seth stepped up and stretched out his arms.

Seth accepted Jules's limp and surprisingly light body from Jones. Cradling her against his chest, he wondered at her slight form. Slender and delicate even in her unconscious state, she seemed precious and fragile. And a need to protect her at all costs ignited within him.

Whoa, where had that come from?

He hardly knew her. He shouldn't feel a need to keep her safe. Shaking it off, he lowered himself to the ground as gently as he could, with Jules in his arms.

Her head lolled back and he watched the pulse throb in her neck. He leaned over, placing his face above her mouth and nose. Warm, shallow breaths tickled his ear.

"She's breathing," he informed the men, surprised to hear the relief in his voice.

"Thank God." Seth glanced up at his partner's whispered words.

Jones stared down from inside the container, seemingly unaffected by the rank stench emanating from beneath his feet. His hands gripped the side of the container and he appeared transfixed by the sight of Jules's unconscious body.

Music started.

"Ah damn," Gareth muttered. "It's her cell phone. It's why she jumped in the trash can in the first place."

The ringtone jolted Jones out of whatever catatonia he'd slipped into. He spun around and disappeared behind the green wall. When he popped back up, he clutched a phone between his fingers. A frown dug a line between his eyebrows.

"We've got a problem," he intoned, glancing from the ringing phone to Jules and back again. He dug into his pocket, pulled out an evidence bag, and dropped the cell in.

"What are you doing?" Gareth asked, his voice cracking.

Jones glared down at the beat cop. Quite possibly, it was the most ferocious expression the kid had ever displayed. Gareth shifted his weight, then increased the distance between them by two steps.

"Officer Gareth, did you look in here before you allowed a civilian to climb inside?" Jones asked, his expression grim.

Invisible bands tightened around Seth's chest.

"I didn't *let* her in. She jumped. I tried to stop her. What did you want me to do? Shoot her?" Gareth fisted his hands at his sides.

Jules stirred to consciousness in Seth's lap. He glanced down. She blinked a few times before lifting a hand to shield her eyes.

"I've got you, *precious*." He covered her hand with his. "You're safe now, Jules."

"Did you get the license plate?" She choked out the strange question, rubbing her throat with her free hand as if it pained her.

"What?"

"Huh?" Her emerald eyes were wide and dilated as she stared up at him. She appeared unaware that she'd just spoken. "Jules?"

"Y-yes?" She blinked as if coming out of a trance.

She started to sit up, then her face paled and she swayed. With a hand on her shoulder, Seth urged her to lie back down. "Just rest a moment."

"Detective English, you need to take a look at this," Jones called from his position inside the bin.

"What?" Seth glanced up to see Jones staring. A mixture of concern and annoyance darkened his features.

"You'd better come see." Jones hiked a thumb over his shoulder.

"Gareth, get over here and keep an eye on her." Seth slid Jules off his lap, laying her gently on the ground. Pointing a finger between the idiot officer and Jules, Seth added, "And don't shoot her."

A tic worked in Gareth's cheek, but he nodded.

Seth crossed to the Dumpster. The stench had intensified now that the lid lay on McGivern's back doorstep. Clutching the side of the Dumpster, he peered inside.

Jones squatted down. Pulling a pen from his pocket, he flicked away a broken foam plate. A vinyl skirt encasing the body of a woman, mostly buried beneath the garbage, came into view.

Hairs rose on Seth's arms.

Jones stood to his full height, which only made him appear slightly shorter than a giant since he stood on a mountain of rotting food, and glared at Gareth. "Did you allow anyone else in here?"

"Of course not!" Gareth answered through clenched teeth, his hands fisted at his sides. "I *didn't let* her in! Besides, this isn't even part of the crime scene." He pointed to the yellow taped area. "That's where I was told the crime scene was. What the hell is going on?"

"Never mind," Seth interrupted, waving the young officer into silence. Turning back to Jones, he asked, "Is she fresh?"

"She's cold," Jones answered at the same time Gareth asked, "Is *who* fresh?"

Gareth abandoned his post near Jules and peered into the Dumpster. His eyes widened. "Oh. Shit."

Indeed.

"Get back to your post." Seth dismissed the soon-to-be meter maid. He focused on activity within the bin. "We can still limit the damage to the crime scene. Provided no one else contaminates it. Jones, radio Harmon and get him to bring more tape. Tell 'im to call in the ME."

Jones nodded, made a quick radio call, then dropped to his haunches. He poked at the area surrounding the body, clearing away some of the debris. "Looks like she's been in here awhile. Rigor's already set in. Need the ME to know for sure how long."

Behind them, Gareth yelled, "Wait!"

THE WORLD SPUN around her as Jules's vision ended. Man, she hated that feeling. What was with the ghost sending her the awful memories of the murder, *again*?

It had been identical to the vision she'd had last night. The trunk of the Buick—although, come to think of it, she had no idea how she knew it was a Buick—was the same, just like every other second of the dream.

Didn't the specter have someone else to haunt? Like the murderer? Why couldn't she go stalk him?

And why couldn't the visions come without the intense physical need to . . . A spasm of warning ripped through her rebellious stomach and sweat beaded on her face.

"Arrggh." She bolted upright.

"Wait!" Officer Chaz Gareth reached for his gun.

Gasping in surprise, she pushed to her knees and nearly stumbled again. She clutched her belly. "Excuse me."

The patrolman grabbed her arm, none too gently.

"Lady, you need to wait right here. You're a—" He cut himself off.

He must have seen the look on her face because he practically shoved her away and sidestepped to clear her path.

Jules raced back to the florist shop. With one hand over her mouth, she tried to stave off the inevitable. As long as no one else slowed her down, she'd make it to the bathroom without mortifying herself by yakking all over the loading dock.

Behind her, shoes slapped the pavement in rapid staccato taps. Someone was chasing her. Assuming it was the young patrolman, she kept going.

"Hey," a familiar voice called out. "Stop running! Juliana . . . Jules, we need to talk."

Seth the Cop's voice penetrated her brain at the same time the normally delicious aroma of sandalwood battered her senses.

Dang and darn!

The scent intensified her need to hurl. Bile rose in her throat. Another spasm wrenched her stomach.

She flung open the back door. The door buzzing swept relief through her system because she was going to make it.

Then he caught her by the shoulders, pulling her to a shuddering halt.

She spun, pushing at the cop's chest. His beautiful coffee-colored eyes were dark with concern and agitation. She shook her head and gulped uselessly.

Oh, no! Please, God, spare me just a little dignity.

"I'm gonna be—" was all she managed to say. She tried to turn away, but he caught her by both arms this time. She flung her hands against his chest to keep some distance between them, hoping it would be enough.

It wasn't.

To her utter mortification, she puked all over his tan slacks and black loafers.

THE APPLAUSE STARTED the moment Seth walked through the front door of the brick police station on Seventeenth Street. Catcalls and whistles were accompanied by a dozen officers holding their noses and pretending to gag.

Dealing with the dregs of society all day, cops enjoyed nothing better than a chance to blow off steam, especially when it came in the form of ribbing a brother in blue.

For that reason, and the fact that Captain Peterson had called him into the station, Seth accepted the ribbing with as much good humor as he could.

"Losers." Seth made sure to add an over-the-top growl to his voice. "Go bust a felon or something."

As he expected, they laughed at him and went back to work.

He made his way through the lemon-scented main office. The desks sat two by two facing each other with flatscreen computer monitors on top, back to back. Twenty desks sandwiched into the square office space that consisted of five rooms. The main office, a small room for interrogation, Captain Peterson's office, and the locker room were connected by doors on one wall. At the opposite side of the main room lay the entrance to the holding cell. Every wall of the station was covered in vintage eighties-style wood paneling. Framed pictures of the response workers raising the flag at Ground Zero, the president, and sailboats hung in frames around the main room.

"Great job getting that witness to spill her guts," Detective O'Dell called out.

He clapped a hand on the shoulder of Detective Reynolds, who stood with his arm propped on top of the water cooler.

"Good thing it's now a homicide investigation or he might have made her *spew* her story again and again," Reynolds added, then playfully elbowed O'Dell in the ribs.

Both men wore smug grins. Both had been Seth's partner at some point in the past five years. And both were now partners in the homicide division.

"You're here?"

Seth turned his back on the idiot brothers from different mothers and found Jones holding an open folder and frowning at it. "I am."

"I thought you were going home to shower."

Seth glanced down at his obviously clean suit and back at the younger detective. But Jones wasn't looking at him. He appeared engrossed in a file. "Whatcha got there?"

"My notes from the crime scene."

"We'll take that." Reynolds reached to pluck it out of Jones's hands, but the kid was too fast. He closed the file and held it against his chest. His expression all but dared Reynolds to reach for it again.

"We need to talk." Jones turned to Seth and said in hushed tones, "First, I learned the part of Atlantic in front of the parking lot was closed for street cleaning between four and seven this morning. I found a flyer and contacted the department of sanitation. They confirm no cars could have gone in or out of the lot during that time."

"Good," Seth said. "Anything else?"

"Yeah." Jones frowned and lowered his voice even more. "The body in the Dumpster was our tramp-stamped robber."

"Crap." Seth didn't know why he was surprised. "So instead of robbing McGivern's, they used it as a dump site."

"Seems so." Jones frowned then added, "But why trash the place and not take anything?"

"Well, if the vic was part of the gang, perhaps they had a difference of opinion? Maybe they trashed the place to stage the robbery, hoping we'd focus on that and not search for the body in the Dumpster."

"Maybe, but they haven't been above taking cheap stuff before. I'll have the owners carefully review their inventory to be sure nothing is actually missing. I just can't see the burglars casing the place just to dump a body and take nothing, ya know?"

"Agreed!" Reynolds chimed in. He gestured to O'Dell. "And while you two are searching for jewels that may or may not be missing, O'Dell and I will solve the murder that actually happened."

Jones pressed his lips together, then turned his back on Reynolds.

Seth ground his back teeth but didn't say anything, too focused on what this twist could mean to his chances of being allowed to finish this case.

No doubt the case would be turned over to homicide and his chances of promotion would evaporate. Unless he and Jones could convince the captain to let them remain the lead detectives.

Peterson stuck his head out of his office. "Jones, English, Reynolds, O'Dell . . . get in here."

He disappeared back inside without waiting for a reply.

Seth shared a wary glance with Jones, then led the way past the empty secretary's desk and into the captain's office. Two faded blue leather chairs sat opposite of Peterson's desk. Reynolds and O'Dell all but raced to claim them, smirking at each other as they settled into the seats.

Seth perched on a corner of the credenza while Jones closed the door then stood at parade rest on the opposite side of Reynolds and O'Dell.

"What happened this morning?" Peterson dispensed with pleasantries.

Since he'd been the lead detective on the scene, Seth

recounted what happened after he'd arrived at McGivern's Jewelers. When he explained about Jules vomiting on him, O'Dell and Reynolds snickered.

"What did you do with her?" Peterson asked, as if not hearing them.

"She was covered in muck from the garbage and clearly physically incapable of being interviewed. I let her go home."

"You did what?"

"She's my neighbor. I know where to find her." Going against procedure didn't endear him to the captain, so he spoke fast to avoid the full brunt of his superior's wrath. "I have someone assigned to watch her until I can get back there."

"Are you getting soft? So what if she's sick? Interview her." Captain Peterson frowned. "I'd expect you of all people to take this seriously. What if she's our killer?"

"She's not our killer, sir."

"How can you be sure?" Peterson shook his head. "According to the preliminary ME report, the victim died sometime between three and seven this morning. And according to what your partner learned, the street was closed off for cleaning from four until seven. So unless you were with her between three and four a.m.—"

"I was," Seth answered quickly, then frowned at what it must have sounded like.

"Come again, Detective?"

"I was with her from eight minutes after three until approximately three forty-five this morning. There's no way she could have killed the victim and dumped her body in the eight minutes before or the fifteen minutes after I was with her."

"Wow, he's quick," Reynolds said.

"Talk about wham, bam, thank you, ma'am," O'Dell added.

"If you two are done," Captain Peterson snapped, but his lips were pressed together as if he were stifling a grin. Turning back to Seth, he asked, "How could you possibly be sure of the time?"

"That's when she was in my apartment."

"No wonder she puked on him this morning," Reynolds said with a laugh.

"She was hung over," O'Dell added with a smirk. "Late night at the bar?"

"She woke me up, assholes. There was no alcohol involved." *I think.* Seth glared at his former partners, then glanced to his captain. "The witness was in my apartment last night, then I escorted her home at three forty-five."

"And you're certain she was in her home?" Peterson asked with a frown.

"I am." Seth paused, expecting more questions, but when none came he added, "At most, sir, she's a material witness after the fact."

"There's no way she could have known the victim was in the Dumpster?" Peterson ran a hand over his glistening bald head.

"No, sir," Jones interjected. "I'd say she had no idea there was a dead body in there when she jumped in. Otherwise, she gave an Oscar-worthy performance in that container. I think my partner is right, she couldn't be involved in the case."

Captain Peterson's eyebrows lifted at the vehemence in Jones's words.

So did Seth's. If he didn't know better, he'd swear Jones had a soft spot for the woman.

Pushing on, Seth added, "I'll interview her when she's—"

"Able to stomach the sight of you," Reynolds interjected.

"Feeling better," Seth finished, ignoring the comment. "Captain, I've known her family a long time. I have a rapport with them. I'll get her story in the morning."

"Fine." The captain nodded, then pulled a handkerchief out of his desk drawer and mopped the sweat from his head. "Jones, share your findings from the scene."

Jones nodded. "The body of a woman aged twenty to twenty-five was found in a Dumpster. Body was in full rigor when discovered. Marks on the neck indicate the cause of death was likely manual strangulation. As you already know, the TOD was between three and seven this morning. Still waiting further findings from the ME to confirm cause of death. Body was found without identification."

"Physical description? Distinguishing marks?" Peterson asked tossing aside the damp cloth and jotting notes onto a pad on his desk.

Jones continued. "Distinguishing mark was a single tattoo on her lower back near her spine: a green snake wrapped around three red roses. At first glance, the woman appeared to be a brunette. However, when the body was moved, the wig fell off. The vic had shoulder-length blonde hair. She was five-seven. Eye color brown."

"Have you run her description against the list of missing persons' cases?"

"Yes. No match. We do know one thing." Jones paused then added, "She's a physical match for one of the robbers in the Diamond Gang."

Captain Peterson tapped his pen against his lower lip. "English, give me your report again from when you arrived on the scene."

Seth recounted his experiences again. Despite knowing each word moved him closer to losing his case, he answered respectfully. The captain nodded and held a hand up to silence the group as he wrote notes.

Seth's mind raced. He needed to find a way to keep this case. This was his ticket out. Without it, he would probably have to wait another year or more before being offered another opportunity to take the sergeant's exam.

"Captain." Seth waited for Peterson to look at him. "I know this complicates matters, but I believe that Jones and I should have first crack at the murder. It's tied to our burglaries. I have a meeting scheduled for later today with someone who claims to have inside knowledge of the heists. We're close to solving the burglaries. I'm positive this murder is tied to it. Just give us a week. We'll have the burglaries wrapped up and bring in your killer."

Reynolds bounced in his seat. His ruddy complexion darkened as he narrowed his eyes at Seth. His focus quickly shifted, as did his expression. He turned to the captain and plastered his best bootlicking grin on his face.

"With all due respect to my former *partner* . . ." Reynolds nodded at Seth. "This is now a homicide investigation. If English and Jones want to continue working the burglary part, that's fine. But homicide is our division. We don't need amateurs screwing up *our* case any further."

"Sir." Seth sucked in air between his teeth in an effort to reign in his mounting irritation. "We were on the scene. We've gone over every single detail of the burglaries and we know this body is one of our suspects. We need time to solve the case."

The captain tossed his pen onto the desk then laced his fingers together over his portly belly. "Reynolds, you and O'Dell want the murder?"

"Yes," Reynolds and O'Dell replied in stereo.

"But you'd be willing to give English and Jones here full access to the crime scene so they could continue their investigation into the burglaries?" the captain asked in an almost bored tone.

"As soon as we're finished wrapping up the murder scene this morning, they can have at it," Reynolds answered emphatically.

"Hmmm . . ." Captain Peterson picked up his pen again and resumed tapping.

Seth wanted to argue, but he'd already pleaded his case. If Peterson didn't give him the case, he'd just have to work it himself. He'd solve it before his brown-nosing ex-partners. Nothing was going to interfere with him taking the sergeant's exam.

After all, he'd started this case. He would finish it.

Before them.

Now he just needed to get Jones on board. He glanced over at his partner. Determination blazed in Jones's eyes and then he gave a curt nod.

No mistaking the fire there.

He and Jones were on the same page.

Seth's heart rate slowed. He hadn't even noticed it had been racing until the pace decreased. Hope had his temper cooling. He glanced back at his captain.

"Well, in that case," Peterson said, "I've made a decision. Jones and English have one week to solve the murder and the burglaries."

Seth barely stifled his satisfied grin.

"But, Captain!" Reynolds began to argue.

Peterson held his left hand palm out to silence the outburst. "Not up for discussion. You two are already working five other cases. We're going to give English and Jones a crack at this."

Captain Peterson pointed a finger at Seth then swung it

back and forth between him and Jones. "One week. That's it. Solve the murder, recover the diamonds, and bring in the thieves."

Or else. He didn't say it, but the words etched themselves on Seth's soul anyway.

CHAPTER 5

"A NEW TWIST in the Diamond Gang robberies. A body was discovered in a Dumpster this morning by a worker of this store." The newscaster waved to the façade of April's Flowers before the camera zoomed back to her. "The police haven't released the name of the worker, but News Channel Five has learned—"

His iPhone rang, cutting out the live news feed. The screen darkened briefly. "Blocked" appeared in bold white letters on a black background.

Glancing around, he assured himself of privacy, then answered in an undertone, "What do you want?"

"Did you see the news? The body . . . it's Aimee-Lynn, isn't it?"

Say her name louder, you asshole. Maybe someone will hear and nail us for this.

"Yes," he hissed, then winced as the fool cursed in an octave unnatural for a grown man.

As much as he wanted to tell the imbecile to get over

it—she got what she deserved—he couldn't. He needed the man's help a little longer.

"We have another problem. They knew each other. How else would shop girl have found *her*?" He didn't dare say Aimee-Lynn's name. He wasn't alone and couldn't risk someone over-hearing him mentioning it. He lowered his voice to barely a whisper, "Word is *she* had shop girl's cell. How'd she get it?"

"I don't know." His partner paused, then asked, "You think Aimee-Lynn told the flower shop girl about the gems?"

"Perhaps," he replied. "Or gave them to her. Either way, the new girl might be our best lead."

Two people strode toward him. He bowed his head and stepped out of their way. Moving away from the crowd toward the shadows, he added, "Follow her and find them. Before I have to do something else you'll regret."

"You don't need to come back in today, Juliana." April's voice sounded strained through the receiver. "I'm heading out with Ernie. We'll be gone most of the afternoon. Diana's running the store. The locksmith just left April's Flowers. The super is out of town until Wednesday. I left a message but he said he'd change the locks when he returned. Cheap jerk won't pay for a locksmith and threatened to charge us if we changed it ourselves. Just keep my apartment key since I won't need it in Florida. Tonight, I'll give you a copy of one of the new shop keys. Don't feel obligated to come back right now. I want you to take care of yourself and rest."

"I'm fine really." Jules hated to hear the worry in April's tone. "A shower and a nap were all I needed. I feel much better. Besides, I promised I'd review the upcoming bookings before you left."

"We can do that tomorrow." April paused, then added, "Or I can always put off the trip by a day or two."

"No, don't do that." Jules shook her head even though no one could see her. Grabbing a brush, she ran it through her hair with one hand while holding the cordless telephone with the other. "I'm coming in. Leave my key with Diana and I'll get it from her. Trust me, I'm rested. I'll review the bookings this afternoon and be ready to talk to you tonight if need be. You don't need to postpone your trip. Tell Diana I'll be there in about twenty minutes. Bye."

She hung up the phone. She'd already lost half the day. After her little Technicolor show on Seth's trousers, she'd allowed him to drive her home. At least he hadn't tried to question her. In truth, the four-block drive had been quick and loud. His little car clanged and moaned, making it next to impossible to carry on a conversation with the windows down.

And they needed to be open. Between her garbage-encrusted clothes and his vomit-laden pants, only someone born without a sense of smell could have handled the stench.

Wonder if he'll ever get that stink out of his car?

She winced and focused on getting to work. She locked the apartment with keys April had loaned her after the Dumpster disaster and slipped them into her front pocket before hurrying down the apartment stairs. She'd barely opened the building's front door when she sensed she wasn't alone. Her back stiffened and a prickly awareness skated down her arms.

She froze in place and glanced around, expecting a ghost.

"Headed somewhere?" Officer Chaz Gareth called out. He leaned against the wall of her building with his arms folded over his chest.

The tension melted away at the sight of a living person. She gave him a weak smile. "Yeah, back to work. Sorry about earlier."

"Hey, at least you didn't ralph on me." He pushed away from the building and gestured to his police cruiser parked across the street. "Come on, I'll drive you back."

An alarm gonged in her chest and she sucked in a breath. It wasn't his fault that he drove a police cruiser. Or that she'd had one ride too many in them to welcome another. But she couldn't think of a way out of it. "I-I'm headed back to work."

"I know that," he replied with a chuckle. "That's where I was offering to take you. That's not a problem, is it?"

"No. That's great." She smiled and hoped it didn't look too plastic. "A ride to work would help. Thanks."

She followed him over and climbed in. As soon as she buckled up, he pulled onto the road so fast, she clutched at the dash for support.

He laughed. "Don't worry. This baby can do ninety and still turn on a dime."

Not something I really want to see. "Are you going to interview me now?"

"Nah, that's for the detectives to do. I'm just helping a damsel in distress."

"Okay." She chuckled. "Thanks, but I'm fine."

"All that work, and you didn't even get it," he said as they jerked to a stop at an intersection.

"Didn't get what?" she asked, bracing both hands against the dashboard. She was sure she'd leave fingerprints in the vinyl.

"Your cell. They confiscated your phone as evidence after they found that body." He stepped on the gas.

She slammed backward into the seat and her hands fell limply into her lap. "Oh."

They traveled a few hundred feet before Chaz whipped the steering wheel to the right and brought the car to a jerking halt in front of April's Flowers.

"We're here, milady." He waved toward the shop.

"Thanks for the lift." Not that she ever planned to let him drive her anywhere ever again.

Opening the door, she stepped one foot out when Officer Gareth grabbed her arm. "Next time, leave the Dumpster diving to the professionals. Have a nice day." He winked.

She hopped out of the cruiser and closed the door. The car zoomed away almost before she'd released the handle. Standing on the curb in front of April's Flowers, she watched him zip around a corner and out of sight.

"Jules?"

She turned to find Mason Hart sauntering up the sidewalk.

Not him again.

She thought she'd gotten rid of him when she'd blocked him from copping a feel at the Pimp and Ho party last night. Apparently not.

Although nine years had passed since they first met, he looked very much the same. Just older. And more attractive. Something he no doubt still used to his advantage.

In college they had been complete opposites with nothing in common other than they both wanted an A in chemistry class. As a geeky horticulture major with a bad haircut and no figure to speak of, she held little attraction for the quarterback of the football team. But somehow they'd been friends. At least until she met Billy in her senior year.

Last night at the reunion, however, dressed in her FM boots and her killer bustier, she'd had an up-close-and-personal run-in with her old friend. And it had been more than friendly.

Embarrassment scorched her cheeks at the memory. "You're right. Let's do it. Let's do it now. Tonight," he whispered into her ear just before his lips closed over her right earlobe. She yelped in surprise and spun around to face him. It was hard to tell in the dark who looked more shocked, her or him.

Now he was outside April's Flowers. *Man, it feels like God has it in for me today.*

"Mason, what are you doing here?" She tried to ask the question brightly but her voice sounded high-pitched to her own ears.

"I'm ordering flowers." He opened his mouth and closed it again. "What are you doing here?"

"I work here."

"You work *here*?" He spread his arms wide briefly, gesturing toward the shop.

"Yes, I'm the manager." With that she turned and strode toward the front door.

"Jules, wait." He followed and pulled her to a stop. "About last night. I'm, uh . . ." His words trailed off, as if he were unsure how to continue.

"We don't have to talk about it. In fact, I'd be thrilled if you never brought it up again." Jules patted his fingers with her hand until he released her, then continued up the four concrete steps to the shop.

"In my defense, you were smokin' last night," Mason said as he reached around her to open the door. "Come on, tell me. You *were* secretly that hot when we were lab partners, weren't you?"

"Not then or now." She snorted. "Come on, I thought we were friends. You never hit on me in school. And I preferred it that way. I always liked being your friend rather than one of your conquests."

She practically bolted inside, crossing the floor in hurried, sure steps.

"Jules, wait." He stopped her from ducking behind the counter by placing a hand on her arm.

She glanced back to find his cheeks mottled red. "Last night really *was* an accident. In the dark, from behind you . . . you looked a little like my fiancée. I swear I wouldn't have touched you had I realized."

"You're engaged?"

When his cheeks darkened even more, she could see a bit of the boy she once knew. This wasn't the quarterback looking to score with all the cheerleaders. This was Mason, her friend. And when he gazed at her with sincerity in his blue eyes, the embarrassment she felt over last night's little debacle faded.

"I really am sorry. You have no idea how much," he said, clearly as uncomfortable with the situation as she.

With a half-laugh she admitted, "It's fine."

She'd have agreed to almost anything to end the embarrassing conversation. Again, the story of her life these past few years. The only intimate touches she'd received from anyone had been police pat-down demonstrations from hot cops and accidental kisses from old friends.

Shoving away the unwanted thoughts, she sidled out of Mason's reach. She moved around the counter, grabbed an apron, then put it on.

Mason glanced around the showroom then back to her. "I thought your boyfriend convinced you to become a teacher."

"Good memory." She smiled. "I did that for a while, but it wasn't really for me. I run April's Flowers now and I'm much happier."

"What happened to the boyfriend? Did you two ever get married?"

Before she was forced to reply to that really uncomfortable question, Diana rushed out from the back room. "Oh, Jules, I didn't know you were here yet." Reaching into her apron, Diana pulled out a key and handed it to Jules. "Miss April said to give this to you."

"Thanks." Jules tucked it into the same pocket as the other two keys.

Diana glanced at Mason and moistened her black lips in a

manner too seductive to be appropriate for a teenaged girl. She held out her hand to him. "Hi, I'm Diana. I do all the floral designs. Can I get you anything special?"

"Actually, I'm here to see my friend, Jules." Mason nodded to Jules.

"Oh." Diana's come-hither look vanished and she released his hand at the same time the silver entry bells chimed announcing a new customer. "Excuse me." Diana headed off to help the new arrival.

"She seems . . . unique." Mason stared off in the direction where Diana had hurried.

"She's a great kid." Jules grinned at him when he met her gaze again. "So what can I do for you? Picking up flowers for your *fiancée*?"

"Yes, I'd like two dozen long-stemmed orange roses." Jules checked the inventory book, not surprised to find that was her entire inventory of orange roses for the day. Making a note to order more, she then went to the refrigeration case to retrieve his order while he continued to talk. "Last night with you was supposed to be my apology to her . . . well, if you had been her."

"That explains a lot," Jules replied, carrying the wrapped flowers back to the counter.

"Unfortunately, I think she saw what happened." He grimaced. "I can't get her to return my calls today."

Ouch.

Still, Jules couldn't help flashing hot and cold at the memory. While there was zero attraction between them, she was woman enough to admit that if the right man had delivered an *apology* like he'd delivered last night, any slate he'd dirtied would've been wiped clean.

But doing that to the wrong girl in a case of mistaken identity? Not so much.

"I'm sure she'll understand once you explain," she said.

"I doubt it. I'm hoping when she sees me with the roses, she'll at least soften enough to listen before she slams the door in my face." Mason blew out a breath and shook his head. He cleared his throat and his charming I-can-get-away-with-murder grin was back on his face. "Jules, let me take you to lunch. I want to make up for the ki—"

"That's very sweet." She cut him off before he could mention exactly what had transpired between them. Although Diana and the new customer were at the other end of the counter, the last thing Jules needed was for them to overhear. That would just make last night's mortification complete. "Mason, you said you wanted to order flowers. We really should get to that. I'm sure your fiancée will love them. Shouldn't you be taking her to lunch?"

"Yes, but—"

"Jules, do you have the special arrangement book I showed you this morning?" Diana interrupted, searching through a pile of black, nine-by-twelve portfolios. "I can't find it in my stack."

"Check in the back, I'll look here." Jules bent down to search. She yanked a book from the middle of the heap beneath the counter. She stood and nearly clocked Mason in the face because he'd leaned so far over, as if watching her. Jules gasped in surprise.

Unfazed by the near miss, he grinned at her. "Jules—"

"Hang on, Mason." Jules held up a finger to silence him. Calling out to Diana, who'd disappeared into the office, she said, "It's here."

"Okay," Diana yelled back. Then the office phone rang. "April's Flowers," Diana answered.

Crossing to the customer, Jules opened the portfolio and set it down in front of him. The soldier, by the look of him, wore a blue camouflage uniform that was a size too big. He gave her a tight-lipped smile.

"Here," Jules said. "Have a look at this one. It's got our best designs in it. Diana'll be right back to help you."

"Thanks," the young man mumbled with a lisp.

Jules moved toward the other end of the counter and Mason followed. He ran a hand through his perfect blond hair. Instead of mussing it, he gave it that sexy, just-rolled-out-of-bed look. He grinned at her but somehow this smile seemed a bit contrived. "Lunch?"

"Mason, I really appreciate the offer. But shouldn't you be trying to win your fiancée's forgiveness and not mine? Buying her flowers is great but you really should be taking her to lunch, not me. I'm fine, really. No harm done."

An odd look crossed his face. "Come on, I could use your help. If the flowers don't work, I'll need advice. She's not your typical woman and I can't afford to lose her. Please? Back in college, you used to be really great at giving good advice on women. Bet you still are."

"Flattery will get you nowhere." She sighed. Old Spice filled her senses. For a hot guy, he always wore that old cologne. Then again, it had had a resurgence a few years back. "Look, I can't do it for a couple of days but give me your number and I'll call you. Lunch would be nice. Maybe by then you and your fiancée will have made up, and you can introduce me to her?"

Mason beamed at her then chucked her under the chin the way he had when they were freshmen. He pulled a business card out of his wallet and handed it to her.

She started to put the card in her apron, but Mason frowned at her. "You are going to call me, aren't you?"

Something in his tone tugged at her heartstrings. She almost felt sorry for the guy. Plus, had she tucked the card in her apron, she might have lost it. "Of course I'm going to call you. We're friends."

As she spoke, she pulled out her purse from where she'd left it earlier in the day and set it on the counter. It landed with a thud.

She opened it, dropped in the card, snapped it closed, then quickly returned it to the spot beneath the counter. When she glanced up, both men shot their gazes to her. Awareness prickled on her skin.

Was it her imagination or had they just shared a look?

CHAPTER 6

BY EIGHT FORTY-FIVE Sunday morning, Seth was ready to delve into the secrets of his very sexy neighbor.

No, he shouldn't think of her as sexy. It wouldn't serve him well to let his attention wander from solving his case.

Jules is a person of interest. Nothing more.

So what if he'd decided to finally wear that ridiculously expensive shirt Theresa bought him for his birthday? The one she said made him look like a *total hottie*. And ten years younger. Closer to Jules's own age.

Sure, all he wanted was to interview her.

Even he didn't believe that.

He knocked on his neighbor's door and waited. It swung open. His heart rate sped up . . . until April, not Jules, appeared.

Then the smell of fresh coffee hit his senses, reminding him he hadn't yet had his first cup of the day.

"Good morning, Seth. You're early. Dinner's not for hours yet," April teased with a smile. "Run out of milk for your coffee again?"

Without waiting for a response, she turned and waddled

back into her apartment, dodging between cardboard boxes stacked in two long rows in her living room. He followed her inside, closing the door behind him.

"Right, dinner. I'll be here. It was sweet of you to invite me. Are you sure you want to cook? My mother would love to whip up something for your last night in town."

His mother ran the best Greek restaurant in the city. And she lived for cooking for family and friends. Asking her to prepare a going-away dinner for April and Ernie would delight her to no end.

"Thanks, but no. I really want to cook one meal for Juliana before we head out. Lasagna's her favorite." She opened the refrigerator door, pulled out the milk, then closed the door with her hip and turned around. Holding out the carton, she said, "Where's your mug, or did you run out of coffee too?"

"I didn't come by for milk." He glanced around the empty kitchen, noting the coffeemaker was on and the pot still half full. "But a cup of coffee would be great."

April must have caught him eyeing the pot because she had moved before he'd finished speaking. She poured him a cup and even added a splash of milk to the mug before returning the carton to the refrigerator.

"Thanks." Seth accepted the cup and took a sip. Hazelnut roast exploded on his taste buds and he sighed. "Delicious as always. You make the best coffee I've ever tasted. Just don't tell my mother I said that."

"Ernie makes me promise the same thing." April beamed. "Your secret is safe with me."

"Where is Ernie? I thought I heard him talking to Mrs. Himmel downstairs this morning."

"Her car broke down, so he gave her a ride to church. He should be back around lunchtime."

Seth took another sip of coffee then admitted, "I actually came by to talk to Jules about yesterday. Is she up yet?"

"Seth, about yesterday." April paused then offered him a wan smile. "You know she's going to pay to replace your shoes. She told me she was going to talk to you about it later today."

"She wants to buy me new shoes?" He couldn't quite keep the incredulity out of his voice. "That's not necessary."

But it was *very* considerate.

"She felt terrible about what happened and told me that she was pretty certain she'd ruined them. She thought she could have your slacks cleaned but doubted the same was true of your shoes."

"Yeah, I didn't bother to bring them into the building." He scrunched up his nose, remembering the stench as he tossed them into the Dumpster behind their apartment complex. "I do appreciate her offer. Still, it's not necessary."

He glanced around the open-floor layout of the apartment. If boxes didn't line every wall, April's place would be very similar to his floor plan, with an eat-in kitchen sharing space with a living room. Except where he had watercolors by local artists on his walls, she had photographs. One in particular caught his eye.

Setting down the mug, he crossed from the kitchen to the living room to stare at the framed picture of Ernie, April, and a teenaged girl with a familiar face. The three people sat on a sand dune in matching outfits of white shirts, blue jeans, and sandals. Even their smiles were identical. Bright and wide. As if they'd just shared in a great joke.

"Is this new?" It couldn't be. Ernie looked about ten years younger in the portrait.

"Kind of. Ernie hung it there about a week ago." April waddled up beside him and stared up at it. "Juliana took the picture when she was seventeen. We were on vacation and she set up the camera on a tripod and made us pose. The original picture was ruined when Mrs. Himmel's cat used my picture box as a litter box last year."

Seth winced. He remembered that cat clawing through more than one screen on a hot day last summer. And all the neighbors who fell victim to Mrs. Himmel's senile cat had something ruined. Including him. Except the cat only destroyed his screen, which was why he didn't have one in his window two nights earlier.

"So where did this one come from?" he asked, gesturing to the large portrait.

"In all the packing, Ernie found the negative. He knew how much I loved that picture, so when Juliana came home, he presented one to each of us. This one belongs to her."

Seth turned to examine it again. "Her eyes aren't green here."

"Oh, right." April gave a wry grin. "That picture was taken right before her eighteenth birthday when she was heavy into her assimilation phase."

"I've heard of a rebellious phase, but what's an assimilation phase?"

She grinned. "Well, all children go through phases. While most children want to be different from their parents, sometimes adopted children want to be more like them. Ernie called it her assimilation phase."

"And since you and Ernie adopted Jules, she wanted to be more like you?" Made sense to him.

"You got it." Her eyes softened as she glanced at the portrait. "Juliana dyed her hair blonde, wore colored contacts, and even called us Mom and Dad for a bit. But her hair never went completely blonde; her red always shined through. And she hated wearing the lenses. Plus, she felt like she was betraying her own mother by calling me 'Mom.'"

"So where's Jules been for the past several years?" He turned to face April. "I mean, you've mentioned having a daughter, but I'd never met her before two nights ago."

"She's been away." April frowned and chewed on her lower lip. "Finding herself."

Before Seth could ask about her curious answer, his cell phone rang. He glanced at the caller ID. Jones.

"Excuse me a moment, April. I need to take this." He moved away in an effort to gain a little privacy. "English here. What do you have for me, kid?"

"It's not Jones," the captain barked in his ear, "it's Captain Peterson."

"Sorry, sir."

"Just kidding, it's me." Jones laughed.

He picks now to develop a sense of humor?

"Damn it, Jones, stop screwing around," Seth hissed into the phone. "If you've got something for me, then get to it. Otherwise, stop wasting my time."

"Right, I apologize, Detective." Instantly, Jones sounded like his typical stoic self. "Good news is I checked out the local tattoo artists in the city and found one who identified our vic's ink as his artwork. Bad news is, he only had a first name for her. Hang on—" Jones must have placed his hand over the receiver because muffled sounds came through for a moment before he returned and said quickly, "Captain Peterson wants an update here in his office in fifteen minutes on what we've come up with since yesterday."

Great. Nothing. Seth had come up with exactly nothing since yesterday. And getting nowhere fast right now.

"I'll be there." He didn't bother saying good-bye, but clicked off his cell. Time to get down to the last bit of business before he left. "I hate to ask you to do this, but can you wake up Jules? I promise not to stay long if she's still sick, but I need to go over what happened yesterday with her before I meet with my captain."

"Oh, Seth. I'm sorry. Juliana isn't here. She left before you arrived."

Seth frowned. "Where is she?"

"Oh, well, I don't know how to reach her right now." April smiled but it seemed a bit forced, then she made her way around the living room as fast as she could waddle. "She doesn't have her cell phone, you know."

Seth pivoted on his heel, keeping her in his line of vision as she collected her jacket from the coat hook near the front door, checked her pockets, dug out her keys, and jingled them.

In all the years he'd known April, she'd never acted uneasy around him. Until now.

"April, is everything okay?"

Another forced smile. "Of course. Look, Juliana had an appointment this morning. But I know she'll be at the shop by nine thirty."

"Ah." The last thing he wanted was to arrive at the station with nothing to show for the last twenty-four hours. He'd ended the call too quickly to hear what exactly Jones had learned from the tattoo artist. Maybe if he hurried, he could reach the station in time to discuss his partner's findings with him. Better to walk into the captain's office with a lead than with nothing at all.

April's watch beeped.

"Ugh, I'm sorry." She flicked her wrist and her eyes widened. "I'm gonna be late if I don't head out now."

He nodded because really, what else could he do? Opening the front door, he held it, then followed her out of the apartment.

They'd barely started down the steps when she surprised him by asking, "I suppose you need to talk to Juliana about that poor woman you found in the Dumpster?"

He snapped his gaze to hers. "I'm afraid so."

"You know she had nothing to do with what happened to that woman." April lifted her chin. Blue fire flared in her eyes. "She couldn't hurt anyone."

"I believe you, April." And he did. It didn't change the fact that he needed to account for Jules's whereabouts before and after she was in his apartment. "But you do understand this isn't personal. I just need to ask her a few questions for my case."

"Anything that happens to Juliana is very personal to me." She paused on the third step and turned to him. Her lips thinned. "Just like it would be for you if it were Theresa caught up in a situation like this."

True.

"April, I could have taken her down to the station for questioning yesterday, but I didn't because she's your daughter. Give me a little credit here. I know she didn't kill that woman." Seth placed a hand on April's shoulder. "It's why I felt confident letting her rest after *she* was discovered in the Dumpster with the body yesterday."

"Thank you for that." April gave him a wan but genuine smile.

He dropped his hand and they started moving again.

She took two more steps down then stopped again. "Seth, please take it easy on her. She's been through a lot. We just got her back home. I don't want to lose her again."

Why would interviewing Jules cause them to lose her, *again*?

JULES HAD ASKED the social worker, Mrs. Harris, to meet her at The Jewish Mother because it was her favorite diner. As a teen, Big Jim and April would bring her there every Sunday morning for a chocolate-covered croissant while they ate fresh lox and bagels.

Just walking inside the building, Jules had an overwhelming sense of home. The place was busy and crowded. Even with every table filled, there was an atmosphere of intimacy and privacy. Perhaps it was because each booth had a high back. Or maybe it was the small tea light candle flickering in a mini hurricane lamp. Or maybe it was the dark wood furniture that lent itself to a homey, cozy feel. Whatever it was, each table nestled between two dark blue cushion-covered seats seemed like a world unto itself.

And Jules couldn't have been more grateful. Because the news she'd just received shook her to the foundation of her soul.

"I wish there was something more I could do for you," Mrs. Harris said as she set her cup of Earl Grey on the table.

Jules smiled despite the cold lump that had formed in her throat. She shifted on the butter-soft blue leather seat. "I really appreciate all you have done. At least I know Shelley ended up with a good family for a while."

"Yes, her adoptive parents dying in that car accident was a tragedy. I didn't even know it had happened until a few days ago. I can't believe five years went by and no one thought to notify me. I spent most of last week trying to track down Shelley's last known address, but according to neighbors, she moved away not long after the accident."

"She was seventeen. Where could a seventeen-year-old go?"

Mrs. Harris gave her a pitying look and shook her head. "It's hard to know. Potentially anywhere."

The truth cut through Jules. Her little sister, lost and alone in the world. Granted, Shelley wasn't a child anymore, but what had she gone through for those last five years? She'd lost her parents not once but twice.

Jules wanted to weep. Weep for the sister who'd lost everything again. And weep for herself. She hadn't meant to, but in one day she'd let her hopes build. Ideas of reuniting with her sisters had taken over every spare thought and threaded through her dreams last night.

Tears stung her eyes but she blinked them away.

"There's still hope, you know." Mrs. Harris smiled and the only lines on her plump, fifty-ish face appeared at the corners

of her eyes, giving her a sweet, grandmotherly appearance.
With her short silver hair in a bob and wearing a red suit from
Talbots, she looked more like a banker's wife than a woman
who worked sixty hours a week helping children find stable
homes.

"I'm sure you're right, there's still hope." Although Jules
doubted it. And truly, hope sucked. "I just wish Hannah's parents hadn't chosen a private adoption."

"You can appeal to the courts. It will take time, but that at
least is an option." Mrs. Harris patted Jules on the hand, then
tugged a card out of her jacket pocket. "Here, take this. It's a
long shot but if anyone can help you locate Shelley, these boys
can. They owe me a favor or two. Just tell them I told you to
call."

Jules accepted the small business card with a logo of a
seagull on the front.

Tidewater Security Specialists:
When no one else can, we will.

"SIX DAYS, ENGLISH. Wrap it up."

The captain's parting words echoed through Seth's brain
like a skipping CD as he made his way from his car down
Atlantic Avenue toward the flower shop.

He hadn't wanted to go to the station before he met with
Jules, but he hadn't had a choice. If that wasn't bad enough, he
learned from Jones that Seth's would-be informant, Aimee-
Lynn, was actually his homicide victim.

Okay, so he'd feared that would be the case since yesterday
when Aimee-Lynn didn't show up for their meeting. But the
idea of telling his captain that only Jones had managed to
make any progress in the case chafed. It didn't help that they
still only had a first name, since the girl had paid for her tattoo
in cash and the artist claimed he didn't have a record beyond
the picture of his work.

Without a last name or at least someone looking for her, the
trail was going cold. His only hope was that Jules had seen
something. Perhaps if she could shed a little light on how her

phone ended up with the dead woman, he'd find out she knew more than she realized.

And he'd get the break his case required.

He needed to get to April's Flowers and question Jules as soon as possible. With lights green all the way up Atlantic Avenue, he stepped on the gas.

JULES WANTED TO scream.

The ghost-girl had materialized near the front door of the florist shop thirty seconds ago. Where had she come from?

For that matter, why was she back?

Jules hadn't seen her since yesterday and thought perhaps the ghost had gone into the light. Or had taken the hint that Jules had no interest in playing *Who Wants to Be a Medium?*

Guess not.

The ghost popped into existence near the front door. She glanced around the shop as if confused by how she got there. At first, she was mostly a transparent apparition with only her head and shoulders fully formed, then slowly the rest of her body became visible. Her hair changed from a short, black bob to shoulder-length and dirty blonde. This time she wore a pair of khaki shorts, a pink polo shirt, and black stiletto boots.

Who does your wardrobe?

The ghost snapped her gaze to Jules as if she heard the thought. Silent and unmoving, she stared balefully at Jules, sending a shiver of unease racing through her. Jules broke eye contact.

At least the storefront was empty. No customers right now meant no risk of anyone overhearing her if she had to speak to the ghost. And given what had happened yesterday when she'd tried to ignore the ghost, the last thing Jules wanted was another round of *The Murder Memory.*

"Please, talk to me." The words whispered through Jules's mind. She glanced up to find the ghost staring at her with a look of intense concentration on her face. Her ghostly lips moved slowly. *"I know you can hear me."*

Dang her crift!

"I can hear you," Jules admitted in a whisper. She glanced

around to make sure no one could hear *her*. Not that anyone else was there yet. April still hadn't arrived and Diana was still in church. "I'm not sure what I can do for you. I really don't do the medium thing anymore."

Okay, she never really had done the medium thing because she'd never learned what she was supposed to do.

Really, what could a living person teach a dead one? How not to be alive? Um . . . no, the ghosts have that market cornered.

The shiver of unease she felt moments ago gave way to warmth and peace. The sensation startled her and she glanced up to find the specter smiling. *"You're funny."*

The ghost's lips didn't move, but Jules clearly heard the girl's thoughts in her mind.

Jules's throat went dry and she swallowed convulsively. Was her crift expanding or did the spirit possess her own form of telepathy? Jules focused on a single thought to see if she could project it.

"Can you hear my thoughts?"

The ghost nodded again. *"Of course."*

Jules's heart beat double time in her chest. She *could* control some part of the gift beyond visualizing castle walls. Granted, it was only projecting her thoughts to a specter, but still . . . she controlled it.

Maybe she could learn to send out a universal message like the bat signal to all specters that she was closed for business? It could be a chance for the paranormal-free existence she'd been hoping for. The thought made her giddy.

Her hope was short-lived. It vanished the moment the ghost-girl's head tilted back and her mouth dropped open. Like before, no words came out. Only the sound of dozens and dozens of fingernails raking a chalkboard screeched as the ghost wailed.

Jules wanted to dig her fingers into her ears but knew the move would be pointless. The ear-piercing scream rang inside her head.

"All right! Stop! I'll help you." Jules shouted her thoughts to the spirit, unsure whether the specter would be able to hear them since she'd barely learned she had a new skill.

The noises stopped with alacrity and the ghost smiled.

She freaking smiled as if she'd won some sort of game.

Jules wanted to slap her. Not that she would have, even if the specter had still been corporeal. Her southern manners were too deeply imbedded to ignore, but that didn't stop her from fantasizing. "Don't do that again."

The specter nodded and her smile faded. Again she glanced around the store as if confused. She reminded Jules of a lost child. *"Do you know what's going on?"*

"Not really." Jules pressed her lips together. She shouldn't be talking to the ghost, certainly not in the store where anyone could come in, but the girl seemed so sad. "We haven't formally been introduced. I'm Juliana Scott, but my friends call me Jules. What's your name?"

"Hi, Jules. My name is . . . I don't know. I can't remember my name." The ghostly words whispered through Jules's mind, immediately followed by a prevailing sense of fear and pain. *"Why can't I remember my name?"*

The pain tugged at Jules, making her want to comfort the spirit despite the fact that moments before she wanted to commit violence against her. "Don't worry," Jules projected. "It'll be okay. It happens sometimes, but your memory will come back. At least, I think it will."

"Oh, when?" The ghost appeared neither pleased nor comforted by her words.

Good question. Jules had no idea. Most ghosts that spoke to her already remembered everything. They just didn't like to share that information with Jules. But there was one other time a ghost had been like this one. Afraid, lost, and confused. When that ghost's memory came back, Jules paid the price for it.

Shoving away thoughts of a past she couldn't change, she projected her answer. "I'm not sure, but I think we need to talk later. I really need to get back to work right now."

The ghost-girl nodded. Silver tears glistened on her translucent cheeks. *"I don't want to be dead."*

"I know." A small lump formed in Jules's throat. "I'm sorry, but I can't help you right now. The store's already open. Someone could come in at any moment. Do you think you can find me later? Somewhere a little more private?"

"But I need you now!" the ghost snapped. Her words sliced through Jules with razor-sharp clarity.

"Take it easy!" Jules projected, silencing the ghost.

Was it possible to start bleeding from the ears because of voices only you can hear?

But the ghost-girl was getting better at direct communication. When she had asked a question, Jules felt no pain. It was only after the specter became upset again and lost control that Jules experienced that searing ache in her head and ears.

With her head still throbbing from the earlier screeching, Jules made a mental note to keep the ghost as calm as possible.

The bells on the front door tinkled gently just before Diana opened the door with a flourish. Dressed in a pink pleated, ankle-length skirt and a button-down white blouse, she hugged an army green duffel bag to her chest and hurried inside.

In her standard combat boots, Diana clomped right through the ghost. The apparition blew apart like smoke on a windy day, only to form again where she'd been before Diana stepped through her.

With a shudder, Diana hurried over to the counter and said, "Let me change into my real clothes and I'll be right back."

"Okay," Jules replied automatically, and turned to watch the girl rush to the back.

"Hey, Jules!" Diana called out. "Can you turn up the heat? You don't want customers to FTAO."

The door to the bathroom closed with a snap, negating any need to respond.

"What is FTAO?" said a husky male voice.

Jules yelped in surprise and turned to find Seth standing on the other side of the counter. She hadn't heard him come in. She frantically glanced around the shop. The ghost was gone. *Where'd she go?*

"Jules?" Seth repeated his question, "What is FTAO?"

She met his gaze and grinned. "Freeze their a— er, butts off."

His lips twitched. "She's got a point. It's a bit drafty by the door, but it's not so bad once you come inside." He paused, then winked at her. "It's nice to see you again. Feeling better today?"

Heat crawled up her cheeks.

"I'm sorry about yesterday." She took in his light green shirt, black slacks, and shiny black shoes. While she was sure the slacks looked better on him from behind—or rather, his behind probably looked excellent in them—he made for a maddeningly distracting male specimen in her shop.

What do I do with the first sex-god-warrior I meet? My impression of the Exorcist.

She repressed a shudder of embarrassment and said, "I'll pay to replace your shoes and slacks."

He laughed, a hearty, rich sound that filled her with warmth. "No need to go that far. Just have lunch with me today and we'll call it even."

"Are you sure?"

"Absolutely." He nodded. "While we're eating, we can talk about what happened at the Dumpster and I can get your statement. I really should have done it yesterday but you looked too ill to be interviewed."

For one brief, incredibly stupid moment, she thought he was asking her out. She'd actually forgotten he was a cop. But of course, a man as hot as Seth wouldn't ask out a freckle-faced florist shop manager.

"So lunch is at the station, I take it." A shiver crawled down her spine at the thought of going near a police station.

He shrugged and offered her another warm smile. "I was thinking we could grab a bite to eat at one of the local restaurants. What do you say?"

Surprised by his offer, she replied, "Sounds wonderful. Do you like Greek?"

Was it her imagination or did he flinch?

"Got a place in mind for lunch?" When she didn't answer him immediately, he prompted, "Anything you like."

"Well, Philomena's has the best Greek food in town. I used to eat there all the time when I was in high school. I haven't been back in years but heard the food is better than ever. You ever been?"

"To Philomena's?" An inscrutable expression crossed his face and for a moment she thought he'd balk at her suggestion. Seth leaned on the counter. Suddenly the space between them seemed infinitely smaller. Intimate. And when she inhaled, sandalwood invaded her senses. "Yes, I've been there. It's always been my favorite place."

"Really?"

"Definitely." He nodded then grinned at her. "Ready to go?"

"Yes," she said, happy that for the moment she could pretend she didn't see ghosts, he wasn't a cop, and she hadn't yakked all over him twenty-four hours ago.

"Great!" He smacked his hands against the counter. "Are you ready for the best Greek of your life?"

If you're on the menu.

CHAPTER 7

S ETH SHOULD HAVE been driving her to the station for questioning. Instead, he was escorting her to his mother's restaurant for lunch. Hell, he'd waited, again, to talk to her when it was convenient. For her.

If he wasn't careful, he'd end up blowing his case. But he couldn't quite believe Jules had anything to do with the murder.

Even though she'd discovered the body, and her phone had been found with the victim, and the victim was a dead ringer for what Jules had looked like the night he'd met her, Seth was positive she was an innocent bystander. In his gut, he knew she was guiltless. Crazy as it seemed, his gut had never been wrong before, so he trusted it.

He just needed to figure out how she'd managed to get mixed up in his case. Then get her out of it.

Jules shifted on the seat next to him. Tearing his gaze from the road, he caught a flash of purple in the neckline of her polo shirt. Her bra was purple today. He suddenly wished someone would jaywalk in front of him so he could slam on the brakes and get a better look at her bra. Great! Like an untried adolescent, he was getting turned on by glimpses of her underwear.

Or maybe I'm just thinking with the head that sits south of my waist?

That had to be it.

Why else would he have offered to let her pick the restaurant and not argued when she'd chosen his mother's establishment? Grimacing to himself, he slowed down and turned left onto Arctic Avenue. When she had requested Philomena's, he should have just urged her to choose someplace else or admitted it was his mother's restaurant. So why hadn't he?

Easy. He was going insane.

Taking Jules to Philomena's could only spell trouble for him. His family would flock around him the moment he stepped inside. Unless . . .

He might be okay if he managed to find a booth near the back. With a little luck, he might even nab a non–family member as his waitress. Simple. All he had to do was put the word out through the server that he wasn't to be disturbed. He could conduct his interview at the restaurant and still maintain his privacy.

Coils of tension started to loosen in his shoulders at the thought of getting through lunch without his family descending upon him. They had been known to leave him alone from time to time if he made it clear that he didn't want them interfering.

Who am I kidding? I'm just going insane from the lack of blood to the head on my shoulders.

His mother's restaurant was only three blocks away. If he hit the lights just right he could be there in three minutes. If not, it could take fifteen and he could possibly conduct the majority of the interview in the car. Then they could just enjoy lunch.

The first light turned red.

"What's with the lambs?" Jules asked, jerking his attention from his thoughts to her face.

She blushed clear down to the swell of her breasts that peeked from beneath the polo top.

He wondered if she blushed all over. He bet she tasted like strawberries. Shaking his head to dispel his wanton thoughts, he tried to focus. What had she asked, something about . . . *lambs*?

"What are you talking about?"

She gestured to the tie dangling from his rearview mirror.

Seth surprised himself by answering, "My mother, despite her devoutly attending church on Sundays, is heavily into horoscopes."

"Ah," Jules replied, nodding her head, but her eyebrows lifted in obvious confusion.

"I'm an Aries," he clarified, but when she didn't do more than widen her eyes, he asked, "You have heard of horoscopes, haven't you?"

"Of course, I have. I'm a Cancer, but what does that have to do with the lambs?"

Seth stole another glance at her as he stopped for the second red light. He needed to question her, not discuss his mother's penchant for giving him presents covered in barnyard animals.

Anytime anyone asked him about his rams, he closed up and wanted to pound something. But with Jules, he could see the humor in it.

Her lips twitched. She wanted to laugh. He knew it. Hell, *he* laughed whenever his mother gifted him with a new ram.

Suddenly, seeing Jules laugh became a high priority. So instead of questioning her, he answered her. "Aries are smart, stubborn, strong, and"—he inhaled before finishing in a high-pitched, thickly accented imitation of his Greek mother—"'as an Aries, my son, *you* are destined for greatness.'"

Laughter burst from her, rich and infectious. Her eyes sparkled and her entire face glowed with warmth, making her more beautiful than she already was. Damn, he liked that.

He liked her.

He shook his head and added in his own voice, "What I'm destined for is a lifetime supply of all things ram."

"Why not just tell your mom you don't like lambs?" Jules asked in a breathless, sexy tone that sent his pulse hammering.

"They're rams." He snapped the tie free and jerked it over his head before noticing it clashed hideously with his green shirt. Ripping it off again, he added with a grunt, "It would kill her if she thought I didn't like her gift."

"So you wear it."

"Yeah," he admitted with a half-smile and dropped it on the console between them. "But what can I do?"

"You wear an ugly tie just because your mother gave it to you?" Her features softened and she added, "That has to be the sweetest thing I've heard in a long time."

"Thanks." He shifted in his seat, as he slowed the car at the second stoplight. "Jules, I wanted to ask you—"

But he didn't finish his question because she said at the same time, "So you must be—"

He cleared his throat. "Must be what?"

The light turned green and he pressed his foot to the gas pedal again before chancing another glance at her. She grinned at him in such a devious manner, he wondered if he'd made a mistake asking. But, at the same time, he couldn't resist finding out. "I must be *what*?"

"Worried about what I was going to say?" Her large green eyes widened in exaggerated innocence. "Don't be. I was going to say that only someone secure in his manhood could wear a tie that awful in public unless he's someone who really loves his mother."

"I can't be both?" he teased back. Damn, he shouldn't be doing this. He needed to at least begin to interview her before they arrived at the restaurant but he was having too much fun to stop.

"I guess you can." She cocked her head; her expression grew pensive momentarily, then her brows lifted and a grin tugged at her lips. She nodded at him in obvious approval, making pride swell inside him.

Seth turned the wheel and pulled into a spot outside of Philomena's.

He cut the engine and turned to find Jules staring out the side window at the restaurant, tugging on her left earlobe.

He shouldn't care if she was nervous. Hell, he was nervous. Suddenly, he found himself praying that his instincts were correct and she truly was an innocent caught up in his case.

Only one way to find out: conduct the interview. He had a job to do and he was determined to do it. Yet he found himself asking, "You okay?"

"I'm fine." She stopped fidgeting and faced him. "Again, thanks for being so cool and not doing this interview downtown."

"No problem." He replied, noting the small shudder that went through her as she spoke. "Police stations make you that uncomfortable?"

"How did you guess?"

"You tug on your earlobe when you're nervous."

"I do?" She blinked.

He couldn't quite suppress a grin as he watched her reach for her ear again. Realizing it, she suddenly dropped her hand to her side.

"Weird, huh? Being nervous about police stations, I mean." She blushed.

"Not really," he said, opening his door. Wanting to put her at ease again, he added, "They make most folks nervous, including me. The food there is terrible."

She laughed.

He hurried around to her side of the car, but she'd already exited. She stood on the sidewalk, staring up at the giant pita his cousin Antony had assured his mother would increase sales. The enormous sign hung precariously from the roof and looked as if it might launch itself at some unsuspecting customer at any moment.

From the way Jules trailed her gaze from the cumbersome pita to the front door and back again, Seth suspected her thoughts ran along the same lines. Jules said, "I don't remember that being here when I was in high school."

"It's fairly new." Resisting the urge to go around and enter through the back door, like he normally did, he captured her by the elbow.

She jumped but didn't pull away.

"Shall we?" He leaned down to whisper into her ear.

"You betcha!" Jules grinned and her eyes twinkled.

Seth opened the door and waited for Jules to cross the threshold. He followed her inside and tried to keep his eyes off her perfect heart-shaped ass.

They were here to conduct an interview. And he needed to get his head on straight before his mother caught him ogling.

·

Otherwise, she'd have them engaged and their wedding planned before the moussaka was served.

THE RESTAURANT WAS a nautical Greek-themed establishment with a homey quality. Flags, rugs, and posters from the Greek Isles decorated the walls and ceiling. Even the muted ceiling fans turning quietly above accentuated the Mediterranean feel.

Jules loved it.

She inhaled the warm aromas of Greek spices, fresh pizza, and lamb. The deli counter to her left bustled with energy. Two women hurried behind the counter, taking orders and passing slips of paper through a window to the kitchen, where a man served up the food on stoneware plates. Unlike most of the mom-and-pop places in Tidewater, which had disposable dishes and utensils, Philomena's used actual flatware and real plates. Blue glasses and hand-painted plates laden with made-to-order food graced the half dozen cloth-covered bistro tables near the front.

Along the opposite wall from the kitchen were booths with navy linens on the tables and white cloth napkins waiting beneath gleaming silverware. The leather seats of the booths shined beneath muted colors of mosaic-style lamps hanging over each table.

A pretty brunette waitress loaded several delicious-smelling meals onto her tray. She bent her knees before propping the overly large tray onto her right shoulder, then straightened. "Thanks, Uncle Antony," she shouted through the open kitchen window to the surprisingly handsome blond cook.

When she spun around, the girl froze a few feet from where Jules and Seth stood. Her hazel eyes wide, she glanced over her shoulder to the women behind the counter, who paid her no attention.

Seth grabbed Jules by the hand, practically dragging her through the small eating area to a booth at the back of the restaurant. She probably should have resisted being hauled around like a child, but she was too curious. The man ran hot and cold, and she couldn't help but wonder what had him nearly pole-vaulting over the tables to the tiny booth nestled against the far wall near the restrooms. It might have seemed an odd choice, but the place was packed.

As they seated themselves, Jules glanced up to see Seth's black brows lower and his mouth flatten into a thin line. He thrust a plastic-coated menu in her face, inadvertently smacking her in the nose with it.

"Oh. Did I hurt you?" he whispered, pulling the menu out of her hand.

Jules gasped when his index finger stroked the bridge of her nose. His lightly roughened skin soothed away any sting she might have experienced and sent her heart tripping. Seth turned his hand over and caressed her cheek with a knuckle.

Just like in the car, her defenses lowered. She reminded herself she shouldn't show weakness around him. He might be the sexiest man she'd ever seen up close, but Seth had a fatal flaw no amount of beauty could fix. He was a cop on a case. A case that involved her in ways someone like him would never believe.

Heck, she hardly believed it herself. But it couldn't be a coincidence that she'd first seen the ghost while in the Dumpster with a dead body.

She needed to be extra careful around him. But careful slipped further from her mind when the left side of his mouth curled into a lopsided grin. He rotated his hand until his palm cupped her cheek and his thumb stroked dangerously close to her lips. She wanted to nibble it. She wanted to stretch like a cat and press her face against his hand in a silent plea for him to pet her more. She nearly did until sanity clawed its way into her psyche.

She wasn't a cat. He wasn't really interested in her for anything other than the case. And this wasn't going to end with a happily ever after.

Straightening so he could no longer touch her, Jules stammered, "I'm fine. I'm . . . good."

She felt bereft without his warm fingers gliding across her skin. If only she could shake off her hot, lustful thoughts. Life could be so unfair. Why couldn't she be attracted to simple, non-police types?

"Welcome to Philomena's," the statuesque brunette said, appearing at the booth. "What can I get you today?"

Jules glanced around but saw no trace of the enormous tray of food the woman had been carrying moments before. What she did see was a distinctly interested smile on the waitress's face as she looked at Seth.

For his part, Seth appeared absorbed by his menu, not even sparing the young woman a glance.

Jules had heard of people staring with their hearts in their eyes but had never actually seen it before. The waitress's gaze had zeroed in on Seth's face and she seemed oblivious to Jules sitting there or even Seth's decidedly distant demeanor.

The girl, who appeared no older than eighteen, seemed to know him. And Seth's refusal to glance up only proved it.

A pang of something hot and sharp hit Jules in the chest. The surprising and unjustified flash of jealousy was so intense she hoped it didn't show on her face. Then again, neither Seth nor the waitress glanced Jules's way for a good thirty seconds.

The waitress's smile wavered and she turned a puzzled gaze to Jules. "Do you know what you want to drink, miss?"

"Yes." Jules grabbed the menu and quickly scanned the beverage section. "I'll have a glass of strawberry lemonade, please."

"And you, Dad?" The waitress turned back to Seth. "Do you see anything *you* like?"

"Coffee." Seth said at the same Jules asked, *"Dad?"*

Relief washed over Jules like a warm wave crashing on the shore. *She's his daughter!* Wait. Why did she care about Seth or his relationships? She shouldn't. She *didn't*. Did she?

Seth groaned and waved a hand in the air. "Jules, meet my daughter, Theresa." He gestured to the waitress. "Theresa, meet my neighbor, Jules."

"Your *neighbor*, Dad?" Theresa grinned at Seth, then turned her head to eye Jules. "Nice to meet you."

"You too."

"Theresa." Seth's voice sounded strained. "Can you bring us our drinks, please?"

"Sure! I'll be right back." Seth's daughter hurried away in a bouncy jaunt as she moved through the restaurant.

He watched her leave, a muscle working in his jaw. Then he muttered under his breath, "This is gonna cost me." Rising from his seat, he added, "Excuse me a moment."

He followed the girl. From across the busy restaurant, Jules watched him catch Theresa by her elbow and usher her into a corner. He spoke rapidly and the girl simply nodded. The smile on her face never wavered even as her curly brown pony-tail bobbed with each nod.

Giving him a quick peck on the cheek, Theresa hurried off. Seth watched her go and then turned and faced Jules. She shouldn't have watched them but his words—*This is gonna cost me*—replayed in her mind.

What could a lunch cost him that he needed to chase down his daughter and have a private conversation? Too many things sprang to mind. And none of them good.

Seth's shoulders were drawn tight and he radiated tension as he made his way back to the table.

"Sorry about that. But Theresa loves to gossip. Thought I'd better stop her before the entire family descends on us," Seth said when he returned. Lowering himself to his side of the booth, he fiddled with his napkin-wrapped utensils before drumming his fingers on the table.

Jules glanced around. "This is your family's restaurant? I mean I knew it was locally owned but I didn't realize when I asked to come here . . ."

"It's okay," he said, shrugging. "I didn't think you knew. Like it?"

"Yes." She smiled. "Your daughter seems very sweet." She paused, then blurted the question foremost in her mind. "How old are you?"

He gave her a wry grin. "Thirty-five. Curious how I have a teenaged daughter?"

She nodded, then admitted, "Sorry. None of my business." Truthfully, she wasn't sure she wanted to know. Because where there was a child, there was usually a mother.

Seth blew out a breath, then said, "At seventeen, I got my sixteen-year-old girlfriend pregnant. Her parents threw her out when she wouldn't have an abortion. She moved in with my mother, my sister, and me. The weekend after we graduated high school, I married Catherine. Six months later, Theresa came laughing into the world. She's been laughing ever since and turning my hair a little more gray every day."

Jules's shoulders drooped and her eyes rounded. "Oh, I-I

didn't realize. Wow. You were a teen father? Did you live with your mother after Theresa's birth?"

"No, I rented the apartment above the restaurant." He hiked a thumb in the air to indicate the ceiling.

She glanced around then back at him. "How did you go from a teen dad living over a Greek restaurant to being a police detective?"

"For the first year I worked two jobs and took college courses at night," he said, shifting in his seat. "A week before my nineteenth birthday, I joined the police academy. Nine months later, I joined the force in Tidewater. I eventually earned my bachelor's degree." He grinned, radiating pride. "Theresa and I graduated the same weekend. She graduated in her little red gown from preschool and I graduated from Tidewater University."

"Oh, that's so sweet." Jules grinned and she rested her chin in her right hand and sighed.

"There's a picture in my bedroom of our graduation day." A devious glint lit his expression before he asked, "You didn't see it?"

Jules's cheeks heated. "Um . . . no."

"Oh, you should come over again sometime and I'll show it to you," Seth said, teasingly.

As much as that idea appealed to her—more than it should— she couldn't help wondering about Theresa's mother. Granted, she hadn't seen a ring on his finger or anything feminine in his bedroom, but still. "You . . . you aren't still married, right?"

"No. I'm definitely not married. Catherine has been gone a long time." He frowned; all humor fled his expression. "And we're not here to talk about me. We're here to talk about your adventure yesterday."

"Right." An uncomfortable silence fell between them. Jules wasn't sure how to fix it. She shouldn't care that Seth wasn't married anymore. It was none of her business. Except it stung in ways she didn't like to admit, that this handsome man wanted nothing more from her than information about his case. It shouldn't. But it did.

Every time Jules started to relax around him, Seth did something to remind her of what he was. A cop. And that was exactly why she shouldn't care about him or his love life.

Tugging at her earlobe, she fidgeted with the sapphire stud in it until Seth cast her a knowing glance. She dropped her hand to her lap, straightened her back, and ignored the automatic pull at her defenses that seemed to perpetually happen around him.

Seth was a threat to her peace of mind. He hadn't brought her here to get to know her. He'd done it to keep her off balance. She'd sensed it almost immediately. But strangely, she also sensed *he* was uncomfortable.

And it was definitely a sensory perception. Outwardly, Seth epitomized calm and smooth. Still, snippets of anxiety pinged off her chest, as if shot from a bow, whenever his gaze met hers.

What kept him off balance?

Theresa returned with their drinks. Her demeanor had changed. Whatever Seth had said across the room had apparently made an impact. Setting the drinks on the table, she barely made eye contact with Jules and avoided Seth's gaze altogether.

"Do you need more time or are you ready to order?"

Despite her shrunken stomach, Jules ordered. "I'll have the Greek salad with the dressing on the side and no bread, please."

"Is that all you're going to eat?" Seth grunted and shook his head. "No wonder you're a twig."

"I wasn't aware you brought me here to monitor my eating habits," Jules countered.

The waitress snorted.

If Seth heard it, he pretended otherwise. "A large Philomena's special and two plates."

Without a word, the smirking girl hurried away.

"You're pushy," Jules said.

"I haven't started to push yet," Seth answered, a grin tugging at the corners of his mouth. Then his lips flattened and he rubbed the bridge of his nose as if it pained him. "Okay, I need to ask you a few questions about yesterday. If we can get them out of the way fast enough, I'm sure we can both enjoy a nice meal. Sound good?"

"Sure," she agreed, and hoped his questions wouldn't require her to bend the truth to avoid having him cart her off to the loony bin. "Go for it."

"Okay." He nodded. "Care to tell me how you ended up in a Dumpster with a dead body?"

Jules's too-tight stomach shrank again as a lump formed in her belly.

"Not really. In fact, I'd prefer to never think about my temporary career as a Dumpster diver ever again. Next question?" She surprised herself with the airy reply.

Seth laughed, then frowned as if bothered that she amused him. Instead of repeating his question, he simply sat and stared at her. Waiting.

Jules shifted in her chair. She could lie, but she had the feeling that despite his lack of ability to distinguish between oregano and marijuana, he was probably well versed at sniffing out a fib. So she settled for a half-truth. "All right. Look, it was nothing nefarious. I'd just put boxes in the recycling bin when I heard my phone, uh . . . singing."

"And how do you suppose your cell got in there to begin with?" He clasped his hands together and leaned closer, resting his forearms on the table. "Did you know the victim?"

"Well, I lost my cell phone and keys sometime Friday night," she answered, focusing on the first question he asked. But she was stumped about how to answer the second question.

I didn't exactly know the victim before she was killed. See, the dead woman you found with my phone is now a ghost who's been following me around for the last two days asking me for something, but I can't understand what it is. Oh, and I'm pretty sure she's the one who tricked me into climbing into your apartment Friday night, but I don't know why.

Yep, that sounded insane even in *her* head.

Perhaps if she could learn a bit about who the ghost had been, she might solve the mystery of how to convince the ghost to cross over or go into the light or wherever it is ghosts are supposed to go, and let Jules live in peace.

"I don't suppose you know the name of the woman found in the Dumpster, do you?" Jules blurted the question before she thought better of it. The surprise that darkened Seth's expression wasn't as harrowing as how quickly he narrowed his eyes in suspicion.

"How did you know the victim was a woman?" He leaned back in his seat, crossing his arms over his chest. "I didn't think you saw the body. Given what we found while you were unconscious, it appeared you had no idea she was in there. So, I repeat, how did you know the victim was a woman?"

"Fifty-fifty guess. I didn't see the body, and believe me, I'm grateful. Just thinking I was locked inside a bin with a dead body makes my skin crawl," Jules replied. She conveniently left out the part where the ghost had held Jules hostage and forced her to relive the dead woman's last moments on earth.

"Oh, right. Good guess." Seth rubbed a hand over his face. Straightening in his seat, he glanced around. "The victim was a woman around your age. Similar build to yours, but where your hair is red, hers was blonde. Sound familiar?"

"No," she answered honestly.

"What about your phone? Do you know when you might have lost it?"

"I'm sorry, I don't have any idea how I lost it." If she did, she'd definitely tell him.

"Did you loan it to someone?" When she shook her head, he asked, "Where's the last place you remember having it?"

"At the reunion, Friday night. Right before I knocked into another hooker contestant in the bathroom."

"DANG!" A FLASH of surprise lit her eyes. Jules's mouth opened to form a small *O*.

Seth had been right to think she knew something. But her line about the hooker had been a bit too loud for his comfort. He glanced around. No one else seemed to have heard her, thank God.

While he understood it had been for a contest, he was pretty sure he didn't want to have to explain that to his mother. Although he'd made Theresa promise not to alert the family that he was in the restaurant, he wasn't entirely sure she wouldn't do it just to spite him for tossing her new fiancé out of his mother's house last week when they'd announced their engagement.

He leaned closer to Jules. "Do you remember what happened to your phone? Did the ho— um, other woman borrow it?"

"Huh? Uh, no." She shook her head and he was momentarily distracted by the red and gold highlights in her hair.

She really was attractive. While her features were not particularly striking separately—except for her eyes—together, they formed a beautiful woman. Even without the corset and leather miniskirt.

His gaze drifted to her lush mouth. Not overly plump like some of the collagen-enhanced ones on the faces of women with too much money and too little self-esteem, but succulent. At least, they appeared that way. He wondered if they were as soft to kiss as they looked.

And I've drifted off topic again.

"What do you think happened to your phone if you didn't lend it?" he asked, determined to conduct his interview.

"Well," she said, tapping an index finger to her forehead. "After I went to the health food store, I went to the reunion. Where they had the contest I told you about." She paused as if waiting for him to agree, but when he didn't she added, "You know *that* contest that had you mistaking me for a . . . you-know-what when we met in your . . . er . . ." Her words trailed away.

A lovely pink flush crept up her cheeks, and again Seth wanted to see if she blushed that way all over her body. Blood thundered through his veins as he remembered every second of meeting her Friday night. Damn, she was going to give him a heart attack if she didn't stop blushing like that.

"In my bedroom?" he asked.

"Shhh!" Jules hissed the sound, a finger pressed to her lips. It was her turn to glance anxiously around.

"What? You can talk about hookers, but blush at the word *bedroom*?" He smiled when her cheeks reddened.

She shrugged. "*Anyway*, I bet I lost my cell in the bathroom. I can't believe I didn't put it together before now."

"Care to elaborate?"

She toyed with the straw in her drink, swirling it around until an eddy formed, before releasing the plastic. Seth watched it spin for a moment until she lifted her eyes to meet his gaze.

"At the party," she said, leaning forward. "Things got a little *confusing*, you might say."

"Confusing how?"

"I, um . . . well." Jules huffed, straightened her spine, and closed her eyes on a long, slow blink. When she opened them again, Seth marveled at the sincerity in their green depths. "At the party, I bumped into this woman. Well, crashed, really. She'd been coming out of the bathroom when I was running in. I wasn't looking where I was going and slammed into her. We both dropped our purses and everything spilled out. I picked up my stuff and tried to help her. She just burst into tears, told me to leave her alone, snatched up her stuff, and bolted out the door.

"I didn't even notice my cell was missing until I was outside our apartment building searching for my keys. You didn't happen to find those in the Dumpster too, did you?"

"No keys, just your cell with a dead woman."

She shuddered. Lowering her gaze to her drink, she fiddled with the straw, then lifted the cup to her lips and took a sip.

Several questions filtered through Seth's mind in rapid succession. For one, why had Jules been running?

"Do you think you might recognize her if you saw her again?"

"Maybe?" She met his gaze again. Confusion and a hint of fear darkened her eyes. "It all happened so fast, and we were both in costume so I'm not sure."

"Would you be willing to take a look at a photo of the victim?"

"I guess." She shivered again. "Will we need to go downtown?"

"Probably not. My partner can send the morgue picture to my phone right now if you want."

Jules glanced around the restaurant then back to him. She'd gone pale. Swallowing hard, she nodded.

"Tell you what, why don't I have him do that *after* lunch?"

Jules exhaled a slow breath and visibly relaxed. "That would be great."

Shifting in his seat, Seth continued his interview. "Was the woman from the bathroom dressed exactly like you?" He thought he already knew the answer but wanted to gauge her response.

"Yeah, pretty close. We both wore leather corsets and miniskirts. My boots were higher than hers, or maybe I was just taller. But what was truly amazing was we both had Prada."

"Why was that amazing?" He tugged his small leather-bound notebook and a pen out of his slacks. He uncapped the pen. "What's Prada?"

"It's the brand of my purse. I didn't get a good look at hers, except for the logo." She furrowed her brow. "At least, I think hers was Prada. I know mine was."

"Again, why is that amazing?"

"Oh, well. They're expensive. You can't even buy them where I lived. At least, not unless you ordered it on the Internet. I guess I should be thankful I lost my keys and cell and not the purse. It's worth a month's salary."

He'd been steadily jotting down her words but jerked to a halt at her last statement. "Forgive me, but you hardly seem the type of person to own something so . . ." He searched his brain for the right term. *Frivolous? Ridiculously expensive?*

"Extravagant?" she supplied with a sheepish expression. She nodded. "I'm not. It's what my ex bought me to convince me to forgive him."

"Didn't work?"

"Not a bit," she admitted. "I divorced him but I kept the gift. It's been in the box it came in for the past two years. I never took it out until Friday night."

"What did he do that was so bad that he tried to buy your forgiveness?"

"I thought you wanted to ask me questions about your case," she replied, looking away.

No, he wanted to know more about her. He *had* to ask her questions about the case. But he could wait to learn more about Jules. Clearly she wasn't ready to share her secrets with him.

At least she was willing to answer his questions about the case. "Okay then. Tell me everything you remember from the incident. What were you doing just before you two collided?"

"I'd just called a cab and was texting April to tell her I'd won the contest."

He glanced down at his notes. She'd run into the woman in the restroom. "You called a cab in the bathroom?"

Jules blushed. "No, I was outside the bathroom when I called the cab. Then I started to text April when I decided to . . . wait, and uh, go to the bathroom instead."

"Where you collided with the other woman?"

"Yes."

"What made you stop texting April?"

When she didn't do more than shrug then shake her head, a prickle of warning lifted the hairs on Seth's forearms. What was she hiding? "Jules, got something else to tell me?"

"No. That's it." Jules reached for her earlobe, then sailed past it and grabbed her shoulder as if it pained her. "Seth, I swear I had nothing to do with her . . . death." She shuddered.

Her voice, laced with fear, incited a need to soothe her, comfort her. Seth patted her right hand. She turned her palm up and entwined her fingers with his. Her soft skin felt like silk against his calloused flesh.

He'd been fairly certain she was an innocent caught up in this before they came to the restaurant. Now he was almost positive.

Still, he needed to finish questioning her. After all, she had met the victim prior to her death. But that too could just mean Jules and the victim traveled in similar circles. Being familiar with a victim didn't necessarily make someone a murderer or an accessory to murder.

"You do believe me, don't you?" The sincerity in her eyes pulled at him.

"Yes, precious. I believe you."

"My name's Jules, not precious."

She reminded him of her real name, just as she had done the night they met and the morning she came to collect her purse. Her eyes narrowed to sharp emerald slits and her stubborn chin jutted out, and she looked absolutely adorable. Precisely why he did it. He preferred her annoyed rather than frightened as she'd been moments before.

"Yes, Jules." Stifling a chuckle, he added, "I know you couldn't have killed her."

"Thank heavens." Relief lit her round, green eyes.

At that moment, his daughter returned with two plates and a large Philomena's pizza.

Jules withdrew her hand from his and they both scooted back to give Theresa room. His normally graceful daughter nearly knocked his coffee cup into his lap while setting the pie on the table. Though he caught the mug before the entire contents spilled, quite a bit splashed over his hand and onto his lap.

Seth jumped to his feet.

"Daddy!" she gasped, then thrust a cloth napkin at him.

"It's all right, Theresa." He tried to sop up the spilled beverage before it soaked into his slacks. It was useless. Unless he wanted to look like he'd wet himself, he needed to go home and change.

The skin on his hand burned. He hadn't even realized how much he'd been doused with the coffee at first. Now that the shock wore off, the pain radiated.

"You might want to put some cold water on that," Jules and Theresa said in unison. He grimaced as his daughter lapsed into a nervous giggle.

The tender flesh between his right thumb and forefinger reddened and grew spotty. He shook his hand in a futile effort to soothe the burn.

"I'm so sorry, Dad." Theresa glanced back at the deli counter and added, "I'll get you some ice." And she was gone.

"Wow, you look like you're going to blister if you don't take care of that fast." Jules grabbed his hand and held it between her slender, cool fingers. Then she glanced at his wrist watch. "Oh, I hate to say this. But I really need to go."

"Now?" He frowned. Her sudden desire to bolt temporarily distracted him from the pain. "We haven't even had lunch yet."

"I know but . . ." Jules glanced around the room as if searching for an escape. "I need to be at the shop. I lost half a day yesterday. I-I really need to get back to work."

"Why the sudden need to leave?"

A line dug between her eyebrows. "I've been out with you for over an hour."

Seth glanced at his watch in surprise. She was right. They'd left the shop more than ninety minutes earlier.

"Oh. Right." Seth shook his head. No wonder she was trying to leave. "Look, have some pizza and I'll take you back to the shop after I take care of this." He glanced down to his hand still in hers.

"I really don't have time to wait." As if realizing she still held his hand, Jules suddenly released it.

Without her touch, the heat seemed to engulf his flesh.

Excusing himself, Seth hurried to the washroom. After five minutes with his hand under the cold running water, his gut quivered warningly. He just knew when he went back to the table, Jules would be gone.

He wasn't wrong.

Theresa returned with a plastic baggie of ice in her hand and a frown pulling between her eyebrows. "Daddy, your friend asked me to tell you she caught a cab back to work. She said she'll see you *later*."

"Thanks, sweetheart." Kissing her on the top of her head he said, "I'll see you for dinner next Sunday?"

"Yes, Daddy." She hugged him. "If you want, you can bring her along. She's . . . nice."

"Theresa." He closed his eyes briefly then grinned at her. Clearly his daughter was as much of a matchmaker as her grandmother. "It's supposed to be just family."

"I know but Yia Yia invited Jovani. So I bet your friend would be welcomed too," she blurted, then hurried away before he could reply.

The last thing he wanted to do was deal with Theresa's fiancé and Jules at his mother's house during Sunday dinner. Now that was an image guaranteed to cause a brain implosion.

Compartmentalizing the unwanted picture, he focused on dealing with his more pressing situation. Keeping the ice on his injured hand, he pulled out his cell, and dialed his partner.

"This is Detective Jones."

"Any more luck with having our tattoo artist track down his receipts?" Guilt flickered through Seth. He probably should have started with hello or something more civil. But he pushed away the thought. He'd spent the last five years repairing his reputation, and in doing so, became known as a hardass. He had no intention of letting his persona slip now.

"None." Jones answered, taciturn as usual.

"I need you to go over to the florist shop and keep an eye on the staff. Make note of who is coming and going." Seth thought about it and added, "And keep an eye on our new friend. She says she doesn't know anything, but she does. Even if she doesn't realize it. Oh, and I need you to send a photo of the vic to my cell."

"Will do, but why the photo?"

"Because I believe Jules met the victim before her death." He ended the call without giving Jones time to comment. Not that he expected the kid would.

Seth needed to stop at his apartment and change before he saw Jules again. This was becoming a bad habit. It might be easier to go naked around her.

And there went his libido again. He tried to ignore it. Tried to convince himself the anticipation licking through his veins had nothing to do with sex. It was only because he was certain she was involved with the case. It had nothing to do with the idea of seeing her again.

Or sex.

Or her purple bra.

Yeah. Right.

CHAPTER 8

JULES FROWNED AT her purse under the counter at April's Flowers.

Why she was still carrying it around, she didn't know. It made her nervous having such an expensive item with her. Plus, after talking to Seth about it at the restaurant, she realized it was time to just let go of the past. Her marriage to Billy had been a mistake. Keeping the reminder, even boxed as it had been, wasn't helping her to move on with her life.

She stared at it and wondered if she should just donate it.

Picking up the black clutch, she traced the letters emblazoned on the front with her index finger. Startled, she traced them again. Although white letters spelled out P-R-A-D-A, someone had blackened the "O" then artfully emblazoned an "A" over it.

"That creep!" No wonder Billy had insisted she keep the purse even after she'd turned down his reconciliation request. He knew it was a fake.

All this time, she'd kept it carefully preserved in the Amazon.com box it had arrived in. Now she wondered how she had managed not to notice sooner that it was a Prada knockoff. Turning it over, she carefully examined it. Furious at first, she couldn't help but laugh.

At least she hadn't forgiven him.

She tossed it lightly under the counter, then jumped when it hit the wood paneling with an audible thunk.

"About time you got back." Diana stomped across the floor in her combat boots. "Miss April said to tell you she'll meet you at home tonight for the special dinner."

Momentarily confused by the girl's words, Jules hesitated. "What? Oh, that's right. She's making her *lasagna de April* tonight. Are you coming to dinner too?"

"I want to, but I can't." Diana sighed and grimaced before continuing to the front window. She dug into a bucket of Halloween decorations. "I have choir tonight and if I miss another rehearsal my mom'll freak."

"I'm sorry. I'll save you some pasta."

"Thanks." Diana smiled then turned back to the window. "What do you think?" Diana set down a witch and two doll-sized scarecrows on coffin-shaped boxes.

Before Jules could respond, Diana yelled, "Wait! Don't look yet!"

She darted forward, rearranged the scarecrows and the witch several times, dangled one scarecrow by an arm and a leg, then retreated a step to examine her work again. A wide grin on her face, she opened her arms in a very showroom-girl style, indicating her window dressing masterpiece.

"Very nice." It wasn't just nice. It was brilliant. Jules never would have thought to hang the dolls like that. It was both aesthetically pleasing and eye-catching. "Looks like you've been busy here without me."

"Actually, I started it yesterday while you were Dumpster diving," Diana replied. "Why were you doing that, anyway?"

"I heard my cell ringing." Jules didn't want to think about being in the garbage bin. Ever again.

"Did you lose it or something?"

"No, I just tossed it in there so I could swim in rotting lo mien. Everyone's doing it," Jules replied with a grin.

"It's true? Garbage is the new vintage?" Diana snorted. "I didn't know you were so hip."

"That's me. Hip." Jules laughed in spite of herself. And this was why she liked Diana so much, her ability to find the humor in most anything. Answering the earlier question, she said, "Yes, Diana. I lost my phone. You know, the phone the police have."

"OMG!" As if suddenly remembering something, Diana slapped a hand to her forehead then giggled. "The hottie cop left you a message. I don't know how I forgot. I mean that guy is H-O-T. Who could forget a man who looks like that being here? Then again, he's no Jake Gyllenhall. Now, if *he* walked in here—"

"*Diana*, what did the cop want?" Jules asked. Her heart raced. How had Seth beat her back to the shop?

"Oh, right. Well, Mr. HC has been by twice to see you. At least, that's the excuse he gave. But I think he likes me. KWIM?"

KWIM? Ah. Know what I mean.

With effort, Jules didn't smile.

Diana was about the same age as Seth's daughter. Somehow she doubted Seth would be attracted to a Goth teen who spoke in text-speech.

"Officer Masculine Perfection is back!" Diana shoved the box of remaining decorations into a corner and raced behind the counter. She hopped up and down, then turned to face Jules. Even the heavy ivory powder couldn't disguise the flush on Diana's cheeks. "How do I look?"

"Great." Jules grinned and yanked on an apron, determined not to stare at the front door. Instead, she watched Diana, who busied herself at the cash register and pretended not to watch for the man to arrive.

Masculine Perfection.

Jules had to agree with Diana's description. Her neighbor, with his amber skin, rock-hard abs, husky voice, and sinfully sexy eyes, defined masculine perfection. Glancing down at her apron, she kept her eyes anywhere but on the door as the bell chimed. She may have been enormously attracted to the man, but there was no need to show it.

After all, he *was* the most narrow-minded, conclusion-jumping-to clod she'd ever met in her life, as he had proved the night they met.

Or not.

He definitely wasn't all bad. He did love his mother enough to wear the gifts she gave him. And while many teen fathers accepted little responsibility for the children they created, Seth obviously adored his daughter. And she him.

Plus, he'd been kind to Jules. Considering she had ruined his shoes and probably his slacks, he could have made her feel guilty. Instead, he'd taken her out to his family's restaurant to eat.

Where she promptly ran away as fast as she could, the moment she realized she was softening toward him. No. He wasn't the clod.

She was.

"Feelin' better, Jules?" asked a deep-timbre voice from the other side of the counter.

"Pardon?" Jules glanced up in surprise to see a huge man with sandy blond hair and light mocha skin. She squelched the disappointment in her belly that Mr. HC wasn't Seth and smiled at the man in front of her. "Hello."

"Remember me?" Brows drew together over blue gray eyes.

"Sorry, I'm afraid I don't. Should I?"

She stared hard, trying to place him. He seemed vaguely familiar. An image of her little sister Shelley, as she might have looked as an adult, flashed through Jules's mind.

Weird.

"My partner's Detective English," he said.

Built like a defensive back, he radiated an air of calm and quiet even as he fingered the gold badge dangling from his black suit jacket.

"Right. Of course." She smiled at him and extended a hand. "Yes, I feel much better. Um, I didn't catch your name . . . ?"

"Detective Devon Jones," he answered. "Dev."

"Nice to meet you, Detective Jones."

He gave her a tight-lipped smile. "Dev."

Despite his seemingly easygoing demeanor, Jules had the impression *Dev* was accustomed to being in control. An authoritative air wound around him and made her slightly nervous.

Like Seth, this man definitely met her three *H* rule. But Jules wasn't attracted to him. Perhaps she was getting smarter.

Or maybe she had somehow found a way to turn off her instant attraction for men in law enforcement. More likely it was because her radar had already pinged hard on her unattainable neighbor, who *hadn't* shown up in the shop looking for her.

"My partner asked me to check on you," he said, leaning his arms on the counter between them. "You gave us quite a scare yesterday."

"I'm fine," she answered, her cheeks warmed at the memory of yesterday's catastrophe.

Diana giggled and he glanced over at her. She licked her black-painted lips and arched a brow at the man.

Dang! Jules should have realized the girl wouldn't be interested in someone old enough to be her father, but this guy . . . Old enough to be "mature" and young enough to still be hot.

The man's pupils dilated as he glanced from Diana to her and back again. He blew out a heavy sigh and an inscrutable expression crossed his face. It could have been lust or it could have just been gas. Either way, he needed to go.

"Detective Jones." Jules drew his attention away from the tittering girl. "I'm fine, as you can see."

For a brief instant, when their gazes locked, Jules sensed something coming from him. Dim and vague though it was, it plucked at her proverbial heartstrings. Loneliness and the need for something that had nothing to do with being a police officer shone in his eyes. It was personal. She didn't know how she knew it, but she did.

He stretched out a hand and reached for her. For reasons she couldn't understand herself, she allowed him to touch her. With her hand in his, his need became definable.

Connection.

It radiated through her. She hadn't felt this kind of association in years. Not with anyone who wasn't family. And he couldn't be related to her; she only had sisters.

Didn't she?

Jules twisted her hand free.

He grimaced but didn't try to hold on to her.

Diana huffed loudly.

Jules and Dev both glanced at the girl. To Jules's dismay, the girl smiled and glanced at Dev from under her lashes. The move was even more of a come-on than the blatant sexual smile she gave to Mason yesterday.

"Detective, we're very busy. You know, getting ready for the local *high school* dance. Isn't the homecoming dance this weekend, Diana?"

"Yes," the girl hissed.

Ooh . . . Jules was going to pay for that later. She hadn't meant to embarrass Diana. No, she'd meant to make it clear to *The Hottie Cop* that he was too old to even consider taking the naïve and vulnerable Diana up on her blatant offer.

"So, Detective Jo—"

"Dev," the man interrupted, raising one finger in the air. A questioning look brightened his eyes. He gave his head a quick shake and said, "My partner wanted you to know he has a few more questions."

Of course he does.

"Would you mind asking him to wait until this evening? I really need to get back to work. Sundays are always busy right after church." Jules smiled and stepped back, increasing the distance between them.

As if by divine intervention, the front door bells chimed and four customers filed in.

Dev glanced over his shoulder and straightened. Tapping two fingers on the counter, he said, "I'm sure that won't be a problem."

"Thanks. I promise to make myself available to him tonight."

A small smile curled the corner of his mouth and she realized how that must have sounded. "Oh, no! I meant I'll be sure to find him after work, so he can finish questioning me."

"I know what you meant," Dev replied with a laugh before he spun on his heel. His long strides ate up the distance to the door.

As Jules watched Dev depart, an image of Shelley's face flashed through her mind. Young and sweet, she'd been seven the last time Jules had seen her. With bright red pigtails and big blue eyes, she was calm and obedient.

Unlike Jules.

Why was she thinking about her sister?

She needed to work. Compartmentalizing her thoughts of Seth and Shelley, and the feelings they both provoked, Jules greeted the first customer. He wanted a dozen cash-and-carry roses.

"Coming right up," Jules said with a grin.

Heading to the refrigeration case, Jules glanced at Diana. The girl narrowed her eyes and stalked over. Okay, to the customers in the shop she probably appeared to simply walk, but they couldn't see what Jules could. Diana's eyes narrowed to slits and glaring poison-tipped arrows.

Diana reached Jules's side, and while pulling out a preordered arrangement of carnations, she hissed between clenched teeth, "I'm not in high school. I'm homeschooled. And I saw him *first*."

With that, she whirled away. A bright smile on her face, she carried the arrangement to the customer she'd been helping. Jules returned to selecting the roses for her customer.

Even if Jules had been interested in Dev, he was much too young for her. What was he, twenty-four? Now Seth . . . He was a man any woman would want to nibble on.

Grabbing the rest of the roses, she gently bundled them, tying a purple satin ribbon around them, and then froze.

No more thinking about Seth's hotness! She refused to allow her foolish and seriously-lacking-self-preservation heart to lead her again. She needed to take care of business. First the store, then the ghost, and then find her sisters, in that order.

Love, lust, and sex were off her to-do list.

THE REST OF the day flew by with the steady stream of Sunday customers. By five in the evening, Jules's stomach rumbled. She regretted skipping out before eating any of the lunch Seth had ordered. The pizza at Philomena's had smelled delicious but she'd needed to put space between her and Seth.

She'd seen a side of him that made him not only human, but yummy. Just thinking about him, her heart sped up like she'd just run a marathon. That so wasn't good for her state of mind.

He embodied the perfect male. Loyal to his family, a loving father and devoted son, handsome, charming, sexy, and funny, Seth would have been perfect if he hadn't been a cop.

Dang! Why couldn't he be a plumber?

This attraction was wholly inappropriate. Still, she couldn't deny that seeing the tuft of dark chest hair peeking out of the top of his green shirt made her insides quiver. The man was sexy with a capital *X*. Even the dash of gray in his hair at his temples was a turn-on.

"I've cashed out and locked up the back." Diana handed over the cash bag and the daily receipts. She'd washed her face and changed back into the pink skirt and white blouse from earlier. Despite changing her clothes, her mood hadn't improved. She'd glared at Jules all afternoon.

"Diana, I really didn't mean what I said earlier. Not the way it sounded." Jules accepted the cash bag, laying it next to the register. She turned to Diana and inhaled a hopeful breath. "Detective Jones is too old for you."

"You're not my mother." Diana emitted a sound of disgust then nodded toward the door. "Do you want me to do anything else? If so, you'd better hurry. My *mom's* outside waiting."

Through the glass, Jules could make out the parked blue Mazda SUV.

She gave up on trying to make the girl see reason. "No, thank you. We're all finished. I'm heading out as soon as I go over these." Jules waved to the bag of receipts. "Have a good night, Diana. I'll see you tomorrow morning. Oh, did April ask you about helping me do inventory on Tuesday?"

"I'll be here." Diana glared, as she had every other time they'd made eye contact since Dev's visit. When she wanted to, the girl could deliver death rays with her eyes that would have made a super villain proud.

Diana shrugged then stomped toward the door, calling out over her shoulder, "Math's my best subject. You won't find a mistake."

She was right, Jules discovered after she'd counted the cash, credit card receipts, and checks. Diana was both a creative wiz and a math one too. She hadn't made a single error.

Stuffing the money and receipts into a plastic bank baggie, she signed her name across the seal. She shoved the plastic bag into a locking canvas one, then placed the bags in the safe in April's office before returning to the counter to collect her belongings.

Jules untied her apron and shoved it under the counter. She pulled out her purse and examined it.

"You must give it to him." A cold chill went down Jules's spine at the ghostly words drifting through her mind.

She glanced around the room. The ghost floated in a seated position above the pirate chest full of stuffed animals and Halloween decorations. This time the girl wore a pair of knee-length beachcomber khaki pants and a dark blue tank top. Her aura pulsed a dark, murky red and her eyes shone as if she held back tears.

"He won't stop. Won't stop," the specter whispered, desperation drawing out every syllable. Each word tumbled over the previous one, creating a cavernous echo. *"He'll kill anyone . . . kill anyone . . . to get what . . . what he wants . . . he wants. I should have seen it sooner . . . seen it sooner. I shouldn't have . . . shouldn't have done it. But I tried to fix it . . . fix it. Now he'll kill—"*

The doorbell chimed as the door opened. Diana stuck her head inside. "I forgot my mom wants to go on some lame field trip with the home school group Tuesday, so I can't come in to do inventory. But I can stay late on Wednesday."

The spirit evaporated.

"Whoa! You all right?" Diana stepped through the door, the scowl she'd worn all afternoon replaced with an expression of concern. "You look like you just saw a ghost."

Jules grinned wryly. "I'm fine, just a long day. Wednesday is fine. Have a good night."

"You too." Diana smiled, then pursed her lips as if she suddenly realized she was supposed to be annoyed. She spun around and left.

Hmmm . . . Diana can't hold a grudge for more than a few hours. Relieved at the thought, Jules set the alarm and exited the shop.

The waning afternoon sunshine cast long shadows of the buildings across the parking lot, making the area seem both inviting and a little magical. A gentle, cool breeze blew, lifting her hair. The scent of roses and sea air mixed together and soothed nerves she hadn't realized were exposed.

Jules hurried down side streets; paying little attention to the world around her, she focused on trying to communicate with the ghost again. Perhaps, this time the ghost might be more forthcoming about what she really wanted.

"Are you there?" Jules sent out a mental push.

Chirping birds were her only answer.

Clutching the purse more firmly in the crook of her under-arm, she tried again. *"Ghost-girl, are you there?"*

Damning her persnickety crift, Jules grimaced and silently repeated the question. Perhaps, her attempt to multitask inhib-ited her newfound ability. She'd been standing still in the store when she discovered she could wing her thoughts out to the ghost.

Maybe if she just stopped, got off the road and out of sight, then she could concentrate.

Spying an alley that appeared deserted, she headed toward it. She'd barely neared it when she heard a voice, calling out.

"Hello. Can you hear me?" The feminine voice was gentle and melodic. Ethereal and ghostlike, but not the spirit Jules had been trying to reach.

Dang! Am I going to channel every specter in the tri-city area?

Jules should just walk past and ignore the ghostly call. Nor-mally she would have, but for reasons even she couldn't explain, she didn't. Instead, she stepped into the unknown alley.

The stench of rotting garbage combined with urine burned her nostrils. Clapping a hand to her face, she choked and glanced at unfamiliar buildings that surrounded her on three sides.

Shafts of sunlight splintered on cracked windows. Dented doors dangled precariously by their hinges. Graffiti and smoke damage marred the walls, giving the buildings an abandoned feel. Three dingy green Dumpsters were shoved into a corner. Crumpled cardboard boxes, broken bottles, and filthy clothing littered the tiny alley.

"Hello?" Jules called out, then wished she hadn't.

Something was wrong. The air around her crackled like static electricity. Despite being outside, a claustrophobic feel-ing swamped her. Whipping her head from side to side, she half expected to see the crumbling walls close in around her.

"Do not fear, child," the disembodied voice spoke again. Her gentle, melodic tone made the words comforting. *"You are safe here."*

"Where are you?" Jules searched the dank alleyway.

Moving slowly through the grimy dead-end street, she glanced around again. "Show yourself. I'd feel a lot better if I could see you."

Nothing answered her.

She looked up when she should have looked down. Jules tripped over a broken bottle and stumbled against a small mountain of old dirty clothes. A black cat had been sleeping on the ratty laundry. It popped its head up and bellowed a loud *meow* at her.

Jules's stomach leapfrogged with her heart into her throat and she squelched the urge to cry out, then chuckled at herself.

"Seen any ghosts down here?" Jules asked the green-eyed cat, then shook her head. "Great! I'm losing my mind. I'm talking to Garfield now."

The cat hissed at her as if insulted by her reference to the cartoon feline, jumped down from the clump of clothing, flicked its tail at her, and then bounded down the alley out to the street.

Jules straightened , pressing her hand against the mountain of torn, smelly clothes for support.

The clothing pile moaned and shifted.

Jules yanked back her hand. A panicked scream caught in her throat.

A man with a matted beard and equally tangled hair rose up from the pile of old clothes. A waterfall of tattered, stained jackets and shirts flowed to the ground, pooling at his feet.

An icy finger brushed beneath the collar of Jules's shirt. Her stomach clenched and she turned around. Only the wall faced her. *"Do not be afraid."*

Yeah, right. Jules sent out another mental push. *"Show yourself, and I won't be."*

Again, the ghost didn't appear. *"I will . . . soon."*

The rational part of her brain told her to run but her danged legs wouldn't listen. Instead of bolting away, her feet moved as if encased in invisible cement. Heavy and slow, she plodded down the alley. She'd barely made it to the middle when all light was sucked into a black vortex.

Although she remained on her feet, the world around her shifted. Another icy digit touched her, this time behind her ear.

She spun around to see the homeless man had given her his back and huddled in a corner near the Dumpster.

Dread ripped down Jules's spine, igniting the instinct to struggle. The impulse to run, to escape, warred with the single logical cell working in her brain. Fighting wouldn't work; if she wanted this to end, she needed to hold still and let the specter have her say.

At least, she hoped that would work.

Jules forced her body to relax and accept what was happening. She focused her mind, clearing it of any stray thoughts, then waited for the whispering to resume.

The physical world withdrew. Birds stopped chirping. Noisy traffic from the street beyond the alley's mouth faded. Everything auditory melted into a vast void. For a nanosecond she found peace in the sublime silence.

"Do not fear. He would never harm you. You are safe here." The melodic, gentle voice spoke again. Her words were soothing, hypnotic. *"I only need you to deliver a message. One he desperately needs to hear."*

"I'm listening," Jules said into the still alley.

"Go to him. It's been so long since he's had kindness. Please."

Despite her uncertainty, Jules obeyed. She moved slowly until she knelt beside the cowering man. She stretched out a tentative hand and rested it on his stiff, dirty sleeve as she spoke. "It's okay. I won't hurt you."

His weathered skin was thin and wrinkly. His unkempt rust-colored hair hung past his shoulders. Still, he smiled, then gently patted her hand with his.

At his touch, a lifetime flashed through her mind like a rapid-fire slideshow. It moved so fast, she shouldn't have been able to see it all, but she comprehended it just the same. It was his lifetime. Complete with a millennium's worth of pain squeezed into forty-nine years.

A burning-hot desert on the other side of the world. A chaplain and his commander walking toward the mess tent. Unbearable news. His wife and only daughter died in an apartment fire, hours before he woke.

He crumpled to his knees. Hours and days blurred past in a haze of pain.

Two coffins: one large, one small. A funeral attended by hundreds but he stood apart.

Alone.

Years slipped by with no one to hate but himself. His single thought, he should have been there . . . to save them.

The slideshow changed. Now the bitter memories interwove themselves with his fondest. His wedding day. His daughter's birth. A family trip to Disney World.

And each sacred moment fed the self-loathing.

When the heartbreaking moments of his life finished playing through her mind, Jules stretched out her arms and wrapped them around him in a gentle hug.

Then the melodic voice whispered, *"His name is Samuel."*

Jules glanced up to find a beautiful woman in a white summer dress.

Whole but transparent, the spirit shimmered in and out of sight, like sunlight shining between leaves on an elm tree. She hovered a few inches above the ground. An aura of silver white light surrounded her and made the ends of her chestnut hair sparkle.

A pervading sense of peace filled Jules and she couldn't help smiling.

"Thank you for heeding my call."

"He's a wonderful person. I'm sorry for his pain. And yours." Jules sent out the mental push to the ghost, who smiled in return.

What was Jules doing talking to a ghost? She knew better than to engage the paranormal world. And yet, she couldn't resist the need to help these two people. The ghost in front of her wasn't the phantom who'd been haunting her.

No, this one was Samuel's wife and she radiated peace. How could Jules deny this gentle spirit anything?

The wife moved her hand, as if caressing Samuel's cheek. He froze, seeming to sense her presence. He cocked his head slightly and closed his eyes as if to heighten the sensation.

A pained expression crossed the ghost's face, and she withdrew her hand then turned her attention to Jules. *"I'm sorry to send you so many visions at once but, I needed you to see my husband as we knew him. Before we died . . . and after. He wasn't always like this. Samuel is a military hero. Our hero.*

*He should be honored. Not ignored. And not forgotten. He has
a higher purpose than this."*

The wife spread her arms wide, gesturing to the alleyway.

"Momma?" called a sweet, childlike voice.

The ghost-wife's form shimmered brighter, and for the first
time, Jules noticed a second smaller form beside her. A child,
no older than five, with straight blonde hair and piercing blue
eyes—her father's eyes—took her mother's hand in hers. With
a hopeful expression on her innocent face, she asked in a small
voice, *"Will he come home now?"*

"Not yet," the mother replied to her daughter, as if Jules
couldn't hear them. *"He has something very important to do.
But we can take him home soon."*

"Then he'll be free?"

"Yes, Penny, then he'll be free." She turned a gimlet stare
to Jules. *"My name is Moira. Can you please deliver my message? He needs to know . . ."*

Jules listened carefully to Moira's speech. She'd nearly
memorized it when Samuel pulled away from her without
warning.

What the heck? Jules had barely hatched the thought when
her physical senses burst through the haze of serenity with a
deafening clamor.

Jules dropped her purse and clapped her hands to her ears
at the cacophony of noises. Then her olfactory senses kicked
in. Fetid air filled her lungs and she gagged.

Wow, how could she have forgotten about the rotting garbage in the alley?

A gentle hand touched her at the base of her spine. Jules
turned to see Seth staring into her face with concern. Despite
the sounds still beating a tattoo against her eardrums, she lowered her hands.

His touch seemed to lessen the aftershocks of her crift, as
if by caressing her skin, Seth drove back the harsh return of
her physical senses. The sounds around her dulled to normal.
The stench of the alley no longer overwhelmed her sense of
smell. Even her gag reflex settled instantly.

She didn't have time to wonder how this was possible
because he asked, "What are you doing out here with him?"

Turning around, Jules saw the homeless man no longer

huddled near the discarded clothes. He watched them with a wary expression on his dirt-coated face.

Despite his grimy appearance, he exuded an air of defiance. And fear. His back ramrod straight and his arms crossed over his chest, he clutched both elbows. He hunched his shoulders, but his feet were spread wide as if he could spring into action at any moment. But it was the rapid shifting of his eyes that was the most telling.

He darted his gaze repeatedly between Jules, Seth, and the mouth of the alley.

Cautiously, Jules move closer to him, two steps at a time, until they stood three feet apart. She couldn't miss the sound of his stomach rumbling. Her stomach ached in sympathy.

The bravado in his stance dissolved and he shuffled backward until his back pressed against the wall. Slowly, he sunk to a seated position, drew his knees to his chest, and wrapped his arms around himself.

"Juliana, did you hear me?" Seth caressed the backs of his fingers down her cheek. "Are you okay, precious?" he asked in a low tone. His breath feathered across her ear.

With a quick glance at Samuel, she nodded. "I'm fine. Just delivering an old message."

Knowing he couldn't possibly understand—heck, she barely comprehended it herself—she sidled out of Seth's touch and headed toward Samuel.

Two days ago, she'd sworn off helping any ghost, and today she was a walking cell phone for the dead.

She took both of Samuel's trembling hands into hers. He kept his gaze lowered to the worn hole in the top of the brown leather shoe on his right foot. Her chest tightened with sympathy. She pushed herself to speak Moira's words in a way that wouldn't necessarily make Seth or Samuel believe she was completely insane.

"Moira and Penny always knew you loved them. They wouldn't want you to suffer any more. Samuel, I know it's hard to hear, but it was their time to go. Not yours. You need to forgive yourself because you couldn't have saved them. They don't blame you—"

Samuel winced, releasing her hands.

The declaration was one the average person couldn't make,

so she amended, "I'm sure they don't blame you. You're a war hero. I bet they were very proud of you. Do you really think they would want you living in an alley with a black cat as your only friend? Don't you know you're destined for so much more?"

Samuel blinked and silent tears rolled clean tracks down his grimy cheeks. Wordlessly, he scrubbed his face, smudging the once-clean streaks. He nodded and turned away. His stomach rumbled loudly.

"Help him, please." Moira and Penny stared at her imploringly, but Jules was already moving back to Seth, who must have picked up the purse when she dropped it. She took it from him.

Digging into the clutch, she pulled out all the money she had. Fifty dollars wasn't much, but it would get him a decent meal and maybe a room for the night.

"Samuel," she called to him. When he turned, she pushed the cash into his hand. His fingers brushed hers as they wrapped around the money.

"Thank you, Miss . . . ?" His voice was gravelly, as if not used in years. The tender smile on his face gave him the appearance of a man decades younger.

"It's Jules. And you're welcome, Samuel. I just wish I could offer more. Is there anything else I can do?"

Seth stepped forward. "There's a new shelter on Fifty-eighth Street. It's clean with hot showers, good food, and friendly service. The doors opened at four. I can drive you. Drop you off at the front door?"

Samuel gave a wan smile and shook his head.

With a tight-lipped expression, Seth nodded his head sharply once, then pulled out his wallet. Aside from the cash he gave Samuel, he also handed him a small card. "It's got my home number on the back. There's been a rash of attacks lately on the homeless in the city. If you need me, call. I'll come. Any hour."

Without another word, Seth took Jules lightly by the elbow and steered her out of the alley. Just before turning the corner, she glanced back over her shoulder.

The ghostly wife and daughter smiled. They flanked Samuel as he settled back down to nap.

Keeping her eyes on them until she rounded the corner, awareness tingled at the base of Jules's neck. She had the distinct impression this wouldn't be the last she'd see of Samuel or his family.

CHAPTER 9

"So how did you know Sam's wife?"

Jules's mouth gaped and she stumbled to a halt at his unexpected words.

The cop continued on for several paces before he noticed she'd stopped moving.

"Jules?" He walked slowly back to her, concern etched in the lines of his face. "Are you all right?"

"You know Samuel?"

"Everyone in our building does." Seth shrugged, then jerked a thumb to the brick structure to her left.

Retracing her steps to the alley, she recognized the back of her building. *Wait! That's not what it looked like two minutes ago.*

The ghosts had called her down her own alley and disguised it as another? It made no sense. What purpose did it serve to show her a scary-looking backstreet?

"I'm . . . home?" Jules stared in disbelief at the back of her building.

Instead of the decrepit piles of charred brick and mortar,

she found multicolored pansies decorating window boxes. While the lump of clothing—which she now knew was Samuel—lay beside a Dumpster, the nauseating stench had disappeared. Gel caricatures of ghosts, pumpkins, and witches clung to pristine windows on the multifloor apartment building.

Breath punched from her body, she blinked several times to be certain her eyes weren't betraying her again. A ceramic pumpkin glowed to life in a second-floor window, prompting Jules to hurry to the front of her building. Pots of orange and yellow mums dotted windowsills and the walkway.

"What is going on?"

"Jules, are you all right?" Seth caught her upper arm and held her still. Moving in front of her, he narrowed his eyes and searched her face, then felt her forehead with the back of his hand. "You're pale. Come sit down."

He tugged her to the front steps of their complex and urged her to sit beside him.

"I'm fine."

"Are you sure? You look lost."

"Well, I was." Jules laughed in spite of herself. He smiled back and she explained. "I am what you might call *directionally challenged*."

"Directionally challenged?" Seth rubbed the back of his neck then sat down on the third step. "You mean you get lost?"

Jules shifted her position on the concrete step, trying to leave as much space between them as possible.

"I mean I get lost *frequently*. Friday night, your window—that kind of stuff used to happen to me all the time."

"What changed?"

"I got married and my husband moved me to Kemmerton, Virginia." When he simply stared at her blank-faced, she added with a grin, "It's pretty rural there. When I left there wasn't even a Walmart in the county yet. But at the time it was great for me. Kind of hard to get lost much with only a few streets in and out of the county. Unfortunately, I still managed to do it for a while. It's why I don't drive. Even a GPS didn't save me from getting lost in a very shady part of D.C. once. I've refused to drive ever since. I still get lost, but I notice it a lot sooner when on foot."

"Your *husband*?" *Figures that would be the one word he'd hear.*

"*Ex*-husband." Jules squirmed. "The one who gave me the Prada." She held the purse up briefly before dropping it back to the space between them. "It's a knockoff, by the way. This is what I get for not taking it out of the box for two years. Turns out I've been preserving a Prad-o all this time."

Seth picked up the purse. Jules showed him the carefully disguised lettering. He frowned, then set it back down again. "Cheap bastard."

"Thanks, I think so." She grinned when he chuckled at her words. "So, what are you doing here?"

"I live here, remember?"

"Oh, right." *Way to sound like a moron.*

He gave her a wry grin. "My shift ended and I'm home for the night."

Jules flicked her left wrist and checked her watch. Seven o'clock? A quick glance upward at the orange-streaked sky confirmed it. Dear Lord! How long had she been standing in that alley? Not wanting to think about it, she turned back to Seth. "I'm really sorry about bolting at lunch. I should have left a note but I needed to get back to work."

He gave her an arch stare, then asked, "You sure that's what happened?" Without giving her time to answer, he said, "Or were you worried about having to see the picture of a dead body right after we ate?"

Okay, that thought *did* make her queasy. "I wasn't keen on it, if you want the truth."

"Can you do it now?" Even as he asked the question, he pulled out his cell phone and scrolled to a photo, then handed it to her.

The face of the woman on the screen was bluish and pale. There were dark bruises on one side of her face, as if she'd been punched, and small oval bruises in the pattern of fingers across her neck.

Bile burned up Jules's throat and she pressed her palm to her lips. She shook her head. "I can honestly say I've never seen that woman alive."

As a ghost was another story.

"Okay, I'm sorry, precious." Seth blackened the screen then

plucked the phone from her trembling hand. Shoving it into his pocket with one hand, he ran his other up and down her arm reassuringly. "I should have remembered you're new to this world. It's not like you see dead people all the time."

Actually . . .

"It-it's okay." But seeing ghosts was a lot easier than seeing dead bodies. They almost never bore the look of death. Granted, they usually appeared in what they'd died in, but their faces almost always had the healthy glow of life.

Jules gestured toward his pocket where he'd stashed his phone. "Do you know her name?"

"Not yet. I have a theory but until I know for certain, I can't say anything."

Jules nodded.

"Thanks for looking anyway," he said, wrinkling his forehead and scratching his right eyebrow. Seth tossed a look toward the alley, then glanced back at her. "Jules, I've got to know. How *did* you know about Moira? She died three years ago. I've lived in our building for five years. I've never seen you before Friday night."

"I honestly don't know much more than her name."

Seth grunted, one eyebrow arched imperiously.

"I had to say something to him, didn't I? He seemed so sad. So alone. No one should live like that. He's a human being and deserves to be treated with respect."

"Yeah." Seth sighed. "Sam changed after the death of his wife and daughter. Before that, he was someone anyone could count on. You did a good thing back there. I think you might be the first person to get him to talk in years. Lord knows I've tried, but he normally just hides when anyone goes near his alley."

"Oh." Jules swallowed. The images she'd seen of Samuel's life made his current situation more heartwrenching. "What happened to them? His wife and daughter, I mean."

"They were killed in an apartment fire." Seth pointed to a parking lot about four blocks over. "There used to be three buildings there. Two of the apartment complexes were old and run-down. Vacant. Their owners had sold the properties to a local landowner. But the third was different. Despite being close to one hundred years old, it was well kept. Its owner was also a tenant in the building and the lone holdout. He hadn't wanted to sell the home that had been in his family for generations. Rent rooms out of it, sure. But he couldn't let it go.

"One day the tenants and the landlord had been fighting to keep their homes, and the next the place burned to the ground. The official finding was the building caught fire due to an electrical short."

"You don't believe that?" Jules shuddered at the implication that the deadly blaze hadn't been accidental.

"*Officially*, I have no opinion." Seth frowned again, his mouth flattening to a thin line.

"Unofficially?"

"I find it convenient that a building the city was on the verge of declaring an historical landmark, which could have saved the homes of eight families, went up in flames two days before the hearing." He gazed at her, sincerity darkening his expression. "There's no proof of arson, just my gut instinct."

Jules's breath caught at his words. What some people called "gut instinct," others called a gift. Or in her case, a crift. Could he truly be special? The thought warmed her, even though it shouldn't.

"A *gut instinct*, huh?" she asked in a teasing tone despite the butterflies in her belly.

"Don't laugh. It's never been wrong." He frowned before adding with a self-deprecating grin, "Too bad I didn't always listen to it."

A shiver of excitement raced up her spine. The way he talked, he might actually believe her if she told him about her ghostly visits. Not that she would. She doubted she'd share the secret of her crift with anyone ever again. However, the idea of opening up to this handsome man seemed less frightening than it probably should.

"We all possess some inner voice," Seth continued, clasping his hands between his knees but leaning his upper body toward her. "Don't you agree? A voice that warns us of danger. And if we'd just listen to it, we could avert a crisis."

"I suppose so." Jules's body drifted closer to his until only a few inches separated them. She couldn't deny the attraction at that moment was more than physical. His words drew her in, caressed her soul. Seduced her spirit.

"That's gut instinct." Seth nailed her with a piercing look as he asked, "Don't you ever have that feeling like something is about to happen or something isn't quite right? And you know if you just turn left instead of right, you'll see what most people would walk past without ever noticing it was there?"

"Yeah." *Like a ghost who hasn't departed.*

Seth nodded and grinned. His delicious sandalwood scent filled her nostrils as he shifted closer without seeming to move. Jules sat mesmerized, first by the laugh lines at the corners of his eyes, then by their twinkling chocolate-colored depths.

"I knew you were smart." His warm breath feathered across her cheek as his voice deepened. "I bet you know all sorts of secrets because your gut tells you to listen when others would chatter on about nonsense. Don't you? Know secrets?"

About my case. Seth's unspoken addendum floated through her mind and Jules nearly flinched. He hadn't actually said it, but she had the distinct impression he'd thought it.

For a second, she had forgotten he was a police officer trying to learn the identity of a murderer. Only a fool—a desperate one at that—would continually lower her guard around a man like Seth. He had one reason for talking to her: to learn what she knew about his case. Frustrated and more disappointed than she wanted to admit, she slid away from him.

Confusion clouded his features and his grin faded. He straightened and placed his hands on his knees, gripping them like a lifeline. He exhaled a word that sounded remarkably like *Crap*.

With her purse in one hand, she tugged on her earlobe with the other and searched for something else to discuss. "Did you investigate it?" When he stared at her blankly, she added, "The fire. You said you didn't believe it was an accident, but it seems to me that if you suspected something, you wouldn't have let it go until you had an answer that satisfied you."

And that thought terrified her.

While he may correctly believe she knew more about the dead woman than she'd admitted so far, her answers definitely would not satisfy him.

"No," he exhaled on a sigh. "I work in the burglary division. Since there was no burglary, I couldn't work the case."

"But you wanted to," Jules guessed, and smiled in satisfaction when he nodded. "What ever happened with the case?"

"Nothing." He grunted and ran a hand through his hair, sending the curls into messy array. On most men it would have looked ridiculous. On him, the effect was annoyingly charming. "No one could do anything," he said. "The fire inspector only found the faulty wiring in Sam's unit and the case was closed. The building owner died in the fire along with Sam's wife and daughter. The lot went up for auction and Hart Construction bought it."

Jules blinked in surprise. "Hart Construction. You mean Mason's father's company?"

"You know Mason Hart?" Seth's gaze sharpened.

"Yes, we went to college together."

He faced her fully and cocked his head. Reaching into his pocket, he again reminded her of a warrior of ancient times. But instead of a sword, he withdrew a little black notebook and a pen. He started to scribble something. "How well do you know him? Were you two lovers?"

A startled laugh escaped her. "That's quite a jump you made. You go around asking every woman if she was lovers with every man she's ever met?"

Seth's cheeks mottled and he shook his head. "No, I don't. It's just that you and Hart went to the same college and he has quite a reputation with the ladies. Something he had in school, from what my sources tell me."

"Oh, well, that's certainly true," Jules agreed, but then shook her head. "I can honestly say I've never dated Mason. And I wouldn't. Not in a million years. I'm not exactly his type."

"Why not?" Seth stopped scribbling and looked her up and down.

Her cheeks warmed and she wished she wasn't subjected to the redheaded curse. Normally, a man staring at her body would have Jules crossing her arms in chagrin, but something about the heat in his gaze held her in place. His mouth curled up on one side in an appreciative grin and Jules felt the ridiculous urge to preen.

While Billy, her ex, had been sweet, Seth was model-worthy hot. And she'd have to be crazy not to feel flattered by his open perusal, at least until he added, "You're female with no visible scars and you're under thirty. That seems to be his type."

Her pride plopped into her belly. "Um . . ."

"I didn't mean it like that," Seth backpedaled. "You must know you're attractive. It's just Mason isn't known for being very choosy—"

Jules covered Seth's lips with her fingers, silencing him. His eyes widened in surprise, then flared to obsidian.

A white-hot flash of desire zoomed from her fingers to her toes and back up to the ends of her hair. She wanted to replace her fingers with her lips and see if he'd taste of hazelnut coffee as he had in her dream.

Instead, she yanked her hand away. She hoped she hid the fact that she'd been as affected by their casual touch as he appeared.

"You seem Hart's type to me," he said. "You're beautiful, sexy, and can stop a man's heart when you climb through his bedroom window at three in the morning." Despite his words ending on a chuckle, they seemed more heartfelt or at least lust-inspired than his previous comment.

Another bloom of awareness started in her midsection and quickly spread through her body. She found herself staring into his eyes. They were warm, sensual, and mesmerizing.

In the alley, his touch left her only feeling peace. Now it sent his desire ricocheting off her chest like arrows from Cupid. Tiny acrobats took up residence in her belly and started performing. She felt positively giddy at his assessment of her.

Oh, this has to stop.

She tore her gaze away from his and focused on his lips. Seth still spoke, but his words were muffled. Her attention centered on the way his mouth moved.

After a lifetime of concealing her crift, hiding who she was came naturally. At least, it did usually. Tonight, for some odd reason, she didn't want to hide. She wanted to lose herself in his eyes, his lips, in him.

Jules flashed hot. A trickle of sweat slid between her breasts. The attraction was wrong, but fighting it didn't seem like the right thing to do either. Her thoughts scattered as she stared at the five-o'clock shadow on his jaw. It added rugged-ness to his sexual appeal.

Her mind had gone wonderfully fuzzy, like being drunk without all the nasty side-effects of being unable to shield herself from ghosts. But it did mean she had to work harder to concentrate. It came easier when he asked, "Have you seen him lately?"

"Who?"

"Mason Hart." Seth nodded toward the little black notebook still in his hands.

"Oh." She gave herself a mental shake. She might be turned on, but he was clearly still in cop mode.

What am I doing?

The sensible, careful persona she'd been trying to adopt since her return to Tidewater had disappeared the moment Seth touched her in the alley. In its place was the wild child Jules had always been. The one who married Billy after knowing him for six weeks, ignoring her family's warnings. The one who foolishly trusted her secret to her cop husband, only to land in jail for her honesty.

Even her line of thinking didn't protect her tonight. Just when she'd thought she'd escaped the tumultuous desire raging between them, Seth stopped speaking again.

He tilted his head to one side and stared at her mouth. His eyes darkened to black, and he unknowingly sent deliciously explicit images winging into her mind.

She leaned her head closer to his. His lips hovered over hers.

"Seth? Juliana? What are you two doing out here?" Big Jim stood poised to climb the steps of their building. Brown paper sacks filled with groceries were nestled in the crook of each arm.

Seth pushed to his feet. Only then did Jules notice his right hand was wrapped in a bandage.

He brushed off his charcoal-colored trousers with his uninjured hand and turned to Big Jim. "Evening, Ernie. Jules and I were just talking. Catching up. Our lunch was cut short, right, Jules?"

"Right," she answered, grateful Seth hadn't gone into more detail.

Big Jim lifted a brow but his eyes narrowed slightly at Seth. "Everything okay? You know Friday night was a mistake, right? Jules here is directionally challenged."

"So I've noticed." Seth turned and winked at her, making her cheeks warm. "Nothing is wrong. Just being . . . neighborly."

Worry eased from Big Jim's expression, and he smiled. "Well, good. Why don't y'all carry the conversation upstairs? April called my cell a few minutes ago. Lasagna's on."

With the haze of lust gone, reality set in. Seth at dinner? In *her* apartment?

King of the bad ideas!

"THE LASAGNA WOULD have been better with organic oregano," April complained as she shifted on the couch after dinner.

Jules was tempted to look at Seth as he came out of the kitchen, but thought better of it. There's no way she could keep a straight face after April's comment.

"I know what you mean, honey," Big Jim said as he returned to the living room and handed April a fresh glass of water. "But dinner was excellent as usual."

"For you," Seth's deep voice said, just before a wineglass seemed to appear from nowhere in front of Jules's face.

She turned in her leather wingback chair to find Seth offering it. She smiled at his thoughtfulness. "Thank you, but I don't drink alcohol."

"I know. Ernie told me." He set her glass on the table next to her. "It's apple juice. He said it's your favorite."

Seth had been interminably polite all through dinner. Not once did he bring up dead bodies or lost cell phones. Now he brought her a glass of juice. He was so sweet, she could almost kiss him. Well, if she thought he'd actually kiss her back.

"It is," Jules replied, smiling. "Thank you."

He delivered a grin that made her heart race at hummingbird speed before claiming the matching chair on the other side of the end table. After he sat down, she noticed he'd brought a glass of red wine with him from the kitchen.

Seth raised the glass, gently tapped it against hers, and drank. Jules sipped her juice.

"How did you say you lost the oregano?" Big Jim asked, settling himself beside April and looping an arm around her shoulders.

"Oh, um . . ." Jules returned the glass to the table and searched for the right words.

Seth distracted her by crossing one long leg over the other and resting his right foot on his left knee. He swallowed a mouthful of wine and cast her a glance that she could only define as *taunting*.

She should change the subject or let the question go, but the wild child inside her couldn't resist rising to Seth's silent challenge.

"Oh, you know, Big Jim, it could've happened anywhere. The other night was crazy from the moment I arrived at the reunion. For all I know, someone could have gone through my purse when I wasn't looking and assumed it was pot."

"Who in their right mind would ever think *you* had drugs?" April laughed.

"Outrageous!" Big Jim agreed with a chuckle.

"I suppose the person who took it feels pretty foolish about now." April brushed a finger at her blonde bangs and addressed Seth. "Are marijuana and oregano very similar? Is it easy to mistake one for the other?"

"Only for innocents like you, love," Big Jim interjected, then laughed. "Seth here would never make such an asinine mistake."

Jules snorted but quickly covered her mouth with her hand and pretended to cough.

Seth said, "Ernie's right. Mistaking one for the other is an error no self-respecting police officer would ever own up to."

Seth sipped his wine and cast Jules a sheepish look.

"On the other hand, it's not like normal people carry around herbs in their purse." Jules used the same words Seth had spoken. "If I hadn't stopped by the health food store on the way to the party, I wouldn't have done it myself. I can see where someone might, in a rush, assume I was carrying an illegal substance in my purse."

"Wise woman," Seth said with a wink that sent her heart skipping.

April waggled her eyebrows. Jules blushed and snapped her gaze back to Seth, who thankfully was looking over at the table as he deposited his half-empty glass. She breathed a small sigh of relief.

It was embarrassing enough that she'd nearly kissed him multiple times, but he'd not followed through once. Didn't her parents know that something developing with Seth was in a race between impossible and never-gonna-happen?

Big Jim and April exchanged one of their patent "spousal glances."

Jules had come to recognize them over the years. The look they shared whenever they were speaking silently. She'd asked them once if they were telepathic, but they'd assured her that they'd been together so long, they'd learned to guess what the other was thinking.

Right now, Jules could guess what they were thinking. They were planning to leave her alone with Seth.

Um . . . no!

April let out a big yawn that would have been believable if Jules had been raised by monkeys on Venus. Still, Big Jim practically leapt to his feet to offer his arm to his wife.

Oh, brother! Do they really think Seth is going to fall for this?

"I guess I should be going too," Seth said, starting to push to his feet, but Big Jim waved at him to remain seated.

"No, sit, stay," Big Jim replied as he helped April stand with one hand on her back. "We've got an early start tomorrow morning. But that's no reason for you to leave. Stay as long as you want. Jules will kick you out when she's ready to go to *sleep*. Right, Juliana?"

"Sure."

She didn't miss the glint in his eye. What did they think would happen when they left the room?

It's not like she'd have sex with Seth on the coffee table. Her heart thumped wildly in her chest.

Must not think of Seth and sex in the same sentence.

"Good night," she called out as Big Jim and April abandoned her and went to their bedroom.

"ALONE AT LAST, *precious*." Coming up behind Jules, Seth couldn't resist inhaling her scent. The faint smell of strawberries hit his senses and shot through his system like an aphrodisiac-laced bullet. Damn, she was turning him into a strawberry junkie.

"So we are. What do you want to do?" She turned to face him. Wide green eyes gazed up at him with curiosity that didn't quite mask her desire for him. That flare of attraction had him reaching for her when he shouldn't.

"Shall we finish our interview?" he asked, stroking a knuckle down her silken cheek.

"What?" She blinked, clearly taken off guard. Then she rolled her shoulders once and slid away from his touch. The heat of her gaze disappeared along with her welcoming smile. She reclaimed her seat. Her expression dulled and she spoke with a crisp civility. "Oh, right. You need to interview me. Fine, let's just get this over with. I'm tired anyway."

What the hell? Why had she suddenly gone cold?

"Jules, I don't want to interview you. I need to." Still, the warmth hadn't returned to her gaze.

"Of course, *Detective.*"

Her clipped tone didn't chafe as much as the pain and acceptance in her eyes. It was the resignation and doubt in her expression that had him moving until he braced his hands on the arms of her chair.

She gasped, but something hot and sensual flared in her gaze. That was what he wanted to see. He was breaking every bit of protocol, but damn, he liked the look of attraction in her eyes.

"Juliana," he whispered, leaning until his lips grazed her cheek as he spoke. "You've driven me crazy since I met you. I'd like nothing better than to kiss you right now and spend the rest of the week exploring your body with my tongue."

She shivered.

He pulled back only far enough to look into her eyes before adding, "But before we can go *exploring*, I need to make sure I've conducted my case properly without compromising my integrity or the case itself. There's a killer out there and I'd hate to be the one who lets him go free because I didn't do my job properly."

He waited. For a moment she just stared at him, then she nodded. "What can I do for you?"

"Ah, precious, that's my girl." He gave her a chaste kiss on her head. Even though he'd just given her a speech about keeping his behavior proper for his case, he'd already crossed the line.

Seth stepped back, released Jules's chair, and put some much-needed space between them. Not an easy task, considering he wanted to wrap his arms around her and taste her lips.

Hell, he wanted to drown in her. But he needed to finish questioning her.

Grabbing his notebook, he said, "Give me a minute to review my notes."

"Take your time." She smiled. "I'll just put away the glasses."

She gestured to the coffee table. Ernie and April had left their dishes. Seth watched as Jules bent over to pick up a napkin that April had left under her water glass.

His eyes trailed up Jules's long, jean-clad legs. The jeans clung to her backside snugly. *I'd kill to be her pair of jeans.*

Seth shook his head to clear his thoughts. Good thing Jules didn't read minds or she'd have slapped him repeatedly by now.

Then he saw the flash of color at the base of her spine as her shirt rode up. "Do you have a tattoo?"

Jules twisted at the waist, tugging her shirt down with one hand. "Yes, why?"

"May I see it?"

She nibbled on her lower lip then slowly gave him her back.

Scooting forward on the chair, Seth raised the hem of her top to reveal the artwork. And it was definitely art. Three intricate roses—one red, one purple, and one yellow—were wrapped in a green banner with the name *Scott* emblazoned on it.

He sighed. For a moment he thought she might have had the same tattoo as his victim. After a second long look, he could see no similarities. Thank God!

"Why'd you get a tattoo?" he asked, tugging her shirt back in place.

"It seemed like a good idea at the time." Although she delivered her answer flippantly, she stumbled and nearly dropped the glasses in her hand.

She recovered quickly and hurried to the kitchen.

He waited for her to return. When she did, he said, "Come on, there's got to be more to it than that."

"I thought you needed to interview me. What does my tattoo have to do with your case?"

She had a point. Checking his notes, he decided to focus on his case, because he wasn't sure he wanted to know why someone as smart as Jules would want to walk around permanently branded with another man's name.

"Earlier, you mentioned that you'd seen Mason Hart recently," he said as she sat back down in her chair. "When exactly was that?"

"Yesterday." She frowned. "Oh, I promised I'd call him today." She checked her watch then shook her head. "Too late now."

Invisible bands around Seth's chest tightened. Jealousy. Oh, he recognized that uncomfortable sensation. Though why the hell he experienced it now, he had no idea. "I thought you told me you two weren't close?"

Jules gave him a frustrated look. "He came in to buy flowers for his *fiancée* yesterday. He wanted to get together and chat. His fiancée is upset with him. He hoped I could give him some advice on women like I used to do in college. That's it. Nothing dark or sinister. I told you, before this weekend, I hadn't seen him in years. Not since I got married."

"Ah, yes, to the cheap bastard who gave you a knockoff purse." Seth knew it was not part of his case, knew he shouldn't ask, but he had to know. "You never did tell me. What did he do that was so bad that he tried to buy your forgiveness?"

Jules tugged on her earlobe. "He didn't trust me. And when it came right down to it, I shouldn't have trusted him."

"He cheated on you?"

"Eventually," she admitted with a shrug. "But the real betrayal came long before that. He didn't know me, not the real me. He had this image in his head of who he thought I should be, but when he was faced with the truth, he denied it. Denied me."

Jules leaned forward in her chair and propped her chin on one hand. At the same time she rubbed at the tattoo on her back. It didn't appear to be a conscious act. And it made him wonder. "You got your tattoo while you were married?"

She glanced up at him, startled. "How did you guess?"

"I'm a cop, remember?" He grinned but frowned when she tensed at his comment. "You really don't like police, do you?"

"Nothing personal," she said, then blew out a breath. "It's just my ex was a cop."

And just like that, several comments she'd made finally made sense. "That's why you get so jumpy."

She neither agreed nor disagreed. Instead she started talking about her tattoo again. "You guessed right, though. Billy was always a suspicious cynic."

"Who's Billy?"

"My ex." She gave Seth a puzzled look.

He gaped at her. "No wonder your ex was suspicious. You have some other guy's name on your back."

"Scott is my last name." She scowled at him. "Jeez, what kind of a person do you think I am?"

A very confusing one. "Sorry, precious. Scott's your last name, which you had tattooed on your back while married to the cheap bastard named Billy."

Jules wrinkled her brow at him then shrugged and continued her story. "*Billy's* doubts about me only worsened when I came home with the tattoo. It didn't matter that I'd gotten it while visiting my parents. Or that he knew the names of everyone on it.

"He refused to believe I didn't have a nefarious reason behind *disfiguring my body* as he put it. But really, three roses with our first names designed into each one and wrapped in a banner with our last name is hardly something to be worried about. How can anyone assume there's something underhanded about that?"

She looked lost as she said, "He never understood why I wanted to find my sisters." Jules blinked her eyes quickly as if holding back tears. "But he always had his family. Mine was taken from me when I was just a child. And out there somewhere are my sisters, Hannah and Shelley. When I told him I'd gotten the tattoo to honor them, he told me to just let go of the past. I had enough family. *Him.*" She balled her fists in her lap. "I should have walked away from him right then. My instincts told me to, but like a fool, I stuck around until he crossed a line I couldn't forgive."

Stretching across the small table, Seth caressed her fists until she opened her hands. He understood her pain. While he couldn't relate to being adopted, he understood her need for family. "I know a thing or two about sticking it out too long."

She glanced up at him. Doubt and need shimmered in her emerald eyes. "Really?"

"Oh yeah," he admitted, stroking the backs of her hands with his thumbs.

She turned her palms up, and he laced his fingers with hers. There was something undeniably peaceful about Jules. Yes, she made his blood pump with her sexy smile and her innocent blushes, but she had a calming effect on him he'd never experienced before. And to his surprise, he opened up to her.

"I told you Catherine isn't around anymore . . ." He let his words trail off. How could he explain Catherine without sounding like a complete imbecile for not guessing sooner what that drug-addicted loon was capable of?

"Yes," Jules said, then gently squeezed his hands, encouraging him to go on.

"Let's just say Catherine found I wasn't enough for her anymore. And in the end she didn't have a choice about living with Theresa and me."

"You left her?" Jules asked, furrowing her brow. When he didn't immediately answer, she added, "Sorry, it's just most people just say they were cheated on but you said she didn't have a choice about living with you."

"You're very observant." He couldn't resist caressing her cheek.

"Thanks," she said wryly. "It usually gets me into trouble."

She met his gaze and there it was. Connection. That sense of warmth and safety shone in her eyes. It pulled at his defenses, making him want to share his secrets. To learn all of hers. And it had nothing to do with his case.

He reached up and stroked an index finger down her silken cheek. "Does being observant get you into trouble, or is it not listening to your instincts?"

She blinked as if the question surprised her, then gave him a sweet, shy smile. "Both, I guess."

He nodded, then glanced back down to their interlaced hands. Touching her felt so natural, it was hard to tell where he ended and she began. This was something his mother had told him he'd find one day, but he'd doubted her, because he'd never experienced it with Catherine.

"She was an addict," he admitted, not surprised to hear the bitterness in his voice. He never talked about her, about what happened, not with anyone. But he couldn't seem to help himself right now. "She was in a car accident not long before Theresa entered high school. Catherine's left elbow was shattered. It took a year of therapy before she had full mobility, but she was never the same. I didn't know it at the time, but she'd developed an addiction to prescription painkillers.

"I started to suspect something was wrong after finding multiple prescriptions from different doctors, but when I confronted her, she promised she was fine. She even tossed out the pills right in front of me. I'd assumed she was better because I hadn't found another medicine bottle in the house. I was so stupid."

"You trusted your wife," Jules argued. "That's not stupid."

"It is when it puts your child at risk," he retorted. Jules's eyes widened and he regretted snapping at her. "I'm sorry."

He started to pull away, but she tightened her hold on him. "What happened?"

Memories of those last two years with his ex washed through him. "Catherine wasn't some street junkie doing smack. She was my wife and Theresa's mother. I didn't want her to suffer from the shame of being sent to rehab if she could stop on her own. But she'd started hiding the drugs everywhere. I just didn't want to believe it."

"What ended up convincing you?" There was no accusation in her voice, no condemnation. She stared at him with caring in those pools of green light.

"The day Theresa broke her leg at school after she slipped off the stage during play rehearsal." He shook his head as shame washed through him. "T had been different for months. Her grades were falling, she'd started getting in trouble at school, and my sweet little girl was angry all the time. But the day she fell, it all became clear.

"For two hours, Theresa sat in the nurse's office waiting for her mother to pick her up. Theresa started shaking and the nurse feared she was going into shock. So she called an ambulance. Thank God, the paramedic knew me. He radioed the station."

"Why didn't Theresa have them call you to begin with?" Jules asked, her thumb running back and forth over his hand. Her touch was light, gentle, and seemingly unconscious.

"I was in the middle of taking my sergeant's exam and T didn't want to interrupt me. It's only held once a year in Tidewater and there are sixty-five applicants for one position. Theresa knew how long I'd studied to earn the invitation to take the test. She didn't want me to wait another year. So she told the nurse I was out of town to keep her from calling the station."

"Wow." Jules sighed and smiled sympathetically. "How old was she at the time?"

"Thirteen, and she already knew what I didn't. Her mother was an addict who had no intention of ever recovering. My little girl spent so much of her youth cleaning up after her mother and I didn't want to believe it. Not until that day."

The familiar hollow opened in his chest at the memory of how he'd failed to protect his little girl. She was his baby and he loved her more than anything, but he hadn't seen what was right in front of him until it nearly destroyed them both.

"What happened?"

"When I brought Theresa home from the hospital she made me promise to take her pain pills with me to work, so her mother wouldn't steal them."

"Poor Theresa. What a horrible request for her to have to make." Jules's eyes misted.

"It was." He nodded. "In the end, Catherine refused to admit there was a problem. I took Theresa, moved out of the house, and filed for divorce. T and I lived in my apartment." He gestured across the hall. "It was smaller than our house, but in just a few weeks, my happy-go-lucky daughter returned."

"Whatever happened to Catherine?" Jules asked quietly. "Does she keep in touch with Theresa?"

"No." He ground his teeth at the memory. "She's . . ."

He hesitated. It wasn't that he grieved anymore. He just never talked about Catherine. Why was he confessing all this now?

"It's okay, Seth. You don't have to tell me if it's too painful." Jules shifted closer in her chair. She grasped his right hand between both of hers. Giving it a sympathetic squeeze, she then lifted his hand to her lips and kissed his knuckles.

That one simple gesture, so sweet, so compassionate, had him finishing the story.

"Even if it had been possible, I wouldn't have let her near Theresa again." He closed his eyes and remembered the flood of blue and red flashing lights outside the house he'd once shared with Catherine. "Six months before our divorce finalized, there was a shooting at my house. Catherine had spiraled out of control after we left. I later learned she'd been having an affair with my partner on the force. The two of them had taken to dealing pain meds out of the house. Among other things. The report stated there was an argument between them over money. They got into a fight over drugs and she killed him with his own gun before she turned it on herself."

Jules's head snapped up. "She's *dead*? She killed him?"

"Pathetic but yeah." Seth said. "I thank God every day that Theresa and I had moved out when we did."

Even the warmth in Jules's touch didn't negate the chill that ran down his back at the memory. An icy reminder of what could happen when he failed to listen to his instincts. Had he not finally heeded his own internal warnings and his daughter's verbal ones, that day could have been far more tragic. He could have lost Theresa too.

They sat in silence for several minutes. "Did you get to retake the sergeant's exam?" Jules finally asked. That was the last question Seth had expected. "I mean, I can tell that you and Theresa went on. She definitely loves you. That was pretty clear at the restaurant. But you've called yourself Detective English several times. Is that higher than a sergeant?"

Rather than answer her question, he said, "It's getting late. We should get back to the questioning."

"Oh, ri-right." Jules nodded but didn't move away from him. Compassion and warmth still shimmered in her eyes. It made him want to reach out and kiss her.

Instead, he pulled away from her touch and picked up his notebook. Scanning it, he realized he'd asked the only remaining question he had on the case. "Well, it seems you did answer all my questions."

"But you only asked me about Mason tonight."

"And you said you hadn't been in touch with him in five years. That pretty much takes care of the rest of my questions." He picked up his half-empty wineglass to finish it off. After talking about Catherine, he really needed a stiffer drink, but wine would suffice.

"I'm really glad you came to dinner tonight." Jules surprised him with the sincerity of her words.

He gazed at her over the rim of his glass. She looked so damned sweet and open. He wanted to kiss her. He wanted to lose himself in her, but what were the odds she'd want to touch him now that she knew what an idiot he'd been? "Thanks for the nice evening."

"Oh, okay then." Jules didn't sound sad, merely surprised.

When she didn't invite him to stay longer, he turned and headed to the door. He'd almost reached it when he realized he still held his wineglass. Spinning around, he came face-to-face with Jules, who carried her own empty stemware. He hadn't even realized she'd left her chair, let alone followed him.

"Seth?"

"Yeah?" He handed her his wineglass.

She stared at it for a moment, then frowned. "I'm sorry you didn't get to take the sergeant's exam."

"I will. I'll get another chance to take the test when I solve this case, *these* cases," he corrected. "The jewelry store thefts and the murder are tied together, I know it. Once I prove that and solve them, I'll be invited to take the sergeant's exam next spring."

Jules leaned forward and kissed him lightly on the cheek. "For luck."

His cheek burned where her lips had brushed his skin. Electricity zinged from that innocent little peck. He craved more. He'd wanted her from the first moment he'd seen her but had denied himself for the case.

She stepped back, but before she could go far, he captured her face between his hands and tilted her head up.

CHAPTER 10

Jules saw it coming. He gave her plenty of time to pull away. Instead she rose up on her tiptoes and met him halfway.

The touch of his lips on hers sent a sizzled excitement down her spine. She savored the feel of his arms wrapping around her body, his chest pressing against her breasts and the heady scent of him.

Oh, how she wanted this man. She knew one kiss and she'd want to drown in his embrace. She'd been right but she hadn't expected it to be this explosive, this needy. But that was okay because he wanted her too.

She could taste it in the sensual way his mouth glided over hers. His kisses were light, like butterfly wings fluttering against her lips. She rose up higher, pressing her lips more fully against his and driving her tongue into his mouth.

He groaned and switched from gently exploring her mouth to feasting on her. His kisses were an intoxicating combination of hungry, gentle, and commanding. Still it felt as if he held back, just a little. Like a warrior leashing his passion.

Her pulse jumped, her hands—still wrapped around the stemware—shook, and her body seemed to come alive until every nerve ending screamed for his touch. She closed her eyes and let herself revel in the sensations pouring through her.

No one ever made her body sing from just a kiss before. Dang! She might need to see a doctor about that. It couldn't be healthy. But boy was it fun. And scary.

"Jules," Seth said, pulling back slightly, but never letting go of her. He shifted to trailing hot, light kisses across her cheek, down her neck and back again.

"Yeah?" she answered, her breath exhaling in staccato gasps at his incredible touch.

"Open your eyes."

Against her will, she listened and was caught in the maelstrom of passion in his gaze. He'd stopped kissing her but was stroking her cheek with the backs of his long, warm fingers. His movements might not have been sensual if not for the hungry look in his darkening eyes. He licked his lips.

Her body pressed even closer to his as if being pulled by a magnet. She couldn't resist rubbing her breasts against his rock-hard chest.

His sexy lips curled into a grin. He lowered his face to hers while his warm fingers massaged the back of her neck. But he didn't return to kissing her.

And she didn't just want him to kiss her. She craved it.

"Don't tease me, Seth," she said.

"Ah, *precious*." He said her nickname like a prayer. "I won't tease. Just one last thing."

"What?" If he didn't stop talking and kiss her again soon, she might just scream.

"I'm officially finished questioning you."

He swooped down, pressing his warm, amazingly soft lips against hers. She melted. He stroked his tongue inside her mouth, and she'd been right. He'd been holding back before. No longer. His kisses were needy, passionate, and so hungry that they enflamed her.

For a moment she let him guide the kiss, then she thrust her tongue into his mouth and fought for dominance. He moaned, kicking up the kiss. He wrapped one hand around her ponytail and held her still as he ravaged her mouth.

And she surrendered to the sensation before she tried to seize control again. She had no intention of letting him dominate her, but his kiss made her knees weak. She wanted to stroke him but the wineglasses in her hands kept her from doing it.

Break the kiss and put the glasses down or keep going?

Seth effectively decided for her when he slid his hand from behind her head to between her breasts. He plucked at one of her nipples through her clothing. Electric pulses ricocheted from her breasts to between her thighs. Her knees went from weak to complete jelly.

She threw her arms around his shoulders, hugging him closer as she drove her tongue into his mouth. Her tongue slid over and under his as their breath mingled. He grunted as he tightened an arm around her waist while his free hand continued the exquisite torture of first her right nipple, then her left.

He started to back up, tugging her along with him. She followed until the wineglasses in her hand clinked against each other between Seth and the door he now rested against.

She needed to put the glasses down before she ended up smashing them against the wood. Glass splinters in Seth's back would definitely kill the mood.

Without breaking the kiss, she ambled backward, away from the door. Moaning when he ran his tongue over her upper lip, she released his shoulders and spread her arms. Blindly, she stretched her arms behind her, searching for the table.

It had to be somewhere close. She waved at empty air as she tried to continue the kiss and put the glasses down at the same time.

"Jules, what are you doing?" Seth panted the words as he trailed his lips to her cheek. Even as he asked the question he kept up the torture on her breasts. Oh my!

Is it possible to orgasm from nipple play alone?

"The ta—ah, ooh! Um . . . need . . . the . . . table," she panted.

Seth yanked back, releasing her completely. Jules stumbled, but before she fell, Seth caught her by the elbows. As if seeing the wineglasses in her hands for the first time, he stared at them.

His dark eyes blazed, even as he glanced from the glasses to the table, then to her face.

"For the glasses?" he asked, but then must have answered his own question, because he plucked the stemware from her hands and quickly set them down.

Pulling her flush against him, Seth clapped one hand to her backside and wrapped the other around her head. The kiss he delivered now made a mockery of the passion in the last one.

As he kissed her, he lifted her off her feet. Walking the few paces back to the door, he spun them both around. Hard wood pressed against her back while warm, muscled male pressed against her front.

He kneaded her backside as he plundered her mouth.

And Jules wanted more. Opening herself to him, she looped one leg over his hip. His hands glided up and down her back. He traced the skin exposed between the hem of her sweater and the top of her jeans.

Dang! He had no such skin exposure. She settled for tangling her fingers in the thick, curly black hair at the nape of his neck and reveled in the silken feel.

Seth trailed his mouth down her chin to her neck and then up to nibble on her earlobe. His hands slid beneath her shirt, touching her bare waist, and she shivered.

Needing more of his drugging kiss, she grabbed his head with both hands and brought his face to hers. He smiled against her lips as, once again, he captured her mouth.

His warm, sinful fingers traced a path from the middle of her back to her belly. She needed his touch on her breasts. Already oversensitized by his ministrations, they ached for naked contact. Without thinking, she wrapped her fingers around his right wrist and shoved his hand up her sweater.

Seth hissed in pleasure then yanked away the lace bra covering her. His touch had her nearly crying out but he covered her mouth with his again. His tongue swept in and out at a driving speed as he started to grind his lower body against hers.

All the time, he rolled and lightly pinched her nipple between his fingers. He pulled and tugged until it was a hard point pressing against his palm, then lightly grazed his hand across it.

"Seth." Jules gasped and arched her back, thrusting against his palm. Desire pooled low in her belly. A rush of moisture at the apex of her thighs made her slick with need. He slipped his other hand beneath her sweater to give her other breast some much-needed attention.

She rubbed the back of her calf against his firm backside, pulling him tighter against her. She was so wound up, she was little more than a huge throbbing mass of aching need and desire.

She whimpered and he softened his touch, only making her crazier.

"Shhh . . . ," he said. "Don't fight it. Just feel, Jules."

"Believe me," she replied. "All I can do right now is feel."

"Good." He made a sound that was a cross between a groan and a chuckle, then he grasped her thigh with his left hand and ground his hugely aroused body against hers.

The act ignited a fire that burned through her. Her body aching for release, she rubbed herself against him more. Just a little bit longer and she'd be flying. A small moan escaped her lips, answered by one from him.

His fingers trailed to the waistband of her jeans. Her belly quivered; heck, her whole body shook. She bowed her back and sucked in her tummy, giving him plenty of room to reach down into her jeans. The act had been instinctual, and the moment she'd realized she'd done it, she tried to straighten.

"Stay," he said, pressing his knuckles against her navel and stroking her skin with the backs of his fingers. "I've got you, precious."

His thumb and forefinger toyed with the button on her fly.

An icy wind whipped through the room. The curtains covering the living room flapped, revealing an open window. The glasses on the table behind them toppled. Glass splintered in different directions.

Then the room went dark. Literally. The lights flickered, and when they came back on, it was as if someone had dumped an invisible bucket of ice water on them both.

"Whoa!" Seth said as he glanced around the space. He cast her a confused stare, then set her away from him.

Jules sighed and had no choice but to uncoil her legs from his hips. Standing where he'd left her, she watched Seth cross the room.

He stuck his head outside, searching for whoever opened

the window. He needn't have bothered. It's not like he could have seen the source anyway.

The ghost did it. Jules was certain. And she had a thing or two to say to that interfering little menace when she saw her again.

"I don't see anyone," Seth said, searching the kitchen. He closed the window, locked it, then turned to face Jules with his hands on his hips. "Keep your windows locked. There've been some break-ins recently."

"But you left yours open?" Jules countered, trying to lighten the mood.

Seth raised a single brow. "And look how well it turned out for the last person to climb through it."

"Wonderfully, from my point of view," Jules couldn't resist replying.

"True." Seth chuckled, then frowned again and crossed his arms over his chest. "Still, you're not me. Keep your windows locked. You're going to be alone tomorrow, with Ernie and April gone. I don't want to have to worry about you."

Then it happened. The ghost materialized. Sort of. She appeared in the windowpane behind Seth, at the same moment the room temperature dropped.

"Brrr . . ." Seth shuddered and glanced around, then took several long strides toward Jules. "There's a pretty big draft coming from the window. Tomorrow you need to call the super to seal it."

"Yes, sir!" Jules gave a mock salute.

"Ha, ha." He rubbed his arms with his hands. "Please, *precious*, call the super tomorrow."

"Okay, I'll call as soon as I return from the airport."

The ghost's aura glowed a brighter shade of yellow than Jules had ever seen it. It was as if she was closer to finding peace or crossing over. The girl glanced from Seth to Jules, her lips moving the entire time.

Jules squinted, trying to read the specter's lips, but she couldn't make out her words.

I don't understand. Jules projected her thoughts quickly, then glanced to Seth, who once again seemed occupied with finding the source of the draft.

The ghost's aura darkened to a murky brownish-yellow and

further to dark, thunderous gray. The color change seemed to suck the remaining warmth from the room.

Jules's skin crawled. Clamping her jaw, she focused all her energy on sending a single thought to the angry spirit.

Please don't scream at me, I swear I'm trying.

To her surprise, the ghost's aura lightened again. Not as bright as before, she appeared bathed in a hazy yellowish-brown glow. A tremulous smile quivered at the edges of her lips.

"Well, you have an early morning," Seth said, suddenly. He turned and crossed the room to where Jules stood by the door. "I had a wonderful time tonight."

"Me too," Jules said, unsure what to do or say next.

Seth solved her confusion by leaning down and pressing a kiss to her cheek. "How about dinner tomorrow night?"

Certain the delight showed in her face, Jules nodded. "That would be great."

Seth smiled wide. "Pick you up at seven." He gave her one last kiss. Not as sinful as the others, but it left her breathless just the same. "Good night."

He opened the door and strode through it. She watched until he crossed the hall and went into his apartment before closing her door.

Pressing her back against the wall, she tried to come up with a reason why dating Seth was a bad thing. Okay, so he was a cop. But at that moment, it didn't seem as terrible to her as it had before. A giddiness bubbled up inside her, then the room went cold again.

Jules glanced over to the window, now covered by the curtains. A faded image of the ghost hovered just inside the room. She mouthed a single word before she faded away.

"Seth."

CHAPTER 11

SETH HAD BARELY stepped into the station when all hell broke loose. And it came in the form of a middle-aged woman in an expensively tailored red suit. She stood at the front desk, yelling at the young officer on duty.

"Someone had better help me, *right now*, young man. Or I swear to *God*, I will see to it that every one of you is fired! Now get your captain on the phone and tell him Iris Masters will speak to him now, or the next call I'll make is to the mayor!"

She slapped something down on the desk, but Seth couldn't see it from his position. The young officer gaped at the woman, then over her shoulder at Seth.

As the highest-ranking officer in the building at the unearthly hour of six thirty in the morning, Seth intervened. "Excuse me, may I help you?"

The woman spun on him. Her short silver hair framed a pretty face. Her light gray eyes narrowed on him. "Are you the captain?"

"No, ma'am. My name is Detective English." He extended

his hand in greeting. "The captain isn't in yet. Perhaps I might assist you."

The woman's features crumpled and her eyes turned glassy as she fought her tears. "My daughter, Aimee-Lynn, is missing and I'm tired of being told to wait to report it."

She held up a picture of a beautiful young woman who bore a resemblance to the victim found in the Dumpster on Saturday. Seth took the photo from Iris Masters. He gestured down the hallway to the interrogation room. "Come with me."

BANG, BANG, BANG!

Jules bolted upright in her bed. Someone was pounding on her front door. Thank God, she'd already driven Big Jim and April to the airport. The racket would have woken them up.

Bang, bang, bang!

She glanced at the clock; it was half past eight. Grumbling, she yanked on a pair of sleep pants and straightened her tank top as she half walked, half hopped down the hall, tugging on her slippers.

When the banging started a third time, she yelled, "Coming! Keep your knickers on!"

Still overtired, she rubbed the sleep out of her eyes, not paying attention to the boxes littering the apartment until she stubbed her toe. With a yelp of pain, she kept moving forward but glanced backward in time to slam her knee into the corner of the coffee table.

"Owww! Shoot!" she hissed under her breath.

Bang, bang, bang, bang, bang, bang.

"Jeez, what's the emergency?" she snapped.

The front door flew open under its own steam but there was no one on the other side. Jules took an automatic step back. Somehow the corridor beyond the door seemed to move closer to her.

Empty and eerily silent, late morning light filtered into the hallway like a spotlight from the large round window overlooking the top of the stairs. Dust motes floated in the rays of sunshine and the world seemed totally at peace.

Seconds later, an icy chill rolled down her back. She glanced around, but time seemed to have stopped. The dust motes hung in the air as if suspended on strings. The morning light changed from vibrant streams to dull shafts of stale sunshine and they appeared to arrow through the icy cold like golden knives pointing to the floor at her feet.

Jules glanced down to her blue-painted toenails. On the floor, in the middle of the light, a series of brilliant, glittery red rocks spelled out the letter *P*. The rocks, maybe rubies, seemed to sparkle from all different directions, until the light they cast grew blinding and painful.

Covering her aching eyes with her right hand, Jules took two steps forward and slammed the door closed, locking it with shaking fingers.

"Give it to him!" The words slashed through her mind. Could mental thoughts alone lacerate her brain? *"Do it now before someone else dies!"*

Clutching one hand to her head, which was now throbbing in agony, Jules dropped to the floor and curled into a ball. Where the hallway had been filled with oppressive light, the living room went unearthly dark. Sound and light were sucked into a vacuum and she was left with the paralyzing reality that the ghost wasn't finished yet.

Then she heard it.

The cry of a baby. Weak, sad. The sound cut through her like a knife.

Swinging her head from left to right, she peered into the blackening room for the infant.

No baby. Only the ghost hovered nearby. Her muddy red aura pulsed around her. Crystalline tears tracked down her cheeks. *"You must do it, today."*

The sound of thousands of nails shrieking down chalkboards echoed in her ears again, sending a rush of tears pricking her eyes. She clapped her hands to her ears and sent a mental plea to the angry spirit. *"Please. I'll do what you want. Tell me what you want me to give and who I should give it to—"*

The ghost screamed. Jules lifted her head in time to see the room erupt into flowing crimson. Red saturated the room like someone had splashed buckets of blood on everything.

The room began to spin. Then the vision started again. The Buick, the desperate search for a way out of the trunk, the smell of blood in the confined space . . . and Jules was there. Reliving the ghost's murder.

Helpless to do more than ride the vision, Jules lay still. Beneath her body, the trunk's carpeting scratched against her skin.

"I'm not in the trunk," she whispered to herself in a desperate attempt to hang on to her sanity. "I'm home."

But as the vision continued, she disconnected from herself and became the victim.

My name is Aimee-Lynn.

The awareness of being someone other than Juliana Scott was enough to pause the vision, like a DVD. Had the ghost spoken or just remembered suddenly? Either way, Jules heard her.

"Do you remember your killer?" Jules winged the question mentally.

Aimee-Lynn didn't answer. Instead, the nightmare started playing again, louder and in a high-def that techno geeks would have killed to produce.

Cold, leather-encased hands squeezed her naked throat. She gasped and wheezed, fighting for breath. As the life slipped from her body, the vision faded. Once again, Jules was in her apartment, alone. Blackness descended, and just before she succumbed to the peace, Aimee-Lynn's voice floated gently through her mind.

"Give it to him and finish what I started."

THE MORNING HAD been a royal pain in the ass. Mondays always sucked at the station. Today transcended from merely sucking into shitsville.

"Christ!" Seth glared at the glossy 8x10 photo, then shoved it into the McGivern's file and dropped it onto his desk. He pulled out his chair and sank into it.

He'd suspected the Dumpster victim had been his tipster, Aimee-Lynn. He'd been right. Worse, he hadn't spent twenty minutes with Iris Masters before he learned it had been her red diamond ring stolen from the Holcomb robbery. Why the hell would Aimee-Lynn steal her mother's diamond only to contact him with information about it? It didn't make sense.

The moment she'd identified Aimee-Lynn's body, her tough-as-nails façade shattered. Captain Peterson had arrived and personally driven the woman home. A sure sign that Iris's threat to call the mayor hadn't been a hollow one.

Now, Seth was back to no suspects and a dead tipster.

Damn it! He was running in circles. Scrubbing a weary hand down his face, Seth yawned. He needed a break in the case that actually might help him. He needed sleep. He needed . . . Jules.

Where had that thought come from?

Probably from his lack of sleep and the fact that he could still taste her on his lips. Whenever he'd closed his eyes last night, he'd pictured her naked beneath him. Several times between midnight and six this morning, he'd debated going back to her apartment and finishing what they'd started.

He couldn't explain why they'd stopped. Well, yes, he could. The window. He was almost certain it had been closed when he arrived. Almost, but not entirely. After all, he couldn't exactly see the window past the boxes in the living room. At least, not until the curtain started to blow in the wind.

Tonight, before they went to dinner, Seth would make sure all of the windows in Jules's apartment were closed and locked. For safety's sake, he'd draw all the curtains too. Any thief glancing in her living room window might see the boxes as a chance for a smash and grab.

And if Jules didn't like it, he might just have to convince her to sleep at his place.

The thought of Jules in his bed brought a smile to his lips.

"Morning," Jones said, dropping his jacket on the back of his chair and sitting down. The man appeared well rested, leaning back casually in his chair. "Anything new on the case?"

Seth grimaced. "Unfortunately. But it requires coffee before I start talking about it."

"None left." Jones shook his head and hiked a thumb over his shoulder toward Reynolds and O'Dell. "They finished off the last of the pot just before I got to it. I've started brewing another."

Seth glared at his two ex-partners who appeared engrossed in an oh-so-mature game of punch tag. "Damn, I could really use a caffeine IV." Since none was available, he focused on their case. Handing the file to Jones, he described his morning. "So we're back to square one."

"Holy shit!" Jones lifted the photo from the file, then dropped it again. He spun to his computer and started typing. A minute later, he sat back in his chair, a satisfied smile on his face. "Want some good news?"

Without waiting for a reply, Jones rotated his monitor on its base so Seth could see it. The heading on the website read "Recently Engaged." The center of the screen displayed a man and a woman, smiling and wrapped in each other's arms. It was Aimee-Lynn and . . .

"Mason Hart!" Seth bounced his gaze from the screen to Jones and back again. "Sonofabitch! Her mother didn't mention him."

"Probably because they broke up two days *after* the Holcomb robbery." Jones scrolled the screen down to an addendum announcing the wedding had been canceled.

"Aimee-Lynn's mother said she'd been withdrawn for the last seven weeks, but that last week it had all changed. What happened?"

Jones shrugged. "Good question. But I've got a better one. Why would someone knowingly keep her mother's stolen diamond ring, only to call the police with a tip about it?"

"And where is it now?" Seth asked with a frown.

Jones scrolled the screen back down until the smiling couple was centered on it. "Where do we go from here?"

"To interview Hart. Let's see if he can shed some light on what happened to his relationship with his fiancée." Seth frowned and gestured to the monitor. "How'd you find this?"

"She was in the society section of the paper two months ago," Jones returned the monitor to its normal position. "I remembered seeing it."

"You read the society column, do you?" O'Dell interrupted.

Reynolds cackled like a hyena. Seth glared at both intruders as they perched their annoying asses on the corners of Seth and Jones's desks. O'Dell fingered the McGivern file while Reynolds picked up the photo.

"Laugh it up, boys, but less than three hours ago, this girl's mother filed a missing persons report." Seth leaned across his desk and plucked the picture out of Reynolds's hands. "We now have the name of our murder victim from the Dumpster."

"You sure?" O'Dell frowned as he looked at the photo. "She seems too pretty to have had a tramp stamp. I thought the vic had one of those."

"I'm positive." Seth frowned at the conversation's odd segue.

"Pretty doesn't make you smart," Reynolds retorted. "I mean, come on, you'd have to be a complete jackass to intentionally mutilate your body to begin with."

"Or young and stupid," O'Dell agreed, then cut his gaze to Jones.

"What's that supposed to mean?" Jones asked, his normally even tone sharp with indignation.

"Back off, assholes." Seth glared at his former partners.

O'Dell and Reynolds shared a surprised glance, then laughed.

"Don't get your panties in a twist, *girls*," O'Dell said, pushing off the desk. He nodded to his partner and Reynolds stood up too. "So aside from learning your victim's name, how is your case coming?"

"Fine." Seth ground his teeth. He knew where this was going. The clock was ticking, and with each passing day his former partners acted more like rabid animals who smelled fresh meat. They wanted his case. Well, he'd be damned before he let them have it. "But we need to get back to work."

"You do that." O'Dell shrugged and started toward the kitchen with Reynolds beside him.

"Assholes," Jones muttered under his breath.

Surprised by his partner's uncharacteristic remark, Seth glanced at Jones. "Ignore them."

Jones's cheeks were mottled red and he rubbed at his left biceps. "That's such crap. I know PhD's with tattoos. Just because you have one doesn't make you stupid."

The kid seemed to take Reynolds and O'Dell's comments personally. Again, out of character for the young detective. "Kid, let it go. They're dicks."

Jones glared at him.

"*Detective* Jones." Seth waited until his partner stopped

glaring. "You're right. I happen to know a bright, beautiful woman with a tattoo of three intricately designed roses. She didn't do it out of stupidity or youthful foolishness. She did it to honor her sisters. She even had their names put in each one." Seth stretched his arms wide, cracking his back. "Don't let the idiot twins rile you."

An inscrutable expression crossed Jones's face.

"You all right, kid?"

"Y-yeah." Jones blinked twice. "Thanks."

O'Dell and Reynolds strode out of the kitchen and past Seth's desk at that moment, heading toward the captain's office.

Seth pushed to his feet. "Time to report in."

"Don't you think we should interview Hart as soon as possible?" Jones asked, rising to his feet.

"Yes, but right now, we don't even know where to find him." Seth tugged on his jacket.

"I do," Jones answered. "He's at the Tidewater Country Club."

That gave Seth pause and raised the hairs on the back of his neck. "Fifteen minutes ago, we didn't know Hart was involved at all. How is it you know where he is right now?"

Jones's expression turned sheepish. "Our mothers were sorority sisters. They kept in touch. The Harts have eaten breakfast at the club every morning for as long as I can remember."

"Your family dines regularly at country clubs?"

Jones swallowed but shook his head. A crimson stain darkened his cheeks. "No, my-my mother's maiden name was McKinnon. It's why I keep an eye on the society section. It's the only way I can keep up with my childhood friends."

Seth's eyes widened. The McKinnons were Tidewater's version of the Kennedys, old money and political power. And it explained much about Jones's taciturn ways. The kid could have thrown his family name around to get what he wanted. He didn't. Instead, he appeared rather embarrassed to admit it at all.

And it gave Seth a newfound respect for his partner. "Okay. Then let's see if we can't get over to the country club before he leaves."

Captain Peterson appeared in his office doorway. A frown

dug a deep wrinkle in his forehead. "English. Jones. Would the two of you like to join me for the morning briefing?"

"Sir, we've just received a tip on the case," Seth said, gathering up his supplies. "We need to go uptown and interview a potential suspect."

"Who?"

"Mason Hart."

The captain rolled his eyes and a tic worked in his jaw. "I know you didn't just tell me the two of you plan to interrogate the son of the wealthiest businessman in the city."

"Captain, Hart might possess knowledge pertinent to our case," Seth explained.

"*Might* isn't good enough." The captain shook his head. "The last time someone started asking that family questions, we got our asses handed to us. You'd better have something substantially stronger than *might*."

"Sir, his mother and mine are old friends," Jones said.

"Do you think he'll talk to you?" The captain asked, clearly not surprised by the information. It made Seth wonder how many secrets his current partner kept from him.

"Although I haven't seen the Harts in years, I bet Mason would be receptive to me." Jones met Seth's gaze levelly, then added, "I can go over there and ask him one or two questions without raising his suspicions. I doubt he even knows I'm on the force."

Seth's stomach shrank. *Jones was asking to go alone?*

The captain ran a hand over his sweaty bald head, sneezed, then said, "English, we need to discuss what happened with Iris Masters. I need you here. Jones, go conduct the interview but be discreet and get your ass back here pronto."

Captain Peterson disappeared back inside his office. This was exactly how it had happened before. His rookie partner was sent to do the actual investigative work, while Seth played office politics.

And the sergeant's exam seemed to slip a little further out of reach.

Still, someone needed to check out Hart as soon as possible. If the rich prick was sniffing around Jules, he might assume she knew more about the murder than she did. Seth couldn't risk her getting hurt.

Turning to Jones, he said, "Make sure you get his alibi for the murder, not just the jewelry heists."

"Of course." Jones stared at him, another enigmatic look on his face.

"Call me the moment you have something." Seth watched the door to the captain's office swing open again and Peterson appeared, his arms crossed over his chest. "If Hart's the killer, we need to know now."

Because if he was, Jules could be in danger.

A RAY OF sunshine cut a warm swath across her cheek and Jules sat up. Rubbing her head, she glanced around the living room. For a moment, she struggled to remember how she got there, then the memory of the vision slammed into her.

She leapt to her feet. *Ooh, stood up too fast.* She swayed, threw out her arms to steady herself, then walked toward the kitchen and glanced up at the clock. Only twenty minutes had passed since she'd first heard the banging on the door.

Thank heavens. She still had time to recover before going to the shop.

Only slightly queasy from the side effects of the vision, she walked across the room and to the bathroom.

She showered, dried her hair, and dressed, all the time wondering what that glittering *P* in the vision could have stood for and coming up empty.

At least this time she'd learned something new. The ghost was named Aimee-Lynn. What Jules didn't understand was why Aimee-Lynn, who'd now been haunting her for three days, still could do little better than cheap parlor tricks when it came to communicating.

Jules headed down the hall and into the kitchen for a glass of milk. Before opening the door, her gaze fell on the business card she'd received yesterday.

Tidewater Security Specialists. *When others can't, we will.*

She'd promised herself that she wouldn't allow anything to distract her from finding her sisters. *No time like the present.*

Plucking the card from beneath the magnet, she carried it to the counter, picked up the cordless phone, and dialed the number on the card.

She expected to hear a recording, so was surprised when a deep, masculine voice said, "Tidewater Security Specialists. When others can't, we will. This is Ian."

"Hi. My name is Juliana Scott. Abigail Harris recommended I call you."

"Mrs. Harris, huh? How's she doing?" Ian asked.

"She seemed good." Jules tapped her fingers on the counter as she spoke. "I don't really know her very well. She's an old friend of my family's. But she suggested I call you and mention her name."

He laughed. "Sounds like Mrs. H. is calling in a favor, then. So what can I do for you?"

Jules hesitated. "I'm trying to locate two women. My younger sisters. We were placed in the foster care system about fourteen years ago. The social workers couldn't keep us together. Mrs. Harris was able to track one of my sisters, Shelley. Well, until her adoptive parents died five years ago. Hannah is a different story. She had a private adoption. Mrs. Harris doesn't know much more than that."

Ian drew in a breath between his teeth. "You're hiring us to locate two women who were adopted by different families fourteen years ago? And you don't know the names of the family who adopted one of them?"

Her heart sank. "It's impossible, isn't it?"

"No, ma'am." Ian paused. Scratching noises floated through the phone as if he were jotting down notes. "*Impossible* is not a word in the TSS vocabulary. It'll take time and money, but if Mrs. H. sent you to us, we can work out a deal."

"You're going to help me?" Hope swelled inside her.

"Absolutely," he said. "Now, tell me everything you know about Shelley and Hannah, starting with their full names and birth dates."

They spent the next fifteen minutes discussing her sisters, his plans for locating them, and the fees. After she'd given him everything he requested, he hit her with a question she didn't have the answer to. "Do you have their social security numbers? That would be the fastest way to locate them."

"No, I don't. We were children when we were separated. I know Shelley had one, but Hannah was only three. I'm not sure she had one before she was adopted."

"No worries," he replied. "I'll bet she did. I'll contact Mrs. H. to see if I can get my hands on it." More note scribbling sounded through the phone. "I think I have enough to get started. Ms. Scott, go through your old scrapbooks, if you have any, and write down what you remember about your sisters and their foster families. Next, gather up any old pictures you have of them. I'll have one of our team members contact you in a day or two."

"You won't be meeting with me?"

"No, sorry." He gave a slight chuckle. "I'm headed out on an assignment to Seattle this morning. But we have several highly trained members at TSS. Any one of them will do an excellent job for you."

When she didn't do more than murmur a noncommittal response, he added, "We mean what we say. When others can't, we *will*."

Buoyed by his words, Jules thanked him and hung up.

Returning the card to the refrigerator, she then opened the door and pulled out the milk jug.

She poured herself a half glass, all that was left in the container, when she remembered she was supposed to call Mason. His number wasn't on the fridge. She'd left it in her purse. Hurrying back to her bedroom, she grabbed the fake Prada then returned to the kitchen. She dug through it, pulled out the gold-foiled card, and dialed his number.

Listening to it ring, she rinsed out the milk jug, then dropped it in the recycling bin behind the trash can beneath the counter.

"Hello?" Mason answered.

"Hi, Mason, it's Jules. How are you?"

"Hi, um . . . I-I really can't talk right now," he said, his voice muffled.

Great! He probably forgot that he asked me to call. "Oh, okay. I was just keeping my promise to call."

"I really appreciate that," he said quickly. "I'm going to be tied up most of today. How about we meet tomorrow morning at the Tidewater Country Club for breakfast?"

"Um . . . that's very generous, but we can just eat at The Jewish Mother." The country club was a little out of her comfort zone.

"It's no problem. You'll like it at the club. Nine o'clock?" he persisted, as if he hadn't heard her counteroffer. There was something in his tone that worried her. An anxious sound, maybe?

"S-sure, the club. That's fine," Jules replied. "Mason, is everything okay?"

"Definitely," he said. "See you then."

The dial tone buzzed in her ear. Jules glanced at the phone briefly then hung up.

Now what?

She'd made the phone calls she'd promised herself she'd make. The shop didn't open for another three hours, and Aimee-Lynn-the-ghost appeared to be gone.

"Aimee-Lynn?" she called out, just to be certain the ghost really wasn't there. She wasn't.

Jules wished she had someone to talk to. Not just anyone but someone who might be able to shed some light on how to make Aimee-Lynn go away. Normally she would have asked April and Big Jim, but they were in Florida. Not that they knew how to handle the situation, just that they were the only people she'd met in the past fourteen years who wouldn't think she was insane-o girl for talking to spirits.

Who could she ask? She opened the fridge to grab a pear for breakfast. She really needed to go to the grocery store today. The only thing left in the fridge was the leftover lasagna from last night's dinner. Unless she wanted to eat only pasta for breakfast, lunch, and dinner, it would go bad before she could finish it. "What am I going to do with this lasagna?"

And in a flash of inspiration, she thought of who to ask for help.

CHAPTER 12

"SHE WAS PREGNANT?" Seth shifted his weight on the squeaky leather chair and leaned forward. Why were they just receiving this information now? "Her mother didn't tell me that."

The captain nodded and held a hand in the air as the ME's voice filled the room through the speakerphone. "No doubt about it. She was about five months along when she was murdered. The fetus appeared to be healthy at the time of its mother's demise."

"Thank you, Clark," the captain said. "Anything else you can tell us?"

"Yes, the victim had a rare disorder called antiphospholipid syndrome, sometimes called sticky blood syndrome. If left untreated, it can produce blood clots. It's especially of a concern when the patient is pregnant, as ours was.

"When the body was stripped, my assistant discovered a syringe in her pocket. Tests confirmed it contained heparin, a common treatment for someone with this syndrome. The injection would have needed to have occurred once daily, but why she chose to do it at three in the morning made little sense to me. Most pregnant women require rest. Shouldn't she have been sleeping around that time?" Clark continued to talk about the victim's exact illness, but Seth tuned him out.

Except our victim was also a jewel thief who spent most of her nights awake.

Seth scrubbed a hand down his face and glanced at his captain. What a waste of two lives. Damn, when he'd thought the victim had been killed for her role in the burglaries he'd felt little pity. No honor among thieves, no matter what people claimed. But what kind of sick bastard kills a pregnant woman?

Seth rose, crossed to the coffeepot Peterson kept full in his office, and poured himself a cup. The captain raised his empty mug in the air. Bringing the coffeepot to him, Seth filled his boss's mug then returned the pot to its stand.

"Thanks, Clark." The captain ended the call and disconnected the line. After taking a sip from his mug, he turned a steely gaze to Seth. "This case has changed. The dead woman wasn't some random vic. Do you know who her mother is?"

"Iris Masters," O'Dell said, straightening his tie. "The Tidewater Parker Foundation's biggest contributor."

O'Dell and Reynolds had been so quiet, Seth had almost forgotten they were there, lurking. Waiting for a chance to snake his case away from him.

"I'm not surprised *you* remember her, O'Dell. She's the woman you told to wait before filing a missing person's case on her daughter Saturday morning," Peterson said, jabbing a finger in O'Dell's direction.

"In my defense, Captain . . ." O'Dell's normal smirk was replaced with a look of genuine concern. "It's standard procedure."

"Not the point." Peterson growled the words.

Seth shouldn't be relieved to learn that O'Dell had failed to help the victim's mother. And in truth, he wasn't. He was disgusted, but it did alleviate some of his concern about his ex-partners stealing his case.

"I don't get it," Reynolds said. "This chick was from a wealthy, influential family. Why would she turn jewel thief?"

"Good question," O'Dell said. "Why would she?"

"No. The real question is, how am I supposed to tell her

mother—a personal friend of the mayor's, I might add—that not only was her pregnant daughter murdered, but she may have had a hand in stealing Mrs. Master's $350,000 red diamond ring?"

"The victim *was* part of the robbery," Seth said. "There's no doubt about it. She may have had a change of heart though. I told you my informant didn't show on Saturday. Well, her name was Aimee-Lynn too. I'm willing to bet my salary my informant is our victim."

"There's something else I don't get. Why did she wait to steal the diamond when it was on display?" O'Dell asked. "Why not take it when it was still in her home?"

All three men turned inquisitive stares toward Seth. But he couldn't answer those questions himself. He had a few theories, but none he was willing to share with the two men drooling like Pavlov's dogs over a chance to take the lead on *his* case.

Unfortunately, he didn't have much of a choice about revealing one tidbit when the captain asked, "Why were you and Jones so eager to interview Mason Hart about this case?"

"The heir to Hart Industries?" Reynolds's jaw went slack.

"Yeah." Seth nodded, then explained about Jones stumbling across the newspaper clipping.

Peterson nodded, then said, "Fine. Now, what about the witness who jumped into the Dumpster?"

"Jules?" Seth asked, surprised the conversation had come back around to her.

"Jules?" the captain repeated. "That a first name or a last?"

"Nickname," Seth answered, then quickly added, "Juliana Scott, but she's clean. She's got nothing to do with this case."

"You're sure?" Peterson frowned.

"Positive." Although Seth did wonder why Hart—*Jules's old friend*—suddenly popped up to see Jules the day after his ex-fiancée was murdered. Yeah, he wondered, all right. And worried.

JULES BALANCED THE sealed container of warmed lasagna on one hand and a tray holding two hot coffees in the other. Clutching her purse tightly beneath her right arm, she made her way outside through the front door of her building and around to the back alley.

Sunshine washed between the buildings, illuminating everything but the deepest corners of the alley. And there, in the far right corner, nestled next to a huge green garbage bin, lay Samuel.

Approaching him cautiously, Jules held out the plate of food, hoping to entice him to come toward her. He didn't. He appeared to be sleeping soundly. Setting the container and one of the coffees down beside him, Jules straightened.

Moira shimmered into being beside her.

Jules turned and faced the spirit. Moira's aura pulsed white as she glanced from Jules to Samuel and back again.

"Thank you," Moira said. *"He went to sleep hungry."*

"Why? I gave him money last night." Jules projected her thoughts to the ghost. "Did someone steal it?"

Moira smiled. *"No. He used it to buy bread for the shelter. He only accepted a single sandwich as payment."*

Jules glanced down at Samuel's sleeping form. In repose, beneath the mountain of clothes, he looked angelic despite the thick smudges of dirt on his cheeks.

"Thank you again for taking care of him," Moira said, then shimmered out of existence.

"Wait!" Jules called out before remembering she needn't have spoken.

Moira returned. *"Yes?"*

"Do you know a spirit named Aimee-Lynn?"

"I'm sorry, I don't know her." Moira shook her head. *"Is she a friend of yours?"*

"No, she's not." Jules shifted the purse under her arm, then sighed. "But she's someone who needs my help. At least, I think she does. I've seen her several times and she keeps sending me visions. But I don't know what she wants. When I try to ask she gets really angry and starts shrieking. Most of the time when she comes around, I end up curled into a ball, trying to keep her from ripping my skull apart from the inside out."

Moira gave her a sad look and shook her head. *"There are a lot of souls out there, lost and searching for a way into the light. She sounds like one of them."*

"Why aren't you there? In the light, I mean." Moira's aura glowed silver, giving Jules pause. "You're the first spirit I've met who seemed totally at peace, but you're here. I thought that kind of peace only came from passing over?"

The ghost shimmered brighter until the edges of her hair sparkled. *"I'm waiting for Samuel. It won't be much longer for him now. He has one more important task, then I'll take him home."*

Jules glanced down again to the sleeping man. He didn't appear sick, but then neither had her mother. One day she was healthy and playing catch in the backyard; the next she was gone. "He's going to die?"

A shiver worked through her.

"It's okay, Jules." Moira smiled. *"His time is near and he's been waiting a very long time for it to happen. Don't be sad."*

Stunned by the news, Jules couldn't do more than stand there until Moira's gentle voice whispered into her mind again. *"I think I see your friend, Aimee-Lynn. She's at the mouth of the alley."*

Jules turned to see Aimee-Lynn floating above the ground. Her aura pulsed light red then vermilion then crimson around her translucent figure.

Spinning back quickly, she projected, "Thank you," to Moira, then headed to the end of the alley, which spilled out onto Atlantic Avenue.

"Aimee-Lynn?" Jules said telepathically. "Can you talk to me?"

The ghost gave her a wan, pitiful smile and nodded. *"You know my name?"*

"Yes." Jules mentally winged out the reply. "If you can hear me, then we can just walk and talk like this."

Aimee-Lynn nodded. Her form appeared more defined than it had before. Today she sported a shiny black corset and loose-fitting blue jeans.

Although still translucent, her figure seemed almost corporeal. The sunshine shone down on Aimee-Lynn's dirty blonde hair and illuminated her blue gray eyes.

Eyes that held pain and fear and a trace of hope.

The pain-filled eyes tugged at Jules's heart, but it was the flicker of hope in the ghostly orbs that pulled her in. Jules might crave a normal life, but this poor, lost soul craved something too. And for whatever reason, she thought Jules held the key to her peace.

A slick, oily sensation of being watched went down her spine. She glanced around Atlantic Avenue then back down the alley. Moira was gone and Samuel still slept. The only other two people around, alive or dead, were Jules and Aimee-Lynn.

Still, the feeling persisted. Squeezing the purse tighter under her right arm, she curled her fingers around it. Using her crift, she projected her thoughts. "What do you remember about what happened to you?"

The ghost smiled. *"When I was alive, my name was Aimee-Lynn Masters,"* she answered, then vanished, only to reappear across the street. *"I was going to be a mother. And a wife."*

Aimee-Lynn vanished again, this time reappearing in the same spot where she'd first appeared to Jules.

"Did you live around here?" Jules winged her thoughts.

"No, I'm from Lancaster, Pennsylvania." Aimee-Lynn paused, as if confused, then added, *"Wait. Yes, I lived here."* She grimaced. *"How could I forget that? My parents divorced when I was young and my mother came to Tidewater. I moved in with her when I went to college.*

"My fiancé and I lived . . . lived . . . I can't remember that part. But we were going to have a baby. A boy." She frowned. *"No one knew about the baby. I wanted to wait until we were married before I announced it. Why did I wait?"*

Aimee-Lynn's aura pulsed to green then blue and back again. She drifted backward, lazily, down the street, like a cloud blowing in the wind. Jules followed her slowly along the cracked sidewalk.

"I'm sorry for what happened to you." Jules focused on projecting her thoughts. "It was you in the car, right? Someone strangled you?"

The ghost's aura shifted from green to muddy brown and she stopped drifting. *"Yes. He killed me."*

"Do you remember who did it?"

"The knight," Aimee-Lynn said with a curt nod of her head. *"I thought my prince had come to rescue me. But he hadn't. And the knight killed me."*

Before Jules could ask for a less Arthur-and-the-Round-Table description, Aimee-Lynn's eyes went wide.

"Jack! Don't!" Aimee-Lynn shrieked. *"What are you doing?"* Aimee-Lynn's panicked voice blared through Jules's head like a foghorn. *"Stop!"*

The final word kept repeating until Jules was nauseous.

"Aimee-Lynn?" She sent out a mental push, but before she could do more than that, something struck her hard in the right shoulder, knocking her off balance.

Jules stumbled forward, even as something behind her tugged at her right arm. Hard gloved fingers dug into her bicep, forcing her to spin around to face her attacker.

"Gimme the purse, bitch!" The man yanked on it.

Acting purely on instinct, Jules threw her cup at her assailant. Her hot coffee splashed into his face. He screamed out in pain, shoving her aside. Jules tumbled to the unforgiving pavement, landing on all fours. The purse smacked to the ground beneath her.

From this vantage point she could see who'd grabbed her. Dressed in a navy-colored hoodie and matching sweatpants, he looked like any other jogger out for a morning run—except for the huge dark stains coating the sleeve of his left arm, the front of his shirt, and the left side of his hoodie.

He shoved back his hood, swiping at his cheek with his hands. His face no longer in shadows, she recognized him but she wasn't sure from where.

Her startled realization had her on the ground longer than she should have been. She shoved to her feet, snatching up her purse as she went.

But he was faster. He grappled with her for the handbag, shouting, "You're gonna pay for that!"

"Are you *kidding* me?" Jules screeched, half in shock and half in terror. "Ghosts, visions of women strangled to death, and now I'm getting *mugged*? Take the danged thing! It's only got twenty bucks in it."

She released it, but her rant, which really was more of shocked outrage than anything else, gave her attacker pause. The bag clattered to the ground between them.

"What did you say?" he asked in a pronounced lisp.

Recognition slammed into her. This man had been in her shop two days ago. She gaped at him.

He must have realized she could identify him because his face, already red and puffy on one side, contorted with rage. He lunged for her.

She ducked, grabbed her purse from the pavement, and threw it at him. The corner of the bag hit him solidly in the nose and smacked back to the ground.

He threw one hand up to cover his now bloody nose while he dove for her, pulling something from the waistband of his belt. Sunlight glinted off a long, silver object. "I'm gonna make you bleed for that."

Panic jolted through her and she turned to run. His fingers grappled for purchase at her shoulder, then an icy pain sliced her left arm.

Determined to survive, Jules kicked back with her right foot, aiming for his knee.

Contact!

He released her with another howl of pain. She tripped over her forgotten purse. With a squeal, she lost her balance and fell. Her hands slapped the pavement as her knees crashed against it.

From the corner of her eye she saw something brownish streak past. It took a moment for her brain to process that the flash had been Samuel. Jules sat up and rotated, keeping him in her sights.

Samuel didn't appear old and decrepit. In fact, he had the fiercest expression on his face she'd ever seen on a living person.

The mugger must not have seen it, because he smirked as Samuel came to a stop in front of him. "You don't want to mess with me, old man," he taunted.

"Bring it," Samuel said in his gravelly voice.

Her attacker raised the six-inch-long serrated knife into the air.

"Watch out!" she called to Samuel, who didn't seem to hear her.

The mugger aimed for Samuel's face, but Samuel threw both of his arms up in front of him in an X and blocked the attack. Then he swung out his right leg, catching the attacker behind the knees and knocking him backward.

Flat on his back, the attacker appeared to momentarily debate attacking Samuel again. Then he jumped to his feet and ran the other way up Atlantic Avenue.

Samuel gave chase until the mugger darted around the corner on 62nd Street, at which point, a police siren blared somewhere nearby and he turned back toward her.

His shaggy matted hair glinted in the sunshine and a much younger version of the man superimposed itself over his body. Short, closely cropped hair set off his strong, shaven jawline. His piercing blue eyes spoke of pride and honor, and his aura glowed a radiant shade of silver white.

"Jules?" said a deep-timbre voice just as a hand touched her shoulder and she jumped.

A quick glance over her shoulder showed Devon "Call Me Dev" Jones kneeling beside her. His sand-colored eyebrows were drawn together over eyes that held concern and something else. He cocked his head to the side and she swore she heard him mutter, "Even up close you could be twins."

"What was that?" Jules had trouble focusing because of the biting pain at her elbow from where she must have smacked it on the pavement. She tried to twist to get a look at her elbow, but couldn't.

"I said, 'I didn't think he had it in him.'" He nodded to Samuel.

"Oh." Her head started swimming from the pain in her arm.

Dev produced a first aid kit and hastily dragged on disposable gloves. then bent closer to her. "Sit still, Jules. Did you get a good look at the mugger?"

His question seemed to include both Jules and Samuel.

"I did," Jules answered without giving Samuel a chance to reply. Not that he appeared readily able to do so. He gasped and wheezed as he limped back toward them. His sudden burst of speed appeared to have cost him more than just the rush of adrenaline.

"Could you identify him if you saw him again?"

"Probably . . . I mean, yes." Jules blinked at the shakiness in her voice.

"Really?" He sounded impressed. Ripping open a roll of white gauze, he started to wind it around her injured arm and said, "Tell me what you remember."

"Well, he wore navy blue sweats with a hoodie." Jules closed her eyes and tried to focus on the memory. "Light brown hair, military cut. White guy around my age, I think. He said, 'Gimme the purse, bitch.' Except he spoke with a heavy lisp."

She shuddered, making her wince in pain as Dev's fingers glanced over her wound.

"You're safe now, Jules," Dev said soothingly, continuing to wrap her arm.

"Wait, he was in the flower shop on Saturday."

"Are you sure?" Dev arched an eyebrow at her.

"Yeah, I remember because he spoke with a lisp then too. But I guess saying that he'd been in the shop doesn't really help you much, huh. Sorry." She nibbled on her bottom lip as a slow radiating pain burned through her left arm with an increasing ferocity. Trying to do anything to blot out the pain she said, "I bet we've got a record of his purchase. When I get to the shop, I'll ask Diana if she remembers his name."

"Maybe I should talk to her?"

"I don't think so," she said, then blew out a frustrated breath. "You're too old for her. She's just a kid."

Dev snorted. "Agreed." He finished wrapping her arm and checked her fingers for feeling, warmth, and color. "I thought I could talk to Diana while you get checked out at the hospital and give your statement to the police."

"No hospital. No police. It's not that bad." She met his disbelieving expression, then glanced down at her arm. The white bandage already had a spot of red blooming on it. Then her purse caught her eye. She held it up for Dev to see. "Look, it's just a cheap Prada knockoff. What are the odds the police are going to catch the guy?"

Dev's brows drew together. "Not good if you won't file a report."

"There's nothing to report." Shaking more from the fear of going to the police station than from the attack itself, she heard herself babble, "He wouldn't have gotten away with much even if he had taken it. Gah! My life is more cursed than usual. I mean, there's hardly any money in it. I can't believe this. Why would anyone want to steal it?"

"It's the city," Samuel said. "People rob the homeless here."

The thought sickened her. Or maybe that was due to the pavement swimming before her eyes. She dropped her clutch and reached for her head with her free hand.

"Jules, you've got a pretty nasty cut. Why don't we talk about this in a minute? Lie back and let me help you." Dev cupped one hand behind her head and helped her recline. The cement sidewalk felt cool against her head. "Do you hurt anywhere else?"

"No," she replied, then looked at Samuel. "Thank you. I think you just saved my life."

His dirty cheeks mottled darker but he didn't reply.

Dev's concerned face hovered above hers while he ran his hands over her head, neck, shoulders, and arms, checking her for other injuries. His gentle touch was light and impersonal. Through the examination she watched his face.

He appeared to be lip-synching an old En Vogue song, popular in the early nineties. He mouthed, "Before you can read me, you've got to learn how to see me."

Or maybe she was dreaming, because the next thing she knew, she opened her eyes to see a paramedic shining a light into them.

CHAPTER 13

"WHAT DO YOU mean Jules was mugged?" Seth stomped on his brake and glanced up at the green traffic light, ignoring the angry sound of horns blaring behind him. He made a U-turn and headed back up Atlantic Avenue.

He'd called Jones to give him the update about Aimee-Lynn's pregnancy when Jones blindsided him with the news that Jules was injured in a botched mugging.

"Like I said," Jones explained, "I was headed to the country club when I saw her. Someone taught the girl to fight. She threw a cup of coffee in his face and nailed him in the knee with a deliberate kick. When he kept coming, she threw her purse like a hatchet. I think she broke the bastard's nose. It was beautiful."

The admiration in Jones's voice surprised him. Seth asked, "Where were you when you saw this?"

"Driving down your street. I blew through a red light to get to her." Jones paused, then added, "I flipped on my siren to scare him off, but he didn't care."

"Jules was home when this happened?"

"Not quite, about a half-block down. She'd just come out of an alley."

"Sonofabitch! I just passed that part of Atlantic Avenue. How did I not see her?"

"You were here?" Jones repeated as if confused, then continued before Seth had a chance to answer. "Sam, the homeless guy, gave chase but her mugger got away. Right now the EMTs are here trying to convince her to go to the hospital, but she's refusing. She keeps asking if they can just stitch her up here. Says she's gotta go to work."

"Of course she does." Seth cursed under his breath as he found himself behind two cars driving under the speed limit. "I'm on my way to you right now. Hang on a minute."

Even with his cell on hands-free mode, Seth needed to focus on the road. The drivers of the two cars in front of him were leaning out their windows yelling to one another, paying more attention to each other than to the street.

Normally Seth hated driving police vehicles, but today he would have killed to have a siren and blue lights going. He pressed his palm to the horn again and held it there until the drivers made room for him.

One car dropped back. Seth snaked his Honda between the two cars before he zoomed through a yellow light. Once through the intersection, he let his foot off the gas marginally and continued his conversation with Jones. "How badly is she injured?"

"It's not life-threatening but . . ." Jones's voice trailed away. Probably because he saw Seth at the same moment Seth saw him.

Spotting a space, Seth slid his car into it and threw it into park, barely remembering to yank his keys from the ignition before he jumped out. He clicked off the phone and hurried across the street to where Jules sat in the back of an open ambulance.

Jules's red ponytail hung askew, wisps of hair blew into her eyes, and she kept rubbing her skinned knee through the tear in her jeans. One sleeve of her sweater dangled limply, split from elbow to shoulder, revealing her bloody, bandaged arm.

Seth broke out in an icy sweat.

"No, I'm fine, really," Jules said to the EMT. Although

trembling uncontrollably, her voice didn't waver as she spoke and she seemed determined to have her way. "I can't go to the hospital right now. The shop opens in two and a half hours. Can't you just stitch me up? I promise I'll get a tetanus shot tomorrow when I go to the doctor."

"Miss, you *need* to go to the hospital. Now." Seth's blood chilled at the EMT's words. The man's blue jumpsuit uniform bore the name Jeffers. His jaw tight, he said through clenched teeth, "I cannot stitch you up out here, and until you get those stitches, you're going to continue to bleed. I realize you have a job to do but so do I. It would make my job much easier if you would stop fighting me and get into the ambulance. The police can get your statement at the hospital."

The moment the EMT said the word *police*, Jules blanched. Panic widened her eyes. Seth knew her ex—a cop—had done a number on her, but until that moment, he'd had no idea how much. She wasn't just leery of police; she was downright terrified of them.

It made Seth want to know exactly what good ol' Billy had done to elicit that kind of reaction. And beat the crap out of him for it.

Seth wasn't surprised when Jules repeated, "I'm fine, really."

She wasn't, but she would be. Seth would make certain of it.

He called out to her, "Hi, Juliana."

She glanced over at him and smiled. A weak, grateful smile that warmed him in ways it shouldn't have.

"Seth, please tell this nice gentleman I'll go to the doctor later."

Okay, he understood the fear of the police, but why the hospital? He could fight her or take a less combative approach. He opted for keeping her calm.

Turning to the EMT, Seth said, "It's all right, Jeffers. I've got it from here. I'll get her seen and make sure she doesn't overdo it before she gets her stitches. Thank you for your help."

In no time, EMT Jeffers had her signing a Refusal of Care form and cleaned up his mess. Seth helped Jules down from the ambulance.

They'd taken two steps when she jumped. "Wait!" She turned around and snatched her purse from the floor of the vehicle and tucked it securely under her arm. She turned back to him, smiling. "Thank you, Seth."

"It's my pleasure, Jules. Come on, I'll give you a ride."

Seth ushered Jules to his car and held open her door for her. Catching his partner's eye, he wondered at the expression on Jones's face. Seth started to walk toward his partner but the man waved him on. Jones lifted his cell in the air and tapped on it. Moments later, Seth's phone buzzed.

Glancing down, he read the text. Take care of her. Am finishing up here. She doesn't want to file a report. Not much left to do. Hart has probably left TCC but will check and meet you back at the station.

Rather than waste his time tapping out a response, Seth just nodded. When Jones returned the gesture, Seth climbed into the driver's seat next to Jules.

Although normally fair-skinned, she appeared paler than usual. Her lips flattened in a grimace of pain. Automatically he reached over and checked her white bandage, which had a large red stain growing on the outer side of her arm between her elbow and shoulder.

Despite guessing the response he'd receive, he asked, "Where to now?"

"I really need to go work," Jules said, relief evident in her voice.

Her stomach rumbled.

He nearly grinned. He'd been hoping for a way to steer her in the direction of the hospital without technically resorting to kidnapping. Still, given the pinched look of pain she couldn't quite keep off of her face, he'd have done it if he had to.

"Sounds like what you need is an early lunch." Seth smiled. "I've got an idea. How about I take you someplace with friendly service and great food and give you a shot of what you really need after a morning like yours. We can talk about what happened along the way."

Tears sprung to her eyes and she blinked repeatedly. Looking down at her hands, she said, "I can't believe I'm shaking."

"I can't believe that's all you're doing, precious. You're amazing." He stroked a finger down her chilled cheek. When she gave him a noncommittal shrug, he added, "Jones told me what you did. Most people would be crying or screaming by now. Hell, you fought back." His stomach shriveled. His hand shook. Still, he didn't stop touching her. He needed to reassure himself she still sat there, next to him. "You're incredibly brave."

"Th-thank you." She snapped her gaze to his. Her wide, emerald eyes swam, but not a single tear fell. Jules went quiet for a moment before clenching her jaw again. "You promise you'll take me to work after we eat? If not, I'm getting out of this car and walking to the shop."

Despite her flippant tone, he could see the fear in her eyes. Feel the fine tremors racking her body. She'd been terrified. And still she'd fought.

Pride, warm and vast, spread through him.

"April and Big Jim are counting on me." Shying away from his touch, she twisted in the seat to face him. "I can't let them down because of this." She gestured to her injured arm. The stain on her bandage was darker than before. And larger.

Starting the engine, he chose his words carefully. "I promise you'll get to work before the store opens."

"WHAT IN THE hell have you done?" He balled his fist and punched Jack in his burned, puffy face twice before he reigned in his temper. Blood poured from the bastard's nose and right eye. No less than he deserved.

Jack fell back against the piling, whimpering.

Panting, the smells of copper, salt, coffee, and fear hit his senses, ratcheting up his fury. He flexed his hands, itching to throw another punch.

Instead he listened to the echo of waves crash against the shore from where they hid, ensconced in shadows beneath the Seventeenth Street pier. A sharp contrast to the rage thundering a tattoo between his ears and Jack's pathetic pleas for clemency. "Please, you said we needed to do something. You *said*—" His lisp grew more pronounced in his distress.

"I said, 'Don't be stupid!'" He grabbed Jack by the shoulders, shaking him until his head wobbled like a rag doll and thunked against the aged wooden column. "She can identify you, *asshole*! It's been two hours and already every cop in this city is out looking for a thug in a blue jogging suit who speaks with a lisp. *Thound* like anyone you know?"

He shoved Jack against the splintered wood, not caring when a stream of blood trickled from behind his left ear where his head had struck the piling.

"I'm sorry. I'm sorry." Jack dropped to his knees in the sand like a supplicant begging forgiveness. "She didn't even know what I really wanted. She thought I was after her purse. I can still do it. I can get it, please!"

"You *can't* get it!" he said between clenched teeth. "That damned detective will be watching her now. He showed up on the scene before you even called to tell me what an utter fuck-up you truly are."

Jack groveled nonsensically as waves splashed over him. Crouched in the sand as he was, the water doused his pants up to the hem of his sweatshirt.

The little pissant would roll and confess everything within minutes of being arrested. Hell, the wimp had cried like a baby torn from the breast when Aimee-Lynn died.

Only fear and the need to save his own worthless ass had kept him quiet. All that would change if Jack were arrested. Given that the coward had no place to hide, it wouldn't be long before he was caught.

I've come too close to lose it all now.

He removed his gloves and shoved them into his pockets, then pushed up his sleeves.

Above, the pier creaked and groaned as shop owners opened their doors for the day's business. Jack flinched, casting a fearful eye heavenward.

Little did he know, the true danger came from the ocean lapping at his knees.

JULES DUG A fingernail beneath the bandage and scratched lightly, careful to avoid both her stitches and the tender part of her body. Gah! Why was it a body felt great until the moment a bandage was put on?

A shot of what you really need.

It was a good thing Seth had stayed out of sight at the hospital. She'd been so furious that he'd tricked her into going there, she might have been tempted to give him a shot of something in his backside.

Still, she could only be so angry with him. He'd been right to make her go. The injury, which she hadn't been able to see, *was* bad enough to warrant sixteen stitches. And a tetanus shot. Where her arm didn't itch and throb from the assault, it ached from the shot. Thank heavens the nurse did it all in the same arm.

At least Seth had delivered on his promise of good food. Too bad Jules had needed to eat one-handed in the car on the way back to April's Flowers.

She leaned over the workbench and looked into the show-room. Where had Seth gone? While she appreciated that he'd given her space once she'd arrived at work, she hadn't seen him in thirty minutes. Had he left?

Jules shifted off the stool where she'd been trying to wrap roses one-handed, a near-impossible task. The moment she stood, her arm itched like she'd been bitten by a dozen mosquitoes.

Unable to stand it, she grabbed a six-inch floral stick from the workbench and attempted to wedge it beneath the bandage to scratch the wretched itch. The danged stick snagged on the gauze. The green dowel protruded from the top of her bandage like a stem stripped of its leaves. She tugged and twisted, but the more she tried to remove the rod, the deeper it lodged.

"Can I help?" Seth's amused voice floated in from the open doorway.

She turned her head to see his lips twitching. Amusement sparkled in his eyes. It would have been nice if she could have found the annoyance she had felt at being tricked; instead, her idiotic heart leapt at the sight of him.

I'm insane for reacting like this.

"I've got it," she said, frowning at the dowel.

"Still mad at me for making you get stitches?" He chuckled.

"And the tetanus shot," she reminded him. When he didn't do more than stare at her, she gave him a mock frown that had him laughing. Her heart light at the sound, she admitted, "No. I'm not mad. You were . . . right."

"Bet that was hard for you to admit." He winked at her.

"You have no idea." Her cheeks warmed.

This attraction didn't make sense. They'd only known each other for a few days. Why was she so happy just to see him?

Okay, he was thoughtful. And sweet. He didn't even press

her to go to the station to file charges. He'd offered to take care of the paperwork for her. Cop or not, Seth truly was a gentleman.

And she was a freak with a stick stuck up her sleeve.

Blushing, she stared at the rod, then tugged again. It didn't do more than make her arm burn. "Dang."

"You sure I can't help?" He moved closer to her but stopped when she shook her head. A moment of silence passed, then he asked, "Jules, would you be willing to meet with a sketch artist later today? I'll go with you to the station."

So much for Seth not pressuring her.

"I don't see the point," she said. "I told you and Dev what I saw. Can't you tell her?"

"But *you* saw your mugger. We didn't. You really need to be the one who talks to the artist." He crossed his arms over his chest. "Would you feel better if I had the sketch artist come here?"

"Can you do that?" Jules sighed, inadvertently inhaling his delicious masculine scent. Great, now her whole body sizzled with awareness of him.

"Yeah. I'll arrange it," Seth said.

But she focused on the way his lips moved.

As if noticing her stare, he gave her a cocky lopsided grin and licked his lips. It made her hungry for another taste of them. Oh yeah, he also kissed like a conquering warrior.

Her lips actually tingled at the remembered sensation of his mouth on hers. It had been hot and sweet and she wanted to do it all over again.

I'm a masochist.

Blushing, she gave him her back.

His feet slid across the tiled floor. Moments later, his breath feathered across her ear. She didn't need to look over her shoulder to know he stood directly behind her. His heat radiated against her back and she struggled to remain upright. To not lean into all the warmth that seemed to beckon her closer.

"Let me help you, precious," he whispered in husky tones. His arms wrapped around her waist and tugged her closer until her back was flush with his front. And oh my, he smelled even more delicious up close.

Gently, he turned her in his arms until they stood thigh to

thigh, chest to chest. His eyes no longer twinkled with amusement. Instead they darkened with banked heat.

"Hold still," he said in a tone so deep and gravelly it made her shiver. "One day you're going to have to tell me why you're so afraid of the police."

"I'm not!"

"Shh . . ." He kissed the side of her head. "You are. I know it. I want to know why, but I can wait. I'm just glad you aren't afraid of me."

He was right. Jules wasn't afraid of him. Anymore. "Not right now, okay?"

"Soon?"

"Soon," she agreed.

One side of his mouth quirked up at the corner but otherwise he showed no reaction. "Don't move."

Carefully, he twisted the dowel between two fingers while he used his other hand to loosen the bandage. In seconds—several long she-couldn't-remember-how-to-breathe seconds—she was free.

He dropped the stick on the workbench then pulled Jules into his arms. His touch was gentle, his movements measured and sure. And it made her heartbeat skip into triple digits.

"Thank you," she whispered, then licked her lips.

"You're welcome." His eyes darkened even more but he didn't make a move. Instead he said, "I'm working."

"So am I." She grinned at him. Rising up on her tiptoes, she tilted her face toward his.

He hesitated briefly, then lowered his head until their lips nearly touched. He didn't kiss her right away. He smoothed his hands up and down her back, pulling her tighter against him. Yet he took care not to touch her injured arm.

This close, she could feel his arousal pressing against her lower belly through his slacks and she couldn't resist sliding her body against his.

He groaned, licked his lips, and his hands moved a little less gently along her back. Seth might normally be in control, but at this moment, his control was slipping.

Her head swam with the heady sense of power. She wondered what he'd be like completely out of control. Last night she thought she'd experienced a taste of it. And like a narcotic, it made her crave more.

She wrapped one hand around his neck and pulled his mouth close enough to brush her lips against his. When he parted his lips on a moan of pleasure, she slipped her tongue inside and nearly moaned herself. He tasted of hazelnut coffee.

Her new favorite flavor.

He backed her up until her hips met the workbench. While her left arm had ached and throbbed only moments before, it didn't hurt as much now. She slid her uninjured arm down his body and wrapped it around Seth's waist. His hardness rubbing against her through their clothes heightened her excitement.

He shifted and his warm, large hands gently clasped her face, angling her head for the best access. He attempted to take over the kiss. But with every thrust of his tongue, she parried. The give-and-take of their kiss, the need to experience every nuance, every delicious moment, left her breathless. She turned her face to suck in air. Seth slid his mouth from her face to her neck and suckled gently. Shivers of electricity bolted through her.

"You taste so damn sweet. I could lick you all over," Seth said against her neck. His hands trailed from her face to her shoulders and down her back. Almost before he'd whispered the words, he'd sent the fantasy winging into her mind.

Sexy and erotic, she wanted to revel in it. Heck, she wanted to strip him naked and experience it live.

As quickly as the images flashed in, they disappeared. Like a movie reel snapping at the theater, the fantasy zapped out of existence.

Then everything happened at once. Seth's cell phone started ringing, the room temperature dropped, and Aimee-Lynn started shrieking incoherently.

Jules's eyes flew open. The angry spirit hovered behind Seth. A crimson aura pulsed around her.

Hissing in pain from Aimee-Lynn's wail slicing through her skull, Jules pulled back.

"Juliana, did I hurt you?" Seth examined her bandaged arm.

"It's okay, I just need a minute," Jules said, then gestured to Seth's ringing phone. "Do you need to get that?"

She could barely hear herself speak over the ghostly cries shredding her eardrums.

Jerking the phone from his belt, Seth glanced at it and frowned. "Yeah, I do. Will you be all right?"

"Yep," she replied.

He kissed her on the cheek. "I'll be right back."

She was pretty sure that was what he'd said just before Seth strode out the back door, but Jules hadn't actually heard him. The spirit's cries blocked out all other sounds.

Jules hurried from the back room to the front and gasped. Aimee-Lynn's murky red aura bled all over the showroom.

"Aimee-Lynn!" Jules focused her thoughts on reaching the angry ghost. "Calm down, I can't understand you."

Jules sent out the mental push repeatedly, but Aimee-Lynn didn't appear to hear her. The shrieking continued, then the ghost gestured wildly.

At first, Jules thought Aimee-Lynn was trying to communicate with her. It took a moment for realization to sink in.

Aimee-Lynn appeared to be communicating with another ghost. One that Jules could barely make out. The second specter was little more than the silhouette of a man lying spread-eagle on the ground in the middle of the room. He jerked and shook as if he were being attacked by some unseen force. He slid violently left and right as if unseen beasts had latched on to his limbs and were playing tug-of-war.

Death-Bearers.

Terror sluiced through Jules. The Death-Bearers were the beasts that chased after evil souls and dragged them into hell. She'd learned about them after she'd seen them drag off her father's business partner when she'd been nine years old. And she'd had nightmares for weeks afterward.

Aimee-Lynn's wails reached near-glass-shattering decibels and the temperature in the room dropped about fifteen degrees.

Unmitigated rage and anguish hit Jules in the midsection like a punch.

The man's silhouetted figure stopped jerking and he was dragged past Jules. A Death-Bearer glided close enough that her nose burned from the stench of sulfur. Its wicked presence had the hair on her forearms standing on end.

Jules wrapped her good arm around herself and fought to erect her mental shields. Her castle. She visualized the cold granite walls, high turrets, deep moat, and heavy drawbridge. And in front of the castle in a suit of gleaming armor stood Seth, sword drawn and ready to fight.

The cold menace dissolved at the same time the male silhouette vanished.

The room fell silent so fast, Jules's ears popped. Instantly, the red aura washed away, replaced by the vivid greens, oranges, yellows, and blues of the plants and flowers in the showroom.

"He was my friend," Aimee-Lynn said in a small voice. The spirit stared off in the direction the ghostly man had been dragged before he vanished. She appeared to be talking to herself. *"He didn't deserve that."*

Jules didn't know who the friend was, but she bet he deserved where he was going.

Justice might be blind, but Karma's a bitch with a big stick. But Jules kept that thought to herself. At least, she thought she had until the ghost spun on her and pointed an accusatory finger.

Rage blazed in the spirit's eyes and her mouth worked, but instead of words or shrieks, the only sound Jules heard was the hum of the refrigeration unit.

She took a step toward the ghost, wanting to help her. Jules winged her thoughts. "Aimee-Lynn, you need to calm down. I can't hear you."

"What are you doing here?" Diana said, striding in from the workroom.

Jules jumped in surprise. Aimee-Lynn vanished.

Her street clothes bundled under her arm, Diana had already dressed in her usual Goth gear and donned her April's Flowers apron.

"I didn't see you come in. When did you get here?" Jules said, surprised her voice didn't squeak.

"About five minutes ago." Diana shoved her clothing bundle beneath the counter, then added, "I rode my bike, so I came in around back." When Jules didn't do anything more than stare, Diana added in a tone that said she thought Jules was mentally deficient, "So I could lock it up in the back room. You feeling all right?"

Honestly, no. Jules started to put her hands behind her back, to hide their trembling before Diana noticed. Pain lanced up her arm because the motion pulled at her stitches. She let go and lightly patted the sore spot.

"What happened to you?" Diana asked, coming around the desk to where Jules stood with her back to the refrigeration case. "I got the message we were opening an hour late but I didn't hear why."

"I was—"

"WTF!" Diana cut her off. Eyes wide, she raced past Jules and yanked open the door of the refrigeration case. "These were perfect when I closed out last night, I swear! How did this happen? The chiller's still working but *all* the flowers are dead."

Jules gaped at the withered and brown roses, carnations, and calla lilies inside the case. The flowers had been vibrant when she'd arrived.

A cold, invisible finger stroked down the back of her neck. Jules didn't need to turn to know it was Aimee-Lynn, but she did and swallowed hard at the sight.

In the past few days she'd seen the spirit angry, sad, frustrated, even afraid, but never had she seen the ghost as furious as she was now. Aimee-Lynn's aura shifted from maroon to black and back again. An icy wind whipped through the room.

While Diana continued to fuss and search through the case for a viable flower, Jules braced herself. If Aimee-Lynn had the power to suck the life out of plants, who knew what else she was capable of in this state.

Determined to shield Diana from any harm, Jules took two silent steps toward the angry specter, who hovered in the middle of the showroom floor looking as if she might explode. She sent out a mental push. "What can I do?"

Aimee-Lynn's aura rolled around her in thick black waves and she shrieked, *"Give it to him. Now!"*

Overhead, the string of muted colored lights crisscrossing the room burst in rapid succession like firecrackers on the Fourth of July. Diana screamed and covered her head. Jules dove to cover Diana to protect her from the flying shards of glass.

CHAPTER 14

"J ULES!" SETH CALLED out as the back door slammed. "Juliana! Answer me, damn it!"

She glanced up, her heart racing, and more than a little relieved to hear his voice.

Seth rushed into the room, his gun drawn. A warrior expression on his face, he peered around the demolished front room. As usual, he seemed to take in everything at once. The showcase room in near ruin, the sunlight streaming in through the front windows, the dead flowers in the refrigeration case, and Jules covering Diana's body with her own.

"We're fine," Jules said, pushing to her feet as Seth holstered his weapon.

"Speak for yourself," Diana intoned, accepting Seth's proffered hand. Once on her feet the girl gave him a tremulous smile. "I thought someone was shooting up the place for a second."

"No one shot at us." Jules wrapped a reassuring arm around Diana's shoulders and hugged her.

Diana accepted the comfort momentarily then shrugged

off the touch with a hearty sigh. Glancing at the dead flowers and broken glass scattered across the floor, she said, "I guess I'll get a broom."

"Bring me one too, please," Jules called out as Diana headed to the storeroom in April's office.

Seth shoved up Jules's sleeve, making her jump. "Hey!"

"Hold still, precious," he said, his voice gruffer than usual. "I'm just checking your stitches."

Funny, until he reminded her, her arm hadn't hurt. Now the pain radiated and she wanted some ibuprofen. Fear still had her chest constricting, but she needed relief. She needed . . . Seth.

"You can kiss it and make it better," she said, half-joking.

He frowned briefly, clearly not in the mood to play. Then he surprised her by pressing his lips lightly to her bandage. "Better?"

"Much." She lowered her sleeve and stared at the green aura pulsing around him. "Seth, is something wrong?"

He gestured to the showroom. "Besides this?"

"Yes. You seem . . . different." No, the green aura around him implied protection. Although, why was she seeing it again? "Wanna tell me why you came running in here with your gun drawn? Surely you didn't think we were being shot at?"

"I heard you two screaming." He gave her a wry grin. "Thanks for the vote of confidence but I *do* know the difference between light bulbs popping and gunshots."

"You sure?" she teased. That she was able to joke at this moment amazed her. Inside she was shaking, but with Seth beside her, she felt . . . safe.

"I'm sure." He winked, glanced toward the front door with a frown and then down at his watch.

Right. So why was the green light surrounding him expanding?

"Uh, huh." She let the doubt ooze into her voice. "Why do you seem edgy all of a sudden?"

Seth cocked his head but didn't say anything. The front door chimed. Jules faced the door, unsure how to explain the chaos in her shop to a customer, but was saved the trouble when two patrolmen strode in.

Jules recognized the first officer as Chaz Gareth. She'd met him at the Dumpster on Saturday. The second man was a stranger.

"Thank you for coming so quickly, Officers," Seth said. He moved carefully across the blue tiled floor, glass crunching beneath his feet. With each step he took, his aura faded.

By the time he reached the newcomers, Jules could no longer see any color surrounding Seth.

The three men spoke in low voices. Jules strained to hear but couldn't.

Diana returned from the storeroom, clomping over the broken glass. She spared little more than a glance at the two new arrivals before turning to Jules and handing her the broom. "I could only find one. Do you know where the other broom went?"

Good question. "I think it's in the warehouse out back," Jules said. "Why don't you check there and I'll start sweeping."

"Harmon, go with her," Seth said, gesturing to the younger patrolman.

Diana blushed but Officer Harmon didn't seem to notice. Instead, he extended his arm and said, "Lead the way."

After the two of them disappeared out the back, Jules turned to Seth in time to see Officer Gareth take up station just to the right of the front door. With his arms folded across his chest, there was no question that Chaz Gareth was here to stay.

"What's happening?" Jules asked, leaning against the broom.

"Jules, are you sure you've told me everything you remember about Friday night?"

"I'm sure," she replied, ignoring the pinch of guilt she felt about hiding her crift from him.

"What about your mugger?" Seth's gaze bore into her, as if searching for a lie. "Is there any chance he was at the reunion too?"

"I don't think so. Except for this morning, I'd only ever seen him here. And that was Saturday." Tension coiled around Jules's spine. It wasn't so much what he'd asked as it was his intense, coplike tone that bothered her. "Seth, what's going on?"

"A lot," Seth said with a strained smile. "Wait for me to

pick you up after work. I'll explain everything over a gourmet meal tonight. In the meantime, Officers Gareth and Harmon will stay with you until I return. Okay?"

"No. I think you'd better explain to me now, *Detective English*, why you're putting me under proverbial house arrest. And it is *house* arrest, right? My gourmet dinner won't be at the station?" Her hands shook worse. A sick, familiar feeling curdled in her belly.

"No, you'll be at home. You're not under house arrest. This is for your protection." Seth exhaled hard and crossed back to her. He ran his hands through his hair, then scrubbed one down his face. "I don't want you to worry, but about fifteen minutes ago someone found the body of a jogger on the beach. He'd been beaten, strangled, and drowned. Jones is pretty certain it's your mugger."

"Really?" Jules felt the color drain from her face. "Who would do that?"

"I don't know, Juliana." Seth stepped closer to her until their bodies nearly touched. She wished he would hold her, but he didn't. Instead, he lowered his voice. "Precious, it's why I want you protected. Something's not right. Two days ago, your cell phone was found in a Dumpster with a dead woman. Today, you were mugged. Within hours of the stabbing, your mugger is murdered. My gut tells me that's not a coincidence. *Some*one killed both of those people. There's a very real possibility that you could still be in danger."

Jules went cold at Seth's words. She shook so badly, she dropped the broom. Seth caught it and handed it back to her. But when she took it, he closed his warm hands over hers as if to infuse her with his strength.

"Jules, I need you to listen to the officers while I'm gone. Gareth and Harmon are under strict orders not to leave you alone."

"Wh-what about Diana?" Jules couldn't live with herself if anything happened to the teen.

"We're keeping an eye on her too."

Jules thought of Aimee-Lynn and the ghost being dragged off by the Death-Bearers. A sick feeling slid into her stomach. What if her mugger had been that tortured spirit?

Her terror must have shown on her face because Seth laid

aside the broom and pulled her into his arms. Holding her close he whispered, "It's going to be all right, precious."

Seth's warm scent wound around her, calmed her until she could think again. Even though she wanted to sink into his embrace and hold him all day, she sensed his discomfort. He needed to work.

Releasing him, she picked up the broom and arranged her face in the bravest smile in her arsenal. She gestured with her good arm to indicate the floor and room. "Go on, then. I've got plenty to do here."

"Don't worry. You'll be safe here, with my men."

"Who says I'm worried?"

"I do. I know you're worried." He gave her a penetrating stare that made her feel as if he could see inside her. He glanced over at Gareth, who appeared to be preoccupied fidgeting with the badge on his uniform. Lowering his voice, Seth said, "Trust me, precious. I won't let anything happen to you."

"I trust you." And as stupid as it sounded, she *did*.

The question remained: Would he trust her if he ever learned she could see ghosts?

Probably not. He'd probably try to have her committed. Pushing the thoughts away, she asked, "Seth, should I go with you to identify the body?"

"No." Seth shook his head. "You don't need to. Turns out Sam got a good look at him. While you were getting stitched up he went to the station and gave a description to the sketch artist. So you wouldn't have had to do that after all. Plus, how many men out there are wearing coffee-stained sweats and sporting fresh burns on the left sides of their faces? Jones already saw the body. It's why he called me.

"You don't need to do anything this afternoon but take care of yourself and the store. Do me a favor, try to stick to being out here in the main part of the shop. Keep Diana with you. If the killer is around, let's make it harder for him to get near you."

At that moment, the back door buzzed, then Diana returned with a broom in her hand and the patrolman right behind her carrying a dustpan.

"Officers," Seth called out. He waved them over to where Jules stood. Not surprisingly, Diana came too.

"What's up?" Diana asked, her heavily mascaraed eyes wide.

"Tell you in a bit." Jules put up a finger to silence any further questions and nodded toward Seth.

"Officers Harmon and Gareth, meet Jules and Diana." Seth pointed to each person as he named them. "Gareth, you might remember meeting Ms. *Scott* on Saturday, when she jumped into the Dumpster."

Gareth huffed. A muscle ticked in his jaw, then he said sarcastically, "How could I forget? I was written up for her adventure."

"Do we have a problem, Patrolman?" Seth asked, matching Gareth's tone.

"No, sir." Gareth shook his head, then gave Jules something that probably could have passed for a smile. If she were blind. "Ms. Scott, nice to see you again."

Right. "You too, Officer Gareth."

"I'm Zig Harmon," the other patrolman said, offering his hand. "You probably don't remember, but I was there too. I'm glad to see you're feeling better."

"Thanks," Jules replied, shaking his hand. Unlike Chaz Gareth, Zig Harmon appeared genuinely pleased to talk with her.

Both officers greeted Diana in turn.

Seth said, "Good, now that y'all are acquainted, I need to head out. I'll be back here to escort Jules home at six." Without another word, he left.

Through the showroom window, Jules watched Seth climb into his Honda and drive away.

An oily, slippery sensation went down her neck, alerting her.

Someone was watching her too.

No MATTER HOW hard he'd tried, Seth couldn't catch a break. He'd missed Jones at the scene and his partner wasn't answering his cell. He'd called the station, but Jones wasn't there either and the officer on duty stated that Sam had already left too.

Seth headed to Sam's alley to talk to him, but the homeless man hadn't returned.

After searching the surrounding area for close to two hours, Seth gave up and drove to the station.

He'd just arrived at headquarters when Jones hurried in behind him. For his part, Jones looked about as happy as Seth felt.

"I couldn't locate Mason Hart," Jones explained, dropping into his seat. Frustration oozed from his normally calm expression. "He wasn't at the country club, his house, or his job today. It's like the guy just vanished."

"Or went into hiding." Seth rubbed at the ache in his neck. "After you called, I questioned Jules again. She swears she never saw her attacker before Saturday."

"You believe her?"

"Yeah, I do."

Jules had been shocked and frightened when he told her there might be a killer after her. No one could fake that kind of fear. But a thread of warning tickled at the base of his neck like a loose tag on a shirt. She was holding something back from him; still he didn't think it was anything nefarious.

Captain Peterson stuck his head out of his office. "Jones, English. In here, now."

Sharing a glance with his partner, Seth obeyed. Once inside, they found O'Dell and Reynolds already seated.

The homicide detectives itched to take over the investigation. Their barrage of reasons why they should handle the case from this point forward started before Seth and Jones had barely closed the door.

"There's no conclusive evidence that this murder has anything to do with their robbery," O'Dell said. "It's a homicide, plain and simple."

"Except that the homicide victim mugged my witness," Seth retorted.

Peterson turned a sharp glare his way. "I thought you said she didn't see anything. Didn't know anything. Is she a witness or not?"

"No, she's not a witness," Seth explained. "But she was at the scene where we found the first victim and she was mugged by the second."

"Seems to me," Reynolds said, "the only thing tying the two cases together is your *witness*. You sure she's not a killer?"

"Of course, she's not!" Seth ground his teeth, biting back the scathing retort he wanted to make. "She was at the hospital when her mugger was killed. We've got a doctor and three nurses who can verify that."

Seth turned his attention back to Peterson. "Look, Captain, my gut tells me that Jules is in danger."

"Your gut?" O'Dell scoffed. "I think your *gut* is telling you that you're about to lose your case to two detectives who can actually solve it. You'll say anything to keep it."

Seth's jaw ached from grinding his teeth. "Captain," he said, ignoring O'Dell, "you said we had a week to solve the case. I'm just asking that you let us have that."

Peterson sneezed, then said, "You have five more days."

Seth sighed in relief, but his relief was short-lived when his captain added, "But this latest murder appears unrelated. The only tie is your *nonwitness*, Juliana Scott. I'm handing the dead jogger case to O'Dell and Reynolds. Give them her information so they can go interview her now."

To his surprise, Jones argued. "With all due respect, she doesn't know anything. She fought like a cat on crack to protect herself. There's no reason to continue to question her. I documented everything that happened in my report."

"Be that as it may," Peterson replied, "this case belongs to O'Dell and Reynolds. They have the right to question anyone they see fit."

The two homicide detectives grinned.

Seth inwardly cursed them. Jules hadn't wanted to talk with the police. He'd respected her wishes and handled the case for her. Now it appeared she'd have no choice but to deal with the two most arrogant assholes on the force.

Well, he'd be there when she did!

"Why don't y'all follow me over, I'll introduce you," Seth said to O'Dell.

"No. Give them her information," Captain Peterson snapped.

Reluctantly, he did so, then Peterson glanced at the homicide detectives. "Get moving. I want this case closed ASAP."

The door shut quietly behind Reynolds, who'd followed O'Dell out.

"Sit," Peterson said to Seth and Jones. When they obeyed

he continued. "I get the feeling you two have a personal stake in this case."

"No, sir," they replied in unison.

He narrowed his gaze on them, pointing an accusatory finger at Jones. "Your family legacy doesn't give you free reign here, Jones. I don't care that your granddaddy was the chief of police forty years ago. Or that your mama's family owns half the property of the Oceanfront. You will do everything by the book." Peterson swung his finger at Seth. "And I'm giving you a break. Don't make me regret it. Solve the jewelry thefts, find the person who murdered Aimee-Lynn Masters, and close this now!"

JULES CHEWED ON her lip, locking the shop door behind Diana as the Goth climbed into her mother's SUV. Diana had been none-too-happy to leave her bike in the back room and ride home with her mother, but had caved after Jules had explained about the murdered mugger.

At ten minutes after six, Jules grew anxious again. Seth had called to say he was running late, but she wished he'd hurry.

"I . . . I say, Hugh . . . have you met my friend, Harvey?" Zig said in an incredibly accurate imitation of Jimmy Stewart.

Jules returned to the counter where he stood, then hopped up on it and listened. Zig and Chaz had been doing impressions all afternoon.

It had been a great way to keep Jules from worrying. Something she'd been doing since the two homicide detectives had come by earlier. They'd asked so many questions, she'd grown confused about their purpose.

Thank heavens Zig and Chaz had been there. Otherwise, she was sure she would have been hauled down to the station.

"Wh-what do you mean?" Zig switched from sounding like Jimmy Stewart to imitating Hugh Grant in an instant. "Bollocks! That's not an enormous white rabbit behind you. It's an alien with a . . . with a . . . bloody huge knife. I think he's planning to make Jimmy stew!"

"Is this your idea of work?" Chaz interjected, sounding

remarkably like Seth, at least until he laughed. Then Chaz sounded like a hyena. "I thought you were a cop, not a street performer."

Jules laughed.

The front door handle jiggled and her laughter died in her throat. Fear flashed through her as both men snapped their gazes to the source of the sound.

"It's all right, it's only good ol' Detective English," Zig announced in his Jimmy Stewart voice. He crossed the room, unlocked the door, and opened it. "Why, come in. We've been waiting for you."

Seth scowled at him. "I thought you were a cop, not a street performer."

Chaz and Zig laughed with Jules again. For his part, Seth just looked confused. "Did I miss something?"

"Not really," Jules explained as Chaz and Zig put on their coats. "The officers were just keeping me company."

"If you no longer need us," Chaz said to Seth, "we'll be on our way."

"We're through here." Seth managed a smile. "See you in the a.m."

"You ready to go?" Jules asked when he glanced her way. She hopped off the counter and grabbed her purse and jacket from the nook beneath the register. "I'm starving."

He nodded, and in no time, they were back in their building. Seth did a quick sweep of her apartment, then said, "Wait here. I'll be back in a minute." He headed to his apartment.

She wandered through her living room. Alone. She shivered.

Funny, being alone had never bothered her before, but after the past few days, she wouldn't mind steady company for a while. Okay, not just any company. The breathing kind.

"Aimee-Lynn?" she whispered, walking from room to room, flipping on lights as she went. The ghost didn't answer.

Relief at being specter-free drained the tension from her body. Ready to relax, Jules changed into an old, comfortable heather gray sweatshirt and blue jeans.

Three sharp knocks sounded at her front door. She hurried from her bedroom to the living room. Finally! Seth was back.

"Just a sec," she called out.

"Jules, it's Seth. Open—" She pulled open the door to find

him frowning at her. He finished his sentence adding the final word. "Up."

"Hi, Seth."

"You really shouldn't open the door until you've checked who's outside. I could have been anyone."

"I knew it was you," she said, and blushed. "Okay, I hadn't actually *known* but I figured it was you."

"Humor me and check from now on." His frown faded and he held up a brown paper sack the size of a grocery bag. "Dinner's ready."

He strode through the living room, headed for the kitchen, then settled the bag on the table. She locked the door and joined him. Jules pulled out dishes, cups, and flatware, while Seth arranged the large containers on the table.

"You're in for a treat," Seth said, gesturing toward the food. "It's my mother's moussaka and my daughter's baked bread. If you're sweet to me, I'll even feed you some of my special baklava."

He grinned at her wickedly. Images of him feeding her naked winged into her mind.

Her tummy did a little flip that had nothing to do with hunger and everything to do with the sexy man in front of her. She was certain she blushed, because the images winged faster now.

Ooh, if that man ever learned how to control that fantasy-push he did, she'd be in real trouble. But that would require her telling him about her crift and him believing her.

Two things she wasn't sure could ever happen.

Subdued, she grabbed a glass of sweet tea for herself and a bottle of water for him. She sat down at the table. Across from her, the scent of warm bread, spices, and Seth tickled her senses.

He lifted his bottle of water in the air and she touched her glass to it. "To getting to know each other *much* better," he said with barely banked heat in his gaze.

His look sent the blood rushing to her cheeks again. Confusion had her blurting out, "Seth, what's going on here? Are—are we on a date or are you providing police protection?"

He frowned, sipped his water, then sighed. "Last night I'd planned for this to be a date."

"And now?"

"Jules." He shook his head. "I can't seem to think straight around you. You come near me and all I can imagine is stripping you naked to see if your entire body tastes as sweet as your lips."

She shivered at his words. She'd like nothing more than for him to do that. "But?"

"But what?"

"There has to be a *but* here, otherwise we wouldn't still be talking about this. Right?"

Seth pressed the bottle to his lips and took another long draught. "I'm walking a fine line with my case. Since you seem to be in the middle of it—"

"I didn't do anything wrong," she interrupted.

"I know that," he said, setting the bottle on the table and reaching for her hand. His warm fingers entwined with hers. "But you *are* the only link I have to two murders. Had I known that last night, I wouldn't have kissed you. I can't afford to let myself get distracted from solving my case. People get killed when cops get sloppy. I won't risk your life by allowing myself to become distracted."

"Okay," she said, a little shaken by the sincerity in his words. She could fall in love with this man, so easily. If only she had any hope he'd ever believe in her crift. "So I won't distract you. We'll have a nice dinner and you can keep focused on solving your case."

"Thank you," he said with a wink. His expression sobered he added, "Don't misunderstand, Juliana. Tonight, we're just going to talk. But the moment this case is put to bed, I intend to have you in mine."

Her cheeks warmed. Heck, her whole body burned at his words.

"You're pretty damned adorable when you do that. I bet that got you out of a lot of trouble over the years."

"What got me out of trouble?"

"That blush." His gaze tender, Seth released her hand to stroke a finger down her cheek. As if realizing what he was doing, he pulled back and curled his hand around his water bottle. "I'd almost swear you could do it on command to manipulate a situation, but I don't think you know how adorable you are when you do it."

"Wow, jaded much?"

He laughed a short burst of air, then shook his head. "Maybe. But spend enough time dealing with the dregs of society and you'd be jaded too."

"Come on, not everyone you meet is a bad person."

"You seem to be the exception to the rule."

"A high compliment." She laughed. "Well, you seem to be a decent guy too, for a grumpy *cop*."

"Grumpy?" His eyebrows drew together in a caricature of a frown. "I happen to be the most pleasant, giving *cop* living in this building."

"And how many cops live in our complex?" she asked, knowing the answer.

"One. Now, let's eat, I'm hungry." Seth cut a slice of moussaka and served her, then himself.

The aroma of peppers, onions, and garlic wafted up and her stomach growled. "Everything smells delicious."

"And tastes even better. Dig in."

She did. The smell of the food didn't do it justice. Taste exploded on her tongue. "Wow, is that cinnamon?"

Seth had just scooped a large forkful into his mouth, so he could only nod.

Apparently he was as ravenous as she was. They ate quickly and quietly. Before she knew it, she'd finished what he'd served her. She eyed the moussaka, tempted to take another slice, but didn't want to appear piggish.

"You want more?" he asked, a curious expression on his face. He cut another slice and placed it on her plate. When she lifted her fork and took a bite, he said, "It's nice to see you eat. Sexy."

Jules almost choked. "What?"

Seth laughed. "At lunch yesterday, I was afraid you were like most women. You know, determined to be so skinny their bodies are shaped like teenaged boys'. You're not like that. I'm glad. And seeing the way you enjoy the food, it's . . . erotic."

Heat burned her cheeks again. *Dang!* She fought to think of a reply that didn't sound stupid but was saved when Seth changed the subject.

"Jules, why didn't you want to file a report after the mugging?" Seth set his fork down on his empty plate.

"What's the point?" She put her fork down too, her appetite suddenly gone.

"I'm going to make a guess here," he said, leaning back in his chair and folding his arms over his chest. "I think your ex-husband did something worse than simply not trusting you. Worse than cheating. But what? I gotta tell you, my imagination is running wild here. Clue me in. It would have to be something horrible to traumatize you so much that you not only don't trust law enforcement officers, you don't even like them."

"I like you," she blurted, a bit flustered by how right Seth was. "Look, it's not like he beat me or anything. It's . . . it's hard for most people to understand. He just didn't trust me."

"You said that yesterday." Seth straightened in his seat and pushed his plate forward until he could rest his arms on the table. "He didn't trust you and you shouldn't have trusted him, right?"

"Yeah." She pushed her plate aside too and started to rise.

Seth stopped her by placing a hand on her uninjured arm. "Wait. Talk to me. I want to know what happened."

"Why? What does it have to do with your case?" A jittery sensation started just behind her breastbone.

"It has nothing to do with my case. It has everything to do with understanding you better. I saw the way you paled when the paramedic mentioned the police and the fear in your eyes when I told you I was leaving patrolmen at your shop. You don't just not like police; you fear them." He paused, then continued in a lower voice, "I see the fear there now, staring at me, as if you expect me to hurt you. I promise I won't."

Part of her wanted to run, to protect herself from this conversation. From him. And part of her wanted to open up and tell him everything. But experience taught her that the latter could destroy her. Still, the sincerity and warmth in his eyes soothed her and she found herself wanting to trust another person for the first time in years.

"Four years ago, I was a newlywed living in a small town and married to the youngest sheriff Kemmerton ever had." Jules sank into her chair again. She twisted her wrist. Seth let her go.

She pictured Kemmerton with its lush, green hills, lakes,

and riverfront homes. She smiled. "That fall, I started teaching preschool. I loved my kids. Five-year-olds are so excited all the time. They love to learn and play and they haven't yet learned to fear differences."

"Differences?"

"You know, they don't have biases based on religion or gender or ethnicities," she explained. "Anyway, about two months into the school year, one of my students, Michael, disappeared along with his older sister, Martha. They'd been in the grocery store with their nanny when it had happened. There had never been a kidnapping in the county before, so everyone was in a state of shock.

"Two weeks went by without a word. No suspects, no ransom note, nothing. The Amber Alert hadn't helped. It was like they just vanished. Billy wasn't sleeping and was at the station all the time. Parents kept their preschoolers home. The local elementary school was on lockdown during the day. It was horrible."

Seth covered the back of her hand with his and squeezed it lightly, but didn't interrupt.

"I saw an old woman in the grocery store parking lot. Her tire had gone flat and she seemed genuinely distraught. I changed her tire for her and even offered to follow her back to her house. She told me she lived on a farm at the edge of town, that I needn't bother because her grandchildren were there to help her. She tried to give me a hundred dollars for changing the tire, but I didn't take it." She shook her head. "I should have realized sooner something was off. She was jittery, aloof, and kept looking around as if expecting trouble. But this lady looked like your average grandmother. I figured she was just senile or something. Had she been forty years younger, I might have been suspicious that she'd been up to no good. I'd never imagined that a grandmotherly type could be a monster."

Seth frowned and stared at her intently for a moment before he guessed, "*She* was the kidnapper?"

Jules nodded.

Guilt lanced through her and she broke eye contact.

She remembered that unseasonably warm day. Remembered seeing the ghost of a little girl dressed in a poodle skirt, her wide blue eyes filled with an unspoken need. Remembered how she hovered around the old woman and begged Jules to stay with them. At the time, she'd assumed the girl had been the old woman's dead child. How wrong she'd been.

"What happened next?" Seth asked quietly.

Jules fought back the tears stinging her eyes. "The following night, Billy came home stressed and worried. He told me about reports of an ex-con, an elderly woman, who'd been seen trolling the schoolyard before the kidnapping. She'd been sent to prison twenty years before for the murder of a little girl she'd kidnapped on Halloween night. Through a clerical error, she'd been released. And worse, someone had reported seeing her at the elementary school only an hour before I'd helped the old woman with the flat tire.

"As soon as he told me, I explained that I thought I'd met the kidnapper the day before. I described the parking lot event, but he told me I needed to stick to teaching and to stop reading so many mystery novels. He said I needed to leave the police work to the professionals."

"Idiot!" A muscle worked in Seth's jaw. "The best tips we get are from people who are not in law enforcement. He should have listened to you."

Relief flitted through her. "Thanks. In the end, I called the station and delivered a tip."

"What made you so sure she was the kidnapper?" Seth asked.

Jules almost told him about the ghost of the little girl, then thought better of it. "Just a feeling. You know, like your gut tells you things."

"Yes." He nodded. "But I usually have evidence to back up my gut reactions."

"Yeah, well, Billy said something similar to me," Jules said bitterly. "I *was* right, you know."

Jules squared her shoulders, ready to drop the conversation, but Seth surprised her.

"There have been times when I didn't get my evidence until after I listened to my gut," he admitted. "Good for you for trusting yourself."

"Thanks, but it didn't end well." Jules shuddered at the memory. "I thought I'd made the tip anonymously because I used the only pay phone in town. I was so stupid. Everyone knows everyone in a small town. Anyway, the police found the children alive. But the old woman was killed on the scene. She'd been trying to drown Michael when the police kicked in the door. I didn't even know what happened. All I knew was that two hours after I'd made the call, my husband sent his deputy to arrest me for accessory to kidnapping."

"What? Why?" Seth sucked in a breath. His melted-chocolate eyes snapped fury. "You called in the tip. A tip you tried to give to the sheriff himself. Why would he have had you arrested?"

Jules couldn't look at him. She couldn't face the distrust she was sure she'd see in his eyes. It was the same look of doubt and fear she'd seen in Billy's. Pushing to her feet, she swallowed back the unexpected lump that had formed in her throat and carried their plates to the sink.

"Juliana." Seth touched her shoulder gently. "Talk to me. I know you couldn't have hurt those children. It's not in you."

"Billy said the only way I could have known about the old woman, or where to find her, was if I'd been there." More tears stung her eyes and she blinked rapidly to keep them from escaping. "It didn't help that as the old woman lay dying, she said my name to the police. I was condemned before her body was cold.

"I spent the night in jail, terrified I'd go to prison for trying to help. Worse, I'd been friends with all the guys at the station, but that night, they treated me like a rabid animal. One they needed to put down." Her hands shook and she hated herself for the weakness. Hated the memories of that horrifying night. "Michael and Martha's parents refused to believe I could have been involved. They hired an attorney for me and had me out by the next day."

"Thank Christ, someone in that damned county had some sense." Seth turned her in his arms then crooked a finger under her chin. He tilted her head back until she met his gaze. "You saved their babies and they saved you. Thank God, they did."

Warmth and something else filled his eyes. Something tender and powerful. Love?

That look succeeded in breaking her where the memories hadn't. Tears trickled from the corners of her eyes. He drew her close. She sank into his embrace, absorbing his strength and allowing him to rock her as she wept.

Her own husband hadn't had faith in her, but Seth did. Billy hadn't trusted what Jules had just shared with Seth. He'd demanded to know more, and when she'd told him about seeing the ghost, he'd thrown her away.

While she hadn't told Seth everything, he still believed her. Believed in her. If only he believed in psychics, she'd completely fall in love with him.

As it was, his faith in her made her want to thank him, to kiss him, to drink him in.

"Thank you for believing me." Pushing up on her toes, she pressed a featherlight kiss to his lips.

CHAPTER 15

❧

T HE ELECTRICITY SETH had experienced when they kissed
last night was nothing compared to the lightning arcing
between them now. Jules had only given him a gentle peck but
his lips sizzled. The scent of strawberries hit his senses and he
went hard for her.

Jules's story hadn't turned him on, but her strength had.
She'd had good reason not to trust another cop again, but she
trusted him.

Sanity briefly reared its head. He shouldn't be kissing her.
He needed to focus on his case. But he couldn't make himself
stop touching her.

Screw sanity.

Seth sensed she needed this. She needed him. And, God
help him, he needed her too.

Seth leaned in and kissed her again, exploring her mouth
with his lips and tongue. She met him stroke for stroke and it
made him hungrier.

He wrapped his left arm around her shoulders, then slid it

down until it wedged between her back and the counter. At the same time, he looped his right arm around her waist, bringing her body flush with his. She opened her eyes and stared up at him with a hazy look of lust in those emerald depths.

Every fantasy he'd had since he met her came flooding back. He wanted her on the counter, on the couch, on the floor, in a bed, and everywhere in between. Even finishing what they'd started the night before against the front door made his personal top-ten list.

Keeping her wrapped in his arms, he backed out of the kitchen and into the living room. While he wanted her everywhere, for their first time, he wanted a bed. A warm, large bed with plenty of space to give her body the thorough loving he intended.

"Seth, what are you doing?" she whispered, stumbling into him.

"Taking you someplace a little more comfortable." He dotted her cheeks, nose, and forehead with light kisses. With his lips hovering just above hers, near enough to kiss, he said, "Ah, precious. Tonight, you're mine."

He swept his tongue into her mouth, claiming her. He planned to explore every inch of her body. But not out here where the stacked boxes littered most of the free space in the room. *Need to move to the bedroom.*

She moaned into his mouth and drove her fingers into his hair, deepening the kiss. They half-walked, half-stumbled across the room, making it as far as the couch. He went down first and she landed on top of him.

Bed later.

He loved this side of her. At first glance, her slender body appeared fragile, but she wasn't. Jules was strong and tough, and she was the sexiest woman he'd ever touched.

And her kisses were fearless, like she wanted to devour him. The feeling was definitely mutual. Breaking the kiss, he whispered in gravelly tones, "You taste so good, precious. I could spend hours licking you all over."

She shivered in his arms.

He grinned in response. "You like that idea?"

Because it sure sounds good to me.

"Shhh . . ." She cupped his face in her hands and tugged

him back to her, claiming his mouth in a kiss so hot, he thought his shoes would melt off.

He'd never been especially fond of kissing. It was a function to get his lover excited. But when Jules kissed him, it was scorching and eager. He simultaneously wanted to make their clothes disappear and keep kissing her.

Jules shifted and bumped her arm against the back of the couch. Hissing, she jerked away from his touch. The look of pinched pain on her face doused his libido.

"Let me see." He reached for her arm and held it gently in one hand. He shoved up the sleeve of her gray sweatshirt and exposed the white bandage beneath. "Does it hurt much?"

"No, not much," she said, trying to twist out of his grasp.

He tightened his hold just enough to convince her to stop moving. Pressing his lips to her wound, he trailed the kisses up to her shoulder, then to her neck, and finally to the tender flesh behind her right ear. "Maybe we should find a bed?"

"I only have a twin," she said, but a look of doubt flashed in her eyes.

He leaned down and nuzzled her earlobe with his tongue and teeth until she moaned. "We can go to my apartment."

"Oh, that feels good," she breathed. "Or you can keep doing that and we can stay here a little longer."

He pulled back enough to look at her beautiful face. "Precious, it's taking every ounce of restraint I have not to take you right here on the couch like some horny teenager."

"Really?" Delight lit her eyes and she dropped her gaze to his groin.

His cock jumped at her open perusal. Needing to convince her of his word and needing her hands on his body, he wrapped one hand around her wrist and brought it to his jeans.

"Oh. My." She cupped him through the denim and rubbed him until he groaned. Pleasure, white hot and needy, burned through him. His balls sizzled with the need to come. And they hadn't even undressed yet.

"Juliana, you're killing me," he panted.

"You like this?" Her tone sounded uncertain, yet she caressed him as if they'd been lovers for years, as if she knew exactly how to touch him.

His tenuous control threatened to break when she lifted her gaze to his. The contrast of the uncertainty in her voice and the surety of her hands, added to the fact her eyes had darkened to a smoky green, almost snapped his control.

She was a contradiction in terms.

And every bit as turned on by what she was doing to him as he was.

He let his gaze drop to her nipples, which were poking hard little points into her sweatshirt. His mouth watered for a taste of her, but his lips went dry. He licked them and was rewarded by her slamming her mouth against his in a kiss so explosive it made a mockery of every other kiss he'd ever tasted.

She broke the kiss but continued teasing his body to a spike of pleasure and pain. "Seth, touch me, please."

Bending his face closer to her neck, he nuzzled the silken flesh at her collarbone and slid one hand up beneath the hem of her top. "Like this?"

"Yes. Yes, please."

He continued upward until his fingers grazed one distended nipple. A small sound of pleasure escaped her. Tugging the sweatshirt up out of his way, he exposed her breast to his gaze.

"You're not wearing a bra," he said, leaning down then taking the dusky bud into his mouth.

"Ah!" She drove the fingers of both hands into his hair and held him against her.

Rolling his tongue under and over the pebbled point, he licked it. Laved it. Her breasts were smaller than they had appeared in the corset she'd worn the night they met. But they were perfect.

She arched her back, offering him more, and he gladly accepted. He sucked the nipple into his mouth then popped it free, blowing his breath across it. She quivered in response. Then he turned his attention to the other nipple to give it the same loving.

"Off! Take my shirt off." She started to pull her top over her head but stopped when the sleeve snagged at her bandaged arm. Drawing air in between her teeth, she emitted a small cry of pain.

He tugged her sweatshirt back down until it covered her breasts, leaving her belly exposed. "No, we can't do this here."

"Okay." She pushed to her feet and stumbled a few steps before steadying herself, leading him toward the front door. She unlocked it and held it open. "Coming?"

"Not without you," he replied, hurrying to her side. Leaning down, he whispered, "Don't you know it's impolite for a man to come before his lover?"

A burst of air escaped her and she blushed. "And you're a gentleman, of course."

"Of course." He kissed her cheek. "And I'm going to make you come all night long."

Her gaze darkened. He brushed his lips against hers then headed toward his home.

Seth had nearly reached his front door when he turned to see Juliana disappearing back inside her apartment. In three long strides, he ate the distance and caught her door before it swung closed. "Juliana, what are you doing?"

"I forgot my purse and keys," she said. He held open the door and watched her disappear down the hall into her bedroom. She needed to hurry. His erection was close to popping the buttons on his fly.

She returned moments later, a confused expression on her face. "I could have met you in your apartment."

"Yes, but a gentleman escorts his lady to the door."

"And here I'd been picturing you more as a conquering warrior," she said, then blushed. "I can't believe I just said that out loud."

He leaned over and kissed her until she started groping him again.

"Precious." He groaned. "I'm fairly certain that tonight you're going to be the conquering warrior. Keep touching me like that and I'm going to finish right here before we can get to my place."

"We can't have that." Jules bolted across the hall to his door. She tried to open it, but it was locked.

He hugged her back to his front and nuzzled her neck as he unlocked his door, then opened it. Tugging her keys from her hand, he then patted her behind. "You didn't lock your door. I'll be right back. Make yourself at home."

He left to lock her door, leaving Jules alone in his darkened apartment. She flipped on the light in his living room and tried to catch her breath.

Was she really going to do this? Have sex with him?
Heck yes!

When he'd said, *"No, we can't do this here,"* she'd wanted
to weep in frustration. For a split second, she'd feared he'd
changed his mind.

Before he'd said that, she'd sensed his desires and fantasies.
But the moment she'd lifted her shirt, baring her breasts to
him, his fantasies had winked out of her brain. She wasn't sure
why, but she was too excited to care, especially after his promise to make her come all night.

Walking through the living room, she headed to Seth's
bedroom. She dropped her purse on the end table and continued on into the bathroom. She flipped on the light and the
fluorescent bulb hummed to life. Quickly washing her face
and hands, she ran her fingers through her shoulder-length red
hair and tried to sweep some body into it. But it was no use;
her hair was stick-straight.

Her reflection caught her attention. Her lips were swollen
and red, her whole face was flushed, and she had the look of a
woman who had been thoroughly kissed. She grinned, remembering the taste of him. And she wanted more.

Flipping off the bathroom light, she stood in the mostly
dark bedroom and stripped naked. Except for the light from
the streetlamp outside and the light filtering in from the living
room, the bedroom lay in darkness.

She folded her clothes and set them in a neat pile on top of
his dresser beside the bathroom door. Then she climbed into bed.

Manly but soft and inviting, the bamboo sheets were cool
against her hot skin. Sighing, she reveled in the decadent sensation of the exotic material on her naked, needy flesh.

The front door opened and closed, followed by the distinctive sound of a lock clicking into place. Listening to his heavy
footfalls, she silently imagined him crossing his living room,
stopping only long enough to flip off the light, past his galley
kitchen, down the hall, and into the bedroom. His footsteps
paused at the door.

"Jules?" he called in a stage whisper. "Did you fall asleep?"
"No."

"Damn." He moved into the room with a slow, deliberate

gait. "I was looking forward to finding a creative way to wake you up."

"Hang on," she said, feeling saucy. "I'll pretend to sleep and you can show me."

He chuckled. "I don't think so. I want to truly wake you up when I work my magic."

"Ooh," she said, unable to keep the excitement out of her voice. "Well, then I can go to sleep now." She faked a yawn.

Seth laughed again, then the bed dipped.

He sank down beside her and untied the laces to his sneakers one at a time, letting each one fall to the floor with a thunk. Stretching across her midsection, he reached out and turned on the lamp atop the bedside table.

"That's better," he said, propping his hands on either side of her head and staring down at her. "I could just look at you all night."

I don't think so.

She grabbed him and kissed him. He grinned against her lips and she smiled in return. Then she got down to some serious smooching. Driving her tongue into his mouth, she reached for his right hand, placing it on her bared breast.

He groaned into her mouth, then lightly pinched and plucked at her nipple until she moaned in response. When she finally did cry out, he broke their kiss and closed his lips around the aching tip while plucking and pinching the other one.

With each flick of his tongue or brush of his fingers on her breasts, she wound tighter and tighter until she thought she might shake apart with the need for completion. Then he dropped one hand between her thighs.

She spread wide for his touch, needing him to fill her and stop the torture. But he only glided one long finger inside her just enough to coat himself in her moisture, then he started stroking her. Not enough to bring her to release, just enough to keep her spinning with a growing, aching need.

"You're killing me."

"I am not." He laughed. "Just tormenting you. Besides, you're enjoying yourself. And believe me, I'm really enjoying it. You're so damned sexy."

Sexy?

She hadn't realized she'd closed her eyes until she opened them and found him stretched out beside her on the bed. He was still fully clothed except for his shoes and socks.

Oh, this wasn't fair.

Jules sat bolt upright, flipped over, and scooted down the bed until her face was in line with his jean-clad thighs. She yanked at the buttons on his fly. Excitement rippled through her when his erection sprang free.

"Commando?" she asked, licking her lips.

He might have answered her. She wasn't sure because she'd already leaned forward and licked him from base to tip.

"Ah, precious, you're going to give me a heart attack." He gasped between each word.

She might have been to blame for that. Each time he uttered a sound, she licked or nibbled or reached into his jeans to cup his sac. But he was so incredibly responsive to everything she did that he made her hungry to try more.

When he lifted a trembling hand to stroke the hair away from her face so he could watch her take him into her mouth, she nearly froze.

There was something sinful about being totally naked with a man who was still clothed. Especially when teasing him until *he* shook. Keeping eye contact with him, she inhaled and slowly took more of him into her mouth.

His breathing went ragged. His fingers tightened on her head as he guided her up and down, teaching her the best way to please him. The grip loosened after a minute as she caught his rhythm and did it on her own.

He sat up, forcing her to adjust her position in order to keep pleasing him.

Why'd he sit up?

As if to answer her unspoken question, he slipped a hand between her thighs and coated his fingers in her moisture again. Then he stroked her, rubbing the swollen, distended bundle of nerves at the apex of her thighs.

Her heart rate accelerated and her whole body tensed. Squeezing her eyes shut, she slid her mouth down his shaft again and held it there as lights exploded behind her eyes. Reflexively, she sucked hard on his shaft and he groaned loudly. "Precious, stop. I'm barely holding back here."

He tugged away from her touch and slipped his hands beneath her arms, dragging her sensitized body up his before flipping her onto her back and covering her body with his. He leaned back long enough to tug his shirt up over his head.

His beautiful naked chest glistened in the light. He was really about to make love to her. She'd thought he'd been sexy before, but actually running her hands over his naked abs, she realized he was even more so.

Oh, if this is a dream, don't let me wake up!

She tried to help him strip but only succeeded in getting in the way since she couldn't stop touching him. So she focused on freeing him from his jeans.

When her palm came skin to skin with his erection, Seth groaned deep in his throat, then laughed. "Stop helping me! You're going to help us into waiting another hour if you touch me like that again."

"An hour, really?" Jules asked with surprise. She watched him strip out of his jeans, grab a condom from the nightstand, and roll it on. "I thought men only needed twenty minutes."

"Precious, with you, I have a feeling I wouldn't need ten seconds before I'm ready to go again. But you make me come before I can get inside you and I'll tie you down and torture you for an hour before I'll let you come again."

Butterflies in her belly quivered in delight at the thought of him teasing her nonstop for an hour.

He positioned himself over her. With his thighs between hers, he rested his weight on his fists beside her head, and said, "You ready or should I test out that sexual torture idea right now?"

He didn't wait for a response; instead, he slid into her with one long, deep thrust.

She gasped, wrapping her legs around his hips. He lowered his body until his curly chest hair tickled her breasts. He wrapped one hand behind her back, clutching her backside and kneading it with his fingers while he slowly slid back out and then even deeper inside her again. The sensations of both actions nearly distracted her from what he did with her right arm.

Gently, slowly, he entwined the fingers of his left hand with her right one. He raised her arm above her head, pinning it to the pillow beneath her. She turned her head to look at what he'd done.

"Seth, why did you do that?"

He didn't answer but covered her mouth with his. Had the kiss been passionate and full of demand, she wouldn't have been surprised, but it wasn't. It was tender and lingering. Caring.

It brought tears to her eyes. It was a moment unlike any she'd ever experienced. She'd had sex before, but this was the first time she'd ever felt as if someone was making love *with* her.

She blinked back the moisture so she wouldn't make a fool of herself. Wanting to breathe him in, to touch him, she caressed his naked back with her free hand and still he kissed her as he thrust rhythmically.

Like a moment suspended in time, she wanted to make love with him forever, to keep going, but that incredibly needy build of excitement coiled in her midsection. It spread through her entire body until she was straining to reach her climax.

Seth broke their kiss and pressed his lips against her left ear. "Let go, I've got you, precious."

As if to emphasize his words, he pistoned his hips and started pumping harder into her, pushing her higher until she snapped free and was flying.

Seconds later, he plunged deeply inside of her one last time. With a groan of pleasure, he shifted his weight to her left side and sank onto the mattress.

Still breathing heavily, he lowered her arm and checked her bandage again as if expecting her to have torn her stitches. His brow furrowed in concern, he examined the dressing so white it nearly glowed.

She couldn't resist teasing him. "It's not like you tied me down this time. I doubt we did anything that could have aggravated my wound. But you could tie me up next time. Or maybe I'll put those handcuffs you used on me . . . on you."

Inside her, he twitched to life.

"Ooh, you are a naughty boy." She laughed.

He opened his mouth wide and playfully bit her shoulder, then laughed too. "I knew you would be trouble the moment I caught you sneaking into my bedroom."

"Right."

"No, I did." He chuckled again. "It's my sixth sense. It always lets me know when trouble's brewing."

"A sixth sense?" She snorted, half-disbelieving and half-hoping. "You're so full of it."

He pulled back until he stared into her eyes. "You don't believe in a sixth sense? Come on, precious. See the world beyond the *monochrome*."

Jules let out a short, nervous laugh, then said, "You know, you've called me *precious* since the moment we met. You go around calling everyone that when your sixth sense warns you they could be trouble?"

"Nope. Only you." He licked a path from her collarbone to her nipple.

She stretched under his caress and tried, unsuccessfully, to tamp down her delight at his use of the term *sixth sense*. "So I'm trouble."

"Oh yeah, precious," he said, kissing her neck again. "The kind I need to spend all night investigating."

AFTER THEY'D MADE love the second time, they'd both fallen asleep. Jules awoke to the erotic tingling of Seth's teeth and tongue stroking the tender flesh between her thighs. Before she'd managed to even open her eyes, he'd brought her to orgasm.

The waking had been every bit as wonderful as Seth had promised it would be, even more so when he joined their bodies together again. Her release came so hard and fast, Jules could do little more than hold on for the ride. It left her replete and drained. While she dozed again, he'd gone back to her apartment and grabbed the baklava he'd brought for dessert.

Seth leaned against the headboard and Jules sat nestled between his legs, her back to his front. They fed each other baklava and talked. She told him about searching for her sisters and he told her about growing up in his mother's restaurant.

"Mama closes the restaurant on Christmas Day and we have a big party with all of my cousins, aunts, and uncles. Now our children come too. It's crowded and crazy," Seth said, then popped a piece of baklava into his mouth.

"It sounds wonderful, being surrounded by so many relatives during the holidays." A lump formed in her throat and Jules had to clear it before she could speak again. Normally she had a love/hate relationship with Christmas. She loved the lights and music but hated the actual day. "April and Big Jim are only children, so it's usually just us for the holidays. Not for much longer, though."

"Are you talking about after the babies are born?" He pressed a gentle kiss to her shoulder. The light brush of his lips on her naked skin made her toes curl.

"Well, yes, but no. I-I told you I want to find my sisters. I spoke to a social worker on Sunday. She helped me as much as she could but then gave me a card for a private detective agency. I'm hoping they'll be able to do more."

"A *private* detective?" Seth frowned, his voice heavy with skepticism.

"I know most cops don't like them, but Mrs. Harris recommended Tidewater Security Specialists." She leaned to the side to look over her shoulder at Seth. "I've tried everything I can think of. I can't do it alone. I-I need help."

"Jules, never apologize for wanting to find your family. TSS is the only company I'd call, because I know the owners. Good guys. I hope they can help you. Don't hesitate to ask if you need me to do anything."

Unexpected tears sprang to her eyes. Jules wanted to thank him for being so supportive, but didn't get a chance. Seth squeezed her gently, his naked chest warm and inviting against her back as he said, "And your sisters are missing out, not having you in their lives. Family is everything."

"You're secretly a romantic," she joked, trying to lighten the mood.

"And you're scared to let anyone else in."

"That's not true." But it had been a few hours ago. Now she wanted to let him in. To show him the real her, the part that made Billy throw her away, and it terrified her.

"Prove it." He sat back and picked up another slice of baklava. "Tell me about how you ended up in the foster care system."

Her mouth went dry. "I told you, my father ran out on us when I was nine. It was right after my mom learned she was pregnant and had breast cancer. And my mom died a year and a half later."

"Juliana, I know the foster care system tries to keep

families together, especially young children. What happened that the three of you were separated?"

She still couldn't bring herself to form the words. The memory of that time still left a gaping hole.

"You don't have to tell me," he said, rolling her hand in his and interlacing their fingers. "I can see it's painful." He kissed her cheek.

It was the offer that convinced her to tell him. If he had insisted, she would have shut down. But she wanted to trust him.

Please, don't let this be a mistake.

"After my mom died," she began. She paused to inhale a breath, hoping it would loosen the knot in her chest, then continued, "Social Services tried to find a relative who would take in my sisters and me, but there was no one. And my father had disappeared long before without looking back.

"So, here we were, three little girls ages ten, seven, and three and a half. We wanted to stay together but there was a *glitch*. A closed adoption had been arranged for Hannah, my baby sister. Before we knew what was happening, she was gone. Then it was just Shelley and me."

She sat forward and drew a great shuddering breath. For several minutes, Jules couldn't speak. Tears clogged her throat but she wanted to show a brave face, so she collected herself. As if sensing her need to be strong, Seth stroked his free hand along her back.

He didn't say anything, just waited patiently.

"Shelley took Hannah's adoption harder than our mom dying. Before foster care, Shelley had always been obedient and well-mannered. After we lost Hannah, she started acting out, running away. It's how we lost our first foster home. It scared Shelley so much, she became the Stepford foster child. It wasn't long before a couple came along and tried to adopt her.

"She would have gone but not without me. I was ten and already over-the-hill in the foster care system. She cried when they came to collect her and didn't stop until they brought her back." Jules closed her eyes against the rage that still bubbled inside her at the injustice. "Who knew children came with a return policy?"

Seth muttered a curse under his breath, then pressed a gentle kiss to her shoulder. "They shouldn't."

She nodded. "Since our foster parents had already replaced her with another child, there was no room for Shelley. So I convinced the social worker to move me to the next foster home with her. We went through this a couple of times before I overheard the social worker talking to the foster parents. They were already planning to have us removed from our current foster home if Shelley didn't go with the next family that offered to adopt her.

"I tried to convince Shelley the new family was a good one. And they were. While the other two families seemed nice, this one really wanted Shelley. They truly cared for her. They wanted me too but couldn't afford to adopt us both. Shelley refused to go with them, until I gave her no choice."

A hollow ache opened in the center of her chest at the memory of Shelley's anguished expression. Jules had tried everything to make Shelley understand she needed to go with this family. Their current foster family wanted Jules out. She'd been caught conversing with ghosts one time too many and her foster parents were afraid her kind of crazy was catching. They had even started whispering that Shelley might go the same way.

Jules couldn't risk her sister being hurt, especially since Shelley didn't see ghosts. She communicated with animals. But so far, the foster parents hadn't noticed that. When they did, Shelley would be labeled a freak like Jules had been.

"What did you do to convince your sister to go with the family?" Seth's voice yanked Jules from her thoughts. "You *did* do something, didn't you?"

"Yes, I told her she was holding me back. I could have been adopted a long time ago if I hadn't had a little sister to take care of."

"That's quite a lie you told." Seth stroked her left arm consolingly. Oddly enough, the touch did comfort her. He kissed her cheek and said, "It must've hurt you terribly when she believed it."

"Well, yeah." She tried to laugh but it came out like a sob. "I lost my best friend and my family all at once."

"So, at ten, you sacrificed being with the only family you had left to guarantee her a chance to have one of her own," he said, admiration in his voice. "So now you search for them."

"And hope Shelley can forgive me." She shuddered.

The baklava stuck in her throat and she swallowed hard, feeling more exposed than ever, despite the sheet covering her.

JULES WAS PULLING away from him. She hadn't moved, hadn't said another word, and still Seth could sense a chasm building between them.

He'd had no idea how hard her life had been. His family had always been there for him, even when he'd screwed up. She deserved the same.

And he'd make damned certain she found her sisters. In the meantime, he needed to bridge the ever-widening distance between them. Searching for a lighter topic, he asked, "Why do you call Ernie *Big Jim*?"

A small chuckle escaped her. "Because he wasn't."

"This has to be good." Seth leaned back again, taking Jules with him. Her bottom nestled snugly between his thighs and against his groin.

"Let's see, after Shelley left, I bounced from foster home to foster home every six months or so. The first three homes had a father-figure named Jim or Jimmy. The fourth home I went to, the guy's name was Oswald or something weird. I called him Jim one day by mistake. He thought it was funny. I thought maybe this time they'd keep me. They didn't.

"Two more homes over a four-month period and I started going to some really crappy foster parents. We're talking they counted the days on the calendar until the foster check came so they could buy cigarettes or lottery tickets."

Seth believed the foster care system could be very successful, but sometimes it just sucked.

"Why didn't anyone adopt you?" He had to know. She was smart, witty, kind . . . and he just bet she'd been a loving child.

"I was *different*."

"Different how?" It wasn't the word she used so much as the tone of resignation in her voice that tugged at the protectiveness he'd felt growing for her since they'd met.

She gave a wry grin.

"Too old to adopt, remember?" she answered a little too lightly and shrugged. "Anyway, the last foster home I lived in was with Little Jim. He was a real winner. Big beefy man, hands like Easter hams, and a mean streak so wide, everyone hid when he was drunk. One day he took a swing at one of the younger boys in the house. I got in between them and he clocked me."

"He punched you? You were . . . what, twelve at the time?"

"Yeah."

He ground his teeth, biting back the litany of curses he wanted to spew. To hit a child, a *girl*, sent Seth into an orbit of pissed he seldom visited.

"Please tell me you reported him." He managed to keep the majority of the venom out of his voice. "Better yet, give me his name and address. I'll visit him personally."

"No need." She shook her head and a dreamy look hazed her eyes. "Big Jim happened to be visiting his mother when Little Jim chased me outside. I crawled into the back seat of this beat-up station wagon across the street. I heard Little Jim bellowing for me but I didn't move.

"This young couple, who looked like they weren't much older than me, climbed into the front of the car. April turned around and gasped when she saw me."

"I'll bet."

"Yeah, well, I don't know what freaked her out more: the split lip Little Jim had given me or the sight of him leaning in her open window to yell at me. He ordered me to get out of the car. That's when Big Jim turned around and looked at me. He told me, 'Safety is a right. Not a privilege. Stay here as long as you like. I'll make sure no one hurts you again.' Then he leaned over and whispered to April.

"Without another word, he stepped out of the car and went toe-to-toe with Little Jim. They looked like David and Goliath. I didn't want him injured because of me. But when I started to get out of the car, April stopped me.

"She promised me her husband wouldn't be hurt. And she was right. No matter how many times that drunk tried to punch Big Jim, he never managed to touch him. When the police arrived, they saw Little Jim throwing punches and Big Jim backing up with his hands in the air."

"They arrested your foster father, then?"

"Yep. When social services arrived on the scene to remove

all eight children to other homes, they said they couldn't find a place for me. I'd need to go to juvenile detention for the night. Big Jim wouldn't hear of it. He and April offered to take me in.

"I kept waiting for them to get rid of me too. I refused to call him anything but Big Jim for the next eight months. But incredibly, a year after we met, they signed my adoption papers."

Jules exhaled a large breath and Seth found himself doing the same. He sat in awe of her. She'd been through hell as a child and still she smiled. No wonder she was so untrusting.

"Probably a little TMI, huh?" she asked, her cheeks reddened.

"No, not too much at all," he said. "You've had such a rough childhood. It's amazing you're as well-adjusted as you are."

"Thanks . . . I think."

"It's a compliment," he assured her. He reached out and stroked her cheek. Pleasure coursed through him when she turned her face into his palm. "You really are precious. How could anyone ever let you get away?"

SHE OPENED HER mouth to tell him that somewhere between two days ago and now, she'd fallen in love with him. And wanted to let him in even if that meant telling him her darkest secrets.

And he believes in the concept of a sixth sense.

Would he believe in her unique abilities or would he be like Billy and her foster families and look at her with fear and loathing in his eyes? It didn't matter that she hated her abilities. Or that she was determined to escape from the ghosts that haunted her.

All that mattered was in the end Billy had thrown her away, like so many others had done before him.

If sexy Seth, the warrior with the melted-chocolate eyes, looked at her as the others had, it might break her.

But if she stayed here much longer, she might lose the fight with that inner child in her that always cried out for acceptance.

Time to leave.

Setting her dessert plate on the end table, she stood and let the sheet fall back to the bed. From behind her, Seth whistled.

"You are quite a sight to behold." She could hear the smile in his voice.

"Yes, and shadows do wondrous things for a woman's figure." She crossed to his dresser, where the lamp light didn't quite reach. Lifting her bra and panties from the stack of folded clothes she'd placed there earlier, she said, "I should be going."

The bed squeaked behind her. Seth's feet smacked the hardwood in several rapid steps, then his arms slipped around her waist and he spun her in his embrace. "Now why would you want to do that?" he asked, his deep baritone voice dropping an octave.

"Don't you need to work in the morning?"

The scent of the honey and nuts of the Greek dessert mingled with the delicious smell of sex and sandalwood. Jules inhaled deeply and burrowed against his chest, despite knowing she shouldn't. Every moment spent in this man's presence weakened her resolve to keep her secrets to herself.

"It's late," she said, giving him the best excuse she could come up with in her fuddled brain. "I should go and let you sleep."

"So you're sacrificing yourself for me, now?" He *tsked* at her, then lightly nipped her earlobe.

The sensation sent a jolt of excitement through her. Instantly, she was wet and ready for him again. She rubbed her chest against his.

He hissed in pleasure, then said, "Come back to bed with me. I won't get a moment's peace without you in it." He dropped his hands to hers and led her toward his bed.

"But your case?" Jules followed with a frown.

He shrugged. "I'll handle it. Tomorrow. Come on, we've talked enough. And I'm wide awake. If you want to sacrifice something for me, then let it be sleep." He tumbled her onto the bed and followed her down. "If you do, I promise it will be the best sleepless night on record."

CHAPTER 16

❦

LATE AFTERNOON SUNSHINE spilled from the high window in the landing of the apartment complex stairwell. It shined a golden spotlight on Seth's front door.

As quietly as he could, he opened it and slipped inside. He listened for sounds as he let his eyes adjust to the dimness of his living room. He'd unplugged his home phone before he'd left for work, so no one could accidentally call and wake Jules while he'd been out.

It had been risky leaving her asleep in his bed while he went to work. But his apartment was the safest place for her, if she couldn't be with him. Not to mention he limited the risk of her leaving by pocketing her keys on his way out at six that morning.

Had she awakened and learned he'd snuck out with her keys, he had no doubt that she would have been livid. But he couldn't risk her accidentally exposing herself to potential danger while he'd been at work.

A yawn seemed to well up from the middle of his body. Damn, he should've gone to sleep sooner last night, but he'd needed to wear out Jules. He counted on her sleeping through the day so he could do his job without worrying about her safety.

Laying both his and her sets of keys on the kitchen counter, he scooped up the note he'd left for Jules in case she woke while he was gone. He tossed the paper into the garbage can on the way to his bedroom.

Seth had drawn the shades just before he'd fallen asleep at four in the morning. He'd hoped she'd sleep all day, given that the shop was closed, and their fantastic marathon lovemaking session last night. A quick glance at his bed and a grin tugged at his lips. Jules still slumbered peacefully, even with the shaft of sunlight spilling across the bed.

He quickly stripped naked, then climbed between the sheets. Still asleep, she rolled over and wrapped herself around him. At her innocent touch, he went hard.

Amazing. He should have been too tired.

They'd made love all night. That should have left him sore, and resulted in him only catching a two-hour nap. Not to mention he'd had a long, frustrating day at work. He should have just stayed in bed given the fact that he and Jones had spent the afternoon chasing down bogus tips.

The only semi-useful bit of information he'd learned had been the identity of Jules's mugger. Jack Kells, an ex-con with a talent for bypassing security systems. The thief had been paroled two years ago and had seemingly kept his nose clean until his attack on Jules.

Another dead end. Another wasted day. And his sergeant's exam invitation seemed to slip further out of reach.

Seth yawned again. He was exhausted. He should sleep, but his body was hard and aching. He was ready to go again. No, he wasn't ready to go exactly. He was ready for Jules. She was special.

Crazy as it sounded, it was true.

They'd talked for hours last night, not because of his case. No, they'd talked because he wanted to get to know her. A first for him.

After his divorce, sex had become a biological function. An itch to scratch, nothing more. Oh, he'd cared for each of his lovers, ensuring they found their pleasure when he was with them. But even the few relationships he'd had since his marriage had ended hadn't been riddled with emotion or the need for more than physical contact.

Jules changed that. He wanted to know everything about her. What were her dreams? Well, he knew that: to find her sisters. What made her laugh? Hmmm . . . he knew that too. As he did a mental inventory of the questions he wanted to ask her, he realized he already knew most of the answers.

Still, there seemed to be something she kept hidden. Her fears, maybe? No, she'd shared those too.

But something had definitely upset her last night after they'd made love the second time. She'd claimed she wanted to leave to let him rest, but he sensed it was more than that. Jules had been ready to run home, and unless he missed his guess, run far away from him.

So why didn't I let her go?

In the past, he never invited a woman to his place. He went to hers. It was easier to find an excuse to leave than it was to ask her to go home. And he always wanted the night to end. But not last night. Not with Jules. And it wasn't entirely because he wanted to keep her safely hidden in his apartment.

No, he'd wanted her *with* him.

Between learning what her ex had done to her and learning about her childhood, Seth had fallen for her. He'd wanted to hold her. Soothe her. Make love to her and make her forget all her pain.

Make love.

His pulse jumped as those two words registered. He'd been thinking them on and off for several minutes but the impact of their meaning now hit him like a punch to his solar plexis.

What they'd shared last night had been erotic, fun, and incredibly powerful. It had been more intimate than anything he'd ever experienced.

She'd been soft and pliant in his arms, yet eager and responsive to his touch. Giving as good as she got, and demanding more. Then when he'd been buried deep inside her and she opened her smoky emerald-colored eyes, so filled with trust and desire, it stole his breath.

The case, her past, his past, all of it had gone away and the world had spiraled down to the two of them in bed. Touching. Caressing. Loving.

Love.

There was that word again. He wasn't a romantic, despite what Jules thought.

Love didn't really exist. It certainly didn't happen after knowing someone only a few days. It wasn't possible. Still, he felt . . . something.

He looked down at her sleeping form. She slept with one hand tucked between her cheek and his chest. Her hair fell over his body like a golden-red curtain. She didn't exactly snore, but her breaths were deep, slow, and steady.

A smile curled his lips.

"What are you staring at?"

Her question startled him but he recovered quickly. "You, precious."

"That's not very modern of you," she said, yawning. "Or me either."

"What?" He pressed a kiss to the hollow on her throat.

"You calling me some generic nickname." Her voice, soft and low, held no humor. "I could be anyone."

"Precious." He nipped her shoulder, hoping she'd open her eyes. She rolled farther away instead. "I told you, I've never called anyone else that. And the name suits you beautifully."

"In that case, I like it." She rolled onto her back and finally opened her eyes. A wide smile spread across her face. "Detective *Lambkins.*"

"Oh, hell no." He looked at her in horror. "You cannot call me that."

"Not masculine enough?" She laughed.

"Definitely not."

She stretched, arching her back. Seth couldn't resist rolling on top of her. The sensation of her perky nipples rubbing against his chest made him ache with need.

Who needs sleep?

Jules slid her thighs around his waist, then pressed her feet against his back, drawing him closer. Her feminine red curls brushed against his bare abdomen. She was already hot and wet for him. Incredibly, he got harder for her.

His body demanded he take her hard and fast. God knew he
needed the rest, but he didn't want to rush this. Even after last
night, touching her was too new. Seth wanted to savor every
second. Lowering his face, he buried his nose against her neck
and hair and inhaled the scent of sex and strawberries.

With only the sliver of the golden sunshine peeking into
the room, she lay mostly in shadows. But a shaft of light drew
a line along the length of her body from her left shoulder to
her ankle. Starting at her shoulder, he traced the sunlit path
with his tongue.

Detouring to her breasts on the way back up, he painted a
path around her nipple but didn't touch it directly. She moaned,
wrapping her legs around his waist again. She arched her
back, clearly trying to guide her nipple into his mouth. He
chuckled against her flesh and brought his hands up to pin her
shoulders gently to the mattress. "Stay."

"Tormentor."

"Maybe," he agreed, then suckled the underside of her
breast. "But you're mine to torture. And you love it."

He curled his tongue around her nipple. She gasped. He
rolled the nipple between his teeth. She moaned. He blew a
warm breath across the dusky pink bud. She shivered.

"You're killing me."

"Mine to torment," he said, licking a path to her other
breast. "Say it. Say you're mine."

"Please don't tease me."

"Say it." He tortured her other nipple as he had her first.
When she shuddered beneath his touch in want of sexual
release, he amped up the torture. Drawing her aching tip into
his mouth, he suckled. Hard.

She dug her heels into his ass, her body bowing.

"Say. It," he said, with her nipple between his teeth, then he
laved the tip and bit down lightly.

"Yours!" she cried out. "I'm yours, Seth. Oh, God! Yes!"

He suckled her until she shook in his arms. Amazed, he
watched her beautiful face as she lost herself in the throes of
her release. "Did you just co—?"

She clapped one hand over his mouth. The light filtering
into the room glittered on her glistening, flushed cheek.
"Shhh . . . pl-please," she panted.

A grin spread across his face; he couldn't stop it if he'd wanted to. And damn, he really didn't want to.

"Proud of yourself?" Her lovely cheeks were pink.

"Very. How many men could say they'd made their lover come with just their mouth on her breast?" He pressed his lips against hers in a scorching kiss. "Don't go anywhere. I'm not through with you yet."

He stretched across her body for the condom box on the nightstand and froze.

The box was empty. "Damn."

I should've bought more on the way home.

"Seth, what's wrong?" Jules propped herself up on an elbow to look at him.

Before he could answer her, his cell phone rang. From the caller ID, he could see it was his partner.

Dropping the empty box onto the bedside table, Seth picked up the cell and answered it. "English. What's up, Jones?"

"Got something interesting to show you down at the station."

"I just got home," Seth said, ignoring Jules's wide-eyed expression. "Can it wait until morning?"

"Doubtful." Jones growled a bearlike yawn.

Seth hadn't been the only one exhausted at work today. Jones had had bags under his eyes and had downed at least two pots of coffee by himself. He hadn't said what had kept him awake and Seth didn't ask. Given Seth's own adventures last night, the last thing he wanted to do was to discuss his partner's sex life.

Jones continued. "Iris Masters came into the station looking for you an hour ago. She showed up with an armful of journals, right after you left. Said she'd thought they were stories Aimee-Lynn made up, but now suspected differently. Seems the girl wanted to be a writer. But the journals aren't fantasies; they're diaries, written in some cryptic prose that makes my eyes want to bleed."

"I can't believe I'm saying this to *you*, but . . . point?"

"There are four references: Daggers, Mitchum, Blue Swan, and—"

"Holcomb," he breathed into the receiver. "Damn, the names of the robbed jewelers."

Excitement and urgency rippled down his spine. It was the break in the case he'd been searching for. Seth crossed to his closet and opened it, listening to Jones the entire time.

"You guessed it. There's also a mention of four masked marauders: the Heiress, the Jack of Fools, the Prince of Hearts, and the Knight of the Realm."

"Knight of the Realm?" he asked, crossing to hang his suit on the back of the bathroom door.

"Hokey, I know, but there's more. There's a detailed plan of how the four plan to prove to Holcomb that his chief of security is betraying his kingdom and stealing from him. It almost sounds like she viewed them as the good guys. Weird, huh?"

"Odd," Seth agreed, crossing to his dresser to retrieve a fresh pair of boxers and socks. He set them on the bathroom sink. "What else?"

"Tons, but it's the last entry you want to read. It's different from the others. Listen—'The Knight of the Realm is not what he seems. He's betrayed us all. I, alone, must seek justice and make this right. I've called upon the English King to help me, and he's promised aid. But I fear the journey on my own. Without my beloved prince at my side, how shall I survive? Whom can I entrust with the sparkling weight of my secrets?'"

Jones fell silent.

Seth checked his phone but the line was still open. "That's it? 'The sparkling weight of my secrets'?"

"Yes, *my liege.*"

Seth wasn't amused. "I get it, I'm the English King."

"Yeah, *you* got it the first time around. I had to read that craptastic piece of literature three times before I could stay awake long enough to even notice your name in there." Jones yawned. He spoke again but his voice was muffled, as if the phone's mouthpiece were covered. "Thanks, Harmon."

Seth turned to Jules, who watched him silently from the bed. Her expression was open, curious. "I gotta go to work," he mouthed.

She nodded, then sat up and wrapped the top sheet around her body, toga-style.

"Harmon just handed me a note from Captain Peterson." Jones returned. "*Whoa!* It says, 'Tell English to get his ass in

here for a meeting at six thirty.' What'd you do to piss off
Peterson so much that he called for a meeting *tonight*?"

"Nothing. I haven't seen him all day." Seth wracked his
brain. He'd left a voice mail for his captain asking to discuss
his concerns about Jules's safety. Surely that hadn't ticked off
his captain. Had it? "I thought Peterson was sick at home."

"Guess not," Jones replied. "But I haven't seen him either.
His office light is out and the door's closed. Guess he's coming
in for the meeting too?"

Seth grunted noncommittally. "Hey, check my desk and
phone for messages. See if he left a reply to my request for a
protection detail."

"For Jules? Never mind, stupid question. Of course it's for
her. Hang on." Several heartbeats passed, then Jones said,
"Sorry. Nothing. Maybe it'll be a short meeting?"

"Let's hope so. I don't like this." Seth wasn't comfortable
leaving Jules alone again. But he couldn't ignore this break or
the command performance issued by Peterson. Shoving a hand
through his hair, he said, "I'll be there in twenty minutes."

JULES COULD HARDLY breathe as she stared at Seth. From the
moment he'd risen from the bed, his aura pulsed a vibrant
emerald green. How could she see his aura and why did the
ability come and go? With ghosts, Jules saw them all the time.
Why was it different with him?

Strong emotions.

The only times she'd seen his aura was when he experienced powerful emotions. And in a strange way, it made sense.
When he was angry or worried to the point of being overpro-
tective, his emotions seemed to radiate from him.

While she didn't see auras around other living people, she
didn't mind seeing his. It only made him more attractive. More
accessible.

He ended his call and turned to her. Standing unabashedly
naked in the middle of the bedroom floor, he tapped his cell
against his chin and regarded her. "Precious, I need to go in to
the station. I don't know how long I'll be. There might be a
break in my case."

"No problem. You go take your shower." She gestured to

the bathroom door where he'd hung a black shirt, blazer, and tie on a hanger. Although she couldn't see it, she bet there were slacks on that hanger too. "I'll let myself out. I need to check my messages anyway. If Big Jim or April called the apartment, they'll worry if they don't hear from me."

"I'd prefer it if you'd stay here," Seth said, propping his hands on his waist. He appeared unaware he stood gloriously naked. "No one knows you're here. It's safe."

"You think I'm in danger?" Jules flinched.

"You know I do." He nodded. "It's why you're here. Let me do my job and protect you."

"Is that why you brought me here last night?" A sick feeling went through her. Could last night have meant more to her than to him? She rose from the bed, holding the sheet firmly around her body with her good arm. "Did you sleep with me out of some kind of . . . of . . . *civic duty*?"

"Jules, don't be ridiculous." Seth reached for her, but she sidled away from his touch. She shuffled to his dresser, where she'd left her purse, clothes, and keys in a pile, last night. Grabbing her clothes and purse, she hugged them to her body and awkwardly searched for her missing keys.

"They're in the kitchen," Seth said. He hadn't moved from his position in the middle of the floor.

"How did they get there? I saw you put them back on the dresser after you brought over the baklava."

Seth closed his eyes on an exhale, then opened them again. "I didn't want you to leave while I was at work today, so I took them with me."

"Who do you think you are?" Jules shouted, shuffling across the floor to stand toe-to-toe with him.

Seth's emerald aura expanded and pulsed like a living thing around him. "I think I'm the only person who believes you're in danger. I *think* I'm the one person who will do anything to keep you safe. And I know that I'll lose my damned mind if one more thing happens to you.

"I told you last night, cops who get involved with people on their cases get sloppy. I'm trying not to be sloppy. I'm trying to protect the woman I adore and do my goddamned job at the same time. So please, stay here and do not let *anyone* in until I get back."

Seth panted as if he'd just finished a triathlon and his aura shifted between barely outlining his body to washing the bedroom in green light. Not once in his speech had he paused long enough for Jules to reply. Good thing.

She doubted he'd have told her what he felt about her, had she interrupted him. And really, at that moment, that was what she needed to know. It was beautiful, freeing. Not quite as good as love, but a heck of a lot better than being his unwanted responsibility.

"Seth," Jules said, shuffling closer to him. She wrapped her free arm around his waist, then hissed in pain as his chest came into contact with her injured one. The clothes and purse fell from her grasp and onto Seth's bare feet.

"Ow!" Seth hopped back, but flung out his hands to her hips, steadying her so she didn't fall. "What have you got in your purse? Rocks?"

Jules glanced down at her clutch lying amid her scattered clothes on the floor, then back to Seth. For a reason she couldn't name, she started laughing. Maybe it was the sight of him standing naked, massaging his big toe. Maybe it was that nervous release that people need after a highly charged moment. Or maybe it was the sheer giddiness she felt as she saw his aura throb green then bright red and green again. "You adore me?"

He stopped massaging his foot and chuckled.

"Ah, precious. I know it's crazy. We've only known each other a few days, but yes, I'm wild about you. I'd do anything to keep you safe. Not because it's my job. But because it's you."

I love you.

Oh, she wanted to say it out loud, but the words didn't come. Instead she kissed him. It was warm and sweet and ended all too soon.

"The prince!" he said, as if solving some puzzle. He glanced heavenward, then back to her. Satisfaction lit his features before his brow furrowed. Gently, he cupped her face in his hands. "Precious, there's one more thing. Your *friend* Mason Hart might be tied to my case."

"What?" She laughed her disbelief. "The burglaries you mentioned? That doesn't make sense. Mason doesn't need money. Why would he rob anything? Besides, his biggest worry right now is that his fiancée won't return his calls."

Seth stepped back, a stunned expression on his face. "You know his fiancée?"

"Just what he told me about her on Saturday when he came to buy her flowers. Why?" A sense of foreboding slithered through her belly.

"The body in the Dumpster," Seth said, slowly, "was his fiancée, Aimee-Lynn Masters."

Jules started trembling. Heck, she wasn't trembling; she was practically convulsing.

Seth steadied her and urged her to sit back down on the bed, cursing the entire way.

"He never told me her name." She shook her head, unable to process the information. "Seth, he bought her flowers. Told me he wanted me to have breakfast with the two of them so she would know Friday night had just been a misunderstanding."

"What had been a misunderstanding?" The bed dipped as Seth sat down beside her. "I thought you told me everything you remembered."

Heat scorched her cheeks. "I didn't mention it because it was embarrassing and I didn't think it had anything to do with your case." Fear whipped through her and she turned to face him. "Please believe me. I didn't know Mason's fiancée was the dead woman."

"Just tell me what happened that you thought was unimportant," he said, sounding all business. "I need you to tell me as quickly as you can."

"Okay, um . . ." Jules tried to will her shaking under control and told Seth about Mason *mistaking* her for his date at the reunion.

"And you're positive you never saw them together?" Seth asked.

"Absolutely." She nodded. "I hadn't seen Mason until I turned around after he kissed my neck."

"Tell me again what he said to you then." Seth leaned over and yanked a note pad and pen from his bedside table. The move gave her a clear view of his naked backside. As delectable as the sight was, it didn't loosen the knots in her belly. "He said, 'You're right. Let's do it. Let's do it now. Tonight.'"

"Any idea what he was talking about?" Seth asked, then immediately followed up with another question. "Did you ask him about it when he went to your shop?"

"No idea what it meant and I didn't ask. I just wanted to forget it. It was really embarrassing. He told me he'd kissed me in the dark, thinking I was her," she explained. Seth frowned at his notebook and she repeated, "Seth, that's all I can remember. You asked me to trust you. I need you to trust me too."

"I do." He snapped his gaze to hers and his expression softened. "I believe you. But now I'm more convinced than ever that you need protection. I can't take you with me to the station, can I?"

She shuddered and all the blood rushed from her head to her toes.

"No, I see I can't." He answered his own question, rubbing her back soothingly with one hand. "You don't have to go there, precious. It's okay."

Seth glanced around his bedroom as if searching for information or inspiration. He shook his head. "If your cell phone ended up with Hart's fiancée after the crash in the bathroom, then what happened to your keys? Did you ever find them? Did you get the locks changed on your apartment door?"

"No," she said, and an icy sensation skittered down her back. "When I tried to call the super about the window, I remembered April told me that he was out of town until Wednesday."

"And it's only Tuesday. Crap." Seth scrubbed a hand down his face. "Okay, that settles it, you cannot go home. Stay here. Keep the shades down and the door locked. Don't open it for anyone. I'll be back as soon as I can. When I come back, we'll sit down and go over every detail you can remember. We'll figure out how to get you out of this mess."

Every detail included seeing Aimee-Lynn's ghost. Could she share her secret with him?

Would he believe her if she did?

CHAPTER 17

FIFTEEN MINUTES LATER, Seth had showered and was in his car headed to the station. The sun hung low, peering like a ball of fire between the hotels littering the Oceanfront district. Without a cloud in the sky to dull it, the brilliant yellow orb was nearly blinding. And the afternoon rush-hour traffic crawled.

He used his time behind the wheel to mentally review what Jones had said.

Aimee-Lynn named four characters in her journals. The Princess, the Jack of Fools, the Prince of Hearts, and the Knight of the Realm . . . she'd left them clues. Obviously, she was the Princess. Could she have really been so pedestrian as to have named her own fiancé, Mason Hart, the Prince of Hearts and Jack Kells the Jack of Fools?

Yes, she could have. She'd named Seth in her story as well as the English King. Okay, so all this was a leap. A gut instinct when what he needed was proof. He needed to get his hands on those journals.

Up ahead, traffic came to a standstill. "Shit!"

Seth glanced at the clock on his dashboard. Quarter past six. If the cars didn't start moving soon, he'd never make the meeting on time. He needed to call Jones. His partner could cover for him until he made it in. Maybe Jones would even consent to reading a few more passages from Aimee-Lynn's journals to him.

Before he could bring up Jones's number, Seth's cell rang. The caller ID read Tidewater Police Station. Seth pressed Send. "Detective English."

"English, where are you?" Captain Peterson snapped.

"I'm on my way to the station, sir." Seth checked his mirrors, searching for an opening in traffic and finding none. "It's rush hour. Atlantic's a parking lot."

"Why in the hell are you coming to the station?" Peterson sounded even more agitated. "You're supposed to be at Tidewater General."

"I'm coming in for the meeting you called," Seth said, tamping down his own annoyance. "What's at the hospital?"

"Forget the meeting, you've got bigger issues. Want a free pass to interview Mason Hart?" Peterson didn't wait for a response. "If so, you'd better get your ass over to Tidewater General. He just arrived there. Covered in blood."

AFTER SETH LEFT, Jules dressed in yesterday's clothes. She checked and double-checked the locks on the front door and the windows to his place, then curled up in his bed.

For an hour she worried about what he might say when she told him about seeing ghosts. Too jittery to sleep, she decided to take a shower.

Although tempted to grab fresh clothes from her place, she didn't want to break her word to Seth. He'd asked her to wait here for him and wait she would.

Still, she hadn't promised him she wouldn't clean up. Sliding to the edge of the bed, she stood up, ready to use his bathroom.

Two steps later, the bedroom went dark without warning. She spun to the window and could barely make out the curtains hanging there. The temperature in the room plummeted twenty degrees, making her shiver.

"Aimee-Lynn, are you here?" Her words came out as puffs of white smoke.

Silence.

"Aimee-Lynn, if you're here, you need to talk to me."

Still nothing.

Grinding her now chattering teeth, she said, "Dang it, Aimee-Lynn! I don't know what you want from me."

"I want you to help me fix it before someone else dies!"

The angry words ripped through her mind like dull razor blades through scarred flesh. Aimee-Lynn's cries grew louder and more incoherent until Jules thought her head might actually be cleaved off from the shrill sound.

Jules dropped to her knees, covering her ears with her hands, and tried to think. She needed to get the ghost calm. Focusing her energy, Jules used a combination of a mental push and her own voice to reach the angry specter.

"Aimee-Lynn, I can't understand you. I can't even see you. But I swear, I will help if you just slow down and talk to me." Jules wasn't sure the ghost could even hear her, but then Aimee-Lynn stopped wailing.

A thunderous gray aura pulsed around the smoky image of Aimee-Lynn standing in a corner near the bathroom door. Taking it for a good sign, Jules continued. "I know you're angry and scared. I know you want me to do something for you—"

"Yes, you must finish it," Aimee-Lynn said in clipped tones, but she'd seemed to have regained her control a degree. Her form took on a more definable shape but still had that hazy, smoky color.

"Yes, I'll finish it, but Aimee, I don't know what *it* is."

"What?"

The temperature in the room warmed by ten degrees and the lights glowed back to life.

Aimee-Lynn shimmered into being wearing a black corset, miniskirt, fishnet stockings, and heels. Instead of blonde hair she wore a shoulder-length black wig

Jules gasped. *"You're* the woman from the bathroom? Seth told me he thought you were but . . ."

"So you hadn't recognized me?" Aimee-Lynn winged the question into Jules's mind.

"No. I guess I should have," Jules admitted. "But you looked a little different each time I saw you."

The chill in the air evaporated instantly and Aimee-Lynn's outfit changed into a pink polo shirt and khaki shorts with white canvas tennis shoes. The black wig melted away and her blonde hair fell across her shoulders.

"Why do you keep changing your clothes?" Jules blurted before she could think better of it.

Aimee-Lynn blinked as if shocked by the question, then glanced down at, or maybe through, her body, then met Jules's gaze again.

"I have to concentrate to wear anything other than what I died in. I refuse to go through eternity looking like a cheap hooker. You know the expression 'I wouldn't be caught dead in that'? Well, now you know where it comes from." Aimee-Lynn's aura pulsed alternating colors of pale pink and true red.

Who knew a ghost could have a sense of humor?

"Are you ready to listen to me now?" Aimee-Lynn paused then added, *"For Seth's sake."*

"Seth?" A tremor that had nothing to do with the chill in the air ran down her spine. Jules asked, "What does he have to do with this?"

"Everything."

"Yes, I'm ready to listen." Jules returned to the bed and burrowed beneath the blankets. Dressed or not, she was freezing because the ghost had caused the temperature to plummet. "I'm all ears. Tell me your story."

Aimee-Lynn sat down on the end of the bed. A visual dichotomy, Aimee-Lynn both sat on and floated above the bed in her transparent state.

Then something weird happened.

Jules's purse floated up from where Seth had left it on the nightstand and landed in her lap with a thud.

"How did you do that?" Jules blinked at the bag then grabbed it with both hands. "I've never encountered a new spirit who figured out how to manipulate the corporeal world as fast as you did."

Aimee-Lynn's aura brightened to a paler pink and no longer throbbed. She shrugged. *"I don't know. Most of the time, things just move around me without me really trying. Making things move or making light bulbs explode is easy. Talking to the living is a lot harder."*

"You're doing a pretty good job, right now." Jules smiled at her. "Just try to stay calm, okay? I don't want stuff breaking in Seth's place."

The spirit nodded.

"So what do you need me for?"

Aimee-Lynn glared and her aura throbbed to a deep shade of red. *"Because I can only do it when I'm with you. No one sees me. No one else hears. No one else even senses me. Except you!"*

The last two words were delivered venomously. Jules squeezed her eyes shut and sucked in a breath, bracing for the assault on her eardrums again, but nothing came. Peeking one eye open, she found Aimee-Lynn's aura had shifted back to a light pink.

A silvery tear glittered on her cheek. *"I hate it here. I don't want to be dead. Always watching everyone but not able to talk to them. My mother keeps calling my name. The first time I heard her, I answered but she didn't hear me. She keeps telling me she'll find my killer and bring him to justice. But she can't. I know who killed me and I know he'll get away with it if I don't set things right."*

"Aimee-Lynn, I need to ask you if . . ." Jules hesitated, hating herself for doubting her old friend. "Did Mason kill you?"

"Mason?" Aimee-Lynn floated a few feet higher in the air as if literally blown away by the idea. *"My Prince loved me. Everything he did, he did for me."*

"Aimee-Lynn, that's not really an answer," Jules said, but Aimee-Lynn didn't pay her any attention. Instead, the spirit said, *"The Knight of the Realm killed me. That deceiving bastard."*

Knight of the Realm? Her Prince?

Oh, dear heavens. This ghost is nuts.

Blanking her mind before the specter heard her thoughts, Jules quickly said, "Aimee-Lynn, if I'm going to help you, I need actual names. Was the killer someone you knew?"

"Yes," Aimee-Lynn said sadly. *"I knew him."*

"What's his real name?" Jules had a glimmer of hope. For the first time since Aimee-Lynn barged into her life, she thought she might be able to use her crift to actually help the spirit. "If you tell me his real name, I can give a tip to the police."

"That won't work." The spirit's aura darkened to a muddy yellow, then she shook her head. Her hair fanned out above her shoulders as if some unseen wind blew it. *"I can't remember his real name. I swear it's like someone poked holes in my brain with an ice pick."*

That was an image forever seared into her mind. *Thanks so much!*

"Some things I remember clearly. Others? Well, I know that you can't just walk into a police station and talk to the first person you see. I just don't remember why."

Jules frowned. She hadn't offered to do that. There was no way she'd willingly traipse into another police station . . . ever again.

There had to be a way to help Aimee-Lynn remember. But how? Jules nibbled on the right side of her lower lip and caught herself tugging on her earlobe.

Hmmm . . . Seth was right about the earlobe-tugging thing.

"It's the reason I had an appointment," Aimee-Lynn said. *"I was supposed to meet the English King . . . I mean, Detective English at the station, but I, uh, didn't make it."*

"You were supposed to meet Seth before you died?"

Aimee-Lynn nodded.

An idea jumped from Jules's lips before it had completely registered in her brain. "How about you tell me what you wanted to tell Seth and I can pass the message on to him?"

Stupid. Stupid. Stupid.

She didn't want Seth to know what an überfreak she was. But she had the sinking feeling the ghost would never leave if Jules didn't do something to hurry her along. And maybe she could find a way to tell Seth without actually telling him? No, if she had to tell him, she'd do it. Better he learn right away what she could do.

Maybe he'd even accept her.

"Okay." Aimee-Lynn's smile vanished and she said darkly, *"Tell Seth, I have the proof he needs. My murderer, the Knight of the Realm, was trying to steal it back when I accidentally gave it to you."*

"Come again?"

"The man who killed me . . . the Knight of the Realm," Aimee-Lynn said more emphatically. *"Seth should know by now about the Knight. I can't remember his name but I know he was a knight who swore an oath of fealty."* Aimee-Lynn's outfit changed again, this time into a flowing blue gown straight out of the Middle Ages. *"You must tell Seth. He'll know what to do about that smarmy coward."*

"Whoa, back up!" Jules swallowed convulsively, her mind still tripping over what Aimee-Lynn had said first. "What was that about giving *it* to *me*? You never gave me anything except a splitting headache."

"You're holding it right now." Aimee-Lynn pointed to the purse in Jules's hands.

Jules glanced down at the black bag. The same one Seth had returned to her multiple times since they'd met. A bad feeling went through her. Very bad.

"Aimee-Lynn, this is *my* purse."

"No, it isn't." Aimee-Lynn shook her head. *"It's mine, I can prove it. Just open it."*

Jules didn't want to do it. Even though she'd opened it at least a half dozen times in the past several days, the idea of opening it now made her nauseous. Taking a deep breath, she unhinged the clasp and pulled the bag open.

Only her ID, a tube of lipstick, and her favorite purple change purse stared up at her.

She exhaled her breath on a *whoosh*.

The contents were perfectly and completely innocuous. She reached in and pulled them out one by one, setting them on her lap. With each object removed, the bedroom seemed to brighten. "There's nothing in here, Aimee-Lynn."

"They're in there. Keep going."

"What's in here?"

"You'll see."

Fear and frustration mounting, Jules stuck her hand inside the purse and felt around. The cheap knockoff was lined with even cheaper polyester that snagged on her fingernails. Yanking her hand out, she glared at the ghost. "What is it you expect me to find?"

"You're not looking hard enough. Look inside the purse again." Aimee-Lynn grinned confidently.

With nothing else to do to prove the ghost wrong, Jules flipped the purse upside down and shook it. Something fell out and plopped onto the bed.

A beautiful white diamond, approximately one carat, sparkled on the bed.

Turning the purse back over, Jules found two more diamonds caught in a hole in the lining. Using her index finger, she poked at the opening, tearing out the crude stitches she'd somehow missed before.

How had she never noticed the crappy lining in the past few days? Easy, because she had given the bag little attention from the moment she realized it was a knockoff.

The thread pulled free and a dozen white diamonds spilled out, along with a red ruby ring.

"Not a ruby," Aimee-Lynn said as if hearing Jules's thoughts. *"That's a $350,000 red diamond ring. My mother's ring."*

"Oh, Aimee-Lynn, what have you gotten me into?"

IT HAD TAKEN Seth two hours to arrive at the hospital. Between afternoon rush-hour traffic and a multivehicle accident closing down three lanes of traffic on 64, it had taken Seth two hours to travel what normally would have been a twenty-minute drive.

He'd arrived and spoken with the head nurse in charge of the ER, a rotund woman in garishly bright neon pink scrubs with a Hello Kitty scrunchie in her hair. Instead of telling him where to find Hart, Nurse Hello Kitty stated there was no record on file of anyone calling the police that afternoon. Worse, Hart wasn't in their system at all.

What in the hell is going on?

It's not like Hart was officially a suspect. So why had Captain Peterson insisted that Seth drive to the hospital? Did Jones relate more to their captain about something in the journals than he'd told Seth? And who reported that the prince of Hart Construction had been attacked? For that matter, why would he have been attacked? Did the man actually know something about his ex-fiancée's murder or the jewelry heists as Seth suspected? Or was it all a big a coincidence?

Good questions, but I'm not going to find the answers from Nurse Hello Kitty.

Seth had thanked the woman, then headed to a private corner in the waiting room to call his captain at the office. Voice mail. Made sense; if the captain was in the middle of the meeting he'd called, he wouldn't have answered his phone. But Jones might.

He called Jones; again he was kicked over to voice mail.

Officer Gareth strode through the front doors of the ER. The patrolman glanced around the room, as if searching for someone. The moment his gaze landed on Seth, the officer hurried over.

"Detective, I've been searching for you," Gareth said.

"Officer Gareth, what are you doing here?"

"Detective Jones told me to find you." Gareth squeezed his eyes closed and rubbed his forehead as if it pained him. "Mason Hart's gone. I was with him until about twenty minutes ago. I'm not sure what happened. One minute he was in the room and the next he wasn't."

"I was told he wasn't here," Seth said.

"Who told you that?" Gareth dropped his hand from his face and shook his head. "He was here. I have him. *Had* him."

Fury snapped through Seth. A week ago, he didn't know the younger patrolman, and this made the second time in as many days the officer had managed to screw up his case.

"How could you just let Hart go?"

"I didn't let him go. He was in radiology with a nurse and a tech getting an X-ray. I was told to wait outside the door. When the tech came out, the room was empty. The nurse and Hart were gone. I've been searching for Hart ever since. I called Detective Jones ten minutes ago to report Hart's escape. He said to stop searching for Hart and find you."

"He told you to *stop* looking for Hart?"

Why would Jones do that?

"I'm sorry, Detective. I had no idea there was a second door out of the room."

Seth turned and headed for radiology, only to notice an exit door just before it. He raced through it. Gareth ran to keep up with him. There was no reason for Hart to run, unless he was guilty of something.

And had the patrolman done his job, neither of them would need to give chase now.

"Where's the nurse?" Seth pulled up short and spun on the

smaller man. They still had a chance of figuring out where Hart went if they could talk with the nurse.

"Sorry, I don't know that either."

Fucking useless. Seth bit back the words.

The patrolman shifted his weight from one foot to the other, then glanced at the black asphalt.

The sight made Seth's gut quiver.

The patrolman was hiding something. What, and more important, why?

"What aren't you telling me?" Seth asked, watching Gareth closely.

"Hart's father showed up a few minutes before Hart vanished." The patrolman looked completely frustrated. Digging his fingers through his closely cropped hair, he glowered. "He said there's no way his son could have been involved in the burglaries or the murder of the Masters girl. And if the police didn't stop harassing his son, he'd call Mayor Bien and then slap a lawsuit against the department. And you in particular."

Seth ground his back teeth together. "Then the younger Hart pulled a disappearing act? Where's the senior Hart?"

"He left when you arrived. I'm surprised you didn't pass him in the parking lot. It's not like you could miss his completely inconspicuous powder blue Mercedes."

"Fine, let's get back to the station."

Seth started toward his Honda. After a few steps, he realized the patrolman hadn't moved. He glanced back to find the younger officer staring up at the hospital. Following the man's line of vision, he squinted to see better through the last rays of the setting sun.

Seth couldn't make out much more than a fuzzy shadowed outline. "You coming, Officer?"

The patrolman snapped his gaze away from the building. He closed the distance between them in several short, hurried strides.

"Detective, what if he's still in the hospital?" The patrolman hiked a thumb over his shoulder toward the building behind him. "I never saw him leave . . . and the ER charge nurse is his cousin."

"She's what?"

"His cousin." Gareth nodded. "What if, Hart, who by all accounts was beaten pretty badly and in need of medical treatment . . . what if he found someone to help him get the medical attention he needed? But not his cousin. She'd be too obvious. But I bet she'd know who would help him."

"You think he's still in there?" Seth asked, but was pretty certain he knew the answer already.

"Yeah, and I noticed something else," Gareth said, pointing to a window on the third floor, nowhere near the ER. "Isn't that his cousin up there?"

Seth turned in time to see someone in neon pink scrubs drawing curtains closed.

WHO SEWS DIAMONDS into a purse? Apparently one loony ghost who's convinced a knight of the realm killed her.

This couldn't be happening.

Think, Jules, think . . . What am I going to do?

"I thought you were going to turn them in to Seth and tell him about the Knight?" Aimee-Lynn, who'd clearly been eavesdropping, cried out.

"I need time to think," Jules said. Her mind raced with fear. These diamonds were related to the case Seth had been working on. The one he needed to solve in order to get the promotion he so desperately wanted. And she'd had them for days.

"I don't see what the problem is. Call him and tell him to come here. Just hurry up and give them to him."

Aimee-Lynn stood up and crossed her arms over her chest, her medieval garb evaporating into the pink polo and khaki shorts she'd been wearing earlier.

"How am I going to explain this?" Jules gestured to the diamonds. "I swore to him I'd told him everything I knew about his case. He's going to think I was lying."

Aimee-Lynn floated six inches above the floor and glided through the middle of the bed toward her. *"If you don't hurry, someone else is going to die!"*

Too much! It was too much.

"Can you see the future, Aimee-Lynn?" Jules jumped, scattering diamonds across the floor. She hurriedly picked them up, and swept them back into her purse.

Not her purse. *Aimee-Lynn's* purse.

Her stomach cramped and the baklava she'd eaten earlier threatened to make a reappearance.

"Calm down!" Aimee-Lynn said, gliding so close, Jules could feel the other woman's aura. *"It'll be okay."*

"So you can see the future?" Jules asked hopefully.

Aimee-Lynn shook her head. Her hair swung lazily, like hair floating under water. *"Not really. But when I'm not here, I go to this room where one wall is like a giant high-definition television of the world. I see the Knight for what he is, a liar, a thief, and a murderer.*

"You know, he told me we were testing security systems, and I actually believed him? Said he needed my help because of my background in gemology. I believed him until I saw my mother's ring in the jewelry store. She'd told me before she loaned the red diamond that the jeweler had already run an extensive test of their security. Then when I learned the ring had disappeared after the robbery, I went looking for the jewels.

"I waited until he was at work, and went through his place. My mother's ring was there. When I told my Prince, he floundered. Said he owed the Knight. That there must have been a mistake. But I took all the jewels and hid them in my purse. I carried them with me every day for weeks, trying to figure out what to do next. I couldn't tell my mother, not without implicating my love."

"So you and Mason weren't part of the Diamond Gang?" Jules shook her head in confusion. "Or were you?"

"I was but didn't know it. I'm not sure my Prince really understood what was happening until it was too late. We thought we were part of a team hired to test private security systems." A red aura pulsed around Aimee-Lynn, it glowed bright and sharp. *"I'd finally convinced him that whatever debt he thought he owed to that blackguard wasn't worth life in prison. My Prince at last agreed to go with me to turn in the diamonds the night I ran into you. We were supposed to be a family. I wasn't supposed to . . ."* Her words trailed off and silver tears glittered on her lashes.

"It was an accident that I gave them to you. Our purses looked so much alike, I didn't know it until the Knight ripped

the purse apart." She paused, then warned, *"He's coming for the diamonds. And he'll kill anyone who gets in his way. I'm proof."*

"Seth?" Jules prayed he was safe. When Aimee-Lynn didn't do more than stare at her, a fierce need to protect him at all costs surged through her.

She may have only known him a few days and she may not have told him she could see ghosts, but she knew one thing. She loved him. And no one was going to hurt him.

No one.

Grabbing Seth's phone from the nightstand, she froze.

"What are you waiting for?"

"I don't know Seth's cell phone number," she admitted, a bit embarrassed she'd just spent the majority of the past twenty-four hours with a man whose phone number she didn't know.

"So call the station."

"Good idea." That number she had. Jones had left her his card at the flower shop. She'd thrown it in her change purse and forgotten about it. She dug it out and punched in the digits.

"Detective Jones, Burglary Division. May I help you?"

"Hi, Detective Jones. This is Juliana Scott. Is Seth, um . . . I mean, is Detective English available?"

"Hi, Jules. You're supposed to call me Dev, remember?" His deep baritone voice rumbled with laughter. "No, the detective isn't here."

"You called him to come to a meeting," she said.

"He didn't come." Dev paused and asked, "He isn't with you?"

"No, after he spoke to you, he told me to wait here and then left."

"Jules, are you home *alone*?"

"Yes, but what—" Jules stopped herself from saying anything more. Seth had told her not to let anyone in. Did that mean she shouldn't be talking to Dev either? And Aimee-Lynn had warned her she couldn't trust just anyone at the police station. Her stomach knotted tighter but she tried to keep her tone light, "Oh well. Never mind, Dev. I've got to go."

"Jules, wait. I need to talk to you—"

She clicked off in the middle of his sentence.

Now what? Too jittery to sit with a purse full of stolen diamonds in the room with her, Jules paced the floor.

"What happened?" Aimee-Lynn asked.

"He wasn't there, I need to wait." Jules struggled to keep calm but she broke in a fine sheen of nervous sweat. "I need a shower."

She did some of her best thinking under the spray. Maybe she could figure out a smart game plan. She shuffled toward the bathroom.

"You're going to take a shower?" Aimee-Lynn snorted indignantly. *"That can't wait?"*

"No, actually, it can't." Jules tugged at the collar of her shirt and sniffed. It didn't smell too bad. Short of stealing one of Seth's shirts, she had no choice but to put on the same clothes after she cleaned up. "Look, I promise I'll be fast. But I can't just sit here. I'll go nuts."

Shutting the door in the ghost's face was more for cathartic purposes than useful ones. Had she wanted to, Aimee-Lynn could have floated right through the white wood.

Stripping quickly, she adjusted the water temperature, then stepped beneath the spray. Once she was fully doused, she grabbed the bottle of shampoo and lathered it into her hair and let her thought processes flow freely.

She could wait here for Seth to return. He knew she discovered the body, and he'd believe she didn't know about the diamonds. It was perfectly plausible that she'd only just discovered the rip in the purse. All she had to do was show him. She didn't even need to mention anything about Aimee-Lynn.

The idea of still hiding her secret pinched. Four days with him and she was already tired of hiding who she was. What she was. Like it or not, she was a psychic.

Question was, would Seth like it? Would he even believe it?

Her stomach plummeted at the thought of seeing Seth look at her with loathing and fear in his eyes.

Focus. Don't lose sight of what's important. Get rid of the diamonds before some idiot decided to arrest her for stealing them. And do it in such a way so that she didn't completely ruin Seth's chances of promotion. From what he'd said, he needed the credit for the case.

Quickly rinsing her body and her hair, she shut off the

water. She'd barely pulled back the curtain when a towel floated in midair toward her.

Aimee-Lynn's image appeared in the bathroom mirror.

"A little privacy, please!" Jules snapped, cinching the towel around her wet body.

"Something's wrong." Aimee-Lynn moved her lips but no sound came out. Her image was more translucent than before and she wore the hooker getup she hated so much.

"Are you okay, Aimee-Lynn?" Concern had Jules moving closer, only to bump into the Corian sink with her belly. Jules stretched out a hand toward the ghostly face in the mirror, then dropped it. She couldn't have touched Aimee-Lynn even if she hadn't looked like a bad hologram from an old sci-fi flick.

"I'm so very tired. I need to go . . . to the other place. I need rest." Aimee-Lynn's mouth moved and the words whispered almost inaudibly through Jules's mind. The spirit's image faded out and came back into being. *"Moving things is easy . . . but I'm . . . sleepy."*

Aimee-Lynn faded out of the mirror again. Jules waited, holding her breath, hoping Aimee-Lynn would come back. When she did, she was a whisper of an image, just a pale gray aura pulsing around the silhouette of a woman.

"Are you in pain?"

The image disappeared altogether, but Aimee-Lynn's word's floated through Jules's mind, high and tinny, like something from an old radio. *"Not pain, per se, more like it feels as if my soul is being sucked out of consciousness. It doesn't hurt but it doesn't feel good either. I'm afraid if I don't find a way to finish this soon, I may lose who I am. I've seen a few people in the other place. Soulless beings with no will or mind of their own."*

"It'll be finished very soon. We've found the diamonds. And before the night is over, I'll give them to Seth. You go and rest. Come back soon."

"I'll try." Aimee-Lynn's image appeared faintly in the mirror again. Her smile was wan and showed her exhaustion. *"Don't forget to tell him about the Knight."*

"I won't forget."

Aimee-Lynn faded away. This time there was no fanfare.

No change in temperature or room lighting. No glass breaking or nightmare vision. Just the sense of someone having been here who was too weak to go on.

Jules swallowed past a sudden lump in her throat. She didn't want Aimee-Lynn to suffer.

Except for those evil souls dragged into hell, Jules had no idea that people could suffer in death.

And here, she'd been trying to avoid this ghost, attempting to ignore her. She had no idea what it took for Aimee-Lynn to appear each time and make her presence known. Or that to finish what she'd started as a living being could cause her suffering in the waiting realm.

Toweling off, Jules dressed quickly and spoke to the empty room, hoping Aimee-Lynn could still hear her. "I'm going to help you return the diamonds. Then you'll be free to move on with your baby, Aimee-Lynn. No more suffering."

CHAPTER 18

TIME WAS WINDING down. Soon that oaf, English, would figure out who the killer really was. He couldn't wait much longer.

In the shadow of an oak tree, he watched the light flick to life in the second-floor window. Curtains rippled as she paced through the living room of English's apartment.

She appeared restless, anxious. She had no idea what anxious was.

He'd been waiting months to find his diamonds, and when he finally spotted the purse in her hands on Saturday, he'd almost whooped with joy. Until he realized he couldn't get near her without drawing attention to himself.

There was no one watching her now.

JULES WAS READY to crawl out of her skin. Seth had been gone for hours. Aimee-Lynn hadn't returned. A purse full of stolen diamonds was in her possession, and she was still wearing yesterday's clothes.

So, the last part wasn't as dire as the rest, but she'd kill to have on clean panties. It was stupid. It was pointless. It was the only thing she *could* control. Picking up the purse—no way was she letting it out of her sight until Seth returned—and her apartment keys, she hurried to the front door and pressed her ear against it.

She checked the peephole. The hallway seemed to be deserted. Sending up a silent prayer, Jules unlocked the door and bolted across the hall.

Like a professional thief, she'd unlocked, opened, and closed her front door in record time. She raced down the hall to her room, yanked out the first pair of clean panties, jeans, bra, and sweater she touched, then ran back toward the safety of Seth's place.

It wasn't until she was locking her apartment that she'd realized how frightened she'd been. And still was. Either someone was in there, or between Seth and Aimee-Lynn, Jules had worked herself up into a good irrational state.

She spun around and slammed into the hard chest of Devon Jones.

Jules tried to navigate around him, but he was a human wall. He backed up with every attempt she made until she'd managed to cross the hallway to Seth's apartment. Clutching the purse between the clothes and her chest, she stuck out her chin and tried to appear nonchalant.

"Excuse me," she said. Twisting the knob, she opened Seth's apartment and called out, "I'm back, Seth! Dev's here." She turned sideways and skirted past Dev's great hulking form. Once inside, she pretended she was straining to hear something from the bedroom, then said, "Dev, he said he'll call you, later."

Dev didn't respond. He didn't even twitch.

"Have a good night!" She swallowed, pasted a please-heaven-let-this-look-real smile on her face, and attempted to close the door.

"Come on, Shelley. Don't be like that," he said, sticking the toe of his expensive leather shoe in the doorway.

Uncertainty flashed through her and she let the door slip from her fingers. He caught it, pushed it wide, and stepped inside, closing it behind him.

Jules backed up, her chest aching from the severe lack of oxygen caused by the terror and disbelief pinging off every nerve in her body. "Wha-what did you call me?"

"Jules, I'm on your side. Don't worry," he said, his hands raised, palms out, submissive. He didn't advance, but held his position near the door. "I don't know what's going on tonight, but Seth made it clear he didn't like the idea of leaving you alone for even twenty minutes. There's no way he'd have done it for two hours. Not without a damned good reason, so I'm not leaving 'til he gets here."

She swung her head slowly from side to side. "No . . . you— you called me Shelley."

His jaw went slack momentarily, then he recovered and rubbed his hands down his thighs. "Oh, sorry. I guess it's because you look so much like your sister, you two could be twins."

WHERE THE HELL had Gareth disappeared to? He was supposed to meet Seth on the third floor but never showed up. To make matters worse, the charge nurse was still in the ER. The nurse they had spotted from the third-floor window not only wasn't her, but she had been opening the curtains for a patient who'd just come out of a coma.

He'd wasted the last two hours searching for Hart and a nurse who was no longer on duty. He had no intention of searching for Gareth too. Riding the elevator to the first floor, he tried to tamp down his irritation.

Seth glared at his dying phone. The battery wouldn't last much longer. He'd forgotten to charge it last night. A mistake he never made. Then again, he'd been distracted by Jules.

The doors opened with a *shush*. Nurse Hello Kitty stood a few feet away speaking with a short, bald man who wore an expensive brown suit. She glanced his way and pointed at him, a frown on her face. The man turned and Seth knew him instantly: Alexander Hart. Mason's father.

Seth exited the elevator, unsurprised when the little man stormed over to him.

"Leave my son alone!" he said in a thick British accent. He gestured to Nurse Hello Kitty. "Elizabeth tells me you've been harassing her all afternoon searching for my boy. Well, he's not here. He has not been here and he is of no concern to you!"

"Yes, he is. I'm conducting an investigation." Seth folded his arms over his chest and glared. "I'll interview anyone I think necessary."

"Not my son, you won't!" Alexander said between his teeth. "The Hart name will not be dragged through the mud. You and your department should look elsewhere. I'll not allow medieval soldiers disguised as police to vilify my child again. My attorney is already preparing a lawsuit."

Without giving Seth time to respond, Alexander stormed away, Nurse Hello Kitty close behind him. Everyone in the waiting room stared at Seth.

Ignoring them, he strode out of the building toward his car. Why had Alexander Hart returned? Was it simply to yell at him?

Something about the man's words bothered him. Not the implication of the lawsuit but the reference to medieval soldiers disguised as cops. Over and over, the words looped through his mind as he crossed the parking lot and climbed into his car.

The answer was there, on the edges of his brain, but he couldn't grasp it. It hung elusive. Blowing out a frustrated breath, he retrieved his cell from his belt clip and hoped it lasted long enough to check his messages.

"Detective, I told you to tread carefully around Hart!" Captain Peterson's gravelly voice boomed in Seth's ear. "What the hell are you doing harassing the Hart family again? I'm giving you a chance and you're fucking it up! Leave Mason Hart alone."

Confused, he called his captain's cell.

"Peterson."

"Captain, it's English." Seth took a breath. "I wasn't harassing the Hart family. I was following up on your request that I check him out at the hospital."

"English, are you high?" Peterson sneezed. "I didn't call you to the hospital. I'm home in bed with this damned cold. The wife's convinced I'm going to come down with pneumonia."

Shit! A lead ball formed in Seth's belly. "You've been home, all night? You didn't come into the station for a meeting?"

"Of course not!" The captain coughed until he wheezed, then took a gasping breath. "What the hell are you rambling about? The only person at the station I've spoken with today is Jones. And you can tell him from me, if you fuck up, he's fucked too!"

That ball in Seth's belly sank to his knees. Then like a flash of lightning, Alexander Hart's words hit him. *Medieval soldiers disguised as cops.* Medieval soldiers were called knights. The fourth person in the ring had to be a cop.

Only one cop had spoken to Seth, the captain, and Gareth: Jones.

Could Jones be in the gang?

It didn't seem possible, but . . .

"Did you hear me, English?" The captain had a longer coughing fit.

"Yes, sir." Seth didn't wait for Peterson to stop coughing. "I'll do that, sir."

Disconnecting the call, Seth tried to reach Jones again. Again, it went straight to voice mail.

Shoving his keys into the ignition, Seth started the car. His mind raced as he peeled out of the parking lot.

Jones had tried to convince him to come to the station first. Then someone claiming to be the captain called him while he was driving to the station and sent him to the hospital to question Hart.

Jones had impersonated the captain before. Could he have done it again? If so, why have Gareth meet him at the hospital? If it wasn't Jones, where was he and why wasn't he answering his phone? And who and why would someone send Seth on a wild Hart chase?

Jules. It had to be Jules. Someone—maybe Jones—wanted Seth away from her. There had already been two attempts on her life. What if someone was watching her? Waiting for the right time to strike?

The lead ball formerly in his knees shot like a bullet up into his belly. Invisible bands squeezed tightly in the space he suspected was his heart. He gunned the engine. Fisting his one sweaty hand on the steering wheel, he used the other to dial home.

The phone just rang until it switched to voice mail again.

Why didn't Jules answer? She wouldn't have left, would she? Of course not, she'd promised him she'd stay put. Unless someone made her leave.

The thought made his stomach pitch.

Crap, he couldn't think like that. She was probably fine. Just sleeping, or in the shower, or watching television too loud, or maybe she just didn't think he'd call her. That had to be it.

Seth hadn't specifically told her to answer the phone, but he did warn her not to trust anyone other than him. Still, he'd feel better when he saw for himself she was safe.

Dropping the phone to his lap, he gripped the steering wheel in both hands and took the exit south on 64 faster than he probably should have. Seth prayed he'd make it home in less than twenty minutes. His mind spun nearly as fast as his tires on the road.

He loosened one hand from the wheel long enough to dial his phone again. This time, he called the station. The line rang once before someone picked up.

"Police station forty-six, this is Officer Harmon. What can I do for you?"

Wasting no time, Seth asked, "Harmon, did you give a note to Jones from the captain?"

"Yes?" The patrolman's voice loaded that single word with confusion.

"Did the captain give it to you?"

"No," Harmon replied. "I haven't seen Captain Peterson all day. I heard he was out sick, but I saw the note on the floor. I gave it to Jones."

"Is he still there? I need to talk to him."

"No, he left a while ago. He said he was on his way to your place."

"Jones is on his way to *my* place?" Two cars ahead, someone slammed on the brakes. Seth hit the brakes to avoid rear-ending the car in front of him, then swerved around both vehicles. "I need backup there, now. At least, I think I do. Damn, I'm not sure. Look, do me a favor and head over there but be ready to call in reinforcements if needed. I'm en route but ten minutes out."

"What's going on?" Harmon asked, then added quickly, "If you don't mind me asking."

"Too much to explain."

His non-answer seemed to satisfy the young officer because he said, "Give me your address and I'll go there now, sir."

Seth rattled off his address and disconnected the call.

His heart beat in a ragged, staccato rhythm. Jules was in danger. The god-awful awareness of it seeped into his bones. Flattening the gas pedal to the floor, he vowed that if anyone broke even one of her fingernails, he'd kill him.

JULES WATCHED JONES circumnavigate the inside of Seth's apartment. She thought about running, but his comparison of her to Shelley kept her from moving. She had to know what he knew. Silently, she sunk down onto the faded denim couch and carefully hid the purse behind her back.

Finally, he returned and made himself comfortable on Seth's couch. She slid away, burrowing against the side of the couch, but his hand shot out and wrapped around her wrist. "You're safe, I just want to talk."

Given that his meaty fingers easily fit around her wrist, struggling was out of the question. For now. She nodded her acquiescence and he released her.

They sat in silence for several minutes before she couldn't take the tension any longer and asked, "How do you know about Shelley?"

"You look so much like her."

She glared at him and he laughed. "And now you really do. She could make a Navy SEAL quake in his boots when she was ticked." Admiration mixed with a hint of sadness in his voice. "I guess I should say *she* looked like *you*, since you're older."

Her heart bounced between her chest and her throat, making speech not only impractical but impossible.

He grinned. "I'm pretty sure I made that same face when I saw you at the Dumpster. For a moment, I thought you were Shelley. But your eyes are green not blue."

"How-how do you know . . . her?"

"We went to college together. She tutored me in English."

Tears sprang to her eyes. "Really?"

Dev nodded, a soft, almost shy smile played across his

face. He twisted slightly sideways, and rested his arm along the back of the couch. "Shelley was my best friend."

"You keep using the past tense." Panic made a balloon swell in her throat. She managed to choke out, "Is she dead?"

"God no!" Horror flashed in his eyes, then he blinked and it was gone. Wearily he explained. "After graduation, she moved back to her hometown, well, the one she'd lived in before going to college. I tried to get her to stay here but . . ." He shook his head.

Dare she hope?

"Does that mean . . ." Jules cleared her suddenly dry throat. "Do you *know* where Shelley is?"

"I do." He nodded slowly. "She lives in a little town in Northern Virginia."

Silly as it sounded, the room spun. Jules leaned forward and cradled her head in her hands, swallowing back tears. "I've been looking for her for so long. I even hired a private detective agency to help."

"Tidewater Security Specialists," he said, rubbing her back consolingly.

"How did you know that?" She stiffened.

"My cousin, Ian, asked me to look into your case for you." Dev smiled. "I haven't been able to reach Shelley yet, but knowing her, she's out communing with the woodland creatures or rescuing birds caught in an oil slick."

Jules took in his lost and lonely expression. She softened toward him. "You're in love with her?"

"Nah." Dev gave her a weak smile. "We've only ever been friends."

Well, he was either lying to himself or to her. Maybe both.

Aimee-Lynn's ghost rose up from the center of the couch between Jules and Dev like a genie from an ancient lamp. Jules jumped back.

"Are you okay?" Dev asked at the same time Aimee-Lynn said, *"Have you done it yet?"*

Jules glanced through Aimee-Lynn to Dev, uncertain how to answer. Before she could think of an adequate reply, Aimee-Lynn vanished, only to reappear seconds later to Jules's right, her aura pulsing a muddy red.

"It's still here!" Aimee-Lynn pointed at the purse peeking

out from behind Jules. The words vibrated through her skull like razor blades on a chalkboard. *"Why didn't you give it to Seth yet?"*

Jules clapped her hands over her ears and squeezed her eyes shut, trying to stave off the pain.

"Jules, what's wrong?" Dev put his hands on her shoulders, shaking her slightly. "Tell me what's going on."

Aimee-Lynn continued to yell at her but the words were no longer intelligible. Just that repetitive razor-blade-serrating-slate noise.

"Stop!" Jules tried to shout, but it came out as a hoarse whisper.

Still, it worked. Aimee-Lynn stopped shouting and Dev dropped his hands from her shoulders.

The silence that followed was interrupted only by the soft thumping of her heartbeat in her ears.

"Ghosts," Dev breathed.

Jules opened her eyes to find him staring at her in wonder.

"Shelley said you saw ghosts as a child. Do you see one now?" He whispered the words, slowly and softly, as if trying not to frighten her or maybe the spirit away.

"Yes." She nodded toward her right.

Aimee-Lynn floated there. Her face drawn, and her image ended at her upper torso and arms. Smoky and transparent, she looked sickly.

Since he already knew what she could do, Jules turned to Aimee-Lynn and said, "I know you asked me to give them to Seth, but I haven't been able to find him. I'll do it as soon as he comes home."

Aimee-Lynn moved closer until she floated just behind the couch. She eyed Dev speculatively and frowned. *"Who's this?"*

"His name's Devon Jones. He's Seth's partner."

Dev sat a little straighter and looked toward the front door, nowhere near Aimee-Lynn, and said, "Pleased to meet you, ma'am."

Aimee-Lynn smiled wanly and nodded. *"Nice to meet you. Finally."*

"She said it's nice to meet you," Jules relayed.

When Dev arched an eyebrow, Aimee-Lynn added, *"Tell him Aimee-Lynn Masters has something to give to him."*

"But you said to only give it, *them*, to Seth." Jules frowned, glancing between the spirit and Dev.

Dev's eyes widened. "Give what to Seth?"

"Don't worry. You can trust this man too."

Not certain the ghost was right, Jules considered her options. Instinctively, she trusted Dev, but giving him the diamonds seemed like betraying Seth. Then again, Dev had no problem accepting that she saw ghosts. Would Seth be as accepting?

"Oh, Jules, it's so beautiful," Aimee-Lynn whispered. *"It's more than just a light. There's my nana. She's waving to me. I want to go so badly. It's warm and wonderful. I've never seen it before. This has to be the right thing to do. Please, I want to take my baby home.*

"Give him the diamonds and tell them what really happened. Tell them, and my mother, I tried to make it right."

Aimee-Lynn's aura, which had been gray earlier in the evening, glowed silvery-white now. It pulsed bright then dark then bright again. The ends of her blonde hair sparkled. She was so beautiful, looking at her almost hurt Jules's eyes.

"It's okay, Aimee-Lynn. Go home. I'll take care of everything," Jules said.

The light faded and Jules was filled with an overwhelming sense of peace. In the distance she distinctly heard a baby giggle and Aimee-Lynn say, *"Thank you."*

Jules needed to clear the sudden lump in her throat. She'd just helped someone. Two someones, really. Aimee-Lynn and her baby. And her crift didn't feel like a curse at the moment. It felt like a gift from God.

The spirits barely departed before Dev spoke. "What just happened?"

"Aimee-Lynn Masters said to tell you hello."

"Aimee-Lynn Masters is *here*?" His eyes widened so much, she thought they might pop out.

"Well, not anymore. She's gone."

Jules regarded Dev and the amazement on his face, then thought of Aimee-Lynn's words. The lump in Jules's throat became a ball of fear.

Giving the diamonds to Seth meant risking he'd think she'd been lying. Or worse . . . crazy. But giving them to Dev could mean destroying Seth's career if anyone ever found out that not only had she had the stolen gems the whole time, but that they were found in Seth's apartment.

"Why was she here?" Dev asked.

"I'll tell you, on one condition." Jules squared her shoulders. As she spoke, she slipped the bag from behind her back and clutched it to her chest. "You have to swear to help me find a way to keep this from harming Seth's reputation."

Dev scowled at her. "If he's done something illegal—"

"He hasn't," she assured him. "But he's dreamed for years of being promoted. Worked for it. Sacrificed for it. If he lost that opportunity because of this, I'd never be able to forgive myself."

"You love him," he said.

"That's not the point." She shrugged, suddenly self-conscious. Truth was, she did love Seth, even though she hadn't told him everything. She only hoped that when she did, he could love her in return. "I won't have him hurt by this. He never knew I had them. *I* didn't even know until a couple of hours ago."

"Had *what* exactly?" Cocking his head, Dev waited for her to answer, but her tongue was suddenly thick and dry. She couldn't have spoken if she'd wanted to. He sighed and said, "You have my word, Jules, if he hasn't done anything illegal, I'll make sure *my partner* is protected."

She unsnapped the purse and exposed the diamonds.

CHAPTER 19

S ETH'S USUAL PARKING space was taken by an old blue
Buick. Swinging his head from side to side, he searched
for an open spot on his street. Given the time of evening, it
wasn't surprising that spaces were hard to come by. Harmon's
patrol car poked out of the mouth of an alley, but the officer
didn't appear to be in it. Jones's black Lexus gleamed beneath
the streetlamp. It too appeared unoccupied.

Swinging his car into the alley next to the patrol car, Seth
killed the engine and jumped out, his gun drawn before the car
door slammed closed. The street appeared deserted, save for
the parked cars. A glance down the alley behind him showed
even Sam wasn't home.

In quick, silent strides, he hurried down the sidewalk and
into his building. The stairwell, still as death, creaked and
echoed with each step he climbed.

The entire time, images of Jules beaten as her mugger had
been or strangled as Aimee-Lynn had been played through his
mind like a horror movie.

He reached his landing. With his hand on his doorknob, he

listened but heard nothing. Twisting the handle, he breathed a small sigh of relief. It didn't budge. Perhaps she was okay after all?

Extracting his key from his pocket, he silently unlocked and pushed open the door.

Jules sat alone in the room. On one end of the couch she had her legs drawn up to her chest, her fingers wrapped over her toes and her forehead pressed against her knees.

Letting the door close with a slam behind him, he dropped his gun to the coffee table, where it landed with a thunk.

Her head snapped up and she appeared startled at first. Her face relaxed and split into a wide grin. Jules was off the couch and in his arms before he'd pocketed his apartment key.

His arms wound around her waist at the same time she looped hers around his neck. Their lips smacked together, almost bruising in the rush. She thrust her tongue into his mouth with a ferocity to match his own. Her sweet scent on his skin and the heady taste of her combined with a rush of relief so strong, he could think of nothing but losing himself inside her warm, welcoming body.

Bearing her down to the couch, he dropped his head to her neck and said between kisses, "I was so worried about you."

Of their own accord, his hands found her breasts and kneaded them.

"Oh, Seth!" She arched into his touch. "I was worried too."

He nipped her neck and placed a knee between her spread thighs. "You're safe, precious."

"Seth, we can't." She pushed her hands against his chest.

He sat up and found lust still hazing her eyes. Leaning forward, he stole another kiss. She eagerly participated, then shook her head, placing a hand between them again. "No, Seth, you've got to listen to me. I'm not the one in danger. You are."

Surprise had him sitting back. "What?"

Jules sighed and straightened her shirt. She slid back to the other side of the couch, as if worried he might attack her again. Crisscrossing her legs, she folded her hands in her lap then delivered, "I found your diamonds."

His jaw went slack. The words were clearly spoken and yet foreign. "You found my . . . diamonds?"

A wan smile ghosted across her face and she nodded.

Panic, fear, and fury ripped through him. "Juliana, I gave you specific instructions not to leave this apartment. Why would you risk your life like that? Do you have any idea how worried I've been? I tried to call but you didn't answer. Why didn't you stay put?"

"Seth, I didn't leave." She winced, tugged on her earlobe, and admitted, "Okay, well I ran to my apartment for two minutes. Maybe that's when you called because I promise had I heard your phone ring, I'd have answered. I've been trying to reach you for hours. I only left long enough to grab some clean clothes." Gesturing to the small stack of clothing sitting on the floor, she added, "But I swear, I didn't go anywhere else."

A dull ache formed between his brows. "Then how did you find the diamonds?"

More earlobe tugging. She appeared to wage an internal battle that ended with a sharp nod of her head. She lifted her chin and met his gaze, and something steely sparked in her eyes. "Seth, I need you to listen to me and keep an open mind. I-I'm crifted."

"Crifted?" He'd never heard such a term before.

"Yeah, I'm gifted or cursed, depending on your perspective. I've seen spirits my whole life. It's not something I tell most people. I mean, what a way to start a conversation. 'Hi, I'm Jules and I see your dead aunt Willa standing behind you.'"

Seth glanced behind him, then back to her.

"It's just the two of us in here right now." She smiled briefly, then said, "I found the diamonds because Aimee-Lynn Masters's ghost showed them to me."

Seth had never had an out-of-body experience before. He'd heard about them in movies, read about them in books, but had always considered such things nonsense. Listening to Jules talk about the ghost telling her their purses had been switched and that Jules had been carrying one with diamonds sewn into the lining for days, he felt his mind disconnect from his body and float up to the ceiling, where he looked down at himself and her.

"So then Dev came by and I gave the purse to him." That sentence snapped him back to himself.

"You're telling me," he said in a voice so calm it frightened *him*, "you've brought stolen diamonds into my home repeatedly. You called the police to report it. Jones was here, collected them, and has now taken them?"

"Well, not exactly." Her eyes widened and she paled. "I called the station looking for you. Dev, um . . . Detective Jones came over because he was worried when he heard I was alone. I hadn't planned to give them to anyone but you. Except the ghost said Dev was safe."

"The ghost of the woman from the Dumpster?" he asked. "The ghost of one of the thieves?"

"Aimee-Lynn wasn't a thief! She was tricked. The Knight, whoever that is, had her and Mason convinced they were part of some crack team sent to test security systems. The moment she realized what happened, she hid the diamonds until she could figure out who to trust." Jules pointed an accusatory finger at him. "Aimee-Lynn thought you and Dev were trustworthy."

The dull ache between his brows spread to encompass his entire forehead. He rubbed the growing spot with his thumb and forefinger.

I'm in love with a beautiful nut case.

"You said your ex gave you that purse." His jaw ached from clenching it. "How could you not know you've been carrying the wrong one since Friday night?"

"I'm not sure how I missed it." She conceded the point, proving she wasn't completely out of touch with reality. "Except like I told you, I never used it before last Friday night. When the purses were switched at the reunion, I hadn't noticed probably because I barely recognized my own."

"So you expect me to believe that you happened to be at a party where your *old friend*, Mason Hart, happened to be with his fiancée?" he asked, his frustration mounting. He doubted she'd seen a ghost, but it was far more likely that she'd been in on the theft from the start. "Hart, who you've just implicated in multiple robberies? But we'll get back to that because you and Aimee-Lynn Masters accidentally switched purses but you didn't know it. And you just *happened* to be discovered in a Dumpster with her body. Added to that, you *just happened* to find the stolen gems in your purse. Because a *ghost* told you to rip away the lining?" He whistled between his teeth. "Did I get everything?"

"Yes." Jules swallowed audibly and closed her eyes briefly, then whispered through a sob, "Tell me you believe me."

"I'm a detective, honey," he said. "I need proof. Can you ask Aimee-Lynn a question for me?"

She shook her head. "I can't. Aimee-Lynn crossed over before you came home."

"Crossed over?" he asked, then wished he hadn't.

"Went into the light." Jules nibbled on her lip, then said, "At least, I think she went into a light. She talked about seeing it. But she talked about her nana too. Hmmm . . ." She shrugged. "Either way, Aimee-Lynn's not here anymore."

She's crazy.

Why had he fallen for *her*? Was every woman crazy or just the ones that held the most attraction for him? Damn, he didn't just suck at relationships; he hoovered at them.

"Seth . . ." She reached for him but he jerked away from her touch. A desolate look washed over her beautiful face, followed by a strange sort of expression of acceptance. "Ask Dev if you don't believe me. He'll confirm what I've told you."

"Yeah, well . . . I've been trying to call him all night." The hard edge to his words appeared to physically hurt her. Her head whipped back as if he'd slapped her. Jules's reaction served to amp up his rioting emotions from frustration to rage. He growled the next sentence. "Stay in town until this is sorted out."

She blanched. "Are you going to arrest me?"

"Not without the diamonds." He shook his head. "Right now, the only proof I have is that you're a certifiable nutcase."

Tears sprang to her eyes, clung to her lashes, but went no farther. She rose to her feet and bent over. Seth, unsure of her intent, snatched his gun from the coffee table, keeping it out of her reach.

Jules flinched; agony flashed across her face. Her eyes swam more, threatening a waterfall of tears, but not a single drop fell. With her gaze on the gun he held loosely in his hand, she retrieved her clothing from the floor.

With the grace of a queen—or of someone completely comfortable in her delusion—Jules crossed the room. She opened the door a crack, then turned back, "One more thing. Aimee-Lynn said to tell you to beware the Knight."

The door closed behind her with a *snick*. The sound pierced his ballooning anger. It radiated through him, echoing, reverberating, stealing the strength from his body. He sunk to the couch. A hollow ache in the center of his chest opened up and he wanted to howl in grief.

The front door slammed open and bounced against the wall.

Jones's big body nearly filled the frame.

CHAPTER 20

"A RE YOU OUT of your ever-lovin' mind?" Jones slammed
the door closed and stomped across Seth's floor. His
face contorted with rage and he practically vibrated. "Did you
just call her a nut case?"

"Where the hell have you been all night?" Seth ground his
teeth in an effort to reign in his temper, then said, "It's none of
your damned business what I said to her. If you'd heard what
she just told me, you'd have said it too!"

"She told you about the diamonds?" Jones's eyebrows knit-
ted together.

"So she did have them all along?" Seth shot a quick glance
at the younger man's hands. "If she gave them to you, where
are they? And where in the hell have you been?"

"I went to my car for my field kit and to document the discovery of evidence while it was still fresh in my head." Jones
reached into the interior pocket of his expensive blazer and
withdrew a plastic evidence bag. Loose white diamonds, a red
diamond ring, and a now-tattered black purse were sealed
inside.

The bag slapped to the coffee table. Jones glared at him. "Anything else you want to ask me?"

Not quite trusting the younger man, Seth continued to dangle his weapon between his fingers and asked, "Did you send me on that wild-goose chase? Are you part of the Diamond Gang?"

Jones blinked. "You *are* out of your mind! Of course I'm not part of it. I'm your *partner*. You know, the one who's barely slept the past few nights trying to help you solve this mystery. The one who worked this afternoon and all night tonight going over those cryptic ass-licking diaries while you made time with the very woman whose heart you just crushed! Why the hell would I give up my entire fucking week to work on this case if I were in on it?"

For a taciturn fellow, Jones certainly has a way with words.

"Then why did you tell me I needed to come into the station?"

Jones goggled at him, then spoke through his clenched teeth. "Because Harmon handed me a note from the captain. The note even said, '*No more screw-ups.*'"

No more screw-ups.

The phrase rang in his ears. He'd heard it before. Where?

"But you didn't show up. Where the hell *did* you go?" Jones continued. "You left Jules alone for hours after telling me you weren't comfortable doing that for twenty minutes. I *thought* I was doing you a favor by coming over here to keep an eye on your girlfriend."

Jones's agitation was too raw to be faked. Or was it?

Seth's mind raced over the details of his case.

"Someone claiming to be Peterson called me while I was on my way to the station," Seth admitted, but watched Jones carefully for any signs of guilt. An eye twitch, an averted gaze, anything to indicate he'd been the one to make the call. "The guy did a great impersonation. Why would someone do that?"

Jones's eyes widened but he didn't so much as flinch. If he hid something, he hid it well. Could he trust his partner after all?

Jones pointed to the purse. "Maybe someone wanted you out of the way to steal this?"

"Jules's purse?"

"No. Not *her* purse," Jones growled the last word. "It

belonged to Aimee-Lynn Masters. I thought Jules told you what happened. Or were you too busy judging her to listen?"

Seth growled low in his throat at the insult. He closed his eyes and rolled his shoulders. "Shit. I must've handed that purse to her at least three times since we met."

In a flash, he saw the future: Jules arrested for obstruction of justice at best if not conspiracy, burglary, and accomplice to murder. But he was her alibi for the murder.

A lead ball clearly labeled *End-of-Seth's-Career* sank in his stomach. No sergeant's exam. No promotion. He might as well hand in his resignation now and apply for a job at McDonald's.

Unbelievable. Where his ex-wife had failed to destroy him, his new lover had just succeeded.

He reached inside his jacket pocket and retrieved his handcuffs, striding toward the door.

"Where are you going?"

"To arrest her." The words tasted bitter on his tongue.

"For what?" Jones stepped between Seth and the exit.

"For burglary, for obstruction of justice, for being a crazy pain in my ass!" Seth glared at the younger man. "Move!"

Jones folded his arms. "Until this moment I had a lot of respect for you. But now I wonder if you aren't just trying to save your own ass by arresting her for crimes you *know* she didn't commit. And there's no law against being a pain in the ass, or I'd arrest you!"

Seth had never wanted to hit another human being as badly as he wanted to punch Jones now. Clenching his free hand into a fist, he warned, "I don't give a damn who you respect. This is not about saving my ass. It's about justice."

"Think about what you're saying, Detective," Jones said, his tone considerably calmer. "Does Jules seem the type to have a half million dollars in stolen diamonds in her purse *and* be stupid enough to hang around the very people searching for them? Did she even once ask you about your case?"

"No." She hadn't. "But she was still hiding something, I felt it in my gut."

"Did she hide from you how she got the purse? Did she tell you that she and the Masters woman met hours before the murder? That they collided in a restroom?" Jones went on, not bothering to wait for Seth to answer. "Did she tell you that she believes that's when Masters got her cell phone and the purses were switched?"

"Yes," Seth admitted, grinding his teeth. This young man had the power to destroy him and Jules. Although why he worried about her, Seth didn't know.

"Tell me, *Detective*, in all the times you handled the purse, you never once noticed the diamonds sewn into the lining?"

"No," he said, resigned. "But I had no reason to believe there would be diamonds in there."

"So why do you think Jules did?"

Good question.

"Jules had seemed genuinely surprised when she noticed the purse was a fake. She even showed it to me." The now familiar sensation of bands wrapping around him, squeezed his chest. "I suppose it's possible that she didn't know about the diamonds. If I didn't see them and *if* she has no prior history with Masters, it could have been a simple case of wrong place, wrong time."

"Thank you!" Jones said in clipped tones.

"But then why did Jules start spouting that psychic mumbo-jumbo about seeing Masters's ghost?" Seth shook his head. "I could have believed it if not for the *I see dead people* reference."

"I swear you're so rigid you make cold iron look pliable!" Jones cursed and threw his hands in the air. "No wonder your other partners wanted transfers."

Jones paced back and forth in front of the door twice, then stopped in front of Seth again. "Listen to me carefully. Jules is a psychic. She does see ghosts. Sees them, talks to them. Gets messages from them. Aimee-Lynn's ghost told her where and how to find the diamonds."

Seth sighed his disgust. "And you believed her."

"Yes, I believe her, and you should too." Jones ran a hand through his sand-colored hair and added, "Years ago I was like you. If I couldn't see it, touch it, smell it, or taste it, it didn't exist. Then I met an amazing woman who could do the scientifically inexplicable."

"Jules?"

"No. Her sister, Shelley."

JULES HADN'T EVEN flipped on the light in her apartment when a sweaty hand clamped over her mouth from behind her.

"Shh . . ." The fetid stench of stale scotch blew across her face.

She had no intention of remaining quiet. Twisting her head and body from side to side, she fought for freedom. She clawed at a leather-jacketed arm but only succeeded in being lifted off the ground by her captor. She kicked backward, aiming for a knee or a leg, but Mr. Scotch Breath just dodged her attempts. Remembering the stacks of boxes in the room, she kicked forward, hoping to knock some over. Instead, her foot connected with a muscular thigh.

A terrifying moment later, the owner of the leg, a second man in the room, produced a fist. It flew toward her face even as her first captor called out, "No!"

Her world tunneled into darkness.

SETH HOLSTERED HIS gun, then rubbed the back of his neck. Tension made his spine ache, and he shifted his position on the couch. Man, he needed a little time to wrap his mind around the possibility that Jules possessed some sort of genetically inherited ESP. "So you're telling me you've actually seen both Shelley and Jules do . . . whatever it is they do? Seen it with your own eyes?"

"Crazy as it sounds, yeah." Jones nodded. "Sitting right here tonight, I watched her talk with Aimee-Lynn's ghost."

"Could *you* see the ghost?" Maybe Jones was crazy too?

"No. But it was weird. I could swear that the air got colder when she arrived. And I had this, um, feeling that we weren't alone anymore."

Seth had that feeling the night he'd kissed Jules in her apartment. But he'd dismissed it as a drafty window because no one *was* there.

"Look, I'm not describing it well. You have to see it for yourself."

"I tried that. I told her to ask Aimee-Lynn a question for me." He sighed. "She told me she couldn't—"

"Because Aimee-Lynn had crossed over before you returned," Jones interrupted.

"Yeah, that's what she said." Seth shook his head. "As she left she told me to beware the night."

It clicked then. Not beware the night. Beware the *knight*.

"Crap, she did tell me something. Either *I'm* going crazy or Jules told me the name of one of the characters in Masters's diary. The Knight. Unless you mentioned it to her."

"Not me. I didn't tell her anything about the case." A spark of recognition lit Jones's eyes. "Wait, she told me Aimee-Lynn had given her strict instructions to give the diamonds only to you or me."

Cottoning onto that train of thought, Seth said, "Crap. I'd been thinking on the way over here that the Knight's a cop. I'd started to suspect someone on the force. For a while I thought it was you. No offense."

"Right." Jones snorted. "Still think it's me?"

"No." A jolt of fear ripped down Seth's spine. He jumped to his feet, running for the door.

"Where are you going?" Jones said.

"If the Knight is someone on the force, Jules could still be in danger. Especially if the Knight doesn't know we have the diamonds."

Seth wrenched open his front door and hurried into the hallway. The familiar musty scent of the old building assailed his nostrils. The hallway lay peaceful and silent. Nothing seemed odd or out of place, except Jules's door.

It stood ajar.

Drawing his gun, he caught Jones doing the same. Quickly and silently, they approached the apartment. Light from the hallway poured through the opening, illuminating the devastation within.

In a single unified move, they swung open the door and aimed their guns into the empty apartment. Stepping lightly over the mess, they checked out the rooms.

"Clear," Jones reported, coming from April and Ernie's bedroom.

"Clear," Seth echoed, exiting Jules's room. Meeting Jones back in the living room, they surveyed the damage.

"Someone was searching for something," Jones said, squatting down near the front door.

He ran two fingers through a spot on the floor the size of a half-dollar, then held them in the air. They were stained crimson.

"Did you check out her apartment before you stormed into mine?" Seth knew he had no right to be angry with Jones, but fear and common sense didn't always go hand in hand. And right now, he was more afraid than he'd ever been in his life.

Jones cursed under his breath. "No."

Surprisingly, Jones didn't hurl an accusation back at Seth, so he did it himself. "It's my fault. I *knew* she was in danger. I shouldn't have left her alone. Whoever has her couldn't have taken her more than ten minutes ago."

"I'll call this in," Jones offered.

"I wouldn't do that," said a gravelly voice from the hallway. Seth turned to find Sam there, a determined look in his eyes. "He'll kill her before you can find them."

SOMETHING WET AND sticky oozed down her neck. Jules opened her eyes and tried to move, but she was in an oddly familiar confined space. Two strips of red light glowed dimly, one at her head and one near her knees. The scent of rubber filled her nostrils. A steady hum of tires on pavement rocked beneath her.

The rocking ended on a jolt and a squeal of tires. She slid sideways and her face slapped against the wall of the trunk. Something heavy and long hit her in the back, making her tight quarters even tighter.

The memory of Aimee-Lynn's murder slammed into her. She was in the same car.

Panic formed a golf ball in her throat. For a moment she lay frozen, too terrified to even try to lift her unbound hands. She didn't want to die like Aimee-Lynn, but the memory replayed itself in her mind.

"Stop it, Jules. Just stop it!" she whispered to herself. "Get a grip and get the heck out of here."

She shifted her weight and brought her right hand to her face, swiping at the blood. Her left arm burned as if she'd torn out her stitches. And unless she was mistaken, her sleeve was sticky. Her right eye throbbed from where she'd been punched. Her legs and arms ached from being crammed into the trunk of a car.

The thing at her back groaned. A tremor ran through her at the deep-throated sound. Pressing her hands against the cold steel of the car, she pushed herself onto her back. Her stitches pulled and threatened to pop, making her cry out in pain. Finally, she lay on her back and stared at the ceiling a scant six inches from her face. Panting with exertion and fear, sweat trickled down her temples.

Terrified to look but more frightened by her own imagination, she swiveled her head and glanced to her right.

It took a moment to recognize the body on its side as Officer Zig Harmon, one of the two patrolmen assigned to watch her at the shop yesterday.

Even in the shadows, his normally youthful face appeared sunken around the eyes. His left shoulder seemed to point both up and backward at once, as if he'd dislocated it. But the blood seeping from it seemed to hint at something else entirely.

"Zig?" Jules whispered and gently touched his face. "Zig, can you hear me?"

He didn't answer. Without putting weight on her injured arm again, she couldn't get close enough to hear if he was still breathing.

Cradling her injured arm to her body, she stretched out two shaky fingers and aimed for the pulse in his neck. A lifetime started and ended before she finally found the weak but steady *thump, thump.*

"Zig!" she whispered urgently into his ear. "Wake up!"

He moaned but didn't rouse. She needed to do something. She'd already seen how one version of this story played out. And she didn't want to star in the sequel.

From Aimee-Lynn's vision, Jules knew there was no release latch, so she turned her attention to the officer, hoping he might have a radio or a gun or at least a pocketknife on his tool belt. Gingerly, she ran her fingers down his shoulder to his belt. The weapons police officers normally carried had been stripped away. No gun, no Taser, even the cord to his radio dangled headless.

"Check his pockets," Moira said. Her face alone peered into the closed trunk. The silver white aura surrounding her illuminated the cramped space.

"Good idea." Jules set to work patting his pockets. She found a cell phone on the third try. Unfortunately, it was wedged between his thigh and the trunk floor. As gently as she could, she pushed Zig onto his back and yanked out the phone.

She pushed the send button and prayed.

THE NIGHT WAS growing stranger by the second. First, Seth was sent on a wild-goose chase. Then Jules told him a ghost showed her where to find a bag of stolen diamonds. Now he and Jones were racing down Atlantic Avenue in Jones's Lexus with a homeless man in the back seat.

"I've got a BOLO on the Buick," Jones said, ending his call and tossing his cell on the dashboard. The BOLO or Be On the Look Out wouldn't do them much good if a cop had taken Jules. But they might get lucky. "Last report of a vehicle matching that description passed here five minutes ago."

"Tell us exactly what you saw," Seth said, splitting his attention between Jones doing a damn good Mario Andretti impersonation shuttling between cars and Sam in the back seat.

"I was sleeping at my Dumpster when a cop and a blond man came around the corner arguing. The blond man carried Jules in his arms. He kept telling the cop, 'I won't do it.' I wasn't sure what *it* was until the cop strode over to a beat-up blue Buick and popped the trunk." Sam clutched the back seat until his knuckles turned white. "The cop pointed his gun at the blond man's head and ordered him to put her in. He put her in the trunk gentle-like, but before he straightened, the cop cuffed him across the back of the skull.

"I thought maybe the blond man had died the way he crumpled to the ground, but no. The cop leaned over, pressed the barrel of his piece against the other man's temple, and whispered something into his ear. I couldn't hear what was said, but whatever it was convinced the blond man to get into the car without another word."

Seth's stomach shrank. Jules was in the trunk of some bastard's car. He could guess who, or at least he thought he knew whose it was, until Sam added, "Then this young officer who barely looked old enough to drive walked up. I don't think he'd seen what I had because he chatted with the cop and glanced inside the car. When he saw the blond man, the first cop said, 'Let it go, Harmon.' But Harmon seemed intent on talking to the blond man. He leaned in the open window and never saw it coming. Bastard shanked him." Blue fire snapped in Sam's eyes. His fingernails dug divots in the expensive leather seat.

"I didn't see anyone when we came down," Jones said.

" 'Cause the bastard cop dumped the guy's body in the trunk with Jules saying he'd make them both disappear and no one but the fishes would know where they were." A look of desolation Seth could identify with crossed Sam's face. "It all happened so quick, I barely got a look at the license plate. I should've moved up the alley faster, but my knees haven't recovered from chasing that asshole mugger yesterday."

"You did the right thing," Seth said.

He had his own guilt to contend with, but now was not the time to deal with Sam's or his.

He had a kidnapper to catch and not a prayer of doing it without divine intervention.

THE SCREEN LIT up.

Four bars.

She dialed 9-1-1.

"Nine-one-one, please hold."

"No, wait!" Jules called into the receiver. She glanced up to where Moira had been moments before and said, "I don't believe this. I've been kidnapped and nine-one-one puts me on hold."

Moira didn't answer. She appeared to have left.

And a Muzak version of "Kids Wanna Rock" played through the receiver.

She couldn't keep waiting. Zig needed help now. Well, she did too, but she wasn't bleeding.

Clicking end, Jules scrolled through Zig's recent calls, hoping they'd be labeled by name and not just a number. There at the top was Seth. Relief rushed through her, but then she worried that he might hang up on her when he realized who was calling. Or worse, he wouldn't believe her.

Best not to chance it.

The next number on the list was labeled Devon Jones. She selected it and hit send.

He answered on the second ring, asking without preamble, "Harmon, is Jules with you?"

"Dev, it's Jules," she said, relieved to know her disappearance had already been noted. "Zig is next to me but unconscious. I know this is gonna sound crazy but we've been kidnapped and stuffed in a trunk."

"How are you calling me from a trunk?"

"That's what you ask me?" Jules replied, disbelievingly.

The sound of her irritated voice through Dev's cell, now on speaker, was a balm to Seth's frayed nerves. If she was ticked, she wasn't mortally injured . . . he hoped.

"Juliana, I need you to tell me in as few words as possible what happened and where you are," Seth said.

And, smart woman that she was, she didn't ask any questions but told them succinctly about being assaulted, kidnapped, and waking up with an unconscious Harmon in the trunk.

"Oh!" she cried out.

"What?" he, Jones, and Sam all yelled at once.

"Um . . . well," she paused again then said, "Moira says we're headed to the old pier near the Tidewater Seafood Packing Company."

A place where no one but the fishes would know where to find them.

"*Moira* says?" Seth echoed at the same time Sam emitted a cry like a wounded animal and slumped in the back seat.

Jules didn't reply to him; instead, she said, "Did you hear me, Dev? The old pier. She's gotta be right, the stench of dead fish is gagworthy."

"Heard you, Jules. Hang on, we'll be there in two minutes," Jones answered, casting Seth a disparaging look.

From the back seat, Sam sniffed then leaned forward. "My Moira?"

CHAPTER 21

TWO MINUTES WAS a long time, one hundred twenty seconds, one hundred sixty heartbeats. In Jules's case, it was roughly the time it took for the car to rumble to a stop in a deserted marina.

The engine cut off.

Jules sucked in a breath, then whispered, "We've stopped. I can't really hear anything distinct—"

Moira popped back in again, a welcome sight. Her blonde hair fanned around her like a mermaid's hair floating in the water. Her aura was almost completely silver now and radiated a peace the likes of which Jules had never known. Despite the dire situation, the sight of all that silver calmed Jules.

"Be still and quiet or they'll hear you." Moira smiled, staring pointedly at the cell.

Jules glanced at it, then whispered, "Put the cell on mute so you can hear."

The phone went silent. From outside, she heard two men shouting and what sounded like knuckles smacking flesh. She flinched and bumped into Zig, who groaned.

"I'm going to go see how far away they are," Moira said, then disappeared.

With no one to talk to, Jules started to shake. The walls closed in, the air grew thick and oppressive. The smell of copper was so strong, she could taste it in the back of her throat.

Moira reappeared. Her silvery aura had darkened to a dove gray. *"They're on the other side of the marina, too far away. But that evil man is coming for you now."*

Tears stung her eyes and for once she didn't fight them; instead she tucked the phone into a shadowed corner of the car and whispered, "Someone's coming for me. In case I don't make it, Dev, I need you to tell Shelley I never gave up looking for her and Hannah."

They must have clicked off the mute because Dev's whispered words came through the phone. "You're not going to die. We're almost there! Hang on."

"Stall, submit, do whatever it takes," Seth interjected. "We're crossing the marina now."

"Seth?" If death was seconds away and they were minutes, there never would be a right time. "I don't think you're going to make it. Seth, I need you to know . . . I love you."

"Ah, precious, I love you too," he replied.

"Well . . ." Tears spilled down her cheeks, choking her words. "I hate that I love such a big, stupid, narrow-minded—"

Her words were cut off when the trunk flew open and she was wrenched out of it by her hair.

JULES'S CRY OF pain lanced through him. Seth lunged for the phone, only to have Jones snatch it up, hit the mute button again, and toss it in the back seat to Sam.

"What the hell did you do that for?" Seth roared his outrage and attempted to grab the phone back from a surprisingly strong Sam.

Jules yelled, but her words were unintelligible.

"Detective, we need the element of surprise," Dev said with a deadly calm voice.

As the older detective, Seth knew Jones was right. And if she cried out, she still breathed. Acting irrationally wouldn't save her. And he'd be damned if he'd lose her now.

They passed beneath the lamppost adorned with a *Welcome to TSP* sign. Jones popped the car into neutral and cut the engine and lights. The car rolled forward in the darkness.

"There they are." Jones pointed to a car with three people outside of it. Two men and a woman. Jules.

The car rolled to a stop.

"Stay here," Seth ordered Sam.

He didn't wait to see if Sam agreed but hopped out with Jones. Keeping to the shadows, guns drawn, they moved stealthily to the scene.

Hart looked like he was taking a good beating. Blood and dirt coated his shirt. Both eyes were nearly swollen shut. The cop had his back to Seth. He recognized the officer insomuch as he knew he *should* know the man. Other than that, until the *cop* turned around, Seth was at a loss.

"She was my fiancée!" Hart shouted.

"She was a fucking thief!" his adversary retorted and threw a punch knocking Hart to the ground.

Hart pushed to his wobbly feet and yelled, "You're the thief. Aimee-Lynn was right. I should never have trusted you."

The cop put his hands on his hips, threw his head back, and laughed a high-pitched nasal laugh. It was the laugh Seth recognized. He'd heard it when he'd picked Jules up from the shop yesterday. Gareth.

Officer Chaz Gareth. The officer who'd allowed Jules to climb into the Dumpster with the corpse. One of the two officers Seth had assigned to protect Jules. The only other person at the station, besides Seth and Jones, who'd been at every burglary scene committed by the Diamond Gang.

Jules! A shadow moved to his left and shells crunched. He whipped his gaze in the direction of the noise.

She crouched low, slowly edging her way toward the sparse trees beyond the lamppost. He didn't know why she didn't just run, until Gareth, gun drawn, charged up and grabbed her by her injured arm.

Her scream of pain didn't stop him from dragging her to the back of the car where he shoved her to her knees beside Mason. Seth must have missed the last punch Gareth threw because Mason was flat on his back on the ground and groaning.

"Give me the diamonds!" Gareth pointed his weapon at Jules.

Then time slowed down and sped up simultaneously.

Mason lurched to his feet between Jules and the gun, his arms thrown wide, yelling, "No!"

"Gun!" Jones yelled, sprinting ahead.

Gareth whipped the gun down Hart's face with a thunderous *crack*. Mason sank to the ground, unmoving. Jules screamed. And screamed.

Seth sprinted, fast and sure, as if he traversed the seashell-encrusted parking lot on a daily basis. Bringing his right arm up, he aimed at Gareth. The bastard's head lined up perfectly in his sights. Before Seth could get off a shot, Jules blocked it.

In that moment, life for Seth stopped. It didn't matter that she thought she talked to ghosts. It didn't matter that she'd inadvertently screwed up his case and probably his career. All that mattered was she was about to die. And without a high-powered rifle, there was no way he could take a shot from this distance without risking Jules.

"ARE YOU GONNA tell me where you hid the diamonds, bitch?" Officer Chaz Gareth demanded, pressing the cold steel of his gun harder into her forehead. "Or do I kill you now?"

Jules considered telling him the truth, that she'd turned the diamonds over to Dev, but she suspected Gareth would just pull the trigger if she did.

Mason moaned softly next to her and stirred to life. He pushed to all fours and spat blood onto the crushed oyster pavement, splattering the white shells with drops of red. "Chaz," he said, in raspy tones. "Chaz, she's innocent in all this."

"Where have I heard that before?" Gareth kicked Mason in the ribs so hard, he lifted off the ground and crashed back down. The sickening crack of ribs breaking ripped through the quiet.

"I'm sorry, Jules," Mason said between gasps of pain. His normally handsome features were drawn and pale. "I didn't know he'd killed Aimee-Lynn until after I saw you had the purse."

"Mason, why would you be involved in something like this? You're rich."

Mason shook his head weakly. The pain in his handsome eyes spoke of something deeper than the physical abuse he was taking. Unshed tears brightened his eyes. "I made a mistake a long time ago. A stupid accident and people died. I'll never stop paying for it."

Gareth kicked him in the chest again and Mason gasped for air. "You're such a fucking wimp." He squatted down between them and screwed up his face. "That fucking sob story again? Christ, man-up or learn to deal with it. You wanted to prove to your father you had the balls to get the Edmunson building. And you did. Then you had to fuck it up and whine, *'Daddy doesn't believe me, Chaz. Help me, Chaz. I'll do anything you ask.'* I fucking helped you then you brought that bitch into my life. Because of you, that damned slut stole my diamonds."

"Aimee-Lynn wasn't a slut," Mason ground out from between his teeth. "You shouldn't have touched her. She was my fiancée. We were supposed to be a family. I'd have died for her."

"God, you're such a pussy." Gareth kicked him in the head, sending Mason flying sideways and skittering over the oyster shells. He didn't move. Jules wasn't even sure he still breathed, but Chaz kept talking as if Mason could hear him.

"I told you that bitch was nothing but trouble. It didn't take her nearly as long as it took you to figure out we weren't testing security systems."

He turned and glared at Jules.

She shivered and tried to back up, but with the car behind her, there was nowhere to go. He sauntered closer to her and again brought the gun to her forehead. She bit down on her lower lip to keep from crying out in pain as the barrel dug into her flesh.

"Now, where did you hide my diamonds?" He smiled a cold, cruel smile.

"You're just going to kill me when I tell you, right?" she asked with a bravado she didn't feel. "Just like you killed Aimee-Lynn and . . . and the guy who mugged me? He worked with you, didn't he? I didn't get it at the time, but he wasn't some random mugger. He knew the diamonds were in my purse and he wanted them."

"Of course, I killed that two-bit piece of shit," Gareth snapped and swung the barrel away from her head. With his hands loosely holding the gun between his spread thighs, he chatted as if he hadn't just beaten Mason almost to death.

"I told them how I wanted it handled but that wimp and Jack panicked when they realized I'd already killed Aimee-fucking-Lynn. No one was supposed to draw attention to us or that purse. But Jack, that worthless sack of shit, fucked up. You could identify him. I knew he'd turn on me the moment he was caught, and I couldn't let that happen."

"But why kill Mason?" She squeaked in alarm the moment he raised the gun to her head again.

"Because with his daddy's money and power, he could get off," he sneered. "Someone like me, a hardworking guy from the streets, they'd lock up forever. That asshole doesn't deserve to be rich."

He swung the gun toward Mason's unmoving body and pulled the trigger. Jules screamed as the shot rent the night. Blood poured from Mason's hip, but he didn't move.

The barrel of the gun swung back at her face and Jules threw up her hands, ready to grab for it. But all she captured was air between her fingers as someone launched himself at Gareth, taking him to the ground.

Samuel's dirty, bedraggled brown coat was all she saw before the gunshot rang out. Both men stopped moving. Samuel collapsed on top of Gareth, and blood spread out from beneath their bodies.

Someone screamed. And screamed. And screamed. It took a moment for Jules to realize it was her.

"Jules." Seth appeared beside her, seemingly from nowhere. With a gun in his right hand, he lightly stroked his left one down her cheek. "Precious, are you okay?"

Dev appeared on the other side of Samuel and Gareth's bodies. He rolled the men apart. Gareth appeared to be knocked out. Samuel breathed shallowly, his long scruffy beard was stained crimson and almost covered the gaping hole in his chest.

Tears burned in her eyes and Jules shoved Seth away,

half-crawling, half-stumbling to Samuel's side. "Oh Samuel, I'm so sorry. I'm so sorry."

Tears blurred her vision as she watched him gasp one last breath.

For a moment there was stillness. No wind, no noise, a pervasive nothingness that enshrouded the entire parking lot. Then Moira and Penny shimmered into being beside Samuel's body. Mother and daughter wept silvery tears.

"I'm so sorry," she whispered around the lump in her throat. "He died saving me. I'm so sorry."

A third light winked into being, soft and silver white. It elongated and reshaped itself over and over. Moira and her daughter flanked the light, watching, anticipation on their faces. Seconds later, Samuel shimmered into existence. Not the man he was when he had died, but the man his family had known him to be. Clean-cut, youthful, and handsome.

He kissed his wife's cheek, then swept his little girl into his arms and hugged her close. The family's collective aura shifted between white and silver. And when the little girl giggled at her father's kisses, her aura sparkled.

"Thank you for giving me purpose again," Samuel said, gazing at Jules. "I stopped living the night my family died. But then you came into my alley and reminded me they were always with me." He glanced at his wife and daughter, then back at Jules. "And now they always will be."

Wet tracks slid down her cheeks as Jules watched the family start to fade. Just when she'd thought they'd gone, the little girl shimmered back. "Tell him he didn't do it. It wasn't his fault."

"Him who?"

The child pointed at Mason. "The fire truly was an accident caused by bad wiring. It wasn't his fault. We don't blame him. He couldn't have saved us any more than my daddy could have." Then she shimmered away.

Then, as it always did, life and sounds returned in a rush. The streetlights were too bright. The sounds of the police sirens in the distance were too loud. And every scrape, bang, and bruise she'd acquired in the past few days scored a perfect ten on the pain scale.

"Jules?" Seth's voice sounded soft in her mind. Had he

whispered? Or was she hearing him in her head? "Precious, talk to me."

Her stomach lurched threateningly. She shuffled away to be sick alone. But she wasn't alone. Seth stroked her back until the violent spasms ended.

She rocked back on her knees and the drugging darkness swept over her.

SETH CALLED 9-1-1 again and demanded an ETA on the ambulances, updating them on the number of injuries. A quick check on Harmon showed the young officer still hadn't regained consciousness.

Squatting down to where Jules lay, Seth removed his coat and wrapped it around her shoulders, then pulled her into his arms.

He stared at her in wonder. Either he was going crazy or she'd just been talking to *ghosts*. He glanced over to his partner, who was monitoring the vital signs of both Mason Hart and Zig Harmon.

"I told you she could see spirits," Jones said, smirking. Pulling his red jacket off his body, he draped it over Hart in an effort to keep him from going into shock.

"I can't believe I'm saying this, but did you just see—?"

"Sam, his wife, and his daughter?" Jones nodded, stood up, crossed over to where Gareth lay unconscious, and pulled out a pair of handcuffs. "Yeah."

"Ever seen anything like that before?"

"Nope. Shelley, Jules's sister, can talk to animals. She told me once that the dead can sometimes make themselves known to the living who *need* to see them and are willing to look." He shrugged his massive shoulders. "Guess you were finally willing to look."

Seth didn't know what stunned him more, the idea of Jules having Dr. Dolittle for a sister or the fact that he was having this conversation as if they were discussing the NFL draft picks.

The sirens in the distance sounded closer. "How much longer?"

"A minute, maybe?" Seth replied.

Gareth finally roused to find himself cuffed and sitting next to the car he'd stuffed Jules into. He glowered at Jules, who'd also finally started to come round.

With her head in his lap, Seth smiled down at her. "Welcome back, precious."

"Am I dead?" Jules mumbled.

"No, thank God."

"Am I under arrest?" She eyed him, suspicion crinkling the corners of her eyes.

"No, love." He shook his head. "You're definitely not."

"Good." She shifted away from him and pushed to her knees. The oyster shells crunched as she moved. Rising to her feet, she swayed, and Seth hurried to her side to steady her. "Whoa, slow down. You've had quite a bump on the head."

She glanced around as the ambulance came blaring onto the scene. Her gaze landed on Samuel's dead body and she shivered. Then she glanced from Mason on the ground with a gunshot wound to Harmon in the trunk. Finally, she looked back at Seth just as two paramedics ran over.

"I didn't—"

"I know," he interrupted. Worried that she was referring to the diamonds or the ghosts, he didn't want anyone else to hear their conversation. "We can talk about it later. You need to go to the hospital first."

"Ma'am, do you mind if we take a look at you?" asked a paramedic as he led Jules toward the back of the ambulance.

Reluctantly, Seth released his hold on her, even though he didn't want to. But as lead detective on the scene, he had a responsibility to fulfill. Still, when she glanced back at him with those wide emerald green eyes full of confusion and doubt, he didn't give a damn what protocol demanded of him.

Striding across the parking lot, he climbed into the back of the ambulance next to her, gently pulled her into his arms, and kissed her. It was meant to be a soft, reassuring kiss, but she broke it off almost before it began.

"Seth, I can't change who I am," she said, clasping her hands together and placing them in her lap.

He turned to the two paramedics. "Would y'all give us just a moment?"

When they exited the vehicle, he reached out and pulled

the door closed. The expression on her face was of resigned acceptance, then she lifted her chin defiantly.

He grinned.

"Precious, I wouldn't ask you to change a thing." He lifted her right hand to his lips and kissed her fingertips. "I love you, just as you are."

"You love a nut case who *thinks* she sees ghosts?" She curled her fingers but didn't pull out of his grasp.

Guilt ate at him. "I was wrong to call you that—"

"Yes, you were," she agreed, no warmth or humor in her voice.

"But I know now what you can do, and it's an amazing gift. One you should be proud of."

Her eyes lit up. "Do you mean it?"

"Yes, and because of it, I was able to put this case to bed. If you hadn't talked to ghosts, I wouldn't have known where to find you in time. Gareth would have gotten away with four murders, including yours."

The thought of Jules dead made his heart shrink.

"But he's not going to get away with it?" she asked, thankfully pulling him from his morose thoughts. "Still, how are you going to explain how you found me?"

"We followed a tip about a kidnapping. It's already covered. And as for Gareth, well, he confessed, didn't he? Jones and I heard him."

The ambulance doors opened and the paramedics returned, effectively ending that conversation.

Shifting closer to Jules, he wrapped an arm around her and did the one thing he told himself he'd never do; he begged. "Please forgive me, Jules. I love you. All of you. Just as you are."

He waited a long, lonely lifetime as she stared at him. Then she leaned forward and brushed her lips against his. "I love you, too, *Lambkins*."

•

EPILOGUE

❧

"**T**HANK YOU SO much for throwing our engagement party here," Jules told April as they carried bowls of potato salad and chips to the backyard.

"It's the least we can do since you won't let us pay for the wedding," April replied, bringing up the same argument they'd been having for six months.

"It's not meant to hurt your feelings, April," Jules explained, setting the dish on the picnic table beside the chips April had just deposited. "It's important to Seth that we do this on our own. I think it's his way of proving he can provide for me."

"Men are so odd." When Jules laughed, April asked, "When does the English clan get here?"

Jules checked her watch. "In about thirty minutes. Seth's mom took Theresa to pick up her bridesmaid's dress, then they'll be over."

Milo made a noise in the bassinet he shared with Maeve. Jules followed April over to the portable crib that was sitting in the shade of a magnolia tree. At four months, the twins were small, but growing and happy. As for April, she glowed.

"Family is everything." April sighed, staring at her infants.

"Yes," Jules agreed, wrapping an arm around April's unfairly-trim-since-she-just-had-twins body.

April gave her a quick hug then headed back to the kitchen to bring more food. Jules followed. The front door opened to reveal Diana.

She smiled and hurried over to hug Jules. "Hi, Jules!"

"Hi, Diana." Jules tried not to stare but it was hard.

The Goth clothing was gone. Diana looked like she'd stepped out of 1985. Crimped hair, teased bangs, denim mini-skirt, lace fingerless gloves, a pink button-down shirt with the collar turned up, and lacy socks with high heels.

"Is Dev here?" Diana grinned wide.

Jules blinked, surprised at the complete lack of black on Diana's body and face. It took Jules a moment, then she replied, "Um, no, not yet. He's picking up Shelley. They should be here in about an hour."

"Oh, I hope he gets here soon. I can't stay long. I've got a hot date later with a guy I met at the community theater. I'd hate to leave without seeing Dev." Diana shrugged. "What can I say, I miss seeing Dev in the shop. That is one fine EOMP. Oh well, where's the food?"

"Out back," April said with a laugh.

Diana waved and hurried to the backyard. April stared after her, then looked back at Jules in obvious confusion. "EOMP?"

"I'm not sure, but I think it stands for *example of masculine perfection.*"

"Ah, makes sense."

Jules grinned. "By the way, I love her new look."

"Last week, I let her borrow a couple John Hughes DVDs from the eighties. Guess they really inspired her." April laughed again.

She sobered and asked quietly, "How's the search for Hannah coming?"

Jules shook her head. So far, TSS hadn't been able to locate her baby sister, but she wouldn't give up hope. "The private detectives are still searching for her."

"They'll find her, just like they did Shelley." April gave her a conciliatory hug, then picked up the bowl of Watergate salad from the counter and strode to the door.

"Dev found Shelley, but I'm not sure who benefitted more there." Jules had to smile. Life was so much better than she'd ever dreamed possible. And soon Hannah would be found and their family reunited at last.

Jules picked up the tray of cucumber sandwiches and followed April. They made their way across the freshly cut lawn to the food tables.

"I think that's the last of it," April said, brushing her hands together. She glanced around the yard. "Now where did Ernie and Seth get off to? They need to bring out the coolers and fire up the grill before the guests come."

Seth and Big Jim came from around the corner of the house. But they weren't alone; another older man and woman followed them. Jules and April headed toward them.

Seth wrapped his arms around Jules and tugged her close. She couldn't resist playing with his curly locks. They were a little longer than usual, because when he hadn't been at the station or home making love with her, he'd been studying for the sergeant's exam. He kissed her quickly on the lips then turned to greet the new couple.

"Jules, this is Captain Dave Peterson and his wife, Dora," Seth said with a smile.

"Pleased to meet you," she said. She shook their hands and continued the introductions. "These are my parents, April and B— um, Ernie."

"We're pleased to meet you too, young lady," the captain said. "We thank y'all for the invitation but we can't stay long. I had some important news to share and felt it couldn't wait."

"What news?" Jules asked, hoping it was what she thought it was.

"Why don't I let Seth tell you?"

"You must stay and have a bite to eat, there's really too much food." April gestured toward the picnic table.

Before they could answer, Maeve started crying. Mrs. Peterson's eyes widened and she asked, "Do you have a baby? I just love babies."

"I have twins," April replied. "Would you like to meet Jules's baby brother and sister?"

The moment April and Ernie led the captain and his wife away, Seth pulled Jules into his arms and kissed her. It wasn't a simple, we're-in-front-of-your-parents kiss. He claimed her mouth as if he were starving and she was the only food for miles. He tugged her close as if he couldn't bear to let her go. Her heart swelled.

"I love you, Seth," she said, leaning back and staring into the melted-chocolate eyes that had stolen her breath the night they met. "Are you going to keep me in suspense? What's the good news?" When he didn't answer right away, she added, "Come on, *lambkins*, you can tell me."

"Ah, precious," he chuckled. "That's Sergeant Lambkins now."

Read on for a sneak peek at the next
Tidewater novel from Mary Behre

GUARDED

Coming in Summer 2014
from Berkley Sensation

"SOMETHING'S WRONG WITH Mr. Fuzzbutt." Beau's angelic voice rang out seconds before the backside of his long-haired, black guinea pig bounced before Dr. Shelley Morgan's eyes. At almost the same moment a cry went up from the back room of the small veterinary clinic.

"Shelley, I need you!" Feet pounded quickly down the short hall before Jack, the veterinary clinic's too-excitable intern, burst into the room yelling, "Lucy is trying to turn Hercules into her Thanksgiving dinner. And this time I think she might just chew his balls off."

"Language! And Thanksgiving's four weeks away," Shelley said, pushing to her feet and sweeping the fur ball known as Mr. Fuzzbutt into her hands.

But Jack hadn't heard her. The intern/groomer/assistant had already spun around and disappeared into the back room. His cries of, "Stop that, Lucy. Get up, Herc," were nearly drowned out by the cacophony of dogs barking.

"Dr. M.? Can you help him?" Beau's voice, still high-pitched from youth, wobbled as he spoke.

She turned to the worried ten-year-old who was small for his age. His large, luminous brown eyes were framed by thick black glasses. His clothes, although threadbare and clearly hand-me-downs, were clean as were his faded blue sneakers.

"Don't worry, Beau. I'm sure he'll be fine. Just have a seat in the waiting area and I'll be back shortly. I'll bring Mr. . . ." she couldn't bring herself to say the word Fuzzbutt to the child, and settled with, "Your little buddy back after I've examined him."

Beau nodded. "Okay, Dr. M., I trust you. But I can't just sit and wait. How about I bring in the bags of dog food from outside?"

"That would be a big help, Beau. You remember where the store room is? Just stack the ones you can carry in there. And don't try to lift the big ones."

Not that the little guy would be able to do much. The last time the clinic received donations, the dog food had come in fifty pound bags. Beau likely didn't even weigh that much. Plus, it had rained late last night and the town handyman she'd hired hadn't had a chance to fix the hole in the shed's roof. So chances were good several of the bags were sodden and useless.

Still he beamed as if she'd just handed him a hundred-dollar bill. "You know it! I'll have the bags all put away before you can bring Mr. Fuzzbutt back. Just you wait."

Then Beau was out the front door. The length of bells hanging from the handle jangled and banged against the glass as he took off around the corner to the storage shed.

Gotta love small towns. Shelley couldn't suppress a grin, even as good ole Mr. F. made a soft "whoop, whoop" noise in her hands. She glanced into his little black eyes and asked, "So are you really sick?"

The eye contact formed an instant telepathic connection. Shelley's world swirled to gray. Still vaguely aware of her surroundings, she focused her attention inward on the movie-like scenes sent from the little boar in her hands.

An image of Beau's anxious face peering between the bars of the cage, filling and refilling the bowl with pellets sprang into her mind. At first, she thought the little boar was repeating the same image over and over, but quickly realized what was happening.

"Oh, so you've been eating," she said. "But Beau doesn't realize it because he's been topping off the food bowl."

The guinea pig "whooped" again.

She chuckled. "Well, you're a pretty wise pig not to eat everything you've been given. Many others wouldn't have such restraint. I'm not sure I would. You sure you don't feel sick?"

The little pig winged an image of Beau snuggling him close and crooning an off-key "Little Drummer Boy." The image was so peaceful she almost forgot she was at the clinic.

"*Shell-ley,*" Jack wailed.

Shelley jumped and turned in time to see Jack burst through the swinging door separating the back hallway from the reception area of the clinic. "Jeez! Jack. You'll freak out the animals."

"Come *on*. I can't stop her and he's just lying there!" Jack gestured wildly with both hands.

Right. Lucy attacking Hercules. Although Lucy was all of three pounds and a *ferret* to Hercules, a one-hundred-pound dog. How much damage could she do?

"It's Wednesday," Shelley said with a sigh. "Although, at least if it starts out like this, it can't get any crazier."

Mr. Fuzzbutt whooped again. *I swear, the little pig's laughing at me.*

"Jack, take Mr. F. and put him in examination room one." She hurried through the swinging white door, which led to the back. Stopping briefly to hand Beau's pet to her too-excitable intern. "There's a small cage in the cabinet under the sink. Pull it out and put him in it then meet me in the dog room."

Without waiting for a response, she hustled to the doggie spa. She usually avoided this area. She'd spent a weekend painting murals of fields, dog bones, blue skies, and fire hydrants on the walls, to give dogs and their owners the impression of a luxury spa. According to Jack and their boss, Dr. Alexander, her hard work paid off. Well, unless she was in there with the canines.

Today, six dogs were there for the Thanksgiving Special, a deluxe grooming, complete with a complimentary toy turkey. Metal cages lined one wall, each with a plush foam bed. The occupants inside them waited in doggy paradise for their turn at the day's scheduled luxurious treatment by Jack. Soft strains of Bach filtered through the air, barely audible over the ruckus of barks, yips, and howls as the canines commented on the show in the middle of the floor.

That was, until one of them caught her scent. Mrs. Hoffstedder's beagle noticed her first. He let out a single, high-pitched yowl, then lowered his head and covered his eyes with his paws. One by one, the other five dogs did the same.

Shelley didn't bother to wonder why they feared her. She'd given up asking that question years ago. It's not like she'd ever beaten an animal in her life. Jeez, she didn't even raise her voice. But almost every dog she'd come into contact with for the past seven years either hid from her or tried to attack her.

Thank God, Jack remembered to lock their cages before he called for her or it would be dog-maggedon as the pooches ran for freedom.

She had to be the world's weirdest vet. Telepathic, she could talk to any animal alive including snakes, hedgehogs, and naked mole rats. Any animal that is, except for the canine variety. She hadn't spoken to a single dog since Barty, her Bay Retriever, died in the car crash with her parents all those years ago.

Dr. Alexander's extremely valuable dog, Hercules, lay stretched out in the middle of the floor. Except for lifting his head to gaze mournfully at her, the large puppy remained still. No small feat considering Lucy, her beautiful cinnamon-colored sable ferret, was steadily chewing on his upper thigh, incredibly close to his testicles.

"You okay, Hercules?" She asked, gingerly kneeling down beside the pair and making eye contact with the dog.

Lifting only his head, he looked at her.

The telepathic connection zapped into place. An image of her prying her ferret off his body followed by him licking his dangly bits in relief flashed through her mind. She had to put her hand to her mouth to stifle a chuckle. Herc let out a loud sigh and dropped his head back to the floor.

Unlike every other dog in the world, Hercules neither feared nor loathed her. He didn't love her either. Usually he ignored her completely. Rarely, he answered her questions but today he seemed to recognize if anyone could save his balls— literally—it was she. The big dog snorted in agreement, but remained still and silently waited for her to rescue him.

"Lucy, why are you doing that?"

The ferret glared up at Shelley briefly but continued to chew.

In that momentary bit of eye contact, another collage of images winged into Shelley's head. Hercules, *the gaseous*, had accidentally sat on Lucy, again, after eating his breakfast. Now she intended to put "that upstart pup" in his place.

"All right, you had your revenge. It's not like he wants to be gassy. Next time try to avoid him after he eats. Let's go." The ferret didn't budge. Shelley prayed for patience and for no blood to be drawn. "Lucy, let go right now. You can't gnaw off his leg. And if you could, he'd be three-legged, wobbly, and end up squashing you anyway. Then you'd be trapped and forced to breathe his stench all day."

Hercules let out a rumbling "woof" of assent and shifted his weight, as if threatening to fulfill Shelley's prediction.

Lucy leapt away from Hercules with a shriek. She raced up Shelley's arm and wrapped herself around Shelley's neck for comfort. "You're all right, girl. Why don't you snuggle with me for a bit, hmmm?"

She patted the ferret on the head then rose to her feet. Hercules immediately began intimately examining his body, reassuring himself that he was still fully intact.

"Wow, how do you do that?" Jack appeared behind her. She turned to find his brown eyes rounded and his mouth agape. "Ferrets are more like cats than dogs. But yours actually seems to understand you. Ooh! They could make a reality show out of you. It could be called *The Ferret Whisperer*."

Shelley swallowed a chuckle, no sense encouraging him. Instead, she spoke directly to the brown and white puppy-behemoth still at her feet. "You're okay now, Hercules. It's safe to move again. Thanks for not eating her."

Hercules sprang to his paws and raced out of the room without so much as a backward glance.

And we're back to ignoring me. The world is normal again.

She chuckled and didn't try to disguise it this time.

"Don't laugh. I'm serious," Jack said. "We could make some serious money if Hollywood ever heard about you." Jack stood arms akimbo in the doorway. His shaggy black hair hung in his face. He jerked his head to the right, throwing the sideways bangs out of his eyes. "I swear, I went near her and that rat tried to munch on my fingers. But *you* . . . You walked in and talked to her like Dr. Freaking-Dolittle. And don't think I haven't seen you do it before. Mr. Fuzzbutt, for example. Yep, your parents mis-named you. You should have been called John Dolittle."

"I'm a woman."

"Jane then."

She shook her head at him. Little did Jack know, she was more like the fictional character than Hugh Lofting had ever dreamed possible. Except, she didn't speak to animals in their own languages. Shelley simply communicated with them telepathically. On the empath level, words were universally understood and all creatures were connected. Well, mostly.

Humans were an entirely different story. And a species she didn't understand at all, despite being one.

"Lucy's a ferret, not a rat. If you're going to be a vet you should know that. And as for what happened in the spa, it wasn't hard to figure out what was going on. Look, she's a good ferret who normally gets along with everyone, animals and people alike. I figured she must have been upset with Hercules. You saw him sit on her last week. And let's face it; he hasn't adjusted to the new dog food well. It didn't take much of a mental leap to figure something like that might have happened again," Shelley said, leaving the back room and heading toward her office.

"Yeah, I suppose so." Jack sounded disappointed, but he rallied. Hurrying down the hall, he reiterated his previous comment. "Still, I've seen you do that with other animals too. It's like you know what they're thinking. Is that how you skipped ahead in vet school? You read the minds of the animal patients. Hey, would that be cheating? Can I learn how to do it?"

"What are you talking about?" Shelley stopped and faced him. His dizzying barrage of questions too much to absorb. She instead focused on the first one. "You can't skip ahead in veterinary school. I graduated last year."

"You're not old enough to have gone all the way through." Jack waved at her. "Hello, you're my age and I'm just getting started. Well, I will start next semester anyway."

"First, you're twenty-one. I'm three years older than you.

Second, I graduated from high school with my Associate's Degree."

"Seriously? *You* took college classes in high school?"

Something about the tone in his voice set her teeth on edge, but still she kept her voice light. "Yes, and you could have done it too. I went from there to the university where I finished up my Bachelor's in twenty-four months because I didn't take summers off. Then I enrolled in veterinary school. I didn't skip anything."

Jack frowned at her then gave her a very obvious once-over. "You're . . . you're a *nerd*? But you're . . . hot. Well, for a vet who dresses like my grandmother."

"Did you just compare me to your *grandmother*?"

Jack just grinned.

Shelley's eyes were going to pop out of her head if she listened to this guy another second. Without responding, she spun on her heel and closed the distance to her office door. Once inside the tiny space, she propped up the wooden and plastic mesh baby gate across her doorway, designed to keep Hercules from wandering in there while she was out. Setting Lucy on the ground, Shelley gave her pet a stern frown then added aloud for good measure, "Behave, I mean it."

Lucy shook her head and sneezed indignantly, then pranced beneath Shelley's desk where her small travel cage rested. After climbing inside, she curled up into a tight ball and did what ferrets did best. She went to sleep.

"What do you want me to do with the guinea pig?" Jack asked. All questions about her age, her clothing, and her career seemingly forgotten. He leaned over the mesh gate rather than crossing into her sanctuary.

Shelley stepped over it, carefully.

"Thanks, Jack. Leave the guinea pig in the examination room. I'll get to him in a little bit. I've got plenty of paperwork to finish before Dr. Alexander returns. So if you want to get started on Mrs. Hoffstedder's beagle, that'd be great."

"No problem," Jack said and disappeared into the back.

The smell of cinnamon and pine cones permeated the receptionist area. The scent was an instant soother for her nerves. Now that the dogs in the spa had settled down, all was quiet. Peaceful.

Settling into the chair, she pulled up the afternoon schedule on the computer. The muscles in her shoulders began to ease. At barely noon, she had an hour before the next client . . . er, guest, was set to arrive. Fifty guaranteed crazy-free minutes.

She exhaled a relieved sigh. A little more tension slipped away.

Breathe, relax. This Wednesday isn't that bad.

"Uh, excuse me . . . Dr. Morgan?" Jack's voice sounded a little too tentative. A little too respectful.

She glanced up to find the young intern standing before her. His gaze bounced around the room. He looked everywhere but at her.

An icy sensation slithered into her stomach, making it shrink. "What did you do?"

"It wasn't my fault," he said, a little too quickly. "I didn't realize you'd left the front door open."

The front door?

"I certainly wouldn't have let Hercules wander through the clinic unattended if you'd told me that the place was open for business," he rushed on. "Or that you had some kid carrying bags of food inside from the shed. I would have locked him up."

"Him, who?" The words were out of her mouth nanoseconds before the answer slammed into her.

Hercules. The dog. *The* dog.

"Are you telling me that Hercules, Dr. Alexander's prized St. Bernard . . ." Her voice pitched higher with each word. "The one he calls his *only true baby* is *missing*?"

"Not my fault." Jack held up his hands.

From behind him came a sound of someone sniffing back tears. "I'm so sorry Dr. M. I didn't see him by the door until after I'd opened it. I tried to stop him. I had him real good for about a minute."

Beau stepped out from behind Jack. His blue T-shirt was torn from the shoulder to the wrist down one sleeve. Worse, he had an ugly patch of road rash on his upper left arm, which disappeared up the torn shirt. His glasses were askew and hanging by a leg.

She raced around Jack and checked Beau's injuries. Pointing at the intern, she ordered, "You, go chase after him."

"Yeah, see, I can't run. Remember, I tore my ACL doing that Mud Run with the Barbie Twins back in September?" He gestured to the brace on his knee. He wasn't on crutches anymore, but that didn't mean he was cleared to go chasing a dog back and forth across town.

"Shoot, shack, shipwreck!" she cursed, kicking off her ridiculous heels. What she wouldn't give for a pair of sneakers and jeans right now. "Jack, help Beau get cleaned up. There's a sewing kit in my desk, get it out and we'll repair his shirt. See if you can fix his glasses. Make sure the rest of the dogs are locked up tight. Do *not* answer the phone for anyone. Let it go to voice mail. And for the love of that St. Bernard, if Dr. Alexander returns before I come back, do not tell him you let his dog escape."

"What do I say?"

"I don't know. Tell him I took Herc for a walk or something."

"Right, like he'll believe that one," Jack scoffed. "Dogs hate you, remember? So maybe you aren't like Dr. Dolittle after all, huh."

"Jack! Focus." Shelley headed for the door then called over her shoulder, "Let's hope Dr. Alexander doesn't beat me back here."

Shoving open the door, sunlight poured in along with a blast of unseasonably warm November air, belying the sodden state of the area after last night's downpour of sleet and rain. Well, at least she wasn't running in her stockings in the rain or snow. This time. Yeah, like that single bit of good news made up for the fact that it was a Wednesday and she was about to run outside on the still wet and most likely muddy ground.

Please let me convince the dog to come back before anyone in town sees Hercules doing his Born Free impression.

That would just put the stale dog treat on her already rancid dog food bowl of a day.

Tidewater Police Detective Devon Jones pulled his black Lexus into the parking lot of Elkridge Veterinary Clinic. He cut the engine, imagining what he'd say when he saw Shelley again.

Her email to him last week had been like a gift from God. He'd been searching for her for weeks. Even going so far as to track down her fiancé—his former roommate—and that was all kinds of a suckfest. Since Camden Figurelle, that rat bastard, was in Africa. In the *Peace Corps*. There was no way to get in touch with him, if it wasn't an absolute emergency.

What the hell was with Cam going into the Peace Corps, anyway? They were supposed to be married by now.

Shells. Shelley Amanda Morgan.

He'd spent the last few weeks searching for Figurelle, since the wedding should have happened last summer. Cam's family had listed the engagement in the society section of the *Baltimore Sun*. Dev read it, marked the date, and noted with some disappointment he hadn't received an invitation. Not that he'd have gone. As much as he wanted Shells to be happy, he hadn't wanted to watch her marry the wrong man.

But she hadn't married Cam. Maybe Shelley had come to her senses and seen the prick for what he was and given him the old heave-ho. The thought brought a smile to Dev's face.

Still, wrong man or not, at least Cam had been a link to Shells. Without the connection, Dev had been stumped in the search for her. It had been by the grace of God that he'd kept his same email from college. The same email she'd contacted just two days ago. Dev pulled his smartphone from his inside jacket pocket and clicked to her saved email. He read it again, although by now he had it memorized.

Hey Dev,

It's me, Shelley Morgan. I know it's been a long time but I could use your help. I heard you're a police officer now but what I need is to use your puzzle-solving skills. Speaking of the police, I remember you wanted to be a police detective. Did that ever happen?

Anyway, I was wondering if I could convince you to leave Tidewater for a few days and come to Elkridge. It's a little town on the border of Suffolk and Tidewater. Great place. Friendly people. Quiet community. Low crime. Sounds like heaven, right?

Well, something strange is going on. I think. See, there's this private zoo. Since I moved here last June there have been a number of unexplained disappearances of animals. I've tried contacting the USDA, but they're no help. It's hard to explain in an email but I just know something is wrong. I've tried investigating this on my own, but I can't piece it together. Plus, I have to be careful how much noise I make. People in small towns talk, you know.

I can pay you for your expertise. A little. If you could come and take a look around. I've got some papers, animal records, and old newspaper clippings. Maybe I'm paranoid and there's nothing really wrong here. But if I'm not, then your time could save the life of an animal. Or ten.

Email me back and I'll give you directions to the veterinary clinic where I work.

Hope to hear from you soon,
Shells

He clicked off the phone and put it back in his pocket. Maybe he should have replied to her email or called first instead of just driving over. But what could he say?

"Hi Shells, long time no see. Can you believe it's been three years since graduation? Time sure flies and all that. While I want to know about this mystery you've unearthed, I'm more interested in the fact that you and Cam aren't together anymore. See, I've been crazy about you since the first time you smiled at me. Had you not been Camden's girl in school, I would have moved heaven and earth to get you into my bed. I also have something you've been looking for. If you'll just come back to Tidewater with me, I'll show you."

Yeah, that would go over really well. He sounded like a stalker or like he was just hoping for a quick and dirty one-night stand. And a one-night stand was absolutely not what he wanted. Although he'd settle for it if that's all he could have.

Dev gave himself a mental shake. He'd come to give her news she'd once told him she never thought she'd hear. Her older sister, Jules, was alive, well, happy, living in Tidewater, and searching for Shelley.

The news of her long-lost sibling should be enough for Shelley to forgive his disappearance after graduation three years ago. But really, he hadn't known what to say. And Camden had made it pretty damned clear that Dev was not welcome in their lives. Plus, it's not like Shelley called him, even once, in all that time.

Okay, so she'd been busy getting her veterinary license and building a happy life with Cam-the-sack. At least, Dev had thought she'd been happy until a few days ago. Although he couldn't quite ignore the pinch to his ego that she hadn't called him sooner. After all, they had been friends.

Christ, he was starting to sound like a freaking girl. First, brooding over *feelings* and worrying about why she hadn't called sooner. Next, he'd want to start a knitting circle.

Okay, so his motives for coming here weren't completely altruistic. He was man enough to admit to himself that if a hint of the spark he'd felt for her back in college still ignited when he saw her again, he'd do it. He'd ask her out . . . this time, no one would hold him back.

He'd use the next few days to let her really get to know him. Help her with her little zoo problem and take her to see her sister, Jules. Maybe then he'd have finally earned the right to spend time with the most graceful, caring woman he'd ever met. Because he certainly hadn't earned it that afternoon all those years ago when she'd been getting mugged while he'd been . . . elsewhere.

Sweat dampened his palms. His silk tie became noose-like around his neck. Digging a finger beneath his collar, he tugged it loose, only to re-tighten it again moments later. He checked himself in the rearview mirror, rehearsed his "I found Jules" speech in his head, and sat for another two minutes.

Enough of the stalling crap.

Dev shoved open the car door and stepped onto the damp cobblestone. His Ferragamos crunched over the wet, gritty street.

With a deep breath, he glanced around the nearly deserted road and took in the picturesque little town. Despite Elkridge's location on the scenic James River—with no elks or ridges in sight—the place lacked one key element Tidewater was known for.

Salt air.

This afternoon, the scent on the warm November wind was rife with apples and cinnamon from the local shops. Refreshing and sweet.

Just like Shelley. Assuming she was as perfect as he remembered. Right. Like she could be anything other than the sweet, shy girl he'd crushed on so long ago. She'd probably be so grateful he came to help her solve her mystery and found Jules on top of it that she'd ask him out.

And now he was dreaming. *Come on, man!*

While he and his partner had wrapped up the biggest case Tidewater had seen all year, there were others that still needed his attention. A few days were all he could afford to spend away from the office. He'd really only taken the five days because he'd foolishly hoped he'd . . . what? See Shelley and she'd finally fall in love with him? They'd run off to Vegas and get married?

Right and we'll have a unicorn and Elvis stand up for us at the ceremony.

Exhaling hard, he started to make his way toward the white washed brick building with the "Elkridge Animal Clinic" sign hanging over the front door.

A huge blurry mass appeared so quickly in front of him, it seemed to pop into existence from nowhere.

Blam!

It flew at his chest, knocking him to the ground. Dev's head smacked the pavement. Tiny stars burst to vibrant multicolored life in front of his eyes.

The something was large and furry, and pinning him. Still he managed to get a hand free. He reached for his sidearm, which . . . Shit! He'd left locked in the trunk of his car.

The damned beast burrowed its muzzle against his cheek and rumbled a deep, throaty growl.

A bear?

Cold fear slid down his neck. Or that might have been the animal's bloodthirsty drool. He might be a city boy, but he'd heard all about bear attacks in little towns like this one. He held perfectly still, eyes closed, playing dead as he tried to get a sense of the animal's size. If it were a bear, it couldn't be more than a cub, given its size.

Relief at the thought evaporated at the next.

Where there's a cub, there's a mama bear somewhere. Throwing caution to the wind, Dev rolled onto his side and into a ball, protecting his head, face, arms, and torso.

The animal seemed to tighten its hold on him. Its breath coming hot and nose-hair curling against Dev's ear.

He was going to be eaten by a bear in the middle of this damned street while everyone in Elkridge was out to lunch. Trying to curl more tightly, he elbowed the beast in a front leg. It yelped.

Wait. Bears don't yelp. Plus, it wasn't trying to bite him. No, it was pawing at his arms, not painfully. *Playfully.*

A long wet tongue slid across his hair, his ear, his cheek. And that growl he heard was followed by a deep woof. A dog, he was pinned by a dog. A great bear of dog, but definitely the canine species as opposed to the *Ursus americanus.*

Dev slowly rolled onto his back then drew his arms away from his face only to throw them up again when a slobbery tongue swiped from one cheek across his nose to the other. "Ugh. Serious dog breath. You need a breath mint, Fido."

Shifting onto his side, he attempted to scoot out from beneath the beast but the dog took it as a game and began licking him in earnest down the neck of his suit. If he hadn't needed a shower before the dog knocked him down, between rolling on the cobblestone and the sloppy dog kisses, he certainly needed one now.

Hoping not to hurt the animal that clearly was looking for a playmate, Dev pushed at the beast's midsection in an effort to make a break for it. He'd barely touched the dog when someone yelled, "Stop it, you big bear! You'll hurt him."

Okay, that wasn't the first time in his life he'd been called a bear. Still, the words stung his pride. He might be considered by the average person to be bear-like due to his large size—he was short compared to some of his cousins—but he wasn't an animal. He was a police detective. A cop. A friggin' hero.

Although, at the moment he was in the least heroic position. Ever.

"Hercules, stop before you hurt him. You bad puppy," the

voice said, closer now. "I'm really sorry about Hercules. Are you okay down there? Give me a minute. I've almost got his leash on him."

Ah, Hercules was the *dog's* name. She was calling the dog a big bear.

The relief coursing through him at the knowledge was quickly overshadowed by a sickening realization. He knew that voice.

There was a distinctive sound of a clink of metal on metal and the dog was suddenly off him. "I'm so sorry," she said; then she laughed. The sound more an exhalation of air than joy. "I'm really, *really* sorry. He doesn't normally do this. But I guess all creatures crave freedom, right? Are you . . . are you hurt?"

His gut shrank at her musical voice. Now? She had to show up and see him covered in dog drool and muck, lying on the ground, pinned there by a playful bear-dog?

Maybe if I'm lucky, she won't recognize me beneath the slobber?

"Dev?" Her voice was closer now. He could feel her breath against his chin as she leaned down to look at him. "Is that you?"

"Uh . . . yeah." Dev lay there for a moment. His arm still firmly over his eyes and his head throbbing. His luck was good for buckets of suck.

"Why bless your heart. Devon Jones, it *is* you." She sounded positively gleeful. "What are you doing down there?"

"Playing possum with Fido." He tugged his arm away and blinked open his eyes. The starbursts were gone but he'd have a nice knot on the back of his skull later. It was already coming up.

And there she was. Leaning over him, her hair a cloud of red curls around her face. Concern and confusion crowded into her sapphire blue eyes. Her pink lips twitched. "Thank God it was you Hercules tackled. How do you do it? You always manage to show up just when I need saving."

If only that were true.

FROM *USA TODAY* BESTSELLING AUTHOR
THEA HARRISON

Rising Darkness

A Game of Shadows Novel

In the ER where she works, Mary is used to chaos. But lately, every aspect of her life seems adrift and the vivid, disturbing dreams she's had all her life are becoming more intense. Then she meets Michael. He's handsome, enigmatic and knows more than he can say. In his company, she slowly remembers the truth about herself…

Thousands of years ago, there were eight of them. The one called the Deceiver came to destroy the world, and the other seven followed to stop him. Reincarnated over and over, they carry on—and Mary finds herself drawn into the battle once again. And the more she learns, the more she realizes that Michael will go to any lengths to destroy the Deceiver.

Then she remembers who killed her during her last life, nine hundred years ago…*Michael*.

theaharrison.com
penguin.com

M1328T0613